Season's End

Betty Fry

DEDICATION

To my husband and my children for allowing me time
and space to imagine alternative realities

1950

"To every thing there is a season, and a time to every purpose under the heaven." --Ecclesiastes 3:1

Prologue

Her skin tingled uncomfortably, her long white fur standing upright with the electric charge hanging in the still air. She was restless and miserable, no more than walking bones with a distended belly and a growing ache in her abdomen. She paced by the stream, flattening her ears with the first distant growl of thunder, met by a closer growl of pain in her loins. She licked at herself, cleaning the discharge that flowed freely now both from her nipples and her hindquarters. She turned back to the exposed roots of the gnarled oak tree where she had tunneled out a soft, cool nest for the birthing and tried to make herself lie still as the spring storm moved in on her.

Resting on her side, she saw the blinding bolt before its noise shook the ground and deafened her. Panicked, she scratched frantically at the earth, trying to hide from the great hollow booms. Her contractions dropped her to the dirt, exhausted and terrified. The first water sack emerged and she instinctively turned to break it gently with her teeth. She freed the puppy, licking it dry, biting the umbilical, forgetting the storm for the moment. She ate the placenta which followed, and relaxed with its nourishment, until the next contractions overtook her. Three more puppies came before the nearby stream broke its banks in a rush of water that seeped into her makeshift den.

The water pushed against her back with prodding rough hands that shifted the soft dirt beneath her, spread its soaking cold into her matted fur, and seeped through to reach the squirming new life at her belly. She edged away from it, but the water rose, icy and heartless, chilling her fever and numbing her pain. The den was thick with mud and cold.

She worried at the newborns, nuzzling them to her, pulling them into the farthest corner, working to keep them warm and dry. Two more births followed but their sacks lay neglected in the mud as she struggled with the babies already clinging to her. One by one, the puppies faded during the long cold night, until morning, when only one continued to suckle at her breast. Even hairless, deaf, and blind, he radiated life and strength. White as winter snow, she called him Yuki.

Part 1, 1995

"A time to be born, and a time to die; a time to plant, and a time to pluck up that which is planted;" -- Ecclesiastes 3:2

CHAPTER 1

Mike leapt from the bed, his heart pounding in his tight throat, and the hair at the back of his neck raised to full alert. The shrill scream that chilled his blood and made his hands shake, still hung on the air. He stumbled into his slippers, grabbed his robe off the bed, and smashed his knee into the dresser as he scrambled through the dark toward Kaitlin's room. A second scream shattered the night with so much terror it caused Mike to gasp as he reached for the doorknob.

The hall light was on and Kaitlin's door stood open. Mike rushed into the room, relieved to see Laurel already there, gripping Kaitlin with her long thin hands and shaking Kaitlin's shoulders as she shouted her name. Mike dropped onto Kaitlin's bed just as her eyes fluttered open.

"It's so cold, so white and cold." Kaitlin's chest heaved with her fear, and Mike's hand tightened on her foot, shaking it through the blankets, hoping to wake her, but Kaitlin kicked viciously, struggling out of his grasp. Kaitlin's arms flung out, striking Laurel with a stinging slap as she twisted on the bed. Mike could see the pulse in Kaitlin's neck throbbing at a breakneck pace.

"Wake up princess. Mom and Dad are here, baby." Laurel shouted into Kaitlin's ear, then wrapped an arm around her daughter and pressed Kaitlin to her chest, stroking her dark hair and rocking her back and forth against her body. "Wake up, Baby. It's just a dream. Just a very bad dream."

Kaitlin pulled back, sitting up by herself, teeth chattering and arms shivering from the remembered cold. "I was so cold, Mom. I was so scared."

Kaitlin began to sob and Mike's heart hitched; it wrenched him to see her cry, always had, but lately there had been so much. He wished it made him angry. Anger he could deal with, fear he could deal with, but seeing Kaitlin hurt was not something he could reconcile. He sat uselessly at the end of the bed while Laurel rocked their daughter and she gradually quieted.

"I know, Baby, but it's just a dream. We're here, see. You're in your own room, in your own bed, it's not real. It's just a dream." Laurel rubbed their daughter's hands, raised them to show Mike how blue and cold they seemed in the dim light.

"Listen, Baby, I'm going to make you some hot chocolate to warm you up. Why don't you pick out a favorite book to read until you start to feel sleepy again?" Laurel stood up from the bed, catching Mike's eye with a tired, frustrated look. She slipped out of the room, while Mike moved himself closer to Kaitlin where he could give her a long hug.

"Okay Sport. Why don't you lie down and I'll give you a back rub while you practice your deep breathing? Slow and easy, okay?" Mike gently moved her waist length, black hair aside and stroked Kaitlin's back, the way Laurel had shown him, listening to Kaitlin's long, slow breaths. It was four in the morning, about the same time as the last few nights when she'd wakened them in the same way. It was unlikely he'd get back to sleep, but she needed her rest. He could feel Kaitlin's shaking fade away and the tense muscles begin to relax.

By the time Laurel returned with the hot chocolate, Kaitlin was calm again. She chose *Tiger Eyes* to read and assured her parents she would be all right. Mike and Laurel wished her goodnight and slipped out of the room, leaving the lamp on and the door open.

Laurel leaned her long, slim torso into Mike's chest. Her short dark hair tickled his cheek as she turned her face toward him. She sighed deeply and he was surprised at how darkly the circles were etched into her skin. "How long can this go on?"

Mike held her there, but shook his head, his helplessness overwhelming him. He shuddered again at the memory of Kaitlin's terror. He wanted warm milk with brandy to put himself to sleep -- wanted it badly. He shook off the thought and followed Laurel back to their bed where he would lie awake until the alarm clock roused him for duty at the Whidbey Island Base.

***

The view from the recreation room windows was oppressive, just a few bare trees and a sloping lawn that led down to an old manufacturing plant. The aged stone building stood cold and dingy against the gray sky, a stream of dirty smoke drifting up to blend in with ragged clouds too tired to spit the icy sleet that had been common these early spring days in Michigan. Sooty snow pocked by salt and chemical deicers was banked against the edge of the parking lot. Shoots of green struggled through the matted winter sod. Donna Jean turned to her companion, a sight no less depressing.

The old woman's dark hair hung limply around her puffy face. She stared straight ahead with once-brown eyes, now cloudy with cataracts, lids drooping and half-open. A stuffed toy dog sat in her lap, her hands squeezing it and sometimes punching it. Occasionally her right arm left the wheelchair armrest, her gnarled fingers tapping out a beat as she chanted, "Eenie, meenie, minie, moe. Catch a doggy by the toe. When he's dead, don't let him go. Eenie, meenie, minie, moe."

Carol Ann had sat the entire morning, a pasty lump in a thin cotton housedress, unmoved by bingo, television, or smiling nurses. An eternally stuck record replayed in her mind; its one groove etched so deeply, that Carol Ann could not hear the comings and goings in the day room.

Donna Jean sat across from her sister, slipping back on the cold, stiff plastic of the orange sofa, frowning a little at the pain in her abdomen. From time to time, she reached out, touching Carol Ann's chin and turning it toward her, trying to catch Carol Ann's attention before

11

visiting time was over and Carol Ann would be rolled away for lunch.

"Carol Ann, look at me! Carol Ann, look at me!" Donna Jean raised her soft voice, though the effort pained her. Finally the old woman's head turned.

"Mama's here," Carol Ann smiled as she turned toward Donna Jean.

"No Honey, its Donna Jean. I've come to visit you."

"You're too old to be Donna Jean. You're Mama. Donna Jean's too mean to visit me."

"I'm Donna Jean. I came to tell you the news. Laurel is coming home to help me with the farm."

"Eenie, meenie, minie, moe. Catch a doggy by the toe. When he's dead, don't let him go. Eenie, meenie, minie, moe." Carol Ann's chanting increased in volume, something that often happened when she did not like what she was hearing.

Donna Jean waited for the chanting to ease, "Laurel's bringing Kaitlin with her too. They'll be here in a few weeks. Laurel's going to start taking care of you."

"Eenie, meenie, minie, moe. Catch a doggy by the toe. When he's dead, don't let him go. Eenie, meenie, minie, moe." Carol Ann was shouting now, trying to drown out Donna Jean's words.

"Eenie, meenie, minie, moe. Catch a doggy by the toe. When he's dead, don't let him go. Eenie, meenie, minie, moe." Carol Ann's voice rose in pitch until the chant was almost a scream. The other residents in the room turned toward her and one started to cry anxiously.

An efficient aide, in a white uniform, stepped in from the hallway. "I'm sorry Donna Jean, she's getting everyone worked up. I'll take her down to her room and see if we can quiet her down."

"Listen, Judy. I'm sorry about this. I need to make her understand. I won't be around much longer and I need her to understand." Donna Jean spoke patiently as she always did regarding Carol Ann.

Judy looked at the gaunt woman, patted her thin shoulder, and nodded sympathetically. "I know, Donna Jean, we'll try to help. It'll be different when your daughter from Washington state gets here. She'll probably think Laurel's you."

They both smiled at that sad truth, but Donna Jean shook her head resignedly. There was nothing else she could do now anyway. It all lay in fate's hands.

***

They wheeled Carol Ann back to her room. She liked her room, high and safe. They parked her chair where she could look out the second-story window into the branches of the old maple that grew there, its green leaf buds starting to swell in the half-sun of early spring. When they pushed her close enough to the tree, it was as if she were sitting in its branches, high and safe above the ground where he couldn't get her. High and safe, she could cling to those solid arms of wood and he couldn't get her. He couldn't reach her up here, and if she didn't look down, she wouldn't fall. She wouldn't look down, no matter how hard it was to look away. She wouldn't look down. She would stay high and safe.

The trunk was scratchy and hard behind her. She shifted on the narrow limbs and they bent and swayed with her weight, but she wouldn't look down at it. It was bloated and swollen, black around the torn edges where flesh had been ripped away. If she looked down, the sight would make her swoon and she'd fall out of the tree. She wouldn't look down. She patted the whistle against her chest, lifted it to her mouth and blew long and hard. She tried to remember the dots and dashes for S. O. S. She wouldn't look down and Papa would find her here, still high and safe.

Below, she could hear the dog circling the tree, growling and whining at the bottom. She heard his claws scratching at the trunk of the tree, snapping, and jumping against the trunk. She wouldn't look down. If she looked down, she would see him slathering, see his fangs bared and flashing. If she looked down, she would begin to shake and she would fall out of the tree. She pressed her eyes tightly shut and shifted her weight on the tree so she could hold on longer. She would stay here, high and safe.

Then, she heard his voice. A man's voice, oily and dirty, slipping loosely through the dog's throat. He said things she shouldn't hear, didn't want to hear. She wanted to cover her ears, but if she let loose of her grip, she would fall from the tree. The voice rose and wrapped itself around her like a coiling snake, threatening to choke her and make her fall from the tree.

She could not cover her ears, but she could cover the sound. She began to recite, spilling rhymes and stories into the air, covering the sick, insinuating man/dog's voice with her own. She clenched her eyes shut and made herself a child again, jumping rope on the play ground, playing finger games in Mama's lap, singing to herself in the enamel bath tub in the warm kitchen. She would not hear the voice, she would not look down, she would not fall from the tree, she would stay high and safe.

"Eenie, meenie, minie, moe."

***

"Doctor, I asked to see you today because Kaitlin is getting a lot worse." Laurel sat across from the psychiatrist's desk, hands in her lap discretely hiding a tissue. She consciously composed her face to hide her distaste for the man. "I don't feel we are making any progress with this treatment. Is there anything else we can do?"

Dr. Foote leaned back in his leather chair, rolling away from the desk to make himself more comfortable. "Mrs. Taylor, I appreciate your concern, but you need to understand that sometimes as clients begin facing their fears, they seem to worsen before they get better."

"No, doctor. Kaitlin is only eleven years old. She doesn't deserve to suffer this much." Laurel was confident she had said this assertively, kept the tremor out of her voice.

"Of course, Mrs. Taylor. I am not suggesting that Kaitlin should suffer, I am only asking for your patience. Anxiety disorders often worsen when stress levels rise, as they do when we are close to identifying the underlying problem. I believe that we will soon find the cause of Kaitlin's panic attacks and night terrors and that we will eliminate them."

"Doctor, when you started with Kaitlin six months ago she was having this nightmare once, maybe twice, a week. Now she is having the dream every night. You haven't been there to see how terrified she is. She truly believes she is dying, that she is being torn apart, that she's freezing. I've never heard anyone scream with such fear. I can't take this anymore, and now it's so much worse. Every night we wake up with this; we have to see our daughter in so much pain. There must be a better way to treat this. Is there something else we can do? Can you refer us to another specialist, someone off the base?" Her face reddened, she knew, and this time her voice betrayed her anger, but she didn't care. It was time to be firm with this man.

Dr. Foote stroked his goatee for a long minute as he studied the fingers of his left hand. Finally he spoke. "Now, 'Mother', you know that I have asked you to come in as a family. I think there is something here that you and Kaitlin's father are denying. Panic disorders like Kaitlin's are caused by underlying emotional anxieties. Kaitlin shows the symptoms of someone who has suffered a real trauma; I think it was a trauma of a sexual nature. I think that you and your husband need to confront this as a couple if we are to help Kaitlin." Dr. Foote flipped Kaitlin's file closed and leaned forward on the desk, leaving the weight of his words on Laurel.

Laurel pushed herself up from the chair. Now she was not just angry, she was justifiably indignant. She held her back straight; she would have her say before she walked out on this infuriating quack. "If you are implying that my daughter has been sexually abused by her father, then you are not only a fraud, you are an idiot. My daughter has always had a perfectly normal and wonderful relationship with her father. In fact, my daughter has always been a perfectly normal and wonderful girl until these dreams started, and all you have succeeded in doing is to intensify them, to embarrass her, and to antagonize me. My daughter needs treatment, not pseudo-science. I will be taking her elsewhere." Laurel turned before the doctor could respond, slamming his door on her way out.

**

Donna Jean made her way up the stairs, gripping the

wooden banister, taking each step carefully so that she wouldn't disturb the little peace she had negotiated with her body. The old farmhouse creaked around her, the groans of wooden joists and the flap of loose shingles replacing the laughter and running foot falls, which had once echoed off its plaster walls. Still, she knew it was well built and its stone foundation would stand long after her generation and the next were gone. She sighed deeply at the top of the stairs, holding her side tentatively and wincing a bit with the exhaustion the climb had produced.

She knocked on the bedroom door next to hers. "Sadie, can you help me? I think I'd like to nap for a while."

"Donna Jean, you should've called me before you tried to come up all these stairs. Why am I staying with you if you can't ask for a little help?" Sadie Johnson's dark face frowned as she reached one arm around Donna Jean's waist and used the other to lift Donna Jean's arm around her shoulder. "I told you, you shouldn't be driving into town by yourself either. Now look at you, you're going to make yourself sick before Laurel and Kaitlin even get here."

"Sadie Johnson, you're a good friend, but you sure are bossy. Wasn't I running cattle and planting corn just last year? You've got to let me do what I can for as long as I can do it." Donna Jean sighed, thinking that all her life she had been as strong as she needed to be, and now age and illness conspired to take her strength away from her.

"Besides, I've been a lot sicker than this, and we've gotten by."

"Yes, we've gotten by a lot in this old life haven't we?" Sadie smiled and Donna Jean laughed with her old friend as she helped her undress and slip under the covers of the large four-poster bed.

The afternoon sun came through the big bay window from the west and showered Donna Jean with gold, making her remember other sunny afternoons when the house had rattled with the noisy sound of children and had been warmed by Mama's baking. Donna Jean thought of family long-gone and wondered if you were really reunited in heaven somewhere. She pictured her husband Jonathan with his wavy golden hair and his beaming smile. She fell asleep dreaming of him again.

***

Whaley creased the stiff sheets into tight, fitted corners at each end of the bed, pulled the top sheet over the edge of the brown wool blanket and folded them neatly and evenly across the chenille spread. His gnarled hands were soft but stiff with age, making it hard to get the folds just right. He fluffed the pillow and carefully centered it beneath the headboard before flipping the spread over its soft hill. He sat in the stiff straight back chair beside the bed and watched dust motes dance in the sunbeams that filled the window. An old man, back rounded and chest sunken under his shirt, he waited patiently, hands tucked in his pockets, head bent away from the glare of the bright window. The white lace curtains billowed in the soft morning air, then sagged back against the black bars and fell straight once more.

From the hallway, he could hear the heavy steps of the morning attendant, could hear the clink of her thick key in the old locks. He watched the floorboards beneath his door sink, and heard the key rattle against his doorknob. It swung open and the large woman's broad face followed it, her perpetual growl a little abated today.

"Good morning, Whaley." Miss Dixon's smoker's voice was coarse, husky, sexy even, if you weren't looking at her gray hair and grim mouth. "This is it. Your last day at the old homestead. How're you feeling?"

Whaley stood, nervously scratched at his shoulder, rubbed his hands on his pants, and nodded. "I'm all right. I'm fine." His voice sounded strange to him, flat and dry, a side effect of the medication. "I'm fine. Ready to say good-bye."

"Breakfast first, then you go for the interview. It'll probably be afternoon before you're out of here." She checked his name off her chart but hesitated before she moved on to the next door.

"I think you're ready for this too." Miss Dixon nodded and patted his hand, then turned and left the room. It was the first time in all his years here that she had ever touched him.

Whaley pulled his loose pants higher, tightened his belt a notch and shuffled after Miss Dixon. The other old timers were gathering in the long hallway, some still in pajamas, mumbling to themselves, chewing fingers, and watching the others with frightened, shifting eyes. Several were already smoking cigarettes, pacing and smoking, like they were being held up from some important appointment. White-haired, grizzled, some toothless, they formed a shambling procession from the hospital ward to the cafeteria.

***

Kaitlin boosted herself onto the cold examining table, relieved that she hadn't been asked to undress this time. Dr. Kraemer was young, he wore a white jacket like her pediatrician and he smiled with his eyes from under a cap of sandy hair. The outpatient clinic was a friendly place, decorated in yellows and blues with bright color photographs of children and animals. It wasn't much like the base clinic where she had always gone.

"You don't have to lie down, Kaitlin. I just need to ask you and your mother some questions." He helped her sit up again and nodded toward an empty chair for Laurel.

"Kaitlin, tell me what happens to you during a panic attack." Dr. Kraemer waited, as if he had all afternoon to spend with Kaitlin.

"Well, you know how you feel on a roller coaster? Like you're going to fly right out of the car and get killed, but you only feel that way for a second? It's just like that, but it doesn't stop in a second. It's like you know you really are going to fly off and you really are going to die." Kaitlin kept her eyes down as she spoke, feeling her face grow hot. She lifted her head at the end of her answer, making eye contact with Dr. Kraemer so he'd know she was really serious.

"What happens to your body when you feel this way, Kaitlin?"

"My heart pounds so hard, I can see it moving under my shirt and I can't get enough to breathe. I start panting like a dog, just trying to get enough air. And I feel so stupid because I know there's nothing there to hurt me but I know just as much that I'm going to die, and I get so scared." Kaitlin gulped, swallowing an ache that was rising in her throat.

"Does this happen often, Kaitlin?"

"It used to be just once in a long while, like when I'd forgotten all about them, but lately, its been a couple of times a week. I have to leave class when it happens because I'm afraid I'm going to cry or throw up or something." Now she felt really stupid, but it was true.

"Do your attacks ever happen at a certain time? Is there one thing that sets them off?"

Kaitlin shook her head. "No, I don't know what makes them happen. There's never anything really bad happening; I think I'm just going crazy."

"Well, Kaitlin, it's clear that you are having panic attacks but there isn't any reason to think you're crazy. I have several other patients who have the same thing happening to them. It's just your brain over-reacting to some kind of neural stimulation, like an electrical short that turns your panic switch on at the wrong times. There are some medications we can try that we call beta-blockers. They make sure your nervous system doesn't get to the level where it can short out. Do you want to try one of these?" Dr. Kraemer waited for Kaitlin's response and was rewarded with a warm smile and a quick nod of her head.

"Mrs. Taylor, I'm glad you came to see me. This is not an uncommon condition and it responds well to medication." Dr. Kraemer leaned toward Laurel and whispered softly, but loudly enough for Kaitlin to hear, "You were right to walk out on the psycho-babble you were getting."

Dr. Kraemer pulled a prescription pad from his desk and began writing. "I'm going to recommend that we start with Imipramine. It might make your mouth dry, Kaitlin, but I bet you can put up with that."

"Doctor, what about her night terrors? Will this medication help with that?" Laurel reached for the prescription, a look of relief on her face.

"Well, there is good reason to think it will. Usually these things are related, though Kaitlin's a little old for the night terrors. Let's watch and see if this helps. I want you to come back in two weeks or sooner if anything worsens or if Kaitlin has any problem on the medication."

***

Kaitlin was rounding the last corner toward home when her skin started to crawl with fear. She pulled her bike to the side, dropped it heavily to the street, and stumbled to the curb. She lowered her head between her knees, feeling dizzy with impending doom, then abruptly raised her head, straightened her upper body and forced herself to breathe deeply, watching her diaphragm rise and fall with the long, slow draws. She could hear her heart beating so fast she was sure it would explode in her chest; she began to breathe quick shallow gasps again, panting for air that wouldn't come. She couldn't sit here, it was coming for her. She stood, confused; she was unprotected in the open, she was all alone, she had to run. Abandoning the bike, Kaitlin raced for her house, another two blocks away.

A voice called out to her from a neighbor's house but Kaitlin couldn't slow down, couldn't stop. She raised her hand as she pummeled down the cul-de-sac that led to her driveway. It was right behind her, she knew it would reach out and grab her shirt if she slowed down. She flung herself up the steps, taking two at a time, and pounded on the door.

"Please, let me in Mom." Kaitlin screamed with the last of the breath in her lungs, all the while banging the brass doorknocker. As the door opened, she fell into her mother's arms, wheezing for air, and jerking with fright. Laurel held her there until her trembling quieted and Kaitlin could make it up to her room.

CHAPTER 2

Arnette held the baby out to Donna Jean, its pink feet kicking away the pastel blanket. The baby gurgled little bubbles of spit as it laughed in Donna Jean's arms. "What a beautiful little girl. Yes, you are." Donna Jean nuzzled the baby's soft forehead, enjoying the fresh baby smells of powder and clean cotton. "She's pure delight, Arnette. You must be so happy!"

Arnette beamed, "Well, I guess we done all right, even if everyone said we were too young. Thanks to you for helpin' with the birthin' and all." The teenager reached out to squeeze Donna Jean's thin hand. "I mean, I was awful afraid, until you come in and then I knew it'd be okay."

Donna Jean nodded, knowing the Tingleys didn't have money for doctors' visits or a hospital stay. She worried about them too, wondering where their grocery money would come from.

"How's A. J. doing on finding a job, Arnette?"

"He's got some work lined up at a couple of farms once it warms up. My mama's been helpin' us out and I guess she can carry us until then. You know, I wouldn't do nothin' different. This baby's the most wonderful thing that ever happened to me."

"Well, I think you are going to be very good parents."

"And our baby? Is she going to grow up okay?"

"Arnette, she has years and years of growing to do, but she looks like a smart little girl and healthy too. You're just going to want to look out for her as carefully as you can. She needs you to love her and to protect her and to always be there for her, and then, I think, yes, she's going to turn out perfect."

Arnette closed her eyes and smiled again, as if she were saying amen to all of it. "I thank you so much, Miss Donna Jean. Thank you for seein' us. Sadie said I shouldn't stay too long and tire you out. I hope you're feelin' better real soon." Arnette wrapped the baby in her blanket again, and backed out of the bedroom, nodding her head to Donna Jean, as if she were ending a visit to the queen.

Donna Jean heard the outside door close behind Arnette and a minute later Sadie was looking in on her. "It's about time you gave up these visits. Folks are going to wear you out with all their needs."

"Some of these folks don't have anyone else. I guess a person has to keep moving for as long as she can. Besides, I liked seeing that baby. Made me feel young again to hold an infant in my arms."

"Especially when you can hand it right back!" Sadie fluffed Donna Jean's pillows and helped her into her bed. "Are you going to be all right, old friend?"

"Well, I'm going to be all right for a while more. My Laurel's coming home and bringing Kaitlin. I guess I can spare a little longer for them."

***

"Christ, why does it have to be right now? Everything is going down at the same time. You know I can't get off now. We'll need what I can bring in during the next three months." Mike paced angrily, his green eyes flashing, his fingers deftly buttoning the brass buttons on his dress uniform. The muscles in his jaw tightened and his heavy brows met at the middle of his forehead like storm clouds gathering.

Laurel sat on the bed, looking miserable but determined. "You know I wouldn't leave you alone at a time like this if it wasn't absolutely necessary. I am being literally torn up inside, but my mother has never asked for one thing from us. All the times we've been stationed so far away, she's not once complained. She needs us now, and we have to go." She said it patiently and gently, simply stating the facts, not arguing and certainly not pleading.

"Honey, you know they won't even let me off. They're not going to let any high-ranking people leave during the mothballing." Mike dropped to his knees in front of her, looking into her gentle, vacant eyes, but Laurel stared inward, listening to some message there. Laurel's fragile good looks left her perpetually child-like; wide eyes, full mouth, long thin neck, and slight body. The vulnerability was more than physical, Mike knew. She always carried some sadness she wouldn't share with him.

"It's Kaitlin, too. I don't know what to do for her anymore. Dr. Kraemer has tried two different beta-blockers and she's not getting any better. Her teacher says she's having attacks at school and she's become so withdrawn her work is suffering. Dr. Foote thinks we're a dysfunctional family who've thrust this on her. We're both half-dead from waking her in the night trying to break this cycle, and she's walking around here like a zombie. When my mother called, I thought maybe this is fate. Maybe I have one last chance to help Kaitlin."

"Kaitlin! What can your mother do that these specialists haven't accomplished? What can she do that we can't do for her right here?"

"You don't know my mother very well. Christ, I don't understand her that well myself, but she has a reputation as a healer."

"Are you saying your mother is a faith healer? That she's going to fix everything for Kaitlin by laying hands on her?"

Laurel stared at him for a long time, then answered slowly. "Actually, she's a natural healer; herbs, plants, old remedies she learned from her grandmother. But people around there come to her. They believe in her healing. I think maybe she can help Kaitlin. I think maybe just being in another place might help Kaitlin."

"We promised we wouldn't pull her out of school in

the middle of the year. What kind of set-back is that going to cause? Are you going to break her heart because your mother can't wait three more months for summer vacation?" Mike was frustrated now, but finally, Laurel really looked at him, her mouth set in a tight line, her eyes wet, and her face pale.

"My mother doesn't have three months, Mike. She has pancreatic cancer. She needs us and we have to go now." Laurel's face fractured into lines and tears, her slender neck bending into his shoulder. "She never said anything. All the times we've talked this last year, she's been in treatment, but she never said anything, and now it's too late. There's nothing else they can do. She asked me to come, and she asked for Kaitlin, too."

Mike reached for her, trying to protect her as he always had. Her bird-like fragility was present between them. He put his arm around her shoulders; careful he didn't hold her so hard he would hurt her. He stroked her back and whispered, "I'm sorry. I'm so sorry. Of course you'll go."

Inside, his heart sank into a deep black hole. She would go and he would have to handle this himself. He realized he was terrified. His life was all about going away. His dad had gone away in a uniform and never come back. His mother had gone away into a bottle of pills and that's where she remained. His career was disappearing, sifting through his fingers no matter how hard he tried to hold on to it. A line in a budget column erased, and suddenly he was nothing of value. Now Laurel was leaving and taking Kaitlin when he needed them both so badly. He was a good sailor though; he'd swallow it back and be strong for her.

Mike reached for a tissue and dried her eyes, stroking her cheeks and holding her as if he could not hold her long enough. Laurel's lips found his and they kissed, lightly at first and then harder. They lay back on the bed in a long embrace and talked softly about the turns their lives were taking and what might happen next.

* * *

Kaitlin was twisting in her sheets when her mother entered her room. Gently, Laurel shook Kaitlin's shoulder and spoke her name. She smoothed Kaitlin's hair with her long fingers as Kaitlin pulled herself out of her sleepy cocoon of blankets and rubbed her eyes open, then wrapped Laurel in a tight hug.

"Mom, I had the most awful dream." Kaitlin felt wetness on her mother's face and sat up quickly to look directly at her. "What's wrong? Why are you crying?"

Laurel used the hem of her T-shirt to wipe her face. "I'm sorry, honey. I had a call early this morning. My mother is very sick and needs us to take care of her. You and I have to go back to stay with Grandma Doe for a while."

"Doe's sick? Is she going to die?" Kaitlin was alert now and goose bumps moved down her arms, watching her mother cry like this.

Laurel nodded and said, "Maybe," with her voice cracking.

"We're going right away, without Dad?"

"We'll leave as soon as school is out on Friday. We'll be gone a long time, Kaitlin; you'll have to pack most of your things to take with us. I am so sorry Honey. I want you to use your time this week to say good-bye to your friends."

"Mom! I don't know if I can do that! Everything's so weird lately; I get so scared. I don't want to be away from Dad, away from home; I can't just pack up and leave."

"Kaitlin, I know this is terribly hard for you, but I think this may be a good thing for you too. This is something you will just have to be understanding about."

"Mom, you promised. You said I'd finish the year, no matter what. I've screwed up so much at school lately. How can I be the new kid when I'm like this?"

"Kaitlin, I am very sorry, but this is not something we will argue about. I've had to make a decision and it's as hard for me and Dad as it is for you."

"When do I get to say anything?" Kaitlin turned to the wall pouting.

Laurel flushed red with anger. "I don't have any other choices right now. My mother is dying and she wants both of us. I am not going to deny her that one thing and neither are you." She turned quickly, leaving the room and putting the argument at an end.

Kaitlin's angry tears started immediately. She lifted her pillow and beat it against the bed, then threw it into the dresser. She pulled at her hair in frustration, "Why can't I have a life? When are you going to treat me like an adult?"

Kaitlin sulked into her clothes. She knew only too well that there wasn't any changing things once her parents had made a decision. She remembered other times when she'd been told they were being posted somewhere else and it was pack up and say good-bye. The worst was that Kaitlin had been in Washington state a long time. She had forgotten her own rule and started to call this place home, and right now she needed her friends so badly.

Kaitlin brushed her hair and thought about the bad dream her mother had interrupted. Not the nightmare, but a strange dream that left her uneasy. Great way to start a day, bad dream and bad news. What else would go wrong today?

She wished she could have told her mother about the dream instead of fighting over the inevitable. Maybe it was an omen or something. Mom always wanted to know about her dreams, and with Doe so sick it might be important. There was something about a woods that Kaitlin knew she shouldn't forget, something in a woods that frightened her even though she never saw it. It was as if the woods were watching her and waiting.

CHAPTER 3

Boxes stood stacked around the room, two smaller ones set off to the side to be shipped to Grandma Doe's, the others to be stored in the garage until the house sold and Dad could truck them back to Michigan. The girls emptied Kaitlin's drawers, packing some things, discarding others, and generally laughing over out-grown pajamas and old notes they found. The three sat in curlers and heavy make-up, giggling about boys they liked and predicting each other's futures.

Allison held the cootie-catcher in her hands, "What color do you want?" She shifted the quadrants of the cootie-catcher four times as she spelled out 'blue'. "What number?" Allison shifted again, counting the times. "What number again?" She lifted a flap. "You will marry a television star and have five children."

Karmen fell to the floor, groaning with laughter, holding her stomach and hooting. "Kaitlin! Will you name one of the girls after me?" She rolled away as Kaitlin reached out to kick her.

"I'm going to have five boys so I'll never be tempted to name any of them after you!" Kaitlin picked up an unused curler and threw it at her friend. The three fell back to the floor, exhausted from laughing and stared at the ceiling.

"You're going to write once a week, every week, right?" Allison lifted her feet into the air, bicycling her legs.

"Sure, but I'll probably have to send it by carrier pigeon or dog sled or something so the mail may be a little slow! That's how they do it out in the boondocks." Kaitlin stood, grabbing her friend's feet and pushing her legs down, like a teeter-totter. She didn't want to talk seriously. She wanted to play and pretend this was just another ordinary overnight.

"You hold her down, and I'll tickle her," Karmen said as she jumped into the scramble.

The screams brought Laurel with a tray of hot chocolate. "Settle down, girls. There's still school tomorrow and I promised your mothers that you'd be half-civilized in the morning." Laurel helped them spread out sleeping bags and pillows, kissed Kaitlin good night, and turned off the television. "Don't stay up all night talking either," she added as she pulled the door shut.

The girls whispered around their hot mugs, promising to telephone, promising to send pictures, and promising to always be best friends. Kaitlin read a story to them from her favorite children's book and soon Allison and Karmen were sleeping.

Kaitlin stared at her sleeping friends in the dim light, memorizing their faces. For all the promises that they had made, Kaitlin knew, somewhere deep inside of her, that she would never see them again.

* * *

The big conference table was polished to a glossy shine. Whaley placed his worn sleeves carefully on its surface, trying not to smudge its gleaming reflection of the overhead lights. Across from him sat the examining board, a long row of suits and white jackets, a couple with gray in their hair but most of them much younger than he with MDs and PhDs and other alphabet letters after their names. He kept his eyes lowered respectfully and waited until he was asked to speak.

They shuffled papers from long manila folders, legal size documents reporting his psychological history, the terms of his confinement, and his recent evaluations. Occasionally one or the other of the doctors would murmur a soft question to a colleague, heads would nod and papers would shift again. Whaley's shoulder burned, but he didn't scratch at it. He'd learned long ago the docs didn't like it when he scratched.

The suit at the center of the table, one of the older ones, with broad shoulders and gray in his beard, cleared his throat and began. "We're here today to make a decision on the release of Mr. Donald Whaley, who you see before you. As you know, the closing of this state facility necessitates the transition of its former residents to less restrictive settings. Mr. Whaley has been in treatment on our criminal unit for almost thirty years. His condition upon his arrival was profoundly violent and disoriented. He hallucinated, heard voices, and was self-mutilating. During his residence, he has received a variety of treatments including insulin shock therapy, behavior modification, and medication. He has been quite responsive to the last and in recent years has moved down from the high security violent crime ward on the third floor to minimum security on the first floor of that unit.

"During the last year he has been part of the supervised grounds crew and has been on an open ward locked only at night. It is the opinion of the attendants on this ward and of the ward administrator that he no longer presents a threat to himself or to others. I would also remind you that his original sentencing was for involuntary manslaughter and only for five years. He has currently served just over forty years counting his time of incarceration and his residence with us. Mr. Whaley has paid his debt to society to the satisfaction of the court. It remains up to us to determine if he is prepared to re-enter the community.

"Arrangements have been readied to return Mr. Whaley to the township where he originally resided. He has a daughter and grandchildren still living in the area and they have maintained contact with him during his institutionalization. A rooming house has agreed to provide a place for him and the county has an itinerant psychologist who will schedule weekly visits in his area. Mr. Whaley will receive social security income due to his age and disability.

"I remind you, however, that despite these preparations, the final decision regarding his release remains with us.

"Mr. Whaley, would you please share with us your perceptions of your current condition?"

Whaley looked up, ready, but surprised, when he was finally addressed directly. His eyes moved up and down the row, gauging the receptiveness of the board. One young woman smiled as he made eye contact and nodded to encourage him to speak. Several continued to peruse his file.

"I guess I been feeling a lot better lately. I been working outside and building up my body a little. I seen my grandkids several times this last year and they don't seem to be scared of me anymore and my daughter says I'm doing much better. I take my medicine regular and I ain't seen or heard anything that wasn't really there in a long, long time." This last statement was a goddamn lie but he told it straight and kept his eyes on the woman who smiled.

"Mr. Whaley, you have a long history of self-mutilation. Does that symptom still bother you?"

Whaley felt himself tense, but he hoped the others couldn't see it in his rough face. "Well, sir, I still have some scars that bother me a bit, especially in the cold, but I have a prescription that takes the pain away a bit and I don't mess with them. The doctor explained I have to keep my hands off those old scars so they'll get better."

Another of the suits cleared his throat and when the bearded man nodded at him, he began a different line of questioning. "Mr. Whaley, while you were in prison and again when you were first at the hospital, you attacked and badly injured several people. Why should I believe you wouldn't do this again?"

"Well, sir, in those days I was suffering from paranoid schizophrenia. A voice told me those people were going to kill me unless I killed them first. My psychiatrist says that I was suffering from a chemical imbalance which has since been cleared up with my medication. As long as I always stay on my medication, I'm not going to have those problems anymore. Also, I have to admit that I'm an old man now, I couldn't do that kind of injury any more and I've learned a lot about controlling my own behavior. If I found myself in a threatening situation, I could defuse it and walk away."

"Mr. Whaley, do you feel any remorse for your victims?"

"Yes sir, I always been sorry for what I done, even right after I did it. I didn't feel like it was me hurting those people. It was like someone else just using my body and listening to those voices. It made me sick to see what I done." This was true, sometimes he'd vomited afterwards and always he tried to tear out that rotten festering part of him that spoke the orders he followed.

"I never took no pleasure out of my violent behavior." This was not strictly true, for at the time it was better than any sex he'd ever had, it was just afterwards that he'd felt violated.

* * *

By Friday afternoon, it was all but done. Bulging suitcases, parked in the hallway, almost tripped Mike as he came through the front door. In the kitchen, he saw Laurel and Kaitlin's airplane tickets tacked to the bulletin board and found the refrigerator and freezer filled with enough food to get him through the first two weeks of bachelorhood. Mike reached around a sliced ham to fish out a beer and pulled a kitchen chair up to the counter. He twisted off the top and took a long draw as he watched Laurel in the back yard, pulling weeds out of her new seedlings.

Mike was surprised by his own melancholy. They'd been separated many times when the service shipped him off to one place or another, but something felt wrong about it this time. He was taking this forced retirement a lot harder than he should. Maybe it was just as well that Laurel and Kaitlin would be gone the next couple of months. Mike had a lot of adjustment to do and maybe they shouldn't have to put up with him as he tried to reinvent himself.

Mike shuffled through the mail and phone messages. The Realtor needed to make an appointment to see the house and set a selling price. "Shit!" he said aloud. It was going to be hard to leave this house, but they'd decided to put it on the market and settle in at Bluehills until Mike figured out what he'd do with his life. Hell, maybe he'd be a farmer; he'd seen a cow once.

Mike grabbed another beer and pushed open the sliding glass door to the back yard. The sun was warm on his face as he crossed the grass and slipped behind Laurel as she bent to pull weeds. He wrapped his arms around her, squeezing her close to him, as if holding her tightly would keep her from leaving him. Laurel turned in his arms and kissed him deeply, her hands entwining at the back of his thick neck. She stepped back, frowning at the smell of the beer, he knew, but she relaxed again and he pulled her closer.

"God, I'm going to miss you. You run up that telephone bill all you want, I'll ask for hardship pay to cover it."

Laurel smiled, "You just be around when I call. I don't want you out with the boys every night or picking up some questionable lady at the bowling alley. You understand me? Just remember, I'm psychic, so I'll know what kind of trouble you're getting into."

"Yes ma'am, and I'll take my vitamins and change my underwear and wash behind my ears."

"Mike," she tapped the bottle. "Don't get carried away with this. I won't be around to keep you out of the brig, you know."

"No you sure won't." Mike stiffened and pulled away. The moment had gone sour. "You have enough to worry about. Don't add me to your list. I can take care of myself."

"Hey, I didn't mean you couldn't. You just don't know how much I'll be wishing I was here with you." Laurel's mouth trembled so Mike kissed it to stop her tears. Gently, he led her back into the house, wishing he could make time stop and keep her here.

* * *

Laurel watched Mike as he left the bed to dress, his

32

muscled body bending gracefully in the late afternoon sun coming in through the skylight. She stretched across the bed, arms above her head; slowly taking in each detail of the room she had long loved and was now leaving. This separation was so hard on Mike and Kaitlin, she wouldn't burden either of them with her own fears and misgivings.

She watched the fan circling in the shaft of light, scattering motes of dust in the warm spring air. The dust danced downward, falling silently on the framed color photographs that decorated her chest of drawers. There was baby Kaitlin, a newborn nestled in her arms. There were Mike and Kaitlin at Yellowstone, laughing as they watched the mud pots boil. There were the three of them in a motorboat on a bright, blue lake; Mike in the middle, his arms around Laurel and Kaitlin. They all smiled, happy and secure.

Laurel had worked so hard to give Kaitlin simple family pleasures that she had lost when she was still too young. They'd made each home a special place, let Kaitlin feel settled as much as possible, spent time together, and kept in touch with Mike when he was stationed away. She'd encouraged Kaitlin's friendships, hosted Campfire troops, and car-pooled to birthday parties. She'd filled Kaitlin's life with all the things her own had lacked; family, friends, and security.

Now, she couldn't tell Mike, and certainly not Kaitlin, how afraid she was to go home. Too many sad and terrible memories lingered at Bluehills. Too many old feelings of loneliness and dread. Laurel loved her mother dearly, but she feared Bluehills deeply, a place, which seemed to steal away whatever was dearest to you. Laurel sighed, and rubbed the goose bumps from her arms. She pulled her sweater over her head and followed Mike into the bathroom. It bothered her that he'd opened another beer, but she didn't want to spoil the short time they had left. She held him long and hard and took courage from his strength.

* * *

It was the crackling sound that made Carol Ann turn away from the window. A young nurse in a white uniform brought her afternoon medicine, crinkling the individual wrapper that encased her syringe. Carol Ann paid no attention to the nurse or the prick of the quick injection. She stared at the cellophane wrapper, and reached out her hand for it.

"You want this honey? You can have this as long as you don't put it in your mouth."

Carol Ann nodded, never taking her eyes off the transparent paper. She snugged it into her palm with her thumb, rubbed it smooth, then fisted her hand and listened to it crackle. Crackle, crackle. The sound nudged at her ears and tugged at her brain, trying to remind her of something. She squeezed her fist again. Crackle. Something bent and dipped ever so slightly in her memory. Crackle, crackle, crackle. The image returned. The sound of wood burning, the orange flames in the night, the smell of flesh, too sweet.

She was home again. They wrapped her in a blanket and carried her to the car; afraid to leave her alone, too hurried to dress her. Papa set her roughly between him and Mama on the front seat while the boys tumbled into the back. He pulled out of the driveway and was a quarter of a mile down the road before Mama reminded him to turn on the headlamps. She whispered it with a shaky voice and at first Carol Ann thought she was talking to her.

Papa slammed through the gears and the car fishtailed around the corner in the icy mud, throwing them against one side and then the other, but Mama didn't scold Papa about his driving. She squeezed Carol Ann's hand so hard it hurt, but Carol Ann didn't say anything either. She watched the black trees hurtle past them as Papa raced his headlights through the night.

Uncle Ross was already there when they roared into the yard, bumping over the log ties that kept the sand out of the grassy lawn. The fire illuminated him in his thick coat and scarf. He didn't even glance at them, just kept staring at the burning remains of the house, wringing his hands and shaking his head.

Mama, Papa, and the boys leapt out of the car. They didn't even close the doors and Carol Ann shivered beneath the blanket and watched the flames dancing on the fallen frame. No one spoke but the fire. It crackled and popped and hissed as it devoured the old cottage.

Mr. Johnson stepped out of the shadows and put one dark hand on Mama's shoulder. "I'm so very sorry, Mrs. Miller. Alana and Ezra was already gone when we got here, God bless their souls." His eyes glistened wetly, reflecting the red and yellow of the flames.

Mama trembled, "Oh, my mother, my father!" A long wail of pain tore itself from her throat, then she turned and buried her head in Papa's chest.

"God All Mighty I wish we'd seen it sooner. My Sadie woke me up and I called the fire department first, then you. I high-tailed it over here. Everything was so far gone; there wasn't nothing we could do. Lord, those firemen won't be here for another half hour as it is. I just wanted to be able to do something, but she'd already collapsed like this. Flames reaching out at us like hands trying to drag us in." Mr. Johnson's face gleamed with wet tears that he wiped away with blackened hands.

Uncle Ross said nothing but he kicked at the melting snow and lowered his scarf long enough to spit at the fire that crackled and hissed back at him.

* * *

Kaitlin stepped out onto the little balcony that looked over the side yard. Pine needles littered the walk into the backyard where Dad was mowing. He was cleaning up for the Realtor to start showing the house next week. Kaitlin wondered if she'd forgotten any hidden treasure she should rescue before they left. She swallowed hard and kept back her tears. There had been too many of those already this week.

Outside, Kaitlin's bike leaned against the house, wet again because she'd forgotten to put it in the shed where the rain couldn't reach it. Leaving the house, she jumped on her bike for one last ride before dark. She took her time, carefully taking in the neighborhood; the beautiful blue spruce trees and tall Ponderosa pines, the gray and brown cedar-shaked homes, and the bushy Rhododendrons almost ready to bloom. Kaitlin watched a squirrel cross in front of her and laughed at the look it gave her from the other side.

Kaitlin hurried on, heading down the hill to the patch of trees and bike trails where all the kids hung out. The trails were curiously empty tonight as she made her way to the far corner where the girls had taken over an old battered tree house. She climbed the low branches that led like a staircase to boards that crossed two strong branches. A red canvas awning, borrowed from someone's patio, shaded the platform. The tree house itself was walled in by new green leaves just coming on with the warm spring. Kaitlin could sit here and make her own special farewell to the good place that had been her home for so long.

Birdcalls echoed through the little patch of trees and she watched as two sparrows argued over an old pan of water they used as a birdbath. When one had managed to chase off the other, it splashed into the shallow water, puffing up its feathers and preening with its head darting under the water. Both the sparrow and Kaitlin were so involved in the pleasure of its bath that neither saw the black and white cat before it pounced, seized the sparrow in its teeth, and leapt away.

The sight caused Kaitlin to gasp, but she watched tearfully as the cat devoured the little bird. She mourned not just for the bird but also for her own life here that was being snatched away just as cruelly.

CHAPTER 4

The plane's tires pounded down the runway as it picked up speed to ascend. Kaitlin wondered if the tires looked like the ones they showed in cartoons; the thumping they made certainly seemed to fit. She felt her stomach lighten and her sinuses swell as the plane took to the air. Kaitlin's ears closed in a vacuum, leaving her alone with herself, trapped in her head and insulated from the rest of the plane's passengers. She traced her finger on the window, pointing out her old neighborhood to herself as the plane rose. She thought of Karmen and Allison left behind at the airport gate and her eyes started to water. Kaitlin used her sleeve to wipe the tears away and hoped that her mother had not noticed. What a baby she had become.

The snowcapped mountains to Kaitlin's left were muted by the ocean's morning mist. Kaitlin kept watching them until she had to turn her head back to catch the last glimpse. The last, she reminded herself. Kaitlin remembered when her best friend Erin had moved to Minnesota three years ago. They had promised to write and Kaitlin did send postcards about twice a year but that was a hard way to keep a friend. These friends were all people she would never see again.

It was the first time Kaitlin had been in a plane and that part was exciting. She could smell coffee cooking in the little kitchen behind her and the stewardess had just passed with a tray of orange juice. They said airplane food was terrible but Kaitlin had not had a bite since getting up at five o'clock and her stomach was growling. She decided that an airplane breakfast of rubber eggs and cold toast would be wonderful.

Kaitlin's stomach fluttered when the plane shuddered. Just like driving on a bumpy road, Mom had told her. The hum of the engines sent a buzz through her whole body, like she was strapped into someone's battery recharger. The tight seat belt held her prisoner and the lights flashed, warning her to stay in her seat. Kaitlin slipped into a quiet doze, thinking about what her new home would be like. Head nestled into a little pillow propped against the window, a blanket protecting her from the blower's draft, she slipped away into a dream of sunshine.

Kaitlin rested on a warm, clean-smelling, pile of straw, gazing into the woods in the distance. The dark trees covered vast hills before her and one lone white bird circled high above the trees, his circles became tighter and lower, like a predator coming down on its next victim. From somewhere a great black crow rose to meet the white hawk and they engaged in mid-air, talons extended, beaks slashing. The white and the black fought as if they would fall together.

Kaitlin woke with a moan, warm drool running down one side of her chin, her mother asking her what kind of soft drink she wanted. Kaitlin shook her head, unable to answer quickly. She was badly frightened but she didn't know why. The dream had seemed so real, but she couldn't understand what had happened. Kaitlin felt as if dreaming it was making it real. She turned back into the pillow, trying desperately to make a new dream, a good one.

* * *

Rawlins knocked at his open door just as Whaley was folding the last of his few pairs of underwear into the shopping bag they'd given him.

"My man! How you doin' Donald? It's movin' day. Are you all right with that?" Rawlins filled the doorway like the football center he'd been in college. He was a wall of a man, with an ebony face that always shone with sweat and a deep voice like a drum. He would have been one hell of a success as a career con, Whaley thought, but he's not bad as a psychiatric nurse either.

Whaley nodded and Rawlins' laugh boomed through the room, rattling the thin glass of the old windows. "I hear you man. It's a little intimidating at first, but you gonna be all right."

Whaley smiled in agreement, snatched the heavy bag from the bed and headed for the door.

"Whoa, man. You don't want to be forgettin' these." Rawlins pulled open the drawer of the bedside table and palmed three prescription drug containers from its depths. "You know when to take these, right?"

"Yes, sir. I wouldn't have forgotten them." Whaley watched Rawlins drop them into the shopping bag. He shook the bag until the bottles dropped to the bottom.

"I know what you're sayin'. Keep the demons away with these and you'll have your life back."

They left the room and Whaley didn't look back. There were no fond memories here. Rawlins' key opened the ward door and they were in the mainstream of hospital traffic, long corridors that connected the main units and the administrative offices. Whaley hurried to keep up with Rawlins. They passed locked doors labeled with numbers that had little meaning to Whaley. The communications system in the hospital was poor compared to what he'd known in prison. No one seemed to have it together enough to pass messages.

The corridor emptied into a main waiting area where family members and agitated clients waited for admission. Whaley felt crowded and his hands began to sweat as they made their way through the people. He was surprised by the garble of foreign languages in the air, by the crying of tired toddlers, and by the insistent drone of women's voices. Sweat trickled down his back under his shirt, irritating the skin there and soaking into his stiff leather belt. Rawlins clapped him on the back and led him to the last door that stood unlocked and open to the damp spring air.

Whaley stepped over the threshold hesitantly, as if he expected alarms to go off. He stared out at the vast green lawn and the blacktopped driveway that led to the city street and the bus stop where staff shuttled back and forth each day.

Rawlins dug into the deep white pockets of his pants and pulled out a wad of rumpled bills and a ticket folder. He reached in again to retrieve a handful of change. "I got a little somethin' here for you, man. Got to get you started off on the right foot. This will tide you over until you're settled in at the boardin' house and your check starts comin' in."

Whaley held out his hand to accept the money and flinched to see his palm shaking in the air between them. His shoulder started to itch and he could feel his blood running up his neck in red tide. Rawlins put his empty hand under Whaley's to steady it and laid the train ticket, the bills and the change into it. Then he gripped Whaley with both hands and gave him a hearty shake.

"You're a good man Donald. You're gonna be okay on the outside. You're gonna do right by me." He squeezed Whaley's hands tightly and gave him a quick wink before he turned to go inside.

* * *

Kaitlin laughed as they boarded the moving walkway and she almost lost her footing with the first step.

"Grab the railing, goose!" Laurel supported Kaitlin as she gained her balance, then hurried to catch up with her, as Kaitlin's long strides took her quickly past other travelers who were leaning on the rail.

"That was fun, Mom! Can we do it again?"

"Sure, on the way back. Come on, let's stow this luggage until the next flight and you and I can explore this little piece of Minneapolis." Laurel led the way to an empty locker, deposited the required coins and pocketed the key.

Kaitlin and Laurel threaded their way toward the main terminal, moving against the steady flow of passengers who were rushing toward their departure gates.

"I think we should pretend we are wealthy tourists who have just won the lottery and do a little window shopping along the way." Kaitlin grinned at her mother, affecting a weak-wristed gesture like some New York prima donna.

"I'm not sure this shopping area is really upscale enough for classy ladies like ourselves but I suppose it wouldn't hurt to look." Laurel led them into a small gallery that stood across from the magazine store.

Laurel stopped in front of a detailed acrylic that depicted a farmhouse surrounded by blossoming apple trees. "It will be good to see Bluehills again. It looks a lot like this in the spring. The orchard blooms, all in pink and white, and the blossoms fall like snow, scattering across the front lawn. Your Grandma Doe's flower beds will be blooming in yellows and reds and you can smell the earth when it's turned over for planting.

"When I was a girl, I used to follow my father's tractor as he plowed in the spring. I'd take off my shoes and trot along barefoot in the rich black dirt. It was always cool and soft, and sometimes I'd find a nest of baby mice that had been turned up and take them home to nurse." Laurel turned to Kaitlin.

"I wish you could have spent more time at Bluehills, and more time getting to know Doe. I know leaving home is awfully hard for you right now, but I'm glad you came with me." Laurel gave Kaitlin a quick hug and tousled her hair to lighten the mood.

"Yeah, okay. Does this mean I can have pizza for lunch instead of waiting for that terrible airplane food?" Kaitlin's cheeks were pink with embarrassment but she was still smiling.

* * *

The loose change felt strange in Whaley's pocket, jingling against his leg as the train rocked over the iron tracks. He checked the contents of his bag, patted the thick bills in his back pocket, and stared at the unpainted gray backs of houses as they flashed by his window. Occasionally a dirty-faced child would wave at him from the sagging back steps of one of those houses. He'd wave back and once he smiled when a skinny, gap-toothed boy reminded him of himself.

His father had been a railroad man and they'd lived beside the tracks themselves. He loved the sound of the iron wheels clacking past and the blast of the train's whistle at the crossing up the road. He used to wait for the caboose and wave at the off-duty conductor.

The old man had gotten him a job in the yards and he'd married his high school sweetheart, a girl from the country. He moved Elinore off the farm and into one of those red-shingled houses along the track on the same street as his Pa. She'd been pregnant and was a lousy cook, but they were so happy until he'd killed the yard boss. Couldn't keep his fists to himself. Couldn't keep a lid on his red-haired Irish temper and that was the end of his life. He'd been drinking beer when he was supposed to be replacing ties and the yard boss had come up on him with a nail-studded two-by-four. He shouldn't have returned the blow. His arms had swelled with months of swinging a sledgehammer. They gave him involuntary manslaughter and he thought he'd die away from Elinore and the baby before he could finish his five-year sentence.

He ran his hand through his short gray hair and absently scratched at his shoulder. Many years ago, he had made himself stop thinking about the day he'd finally be released. Elinore was long dead, his daughter grown up without him. Prison had been a bad place for him; the devil had taken early claim on his soul and made this dreary earth an endless hell. He'd lost his mind somewhere back in the heat of that prison oven and for years they'd been trying to patch him back together. The docs said they were done and he was ready, so here he was on a long train ride to a new level of Hades.

Someone passing bumped against him and Whaley jerked in surprise. He looked up at a pleasant woman who begged his pardon and went on down the aisle. He nodded and looked down to see his hands shaking again. He fished in his bag for the pills that were supposed to keep him calm. He swallowed one dry and rubbed at his shoulder through his thin shirt. He was going home to a room in a boarding house he'd never seen, two hot meals a day, a bathroom down the hall, and three bottles of colored capsules guaranteed to keep the demon inside him quiet.

* * *

Kaitlin's mother nudged her awake just in time to hear the Captain's voice say, ". . . so please return your seats to their upright position. We will soon begin our descent into the Detroit area." Kaitlin sat up quickly, fastening her seat belt and tightening her mouth. She was already in her new state; a two-hour car drive would take her to the farm. Kaitlin leaned over to see out the window to catch the first glimpse of her new home but gray clouds obscured the view. It looked cold and rainy, not at all like the sunny city she had left behind. Her stomach lurched as they hit turbulence and Kaitlin felt much like she did when she had pumped a swing too hard, knowing the seat was suddenly above her and that if she didn't hang on for her life she would fall to the dirt below.

Two heavy bumps and they were on the ground. The plane finally rolled to its destination and the stewardess chimed the signal indicating that passengers could prepare to deplane. It was stuffy with the fans off and Kaitlin was pressed between a businessman's back and her mother's carry-on while she stood in the aisle waiting for the door to be opened. She almost panicked with claustrophobia but her mother kept patting her shoulder and stroking her hair, sensing her uneasiness, and Kaitlin breathed deeply and slowly, stilling her heart.

Finally, the staleness in the air broke and a whiff of fresh, if humid, air flowed to the back of the plane. Kaitlin shuffled forward with the others, saying thank you and good-bye to the crew as she stepped onto the loading ramp. Free of the crowd, she swung her bags from both arms, smiled at her mother, and fairly ran up the ramp to the waiting area. No one was waiting for them at the gate, and Kaitlin was surprised by how dingy and gray the airport was. Well-worn red chairs were anchored in straight rows against the wall and another line of weary travelers waited to shuffle into the plane and take their places.

* * *

Whaley stepped off the train and back into the world

he'd left. Forty years gone, a young man leaving and an old and feeble man returning, but the train station was exactly as it had been. The red brick structure stood as sturdy and untouched as the day he'd been shipped away. Outside the air still smelled of soot, and black cinders sparkled among the rails. Inside the walls were the same pale green, gray with cigarette smoke. The long wooden benches were unchanged over the four decades and the polished oak and brass ticket counters still lined the walls. Only the hum of computer printers had been added.

Across the street on the opposite corner, the Coney Island restaurant sign flashed red and neon blue in the gathering twilight. Its big corner windows highlighted the cook in his greasy apron stirring the thick meat sauce and ladling it over steamed hot dogs and buns. He filled trays of a dozen at a time doused liberally with thin mustard and piles of sweet onions.

Whaley's stomach growled and he calculated how many years it had been since he'd had his favorite meal. He made his way to the restaurant past clusters of young black men who congregated at the corners making furtive exchanges of cash and small white packages. Short-skirted girls leaned against the brick walls of buildings decorated with Spanish graffiti and gang signs, sometimes sauntering out to the curb to lean into the open window of a stopped car.

"Hey what's happenin' ol' man? You lookin' fo' a buy?" Whaley stared into the boy's brown eyes until he turned away. "Ah shit, man's fried already." The boy dismissed him with a backward wave of his hand and returned to his corner. Whaley had seen them all or some version of them before, in prison. Lashing tongues, slow wit, but street smart enough to smell the sickness in him and to back away.

He slid into a vinyl-covered booth at the back where he could see the long narrow stretch of the busy restaurant. He remembered bowls of chili and frosted glasses of chocolate milk he'd shared with Elinore, but when the waitress came he asked only for a bottle of Stroh's beer. The yellow light in the restaurant seemed to bend as his eyes watered and he wiped them with the back of his hand. Just another rheumy-eyed old man he thought and he ordered a second bottle of beer.

The red vinyl of the seat in front of him wavered and reformed itself as he finished off the second bottle. Sinewy forearms rose from the Formica tabletop, hands peaked thoughtfully in front of generous red lips, a wave of blonde hair pushed back from the high forehead. The hands intertwined and Whaley could see the spider legs flexing, ready to pounce. He followed the arms up to the biceps where a dragon coiled, steam whispering out of its flared snout.

Whaley rummaged in his bag, desperate to find the bottles of pills piled at the bottom, but the waitress at his elbow startled him and the ghost vanished as quietly as it had appeared. Whaley ordered another beer and reached under his shirt to scratch at his shoulder that suddenly burned and throbbed.

Part 2, 1950

"A time to kill, and a time to heal; a time to break down, and a time to build up; " --Ecclesiastes 3:3

CHAPTER 5

Alana stood at the edge of the island in the early morning light just before dawn. Her head was covered with a flowered scarf, tied to the side; wisps of gray hair fell over one eye. She turned her weathered face toward the sky, lined eyes squinting with the increasing brightness, toothless mouth held in a close tight line. Her feet ached with cold and exertion in the wet sand, the stream washing up to her toes. She had made the long walk in full moonlight across acres of forest to be here at this special time. She had come to prepare the island for her granddaughter who would someday be old enough to be taught its secrets.

Alana hurried, knowing she had to be back at the cottage before her husband rose from their bed and found her gone. If he knew she had come here, he would beat her; but she would come again even with the beating, because this was what she had to do and because his ignorance would never allow him to understand.

She wrapped an old Indian-print blanket around her shoulders and carried a woven basket, gray with age. In silhouette, she looked as if she might have stood just so a hundred years earlier or a hundred years before that. The air was still, heavy with the smell of water and forest. Small ripples slipped over worn stones and flashed gold flecks in the half-light of early morning. She bent to dip her fingers into the life-giving water that lapped greedily at her small hands, sucking the warmth from her knuckles and sending a sharp jolt of pain up into her elbow and shoulder. Still, she did not pull her hand from the stream.

Alana settled to her knees in the sand, both hands immersed in the heart of the rushing water, waiting for the sunrise above the trees. Her joints protested, but Alana remained, like a statue with eyes closed, waiting for the first rays of sun to touch her and the water with their power. She felt the warmth as a golden glow seeped through her eyelids, chasing the cold night and the icy water out of her bones and out of her thoughts. Sun glinted off the ripples of the stream and the small island was bathed in green and gold as the leaves warmed to the sun's touch.

Alana rose, bringing her wet hands to her face. She washed each cheek with her damp palms and licked cool drops from her fingers, then using the birch branch she had cut earlier to sweep the narrow shore, she moved along the island until she had covered its small circumference. She sang as she swept, a wordless humming that expressed her joy in the first summer day. When she returned to where she had started, she stepped back among the giant old trees, listening to their silent advice and feeling their power run through her. Then, walking without pain, she returned to the shore and surveyed all that was right with this new day.

Across the stream a great hawk, pure white, like none Alana had ever seen, soared high into the cloudless sky and then tore the calm by diving to the opposite shore where a half-grown squirrel ran for the cover of the nearby trees. The white hawk almost speared the squirrel, cutting off its path, but banked at the last moment to mount to the sky again. The squirrel, confused, froze on the sand; eyes bulging from its head, watching the hawk rise above the trees, then dive again. Unable to move, the squirrel watched death reach down with sharp talons and a hooked beak.

Alana turned away, an old woman now, shoulders stooped and head sagging. She chanted an old song she had heard from her grandmother but did not understand. Slowly she walked along the narrow island beach and stooped to gather shells and pebbles into her basket. Hesitantly, she dipped her hand into the water. Carefully so as not to disturb the surface, she drew out a perfectly shaped, almost iridescent black, snail shell. She held her breath as she examined it in her hand, then tucked it into basket, setting it gently between two small stones.

A flutter of wings from the branch above her startled her as the white hawk burst upward from his watching place. A white feather drifted through the budding tree branches and she reached out to catch it just before it could escape in the flowing stream. It too, went into the basket.

Then, resolutely wading into the water, Alana began the long trek that would take her back to the four-room cabin she shared with her husband, a loud argumentative white man. She shook her head, walking slowly and carefully through the thick trees and undergrowth.

Alana knew who the little squirrel was, but she did not know what the white hawk represented. How could she give warning?

* * *

April stood on one shoe in the sand, tugging at the sock on her uplifted foot. As the sock eased its hold, she fell back, catching herself. A little cloud of dust puffed up from the roadside as she dropped to the ground to work on the other foot. The sand slipped under the toes of her bare foot and she leaned her arms against the grassy bank to keep her balance while she tugged on the second shoelace. The gravel lane was empty and its sandy roadside was a cool retreat from the heat of the unusually warm Indian Summer afternoon.

"Wait up! You're getting all the good ones." April hopped up on one foot, trying to take off the second shoe.

"Hurry up, Slowpoke. I'm not going to wait all day for you!" April's older sister Carol Ann had already filled her first stocking; she knotted the end, left the bulging bag of walnuts by the grass and moved forward with the other stocking.

"Leave all the hard ones for me then! I don't care." April moved into the grass, closer to the trunk of the tree where she could see nuts scattered under the branches. Her dark braids swung as she bent to reach the nuts at the base of the tree. More had fallen into the raspberry bushes to the right so she dropped to her knees before reaching into the thorny branches to gather them.

Carol Ann was talkative after sitting quietly in school all day; chattering about how she'd heard Clarence Marrion got orders to go to Korea and his family were sorry they'd ever voted for Truman; how she hoped her fan picture of Elizabeth Taylor would be in the mail today; and how Amy List had told her that *Cinderella* was going to be coming to the Jackson movie house. April let Carol Ann's voice lie on the thick air between them without answering. She was in a good mood, April wouldn't break it.

April parted the green branches to peer further into the brush to see if any more nuts lay hidden there. She dropped to eye level with the ground to scan for more. The earth here was black and moist as the branches came together over her head to make a shady umbrella. Carefully she pushed one hand forward to reach a large nut, and as her head turned to look again, she caught a glimpse of something white and furry. April held her breath and turned her head as slowly as the hands of a clock.

The little patch of white was farther back in the raspberries, so April inched deeper into the prickly bushes, pressing her head into the tangle and moving aside a thorny branch. Now, just an inch from her hand, a blue-eyed, white puppy silently watched her. Their eyes met, bringing a coo from April who was enchanted with the little dog. Its small pink tongue protruded as it panted and it crawled forward bringing its nose closer to April's outstretched hand. She could smell its sweet breath as she slowly brought her hand up to stroke its head.

A rock crashed through the branches, surprising the girl and striking the dog viciously on the head. April jerked her hand away as the sharp rock gouged into the puppy's skull. The dog yowled, and then, seemingly stunned, awkwardly jerked away. April tore at the branches, coming to a full stand.

"What'd you do that for?" April was shaking, both from anger and surprise. "It was just a nice little puppy!" She shouted at Carol Ann and looked around for something she could throw at her, to make her hurt too.

"Get away from there. That dog probably has rabies or something. You're just lucky I saw what you were doing before he could bite you. A wild dog is nothing but trouble for you." Carol Ann grabbed April's shirt and dragged her from the bushes.

April's arms flailed at Carol Ann, her face red with agitation and her eyes brimming with tears. "You can't run my life. I'm not stupid! That dog didn't have rabies or anything bad. Now you've ruined it!" April slapped at her sister's arms but Carol Ann managed to hold her hands down and force her back to the road.

* * *

Yuki crawled away from the bad hurting girl. Her eyes looked nice, she smelled of something warm and sweet, and she made a friendly noise, but she had bitten him hard. His feet moved clumsily and he could smell his own coppery blood. Yuki's sight was bleary; he looked down at fuzzy feet where there should be one foot. His head pulsed with pain and he whined as someone shouted from the roadside. Yuki crept deeper into the bushes and dug at the soft black ground, trying to make a bed in the rich soil. Yuki's eyes closed on black and red grief. He lay dying in the dirt, whimpering occasionally and breathing hard, his claws feebly loosening the decayed leaves and black earth.

Between the waves of pain that throbbed through his head, he pictured the girl's face, dark hair and dark eyes that promised friendship and comfort but lied. Yuki turned his head and gagged up his dinner as his stomach gave in to nausea from the dizziness. He vowed he would protect himself from faces that promise but lie, if he should live to see such a face again.

* * *

Cash shifted his weight into the shovel as he saw the guard swing around in his direction. He threw dirt industriously as McLaughlin strolled by, tapping his stick against the leg of his tan Michigan State Penitentiary uniform, eyes scanning the work gang with a respectful vigilance earned by hard years with hard customers like these. McLaughlin was short but stout, toughened by long days with dangerous men. He was not one to mess with.

"How's it going, sir?" Cash beamed an ingratiating smile at the guard, who turned alert eyes on him, but kept moving without answering. Cash whistled a chorus of *Mockin' Bird Hill*, just to be irritatingly cheerful as McLaughlin moved down the line.

Cash laughed quietly to himself. Yes sir, this could be a pretty good set-up. Out from behind those bars for a little outdoor recreation. Bide his time, behave himself, and one of these days old McLaughlin, or some other uniform like him, would relax at the wrong time and Cash would cut his sentence short. Just shave off a little time, which he surely deserved for his good looks alone.

Cash slouched again as McLaughlin moved down the line, the back of his short cropped hair visible above the sunburned neck, barely shaded by the broad-brimmed prison guard's hat. No reason to waste his energy moving dirt around as long as McLaughlin was looking elsewhere. He pushed the sleeve of his blue work shirt up higher on his arm, revealing the slit-eyed dragon that perched on his thick bicep. A black widow spider rode his hand up to scratch at the arm, its legs drawn along each finger of his left hand. Truly, this was hot work, but conditions could be worse, and the view was not bad.

Cash moved to his right with the shovel where he could see through the trees to the road below. It was about time for the little girls to be coming home from school. Time for Cash's little treat for the day, a stretch of soft thigh from beneath outgrown cotton dresses, maybe a flash of white panties if they decided to race down the dirt road. A small teaser to remind him of the day he would be free to hunt again and little girls would be his to do with as he pleased.

He pushed back his blonde, wavy hair, a sneer growing on his thick sensual lips as he thought about how little girls squirmed under him and how they screamed their high pitched squeals when he drew his knife. How they begged for their mammas and how they cried when he drew the first blood. Yes sir, life was good, but it was especially good drawn from the throat of some half-grown girl, losing innocence and life in the same shrill scream.

Cash continued to shovel half-heartedly, arms moving automatically, shifting his leg to make himself more comfortable, as he scanned the road beneath him, especially hoping not to be disappointed today. He felt his pulse run faster in anticipation as he heard the first shouts from below. Little girl shouts of anger, seasoning his enjoyment.

There, he could see them clearly through the walnut trees at the edge of the road; the little one with braids swinging fiercely at her older sister, a tender morsel with long curly black hair. The fighting added to his excitement, the smaller girl struggling to hit her older sister as the larger girl fended off each blow with her longer arms. Cash felt himself growing hot and looked around to be sure McLaughlin couldn't see him.

Cash licked his lips as the girls moved out of sight, still catching the sound of their argument for a little longer. Yes indeed, the time would come when he would make those tasty looking pieces his own. The dragon's tail twitched along his bicep and a tiny puff of steam rose against his shirtsleeve.

Cash laughed, a dirty snicker that made Sweeney, just down the work line, turn away in disgust. What's your problem? Cash thought. Maybe he'd have to teach Sweeney a little respect before he left.

* * *

April ate alone in her room that night. Mama had sent her there when she had come through the door, still hysterical and screaming at Carol Ann. Mama brought in a plate of mashed potatoes, gravy, and meat loaf for her dinner, but April left it cold and untouched on the dresser. She pulled the quilt over her head and lay sweating and miserable underneath.

April couldn't believe that she was being punished when it was Carol Ann who had been so cruel. Carol Ann, who Mama said had acted responsibly; Carol Ann, who now sat at the dining room table eating peach cobbler and listening to Jack Benny on the radio; Carol Ann, who would cut out a pattern for her new dress tonight. God, how she hated her sister.

Papa came in about eight o'clock to reason with her. He stood uncomfortably in the doorway, insisting that April look at him while he talked. When she wouldn't face him, Papa pulled the quilt down roughly and sat heavily on her bed, his shoes still smelly from milking the cows and his dirty overalls leaving dust on the bedclothes. He rubbed the rough stubble on his cheek and shook his shaggy gray head at her then reached out and held her chin in his callused hand until she looked him in the eye.

"You got no call upsettin' your Mama over this. You know she ain't feelin' well and by God, if you keep this up I'll put you over my knee for sure. Ten years old is not too old for a spankin' and you sure won't be goin' into town with us tomorrow.

"Your sister was right to keep that dog away from you. Those damn things run in packs, killin' animals and carryin' disease. There ain't nothin' to do but shoot 'em. I want you up early tomorrow to help with the chores and I don't want any more mopin' around and no more name callin'.

"If you want a dog, I'll get you one, but you don't go near any wild animals around here. That goes for rabbits or squirrels any other critters you run into. You hear me?" He waited for her to nod, then released her from his grip.

"Yes Papa." April sighed and turned her head to the wall so her pillow would catch the tears running down her cheek. Her shoulders shook with sobs but she didn't let any sounds escape her. Papa left, turning out the light and pulling the door shut a little too hard. Carol Ann would sleep on the davenport tonight and April would have the room alone. April, wrung out of tears, fell into a fitful sleep.

April rose from her bed in the middle of the night, awakened by the yellow glow that filled the window beside her bed. Sitting up on her knees, she looked out to see the moon, rushing toward her, growing larger as it fell forward, filling the sky with its immensity, threatening to crush the farm beneath it. She could make out each crater that formed its face, a stern, unforgiving face with deep-socketed eyes that seemed to stare into her soul. Just as the moon filled her entire window, its mask fell away to reveal the face of a snarling white wolf whose fangs reached down to devour her.

April woke in a sweat of terror, her arms still trembling and her heart racing as she flung herself to the floor to escape certain death.

CHAPTER 6

Yuki was in a bad way when his mother found him, deep in the dank cover of the raspberry bushes. She followed his scent, moving faster when she was close enough to smell the blood and fever. She pushed into the tearing thorns, leaving bits of white fur behind on the overhanging branches. Finally, she could see him, wrapped in a tight ball, unmoving in the black dirt.

Worried, she whined and nosed at him, feeling to be sure he was still warm and breathing. She nuzzled at him until he whimpered from deep inside the hurting place, then sighing deeply, she licked him gently, looking for the wound from which his sticky blood flowed.

She licked the crusty blood from his head, found the deep cut and used her tongue to clean it tenderly, though he whimpered and snapped at her. She placed a heavy paw over his neck to hold him still and probed at the injury until it was clear and open. Her last stroke upset him so; he broke out from under her paw and shook his head to throw her off.

Pleased that he was still strong enough to resist, she took him up by the scruff of the neck and dragged him heavily away to the shelter of the nearby brush pile. She loosened the dirt and repacked it for him before she gently laid him on the soft ground. She nuzzled him against her teat until he began to eat. She nursed him with the last of her milk and waited.

* * *

April swung her tin lunch pail. Once filled with peanut butter, it now carried remnants of wax paper and liverwurst casings. She watched her brothers, George and Ray, cut off the road and go through the fields to the marl bed. Two skinny adolescents, one brown-haired and one blonde, they waded through the last cutting of hay, and across a field of marsh grass, hurrying for their cane poles and bright red and yellow bobbers. They were almost like twins, in the same grade at school, but Ray was the smart one and George had been held back twice. The boys would fish until their stomachs brought them home for supper.

For April, the marl bed was a mystery, a deep pond forever labeled off-limits to the girls. Formed out of an ancient seabed, the marl was a slick white clay made from the crushed snail shells of a time when salt water covered the earth. Papa had quarried the marl until he'd struck a deep spring and the pit had filled with water. Wet marl sucked on a man's feet like quicksand and made a deadly trap if not treated with respect.

Papa said the spring that fed the marl bed drew from an endless lake that seeped under the whole farm, the melt water of the heart of some ancient glacier that had carved Bluehills and its deep valleys, and now lay buried beneath earth. Mama said the water was pure, that it had sprung from a time when men were still animals and there was no evil in the world.

The girls were not allowed to fish or swim at the bottomless pond. Papa deemed it too dangerous and showed them how a long limb would sink out of sight into the white marl that gathered beneath the water. April only knew the water was too cold for swimming anyway, and too deep and black to look into. Sometimes, when she stood alone on the bank, the surface seemed to shift with its own life and left her queasy and cold. She worried about her brothers when she saw them standing at the edge of the strange pit.

She and Carol Ann stuck to the road; April walking yards behind, so she would not have to talk to her sister. They passed the trees where April had spotted the puppy and she listened carefully to pick up any whimper or purr that might come from the raspberry bushes. Blue jays fluttered overhead and scolded them for coming so near. One began to swoop at Carol Ann, making April laugh maliciously until it dove for her head too. She ran, catching up with Carol Ann at the point where the road shifted from soft sand to hard gravel.

"I heard Grandma Alana talking to Mama on Sunday. She says I was right to keep you away from that white dog. She says it's a bad omen or something. She harped on it so long Mama got mad at her and told her to be quiet before Papa heard." Carol Ann looked down to see what effect her words might have on April, but April was quiet, shivering inside, and wondering why Grandma Alana would say that.

* * *

April's father blasted the old truck's horn as he pulled into the driveway, calling all the kids from the house. George and Ray climbed onto the passenger side running board while April and Carol Ann scrambled onto the bumper. They peeked through the narrow cab window and the slats of the back gate to see what Papa had brought back from the auction. Curled up on a pile of loose hay, a black half-grown dog barked back at them. His face and chest wore the markings of a Doberman Pinscher but his ears and tail had not been cropped. Though he still looked young, it was clear he would outweigh most Dobermans by a third again when he was full-grown.

"This is Duke. Damn fella cost me a good healthy calf, but he's said to come from quite a line of hunters. " The dog jumped at the slats, whining to be let out as Papa hollered, "Duke! Get down, sit." The dog sat, still whining and shivering with excitement. Papa let down the gate and the dog was at them, sniffing out each person's shoes and pants, licking hands, jumping up to taste their faces, and even knocking April to the ground. He took off on the trail of a chicken but when Papa whistled and called, "Duke!" he stopped in his tracks and returned to his new master. Papa fished in his pockets for a bit of deer jerky that he flipped to Duke. Papa pressed the dog against his leg with strong stroking hands.

"He comes from the litter of a good ol' coon hound. She was bred with someone's city dog but the pups are bigger and smarter than she was. I'll take you boys out and show you how to hunt with him. We'll train him up for retrievin' too."

The boys each called Duke over and fed him jerky which Papa tossed to them. Carol Ann got a face full of dog breath and went disgustedly back into the house. Mama came out on the front porch to see what the commotion was about. She came down the steps awkwardly, already big with her pregnancy. Her hands pressed against her back to either balance the load of baby or to push back the pain she often felt.

April ran to fetch a short piece of rope from the barn. "Can I take him for a walk, Papa?"

Papa hesitated but a look from Mama made him nod his consent. "Sure, Pumpkin. Just don't tie that rope too tight and pet him a lot when he's bein' good. Don't go off where he's gonna spot some animal and want to take off."

The others followed Papa into the house as he patted his pockets and looked for candy he'd brought home from town. Mama yelled from the doorway, "Don't go too far, April, supper will be on the table in half an hour." The screen door slammed shut and the heavy door swung to as the rest of the family moved inside.

Duke strained at the rope, pulling April forward. April tugged to get him past the barnyard where the cows turned to give him sullen stares. They headed for the creek where April let out a little more rope so the dog could wade into the cold water, lapping at the current and snapping at bits of weed April tossed into the water from upstream. The full-headed milkweed pods had turned brown in the dry fall weather and the sumac on the bank was a brilliant red.

April used her tongue to "tsk" at Duke and he turned alertly looking her squarely in the eye. "We're gonna be great friends, you and me. I'm gonna teach you all kinds of tricks and you'll always be my dog." April hugged the wet dog against her just as he began to shake off his swim in a drenching shower.

* * *

Cash balled the wax paper from his sandwich into a tight missile that he aimed at the back of Bill Sweeney's head, just where his hair and scalp parted company to leave a halo-like circle around Sweeney's skull. "Hey, Old Man, you got a Camel for me?"

"Yeah, I got smokes but not for a sick, pervert punk like you." Sweeney pulled himself up, out of the line of fire and joined a couple of the other men resting on logs they had downed earlier in the day. Short-termers, Don Whaley and Dick Malott, were in for assault on men who needed throttling. Whaley, red-haired, thick and soft, and Malott, tall and stringy; they were cellmates and hung together most of the time, watching each other's back. They gestured for Sweeney to take a seat and the three men sat tiredly, sweat running in rivulets down their smudged faces, hands cupped over dirty knee patches. Sweeney sat facing his friends, but Whaley and Malott followed Cash with careful eyes.

Cash's mouth tightened, white at the corners, while the heat of anger reddened his cheeks, but he stood slowly, strolling in Sweeney's direction and forcing a fixed smile onto his face.

"Now you don't want to turn your back on a fella like me, do you Sweeney?" Cash stood smiling behind Sweeney, shirt still neatly tucked, clean hands hanging loosely near his pockets. He stepped up to Sweeney's back, his cold eyes watching the other two men. Cash pressed one hand on Sweeney's shoulder and moved the other in his pants pocket where it pressed sharply into a space between the ribs below Sweeney's shoulder.

"I'd think you'd want to share those smokes with a friend." Cash leaned into Sweeney, blowing a whiff of mustard and bologna into his face. At Sweeney's back, the sharp blade of a short knife cut through Cash's pants' pocket, through Sweeney's shirt, and into the skin and muscle. Sweeney tightened, winced, but didn't move.

"If I was to turn suddenly and walk away from you, I think you'd feel real bad." Cash kept grinning, turning the smile from Whaley to Malott while he hugged

Sweeney close to him. The men clenched their large hands to their knees but said nothing.

"Yeah, you got 'em. Here's your smokes, you bastard." Sweeney fished out three hand-rolled cigarettes and passed them back to Cash. Fresh sweat beaded on Sweeney's forehead, cold and rank.

Cash reached for the smokes, smiled widely, then twisted the blade into Sweeney's back, jerking the bloodied metal out again. "I won't have to ask next time, will I?" Cash stepped away as Sweeney lurched to his feet with a roar and swung at him. The two tired men beside Sweeney hurried to pull him back as they glared at Cash.

Cash turned his back on them, laughing as he walked away. He tucked two of the hand-rolled smokes into his breast pocket and held the last one in his left hand as he rubbed his bloody right thumb and index finger together, just below the cigarette's tip. A wisp of flame flickered from his hand, catching the paper and tobacco in a smoky burn. Cash laughed louder, deep from his belly, jarring the noonday with his harsh bray.

* * *

Yuki stepped weakly through the opening of the brush pile. His mother washed his ears and nudged him into the gray daylight. Despite the clouds, his eyes burned in the light and a wrenching pain jolted his skull. He stumbled with the pain and struggled to right himself, taking in deep breaths of the fresh, cold air. His nose twitched involuntarily as he picked up the smell of fresh food. He dropped his nose to the ground, causing another wave of pain and vertigo.

Yuki sniffed the dusty ground and picked up the scent of a freshly dead mouse. Hesitantly, he shuffled forward until his nose was buried in the soft texture of the still warm corpse. His tongue flicked out to lick the tiny body, bringing forth a tide of saliva and noisy cramps in his stomach. He snatched up the mouse, crunching the delicate bones between his teeth, releasing warm fluids and rich flavors. He swallowed the gift in one bite that moved satisfyingly down his throat. The bit of blood and bone cheered him. Soon, he would hunt with his mother.

CHAPTER 7

On Saturdays, Papa went into town to do the shopping. He usually took the children with him so Mama could get the floors mopped and do the washing without having them under foot. April stayed home, thinking Mama might need some help. Mama hadn't looked good today, dark bags under her eyes, the color leached out of her face, and her hands rubbing her lower back all the time now. April noticed Mama moved slowly like she was trying not to jar anything loose inside of her.

The others left in a wash of confusion that swept the house clean of their noise and activity. Papa yelling at the boys to get their jackets, Carol Ann whining about her tangled hair, George and Ray arguing about who had earned the right to ride shotgun; then suddenly, it was quiet and still. Mama settled into her overstuffed chair, closed her eyes, took a deep breath, and exhaled with a small moan. Duke lay at her feet and for a few minutes Mama rested there, perfectly still while the radio played softly.

"We'd best get to the chores, April. You come help me find the eggs." She reached up for support and April gave Mama her arm, trying to stand firm as Mama levered herself out of the deep chair. Halfway up, Mama slipped back, caught herself, and gave April a quick forced smile and pulled herself the rest of the way to a stand. "It's okay, Honey. I'm sure glad I've got you home to help me today." Mama squeezed her hand and April went to fetch their jackets.

The barn sat gray and still at the foot of the hill. Its interior made a tapestry in shades of brown, the dirt floor scattered with Rhode Island Reds milling around and pecking at the dirt, the unpainted feed bin standing at the door to the cow stanchions, old leather harnesses draped from nails in the wall, bales of hay stacked almost to the roof, and iron hay hooks and other implements guarding the entryway.

A long braided rope swung from the center beam. In January, the rope would grip an enormous hook hoisting a steer's carcass, skinned and dressed out for cutting into pieces for the meat locker. For now, it hung innocently, its loop a hand-hold for children to swing off the loft and run through space, letting go to land in the soft hay on the other side.

Mama moved to the side of the barn, opening the door to the hen house. Spider webs hung with loose feathers, dust, and dried flies, waved in the draft. There was no electricity here, so Mama stepped gingerly over the doorsill and let her eyes adjust to the dim light. She shooed out the few remaining layers while April climbed the ladder into the hayloft to look for eggs. Duke watched from the bottom of the ladder, putting his paws on the first rung or two and whining after her.

Searching for those holes between the loose bales where chickens were known to hide, April made sure they were unoccupied before reaching her hands into the warm tunnels. If the hen was still at home, April thunked the top of the bales and tried to scare it out but never put her hand in where a sharp beak could peck it. She'd leave those for the boys to get later.

April made her way to the topmost peak of the barn. There, a small paned window looked over the field off to the woods. She liked to climb up to that last high bale where she could rub the grime from the window and take in the long rolling view. She stood there, tottering a little on the loose bale and followed the line of the creek where it separated the cow pasture from the marsh and woods. A branch of water broke off; twisting back into the woods and April followed its path with her eyes.

April's eyes stopped at the edge of the woods when she caught a flash of white. There, at the stream she could see a white dog drinking. It looked warily around between sips, then, as if it could sense her, the white dog turned directly toward her and looked up at the barn. It jumped, as if stung and slipped into the bushes bordering the marsh, its tail flickering out of sight like a match extinguished in the wind.

"April!" An urgent cry shook her out of her daze. It came from below, making April's heart pound as she turned to scramble down from the loft. "April, help me!"

Duke started barking madly, then whimpered at the base of the ladder. April used her feet to push Duke back and off the lower rungs though his claws scratched her legs as she came down. She turned from the ladder as soon as her feet hit the floor. Her eyes found Mama leaning against the barn wall, her skirt soaked in blood that rushed in a stream down to her ankles.

"Mama! What's happening?"

"It's the baby, honey. I'm gonna be okay. You just got to help me get up to the house." Mama reached out for April and draped her arm around her shoulder. "I just got to get up to the phone and call someone."

They started clumsily up the hill, April taking more weight from Mama than she thought she really could. Then, with a little moan, Mama dropped to the ground, fainted dead away. Duke licked at her face, trying to rouse her, but Mama didn't even move when Duke barked in her face. April told Duke to stay and ran for the house, hoping no one was on the party line. She pulled the receiver to her ear and dialed Mrs. Brook's number. It rang a long time before the operator answered.

"Mrs. Brooks, this is April Miller at Bluehills Farm and I have to have help over here right away. Mama's havin' the baby. She's on the ground outside and she's bleedin' awful bad."

"April, you go back out to her. You wet a towel to take with you to wash her face and you take a cup of water and you get her to drink something right now. I'm going to call the doctor for you and I'm going to see if Mrs. Quiggley is home and send her right down." Mrs. Brooks clicked off and April ran to the kitchen to do as she had been directed. She leaned the water pail over the sink to fill a cup with water, then poured it over a dishtowel hanging nearby. April looked out the high kitchen window over the sink to see what was happening and saw Duke circling her mother protectively as she reached up to pat his back. Walking carefully to keep from spilling the water, April hurried down the steps to where Mama lay.

"Mama, someone's comin' right away. You just got to stay where you are and Mrs. Brooks says to drink this water right now."

Her mother didn't answer, but seemed to double up on herself moaning with pain and adding a brighter red to her ruined dress. April moved Mama's head into her own lap, wiping the towel across Mama's face and watching nervously for someone's car to pull into the driveway.

"April, I don't know what I'd do without you. I want you to promise me something right now. If anything should happen to me, I want you to talk to Grandma Alana. I want you to talk to her long and hard and I want you to do whatever it is she tells you to do." Mama closed her eyes after this effort and lay back on April's lap.

"Mama, nothin's gonna happen. Help is coming right now and you and the baby'll be all right. There won't be anything to tell Grandma Alana." April's eyes watered and a tear rolled down her nose where she wiped it away with her hand.

"You just have to tell me that you will listen to Grandma Alana. She can protect you but I can't." Mama spoke so softly, April could barely hear her.

"Of course, Mama! I'll do anything you say." Then April spotted a dusty cloud coming down the road from the west and gently laid Mama's head on the wet towel.

"I'll be right back, Mama. I have to show them where you are. Duke, stay." The dog fidgeted but sat where he was as April ran up the hill toward the driveway.

The Quiggley's black '47 Chevy pulled into the driveway with Mrs. Quiggley at the wheel. April didn't even know the frail looking lady could drive and doubted she did very often. Jeannette Quiggley looked serious and she hustled for the brown heap that was Mama in her winter jacket and bloodstained house dress.

Jeannette must have been a lot stronger than she looked, because together, the two of them managed to carry Mama into the house and to her bed. Jeannette sent April after blankets and hot water and took over nursing Mama. April ran, in part, out of fear. Mama's shrieks chased her through the rooms to the kitchen.

The doctor came almost a half-hour later. April let him in the front door and took him to Mama's room where all was quiet now. The baby had passed; tiny, lifeless, and blue, too early to survive. It lay wrapped in a soft flannel blanket, a cold white bundle resting on Mama's dresser. Jeannette sat on Mama's bed, holding her hands as soft silent tears washed Mama's face. Dr. Faust sent Mrs. Quiggley out and closed the door.

Mrs. Quiggley touched April's shoulder gently. "Are you going to be all right?"

"What happens now?" April asked, swallowing back her own tears.

"Well, your mother is going to need you all to help for a few days. She isn't going to get around so well this first week, and she's going to need you all to be very kind and help her grieve this thing through. The doctor will be by to check on her a couple of times and she's going to be fine again, just a little sore and sad for a while."

"What happens to the baby?"

"Oh honey!" Mrs. Quiggley hugged April to her. "That baby is already home in heaven. Dr. Faust will take his little body down to Stormont's Funeral Home and they'll arrange a burial. Probably just your father will be there but next spring when this is behind you, you'll all go down and put flowers on its grave. That little baby will look down from heaven and know how much you love him."

Mrs. Quiggley's little kindness was more than April could bear. Her face twisted, her mouth quivered, and hot tears coursed down her cheeks. She thought what a black, black day had come to Bluehills Farm.

* * *

Alana woke from her nap, the dream still fresh in her mind and her cheeks still wet from her sorrow. She pushed back the blanket and went to stand on the front porch. She could see the wooden rowboat sitting across the gray lake over the deep hole where her husband liked to fish. He wouldn't be any bother for a while and she could do what she needed without dealing with him.

She found her basket of stones and shells and carefully chose six, one of each color. These she placed in a large clamshell she had cherished since she was a small girl. From the cupboards in her tiny kitchen she gathered dried leaves and small sticks she had set aside, claiming to use them to season food. She placed them in the clamshell, covering the stones and shells, then drew a hot coal from the pot-bellied stove that sat in the middle of the room.

The dried leaves and stems began to smolder as Alana carried the shell to each corner of the room. She raised the white hawk feather she had found and used it as a fan to spread the smoke over all the spaces of the small cabin. As she walked from corner to corner, she prayed quietly, calling for harmony for her child and grandchildren. She then turned the feather toward herself and fanned the smoke first at her feet, then to her knees, to her waist, to her chest, and finally to her head. The herb smoke ringed her head and she breathed deeply, praying for wisdom and courage in what she now knew lay ahead.

* * *

April saw the car first, a white Oldsmobile pulling up the long driveway with Donna Jean in the passenger seat. "Mama, it's Donna Jean, come home for Ray's birthday! And she's with a boy." April thought he looked just like Nicky Hilton, Jr.

Mama pulled back the lace curtain to get a better look at the driver, a young man with dark hair brushed back from his forehead. Mama scowled a little and shook her head. "She better hope your father doesn't see her with that boy. She'd have a lot of explaining to do. Gone away to high school and suddenly she thinks she's all grown up." Mama let the curtain fall back and opened the front door, in time to catch Donna Jean throwing a kiss at the young man as he backed down the drive.

"Mama!" Donna Jean hurried inside, breathless and blushing from being caught by Mama. She was carrying a big white box from the Homemade Bakery. "I hope you haven't fixed Ray's cake yet. Look what I brought from town."

Donna Jean pulled up the cardboard flap to show off the special cake, covered with white frosting and yellow roses. "I saved my bottle money to get it for him." From her pocket, she fished out a box of birthday candles. "And these too! Do you think he'll like it?"

"I suppose he will, honey, but he'll like having you home, the most. What I want to know is why you didn't invite that boy in to have supper with us too. Is this someone you're sweet on?"

"Mama! How would I explain that to Papa? You got to tell him I rode out with the mail truck or something. You know how mad he's going to be. And you got to tell him I'm growing up. Mama, there's a high school dance next week I want to go to. Please ask Papa to give me permission. You know I'll just sneak out anyway if you don't tell Aunt Rona it's all right. Please, Mama."

"Hush, child. Don't be saying things I don't want to know, and don't get any notions about disobeying your Aunt, or your father will bring you back home and that will be the last of any high school at all. April, what are you staring at? Little pitchers have big ears. Now you girls help me get dinner going and we'll make a real party of it."

April jumped up to help her mother, pausing long enough to hug Donna Jean around the waist. "I'm so glad you're home, sis!"

Donna Jean hugged her back, holding on a little longer after April tried to pull away. "Seemed like the right time to come home, like something was calling me back. I just thought it might be the right time to give Mama and Papa something new to worry about."

At supper, they lit all the candles and sang *Happy Birthday* while Ray made a wish and blew them out. His freckled face broke with his wide grin when Papa presented him with a new deer rifle and promised to take him hunting when the season opened on Monday. George punched Ray in the shoulder a couple of times, calling him baby, but offered to shoot targets with him over the weekend.

* * *

On Saturday, the girls went for a long walk in the woods, following the game trails that led back to the wide creek cutting through the center. Donna Jean leading, Carol Ann in the middle, and April at the end making their own quiet parade. They wore scarves tied tightly over their heads, mittens on their cold hands, and wool jackets Mama had insisted they take. It was the first time the three had done something together since last August's hay harvest before Donna Jean first moved to town to live with Aunt Rona and go to high school.

"I can't wait until I'm old enough to live in town and go to high school." April stooped to tie her shoe, admiring the way Donna Jean strode ahead like she owned the world.

"At the high school, you have to take hot showers naked with all the other girls, don't you Donna Jean?" Carol Ann turned to watch April, but she kept a straight face trying not to look shocked.

"Well, just after gym class, but nobody cares what you look like. They're trying to hide too."

"I wish we had running water like Aunt Rona, and indoor plumbing, and oil heat. Must be nice not to have to fetch water and wood all day." Carol Ann stared straight ahead, probably daydreaming of marble bathtubs and flush toilets.

"Sure, it's great if you don't mind living on the third floor of a windy brick building that smells of cabbage all day and if you don't mind sleeping with Aunt Rona, who snores like a train." Donna Jean snatched off Carol Ann's hat, shaking her from her reverie.

"Well, it would be worth it not to get a frost-bitten behind every winter." April and Donna Jean laughed with Carol Ann, agreeing with her sentiments.

The trees had lost the last of their fall color and the forest floor was carpeted with the brown leaves that had already fallen. Mostly oaks with a few maples and walnuts, the trees raised their bare arms like brooms reaching up to sweep the color out of the sky, leaving it gray and cold. Their rough black trunks hedged in around the girls like fence posts keeping them from wandering off the worn deer paths, but the bare limbs let them see farther than usual, making the contours of the land around them clear. The path rose higher until it ran along a ridge that dropped off suddenly to a wide valley, swollen with dark water, beneath them.

The woods were silent, songbirds gone for the winter, the wind still. The girls fell quiet, April holding her breath, squeezed by the heavy cold that seemed to rise from the dark valley below. She closed her eyes, straining to hear any movement or animal voice, but all that came back to her was the soft murmuring of the black creek. The cold climbed up her legs from the nearly frozen ground, weakening her knees and chilling her deep in the pit of her stomach.

"You know, Grandma Alana comes back here sometimes. She says it's an old Indian holy place and I think she fills her medicine bag with plants and roots that grow near that creek." Donna Jean's soft voice warmed the heavy air, easing April's chill.

April opened her eyes, finding her gaze aimed at an open space between the trees on the other side of the water. She watched as a swatch of white slipped between the dark trunks and disappeared. She shuddered with the cold and rubbed her arms to warm up.

"It's creepy back here. Let's keep going." Carol Ann swung out around Donna Jean and shuffled down the path that angled away from the ridge and back toward the road.

The deer came into sight as they neared the road, playing in a field of marsh grass that bordered Papa's cornfield. A magnificent buck led a party of three does and two fawns. His rack was eighteen point, at least, and he stood alert and noble at the edge of the field as the rest of the deer frolicked in the tall grass. The does were large and healthy, and the fawns half grown already. They scampered in tight circles, looking for all the world as if they were playing tag. The girls stood frozen in their tracks watching the game with broad smiles.

Boom! The rifle split the air with a thundering crack that panicked the deer. Confused, they rushed toward the girls, then turned aside as the breeze brought the girls' scent to them. Turning away, the deer ran into the line of fire again and with a second blast, one of the does fell heavily. The doe's scream tore through April like the whine of the big buzz saw ripping through green wood. Sounding exactly like a terrified woman, the animal's agony made April's stomach lurch and twist. She pressed her mittened hands over her ears and moaned with the pain of it.

Donna Jean broke from the trees, racing toward the fallen deer where George and Ray were already standing over the trembling and heaving doe. George was laughing when Donna Jean tackled him, knocking him flat and punching his face hard, before he could shake off his surprise to protect himself.

"You son of a bitch! What the hell do you think you're teaching him? You stupid fool bastard! You killed a Goddamn doe, out of season, when we were right in your line of fire. You stupid pig!" Donna Jean clutched a handful of his coat, pulling George off the ground while she continued to slap his face with each word she spit out at him.

George tore himself out of her grasp, scrambling backwards while Ray grabbed Donna Jean by the waist and held her off of him. White snot ran from George's nose and his face sported red and purple blotches where she'd struck him. "Stupid girl. He's a man now. He can kill any animal he wants. Why do you think Papa got him that gun? You're a damn sissy doe, yourself. Get out of here so we can take care of her." He stooped to pick up his hat and Donna Jean's leg reached out to kick him, knocking him to the ground again.

Ray let go of Donna Jean, turning away and sinking to the ground beside the doe. He reached out a hand to touch her soft side, then drew a knife from the sheaf on his belt and deftly cut her jugular, helping her die faster. Tears streaked down his red face and his shoulders shook as he stroked her soft underbelly and watched her red blood pool on the frozen ground.

CHAPTER 8

November days were short and dark, bringing more bad news about Korea and Mama fretted about her cousin Bob, the marine, being called up for overseas duty. Mrs. Platte assigned *Great Expectations* to the sixth through ninth graders while the younger pupils studied the pilgrims and early American colonies. April hurried home from school, rushed through her chores, and spent the rest of the afternoons training Duke. April taught Duke to climb the ladder to the hayloft, even though he was so top-heavy she had to nail the top extensions into the beams to keep ladder and dog from falling over. April taught Duke to stand perfectly still while she made a forward flip over him. April taught Duke to pull the ice-fishing box with one of the cats spitting and scratching inside. She waited for snow when she would teach him to sled down hill with her.

It seemed to the children that the first snow of the season usually came on Thanksgiving Day, so there was always a feeling of anticipation and a close watch on the sky. Mama rose early that morning to start the pies and by the time April was up, Mama was taking bubbling blackberry and apple pies from the oven. "You girls help me with the dressing. Get these onions cut up while I clean the chickens."

Mama picked up one of the fat headless birds and lowered its body into the black kettle filled with boiling water. She pulled it out and began plucking feathers, reducing the big black and white Brahma hen to a clean mound of baking chicken that would drip fat into the roaster pan for a rich yellow gravy. April looked away, knowing that if she watched too long she couldn't eat it later. The chickens were set aside until it was time to put them into the oven.

Carol Ann and April worked at kneading Mama's bread dough and shaping it into soft white balls for potato rolls. By the time April and Carol Ann had peeled potatoes for mashing and brought up jars of Mama's canned corn from the cellar, they'd lost interest in cooking and were restless for the cousins to arrive.

Papa had set out early making the rounds to pick up folks who would be eating with them. Mr. Johnson, the colored caretaker from Pleasant Lake Camp, and his pretty daughter, Sadie, came with warm peach pies, spiced hot with ginger. Mr. Johnson praised the smell of Mama's cooking and quizzed each child in turn about school and chores. He laughed sweetly, like hot maple syrup, over each complaint they made. Sadie Johnson helped Mama set the table and waited for Donna Jean to come home.

Bruno, a German from the Old Country, the bachelor farmer up the road, came with jars of pennies he had saved for each of the children during the year. His voice was gruff and his hands hard with calluses, but he squeezed a sort of smile out of his unshaven face as he watched the children dump out the jars and begin counting the pennies. For Mama, he brought a big jar of dill pickles he had put up himself.

Papa's Uncle Ross came with this first group. He was a banty-sized, skinny-necked, stingy man who was always included in family happenings though no one seemed to like him much. He had retired at the nearby lake, living in his tent in the summer and in a run-down camp trailer when the weather turned cold. He rented rowboats out to the fishermen, overcharging them if he could.

Grandma Alana and Grandpa Ezra were bickering as they came through the door, but Grandpa Ezra gave it up when he was offered a Stroh's and Grandma Alana joined her daughter in the kitchen. They spoke softly in the corner, then Mama wiped her eyes with her apron and went back to the pots on the stove. Grandma Alana's toothless mouth set itself in a thin line until she looked up to see April with her nose pressed tightly against the kitchen window, watching for snow.

"Oh, Little Squirrel, you gonna frost-bite that little nose of yours and then you'll have to sit inside the rest of the winter, sleeping under blankets like the little bear who lost his skin."

"If I do, Grandma Alana, you'll read to me everyday and let me play with your Cracker Jack toys, won't you?"

Grandma Alana knelt low in front of April and stared at her with wizened black eyes. "If you spend the winter with me, I'll tell you all the stories my grandmother told me, and you will know all the secrets of the animals, the fish, the trees, and the plants. You will be able to read the moon and stars and tell people their dreams." She spoke so quietly that April's Mama couldn't hear her say, "I wish you could spend the winter with me and I would teach you many things."

"Sure, and you'll let me iron your clothes, and do your dishes, and sweep your floors, and anything else you can think of." April laughed out loud, but inside she wondered what Grandma Alana was really saying to her.

* * *

Yuki and his mother snuggled against each other in the cold morning air. They lay in a heap of white fur, curled in two half circles to form a whole. Yuki was already larger than his mother and his appetite grew each day as well. He was a good hunter and kept them both well fed, though the scarce days of winter would not be long in coming, now that the frost had settled into the ground. His mother lovingly tongued his ears and face, carefully tending to the long scar that ran across his skull.

Her attention to his old injury caused Yuki to wince, but he held still. The pain that usually sat just under the surface in quiet moments like this rose to wave its black flag at him, reminding him that life was not kind. He remembered the girl with the young face who smiled as she struck at him. Yuki shifted to his other side to slow the painful pulse behind his right eye. His empty stomach stiffened with the shift, urging him up from the comfortable den and out into the gray day.

Yuki nosed out of the narrow opening they had left for access. The cold air was tainted with the odor of wood fires drifting across the woods from nearby homes. The cold struck his tongue with a bite that spoke of dry snow, longer nights and less game. He moved quickly into the open, nose to the ground as he sought the subtle trail of squirrel, mouse, or rabbit that would make their dinner that day.

* * *

Aunt Rona and her two boys were the last to arrive, having survived a ride with April's sister, Donna Jean. They swept into the house in a rush of voices, arms full of candied yams, jello salads, and green bean casserole. Donna Jean took their coats up to Mama's bedroom, frowning at George as she passed him on the stairway. "Doe," he mouthed back as she glared at him. Still, he'd had two weeks of duty shoveling cow manure, so Donna Jean couldn't begrudge him some animosity.

The youngsters left the adults to their various debates and headed for the barn. George and Ray made sure to properly impress the cousins with feats like gathering eggs out from under the hens and squirting milk in their faces straight from the cow's udder. The cousins fell for the same jokes every time but still laughed at themselves. Sadie Johnson and Donna Jean sat on the rungs of the ladder telling stories about boys they knew and daydreaming about perfect weddings and Hollywood mansions. The cousins and April climbed into the hayloft and swung from a rope like Tarzan, King of the Jungle. Duke amazed them all by climbing right up the ladder behind them, but since he couldn't climb down, he jumped the last eight feet as the rope swung out over the barnyard. When the dinner bell called the children in to eat, they ran like a flock of chickens hearing the corn fly.

The guests and family crowded up to table for the obligatory photograph with Mama showing off her Thanksgiving spread; all of the party pushed into one corner to be a part of the picture. Mama had set out a tablecloth with her best dishes and changed into a fancy lacy apron when it was time to serve. It seemed she spent more time carrying food than eating, not that any one bothered to notice. When the last of the gravy had been mopped up with hot rolls, and the pie and whipped cream had filled all to bursting, the women cleared the table and the men set up card tables for hands of Euchre and Pedro.

The youngsters were back at the windows and when the yard light revealed small specks of snow coming out of the dark night, they were out the door. They put out their tongues to catch the first taste of winter and compare the shapes of snow flakes caught on their sleeves. They talked about building snowmen, and sledding out behind the barn with a kerosene lantern to light the top of the hill. They talked about Christmas coming with its long vacation and hoped to be snowed in before winter was done.

* * *

Cash scraped at his tray, mixing the gluey potatoes with the jellied gravy. The confinement of the last month had darkened his thoughts, leaving him touchy and out of sorts. His eyes moved along the concrete-block walls of the prison cafeteria. Guards with guns were posted on walkways above, eyes scanning for disturbances. Guards with sticks stood at the end of the tables, ready to escort each cell block back to their cages where Cash would sit on his lumpy mattress and feel himself growing old under cold blue lights.

Cash looked over at his cellmate, who sat across from him at the table. He wasn't an innocent of any kind, but the man was young enough and might afford Cash the little boost he needed until he could make the work gang again in the spring. The man was stupid too, and given to irritating habits that started to irk Cash on these gray winter days. If Cash could make it look like an accident or a suicide, he might be able to keep his record clean. If not, Cash would not see the blue sky for a long time to come.

The dragon on Cash's biceps swelled and puffed as Cash tensed his arm, wondering how much strength it would take to strangle a man and make it look like a suicide. He decided it wouldn't be that hard.

* * *

The men gathered in the living room around their card table sniping at each other while the ladies sat at the dining room table going through a box of old family pictures. Grandma Alana told the story behind each sepia-toned or black and white image while Mama faithfully wrote names and dates on the back. They laughed at how funny they'd looked when they were younger and sat silently considering memories of those who were already departed. Aunt Rona's husband had passed away just the year before after a long fight with cancer. She looked at his robust images, patted them a little and set them aside into a special pile. She wanted her sons to see them, too, to remember what their father had once been like. Mama held the baby pictures a little longer than necessary, until her eyes started to tear up and she went to the kitchen to put on a pot of coffee and warm the leftover pies.

The men settled into their game and caught up on news. Papa complained, "Damn dogs been messin' with my traps again this winter. I check those lines first thing every morning and still I've come on two muskrats had their innards eaten into."

Bruno raised an eye brow, "Yah, they been at my hen house too, but my Monk dog, he chase them away. Must be one of them's a bitch cause last week Monk lit out after them and he ain't come back."

"Those dogs are nothing to worry about. I've seen them down drinking at the swimming area, one female and her half-grown pup. She almost come up to me for a handout. Lordy, they're pretty too, both pure white with long silky fur. Even living in the woods, she takes care of them. I suppose some fool summer folk left them behind but I'll have them eating at my table before next spring." Mr. Johnson chuckled at his own joke.

"Well, they better stay away from my place. I got my gun loaded and behind the door." Uncle Ross looked grumpily around the table daring anyone to come at his place.

Papa laughed a great belly laugh joined by Grandpa, Bruno and Mr. Johnson. "What would they want around you? They want some fat old chickens, not a tough old piece of gristle like you!"

"Ha! Ross your garbage doesn't even have enough flavor left in it to smell good to these dogs. I think you're safe enough." Grandpa Ezra took a long pull on his beer and nodded at the other card players.

Uncle Ross sputtered and threw his cards down. "I'm going to get some coffee and some better company." He stamped out of the room toward the dining room as Mama's eyes met Papa's with a resigned Lord-help-me look.

* * *

Yuki ran in stops and starts tracking the rabbit across the field. His breath made small clouds in the cold air as he snorted at the track, keeping his nose down to the ground. Pain rang in his head as it always did when he moved fast, but it didn't keep him from following the rabbit's trail. Ahead, a quick movement in the weeds cut short the chase and a lunge brought him down on the rabbit's back. He devoured the head first, savoring the rich brain matter and the skull marrow. Feeling satisfied, he gripped the remains of the rabbit in his mouth and carried it back to the brush pile.

The rabbit had led him out of the woods and onto new property that he surveyed as he trotted along. A breeze carried the rich aroma of chickens to him, cut through with the odor of man. Marking the edge of the field, he would remember this place when hunger clutched him again.

CHAPTER 9

Alana sat on the edge of her bed listening to the old man snore and watching his chest rise and fall. She slipped her shoes on and reached for her heavy woolen robe. The fire had died out and the cabin was cold. She moved into the main room and methodically piled kindling and small pieces of firewood into the pot-bellied stove. The warm ashes made it easy to get the kindling started and she sat on her haunches poking at the fire and watching its flames. The light reflected off the oily surface of the old man's spittoon, a waft of stale tobacco and spit coming up with the reflection. Fire was an old friend, comforting and familiar. She hoped the warmth of the fire would chase away the cold of her dream.

She was always Crow Woman in her dreams and tonight she had flown above the earth, among the ice crystals that circled the winter moon. She had looked back, finding the paths of red, black, and green that denoted evil, death, and life. She looked down on her daughter's farm and watched as lines of red threaded in among the white. Something very good would be violated soon. The earth turned beneath her and when it returned to familiar terrain, a net of red and black hung loosely over the fabric of green. Crow Woman closed her eyes and soon Alana was awake again.

It was a great burden being Crow Woman when there were no others to speak to you of the signs and warnings you might see. She felt the messages of her dreams but could not put them into thoughts and words to share them, to learn from them, or to gain from them. Tonight's dream brought feelings of dread and a need to counsel others of danger, but they would only laugh at her old woman fears. She could not say what the danger was, from where it would come, or whom it would harm. Her part was only to see, she needed others to know and others to speak. But there were no others, no tribe since the days of her great-grandmother when they were broken apart and her great-grandmother fled to this place of power.

Alana drew nearer to the fire and held in her fear, a wound that was hers to bear alone, buried deep inside her where it gnawed at her lungs and liver. She chanted words she did not know, words that made the shadows pull back away from her and she waited through the long night for the late sun to rise.

* * *

April woke in the night and groaned. She couldn't hold it any longer. As much as she dreaded going out in the cold and the dark, she would have to make the trek to the outhouse. She pulled back the quilt and rubbed the frost off her bedroom window. It was nowhere near light yet, but there was no way she could hold it until morning. She was too big to wake anyone to go with her. She would have to go on her own.

April opened her bedroom door into the dark hall. Duke, asleep by her door, stretched and licked at her hand. April grabbed hold of his neck fur and whispered, "Let's go".

With one hand on Duke's head and one on the wall, April felt her way to the kitchen door that led to the back porch where her winter clothes were hanging. She hurriedly found her boots and coat, then remembering the dark, she returned to the kitchen to hunt up some matches. These she tucked into her coat pocket as she pulled open the back door. Duke hurried out in front of her and April stepped into the blustery night.

The wind slashed into her face with a bitter violence. The skeleton-like maples were whipping frenziedly and scattered snow clouds raced across a dim moon. April patted her pockets to reassure herself that the matches were still there. She wondered if she should go back in for a scarf and mittens but decided that it would be wiser to move fast and get back before she really got cold. She stepped off the porch and started down the hill toward the barn and the adjacent outhouse.

Shadows bounced and deflated around the edges of the pump house, the granary and the barn, making her involuntarily turn toward their movement. Duke skirted the current bush, relieving himself and running on to the barn. A tree branch cracked in the orchard and she could hear a dog dish or chicken feeder rattling as it skidded along the ground. The dark outline of the outhouse stood separately from the orchard and she hurried toward it, thinking of what might be waiting in the shadows under the trees.

Near the chicken coop, Duke began to whine and then to bark and dance in the shadows. Really frightened now, April ran the rest of the way to the outhouse, slamming its door tight and fastening the hook as quickly as she could, despite her usual distaste for the place. She pulled out the box of matches and with a clumsy frozen motion scratched the first match across the rough side of the box. A draft through the door quickly blew out the match though its brief flame assured April that she was alone in the little shack. She wished it was daylight so she could look down the holes as she usually did to make sure nothing was there in the dark.

Now Duke was growling and barking. April could hear him scratching at the chicken-coop door. She could also hear chickens screeching over the sound of the wind and imagined them battering into the walls in their fright. Duke must have nosed up the door latch on the hen house because she suddenly heard the door swinging and bashing into the side of the barn. Now the sound of growling filled the night and the yelping of dogs sent a great shiver through her.

"Duke!" her Papa shouted from the house and a rifle exploded from that direction.

April jumped to the hook, flinging the door open just as a white beast with glowing eyes rushed at her.

* * *

Cash thought through his plan again as he watched Emilio stripping down to his underwear for bed. Emilio was slight, no tough guy, just a greaser who was a little too lucky at cards. He probably used a gun when he needed protection; those skinny arms wouldn't do much in a real fight. Emilio would be easy to take out, almost girl-like, now that Cash thought about it. Cash watched Emilio's long slender fingers and fragile face. Yes, almost girl-like. This could be fun.

Cash laid back on his wool blanket and waited for Emilio's breathing to become quiet and even. He studied Emilio's slender face in its sleep; long black lashes around the lids that were edged with a slight tint of blue visible through the dark skin. Emilio's hair had grown back in, rich black waves that curled over his ears and fell across his forehead. Yes, Emilio was a very pretty boy. This could be a great deal of fun.

Satisfied that Emilio and the other prisoners on the cellblock were sleeping, Cash lifted his pillow and crept over to Emilio's bed. Quickly he forced the pillow over Emilio's head and threw his body over Emilio's. The boy began to struggle, thumping the bed with his kicking, but Cash kept his heavier body pressed against him to reduce the noise and movement.

Cash edged the pillow down just enough to see Emilio's frightened eyes. Yes, it was much better this way, catching the waves of fear that welled up with each flutter of Emilio's long lashes. Cash pressed his mouth to Emilio's ear, pinioning his head against him. His tongue flicked out, catching a taste of sweaty panic from Emilio's soft lobe. Cash opened his lips, using his teeth to nuzzle the ear, then tore a small piece of skin away, feeling Emilio lurch beneath him while the pillow muffled his scream.

"Oh you should be afraid of me, boy. Very afraid." Cash whispered softly into Emilio's ear, watching the terror in his eyes grow. "You think I'm some short-term con, but I am so much more than that. I am older than this prison around us, older than this state, older than the Church of Rome that you pray to. You confess to your priest, but you will give your soul to me. I am more than your death, boy. I am your soul eater."

Cash considered letting the pillow up so Emilio could catch a bit of air and prolong the struggle. He felt himself growing fevered with the power he held over the boy, but recognized that only Emilio's death would bring him the real satisfaction he sought. Cash pressed a knee against Emilio's chest, forcing out any air that remained and waited for Emilio to fall limp, signaling that he had blacked out.

Cash pulled away the pillow and fell onto Emilio's face, his mouth pressed tightly over Emilio's mouth and nose, blocking any intake of air. Cash used his fingers to press against Emilio's neck, feeling the diminishing pulse as the life drained out of him. Cash hovered like that, shaking with his own ecstasy as he absorbed the essence of a two-bit, wetback, card dealer. A spasm shook Cash with the last beat of Emilio's heart. Power surged through him, physically lifting him above the body, levitating inches from the ceiling; smiling, and glowing with a cold silver sheen in the dark cell.

* * *

Yuki's hunger was strong enough to take him and his mother to the field where the scent of chickens and men were strongest. His mother shied away at first but the smell of fresh game drew her forward and she crept inch by inch on her belly until she was close enough that the man odor was overpowered by the promise of food. Yuki followed her lead, whining softly and creeping up to the wooden fence that separated the barnyard from the field.

Stealthily, they crawled under the lowest strands, catching a bit of white fur on the barbs without taking notice. No longer whining, the two moved forward in silence, sniffing for some weakness in the boards that would let them into heaven. A hole large enough for a dog's muzzle admitted their eager noses and they could smell fear as the chickens clucked softly at the intrusion. Using his teeth, Yuki pried at the boards while his mother's paws dug at them, hunger investing them with new vigor. At last the board pulled away with a crack, making both of them jump back before slipping into the hen house.

Overcome with relish, the dogs ripped at the birds, shaking them by the necks and flinging them off to go for others. Feathers flew in the air, some sticking to their mouths; bits of blood spilled onto their tongues, exciting them further. The hens screeched shrilly in the dark, running into the dogs' jaws in their frenzy to escape. Teeth clashed and deep growls added to the din when suddenly their orgy was interrupted by the ferocious barking of another dog.

Yuki's thoughts were a roiling mix of "eat, run, devour, hide, fight, defend!"

With a crash, the door flung open and a black monster of a dog was on them, jaws snapping and claws tearing. The three locked in a snarling dervish of teeth and fur. Yuki lunged for the black dog's stomach but was thrown off as his mother was flung into him, her throat spewing blood over all three. Yuki dove for the black dog's throat but startled when the air beside him exploded in noise, light, flesh, and fur. Yuki fell back, half-blind and half-deaf, making out the mutilated body of his mother.

Filled with terror, Yuki ran, almost crashing into a figure stepping out of a little building in front of him. The girl! The hateful, hurtful girl again. She had killed his mother! Torn with fear and loathing, he ran on, distancing the black dog who stopped with the man's whistle. Yuki ran until he dropped with exhaustion; he lay in the dark; cold, wet, and alone.

* * *

April flew to her father's arms, weeping hysterically and covering herself in shame. She had soaked her nightgown.

Part 3, 1995

"A time to weep, and a time to laugh; a time to mourn, and a time to dance;" --Ecclesiastes 3:4

CHAPTER 10

It was still a long walk to the luggage pick-up where Laurel nervously stationed Kaitlin to guard their bags while she made arrangements for the rental car. With warnings to Kaitlin not to talk to strangers and not to leave her spot for any reason, Laurel boarded the shuttle to the car lot. She sat uneasily in her bus seat, chewing at one thumbnail and wondering what she would find when she was finally home.

Laurel pulled her hair back, tilting her head to one side and then the other to reduce the tension she felt. Laurel knew her mother would not have called them home unless it was absolutely necessary. Even dying, Doe would have left them out of it if she could. Laurel felt a surge of love for her mother, but stronger than that a great dread for what might be happening. All her life, Laurel had seen nothing but misery on that farm; she had seen it take the family one-by-one. Though her mother urged Laurel to leave, Doe was equally insistent that she, herself, could not do the same. Now Doe was calling them back. A shiver ran through Laurel, despite the warmth of the crowded bus.

* * *

Whaley stumbled out of the restaurant, pleasantly plastered and feeling relaxed at last. He checked the address on the rumpled paper he'd carried in his shirt pocket all day and started down State Street in the general direction South 313 suggested. Traffic was light, mostly kids cruising, looking for a pickup. The young toughs on the street ignored him except for some light banter in regard to his loose-jointed gait. Soon the street was empty and he moved past the storefronts and into the residential district.

The moon was high now, a pale yellow moon mostly obliterated by stringy clouds that dropped a light rain. Whaley kept to the inside of the sidewalks close to the huge maples that sheltered the cracked concrete. Few of the streetlights still worked but most of the front porches were lit, providing a thin light that let him dodge the raised ridges of the walkway and the bulging roots of the old trees.

Limbs shifted in the dark and groaned when the wind rose in random gusts. Shadows seemed to swim on the gray sidewalks, like hungry sharks circling his feet. A dog panted behind a picket fence beside him, snuffling under the blunt ends of the fence stakes and releasing a deep menacing growl of frustration as Whaley moved away from the lawn. A heavy thump rattled the wooden fence and Whaley hurried around a dark corner, fear spilling into his gut.

He almost ran into the man before he heard his laugh, an oily, vile voice he'd heard too many times before.

"Out for a walk, old man? It's been a long time since you've been out at night, hasn't it old man? Have you forgotten all the secrets the night knows, old man? Do you think the night doesn't know you're crazy? Stark, raving, mad. A lunatic. A homicidal maniac, isn't it? Do you think you can hide that from the dark? Do you think you can hide it from yourself?"

Whaley clamped both hands over his ears, the shopping bag dragging at his elbow. He walked faster, tripping on the cracked sidewalk, but not looking down. His eyes flew, from tree to tree, to front porches, to parked cars. The man had been right in front of him and the voice still insinuated itself into his ears, weaving through his fingers, and past the curtain his mind tried to draw. Where was he? Where was the demon? Where was the ghost who wouldn't stay dead?

Whaley was running now, a scarecrow of a man, his shirt flapping out of his pants, the bag thumping against his thin frame, his legs folding and catching on the rough sidewalk. His breathing was louder than his pounding heart, but neither over-rode the silky, slimy voice that wrapped itself around his mind.

"We are going to have great fun, you and me. I am going to show you desires you never knew you had, old man." Images flew in front of him; naked bleeding bodies and screaming, cowering girls. Whaley tried to outrun them, but his foot caught on a gnarled tree root that grew out of the pavement. He sprawled, helpless and screaming on the sidewalk.

"Good Gracious, what's happening out here?" Run down heels and baggy hose loomed over him. Whaley looked up thick brown legs to see the cotton house dress lowering itself as thick hands reached under his arms to help him sit up. "What's happened here and who are you mister?"

"I'm Donald Whaley," he croaked and pushed himself up.

"Mr. Whaley! I've been waiting up for you. We expected you hours ago and in a sight better shape than this I must say." The heavy-set woman pulled him to his feet. "You got your medicine with you? Looks to me like you forgot to take your last dose. And mind you, I don't allow drinking in this house. You got to stay sober if you're going board with me."

She brushed him off, stopping at his shoulder. "Old man, you hurt yourself something bad back here. Bleeding like a stuck pig right through your shirt." She pulled him into the yard and led him up the porch steps.

His head swung about, looking everywhere, but the ghost was gone. He saw the numbers by the door, 313, and rubbed them quickly with his hand like one might dip at holy water when entering a church.

* * *

Three left turns at strategic traffic lights put them onto the freeway and at last they were away, flying through a gray afternoon toward her grandmother Doe and the farm. Kaitlin couldn't get over how green everything was. Her eyes almost hurt from the lush brightness that bordered the freeway. Towering trees protected fields on either side, with great ballooning bushes springing up beneath them. Fields of green grass stretched across the acres, interrupted only by close-cropped pastures where cows grazed in groups of five or six. It was as if everything conspired to grow and thrive. Kaitlin enjoyed the feeling and her heart lightened for the first time since she'd known they were leaving home.

Laurel fussed with the radio, trying to tune in the Motown music she'd loved as a girl. Finally, Aretha Franklin singing the last lines of "Respect", followed by Diana Ross & The Supremes singing "Baby Love". Laurel cranked up the volume and they sang with enthusiasm, belting out the words they knew and cracking up when their lyrics were off. Then Percy Sledge romanced them with "When A Man Loves A Woman" and they both thought quietly about Dad, more than two thousand miles and months away.

The Temptations crooned "Just My Imagination" when Laurel finally spoke up. "Are you going to be all right with this, Kiddo? How are you doing?"

"Hey I'm tough. We'll be okay. Right Mom?" Kaitlin looked up at her mother and smiled.

"Sure, Honey. You're special. Just hang in there." But Laurel seemed to grit her teeth as she turned on the window wipers for the light rain that had just started.

* * *

The room was smaller than he'd had at the state institution but it was softer too, with white curtains over the windows and a chenille spread on the narrow bed. The dresser was topped with a white lace doily and a braided rug lay before the bed. He was surprised when he smelled pies running over in the oven and pleased that he still recognized the scent. The doorknob rattled in his hand and the landlady, Ardith Jackson, handed him an old skeleton key when she led him in. He placed his sack on the bed and turned to follow her as she pointed out the bathroom.

"You best be looking after that nasty scrape on your back. There's peroxide and bandages in the bathroom. You help yourself now and buy some later to replace what you use. You look like you had a long hard day, Mr. Whaley. I don't expect to see you until breakfast, which is served at 7:00 AM sharp."

"Thank you ma'am. I'll just clean up and go to bed." His voice came out with an unexpected tremor that made his neck go red.

"You better take your medication if you got any, and I expect you do. First day's always hard. You hear?" Ardith patted him softly on the arm and smiled before she lumbered away down the stairs.

The bathroom light hurt his eyes as he peeled off his shirt and turned to see his back in the mirror. The five long lines of his old scars had split open across his shoulder. He remembered how Cash had looked at him when he'd made those cuts; a look of greed and contempt at the same time. The goddamn scars had festered and burned all these years. Tonight they were not just bleeding; they oozed pus and the edges looked ragged and gray. He balled the shirt into a messy wad in the sink and filled it with steaming water. He rubbed bar soap into the cuts then used the shirt to towel away the crusty ooze. When he could see pink skin again, he splashed peroxide into the wounds and watched them bubble and spit.

He found gauze in the cupboard and used a whole roll fashioning a makeshift bandage that looped around his chest to cover a thicker pad of gauze at his shoulder. By the time he was done, his arm ached from being held high for too long. The color had drained from his face and he was exhausted. He scrubbed the shirt again and laid it over the towel rod, brown stains left accusingly in the fabric.

Back in his room, he found his medication and lined the three bottles up on the lace doily of the dresser. His trinity, he thought. A little altar to worship better living through chemistry. One by one he downed a tablet from each, and finally, unable to move, he collapsed on the bed. The ceiling was lined with dry water spots from earlier days and for a moment a picture almost formed. The shaggy head and long snout of some animal. Exhausted, he fell asleep before the image could register.

* * *

The exit came up faster than either of them expected and quickly led them onto a service street that paralleled the highway. After a mile or so, Kaitlin's mother turned onto a gravel road and stopped to point out an old one-room schoolhouse where Doe had gone to school. It sat neatly back from the road, its clapboard sides painted white and sporting a black and white sign reading 1898. Kaitlin noticed a window had broken out, leaving one empty, black eye to stare after them as they bumped down the rocky track.

The gravel road grew narrower as they went along. Lofty trees seemed to reach over the clearing as if to catch their car and stop them where they were. Laurel slowed down as the tires shifted uneasily in the sandy patches. The lane curved more now, and the rain came down in a torrent, making it hard to see around the curves. They rose with a steep hill and Laurel stopped between the trees to point out the farm off to the east.

An orchard blooming with pink and white flowers cut off the view of the house itself, but below it, a gray barn sagged under its torn tarpaper roof. The fields lay fallow, blotted with weeds and two ruts led away from the barn toward a slow-moving creek at the edge of a wet marsh. Beyond the marsh, forbidding old-growth trees shadowed high hills and cut off the horizon. Closer to them, a bit of blue marked the pond at the foot of a tall sloping field.

"Is this all Doe's?" Kaitlin stared at the woods, remembering her dream and shivering just a little from some small, cold wind. Sometimes she tried to pretend her dreams were just ordinary, but seeing the woods waiting there for her, like a great sullen cat, made Kaitlin cold right to the middle of her bones.

"Yes, and someday it will be all mine, and then all yours. Do you like it?"

"I don't know yet." Kaitlin's feelings were confused, but she was strongly drawn to those woods. Some memory nagged at the back of her head like a tension headache.

Laurel slipped the car into gear, accelerating as they climbed the next hill. They were just cresting the top when something large dodged in front of the car, forcing Laurel to slam on the brakes, sending the car into a slide that put them into a shallow, soggy ditch. Kaitlin covered her eyes as the car's momentum threw her toward the windshield and caught only a glance of something that looked like flashing teeth and fur.

"Did you see that?" Kaitlin demanded.

"All I saw was a blur. What was it?"

"I don't know. I think it was someone's dog."

CHAPTER 11

There was nothing in or along the lane, so whatever had intercepted the car must have fled uninjured. Laurel righted the vehicle with a few forward and reverse turns and continued down the road. The storm abated and a setting sun caught each water drop, making the green fields sparkle. The maples were festooned with new leaf buds, each bright green in the sun. The driveway was lined with yellow crocus and daffodils finally free of the last of winter's dreary snow crusts. The house sat at the end of the long driveway, looking rock-like among the oaks and elms that guarded the yard.

The old stone porch stretched across half the front of the house and its stone foundation continued around the whole perimeter. The white paint and green shutters could use some scraping and touching up, but in general, the place looked neat and respectable for a lady of her age. The large old farmhouse had been home to generations of their family and now it had come down to this, three women, one still a girl, to keep the house up and take care of Bluehills.

Laurel shook her head and grabbed a bag from the back. She took a deep breath before starting up the porch steps, not knowing exactly what to expect inside. She looked back to see Kaitlin staring past the orchard toward the hill where they'd had the near-accident.

"Kaitlin, Doe's waiting for you."

Kaitlin tugged out one of the bigger cases and dragged it up to the porch while Laurel pounded twice with the doorknocker and let herself inside.

"Mama I'm home."

A small black woman came toward them from the kitchen, wiping her hands on her apron. Her lined face smiled generously and she held out her hands to both of them. "Oh Laurel, it's so good to see you. I'm just here to help your mother along a little. She wanted everything to be perfect when you came. I helped her get supper in the oven and she went upstairs to rest just a little 'til you got here." Sadie gave each of them a long hug and took their coats to hang by the register to dry.

"Laurel and Kaitlin! You're already here!" Laurel turned toward the stairs to see her mother, thinner than she remembered, but beaming at them. Doe looked frailer than the last time Laurel had visited her, but better than Laurel expected, except for the dark circles under the eyes and a little more gray at the temples of her close-cropped hair.

Laurel watched Kaitlin make for the top of the stairs, giving her grandmother a bear hug. Kaitlin had grown so much; she made Doe look small beside her. The resemblance between the two was striking, dark complexion, raven hair, and almost black eyes which seemed to look right into you. Their mouths were the same too, generous lips pursed as if holding back a secret.

Doe held Kaitlin's chin up and whispered to her, "Oh, child, I have so much to tell you now that you are here." The smile seemed to falter just a little but her eyes were trained steadily on Kaitlin's as if they were sharing some longtime truth that only the two of them understood. Laurel felt left out, as she often had as a child, knowing there was some part of her mother that was sealed away from her and afraid to ask what it was.

* * *

Kaitlin settled into one of the vacant bedrooms upstairs. Its walls were lined with old pictures, some black and white, some sepia-toned. A bed, warmed by a brightly colored patchwork quilt, stood near the window. The gleaming hardwood floor was covered by a large braided rug that Kaitlin was told had been made by her great-grandmother. A second bed was placed against the opposite wall, matching the first with its bright quilt and pile of pillows. Kaitlin felt as if she were moving into a museum, but at least her old Raggedy Ann looked appropriately placed on one of the big brass beds.

The closet had been emptied for her and at the very back she could see a small square door in the wall which her mother said led to the attic, a favorite hiding place of hers when she had lived here as a child. The room was at the back of the house with a bay window and window seat facing the backfields, the marsh, and the brooding woods beyond. Kaitlin noticed the drawer built into the window seat and pulling it out found old sheet music and several original Nancy Drew books.

Kaitlin stretched out on the pillows that covered the window seat and slowly flipped the brittle pages of one of the old books. A homemade bookmark fell to the floor, still marking the place where the last reader had left off. As Kaitlin reached for the marker, she caught sight of a box pushed under the bed, just visible beneath the edge of the quilt. She dropped to the floor and pulled out the old cardboard container. Opening it, she found dusty photos that had been stored away. She pushed the box back to its hiding place and looked out the window toward the woods.

High on the first hill that crept up from the marsh, Kaitlin could make out a small figure at the edge of the trees. It looked like a small dark-haired girl and a black dog, both staring back at the farmhouse. Kaitlin felt a shiver run through her, then heard the furnace rumble down in the belly of the basement. It must have gotten colder as night came on, she thought, as the cold moved deeper into her bones. She looked back at the distant figures.

Kaitlin's heart started to pound and suddenly, she couldn't breathe. It was as if someone's hand were pressed firmly over her mouth. Unable to speak, she dropped to the floor, rolling herself tightly against her knees. It's not real, it's not going to hurt you, she told herself. But deep in her heart she knew the threat was real, the girl and her dog were real, and they were where the threat was coming from, had come from all these times. She had been so afraid of something that wasn't there before, but now it was there, it was real; she knew this to be true.

Kaitlin pulled herself to the bed, wheezing with her efforts to breathe, she forced herself to slow down her labored gasping. She talked to herself; "calm down, deep slow breaths, quiet heart, slow down." In a minute, Kaitlin was able to stand again. Forcing her feet forward, she went to the window and turned again to the woods. The girl and the dog were gone, vanished in the early evening shade.

The reality of the room returned gradually. Hot air rose out of the register by the window seat and Kaitlin watched it rustle the white lace curtains. Kaitlin could hear Sadie banging pans in the kitchen as she finished getting dinner ready. She strained to hear her mother talking quietly with Doe in the next room but she couldn't make out the words.

Kaitlin rubbed her arms and hung her head down until she felt the blood pooling in her face. Somehow, she had to stop frightening herself. Was the threat real? Now that she was standing and breathing normally, she didn't know, but something was real here. Kaitlin knew Doe was terribly sick, but there was something else about this house that infected the air, some sense of sadness that lay heavily on her. The house always seemed creepy to her when she was younger, but now it seemed to be grieving.

Kaitlin had been here only a few times in her life, but it felt as if she were supposed to be here. It seemed as if the walls had been waiting for her return to tell her unspoken stories that she was supposed to hear. It felt as if small spiders were lurking in the shadows waiting for her to fall asleep so they could scurry out and whisper secrets into her ears as she slept. Slowly, Kaitlin realized what this odd feeling was. She felt as if she were in one of her dreams, but this time she wouldn't be able to wake up.

* * *

Sadie shook her head as she stirred the gravy for their dinner. She thought of the women upstairs and wondered what had ever kept this family on this accursed farm. She'd known Donna Jean, Kaitlin's Doe, all her life, and nothing but grief had ever come to her and the ones she loved, but still the family clung to this land like it was the last piece of property on earth. Sadie remembered her own father telling tales forty years ago that would have driven anyone away from here. It was no wonder all the farms around here had been given up in the Great Depression. Most folks couldn't take the kind of hardship that went with these fertile but unforgiving acres.

Now Donna Jean was dragging Laurel and her little girl back here like it was some fate they couldn't escape. Sadie had argued against it right from the start but Donna Jean just got that resigned look in her eyes and said it was going to happen whether she lived to see it or not, and she was the only one who could help them make sense of it.

Well, Sadie sure couldn't follow Donna Jean's logic but she knew full well that if Donna Jean said something was going to happen, it sure enough always happened. Sadie just hated to see that little girl go through this for the sake of some lost family legacy that Donna Jean imagined to be this important. A little girl like that shouldn't have to watch someone die, grandmother or not.

"Ladies, our dinner is on the table," Sadie hollered up the stairs. "Better get down here before I finish it all off myself." And maybe I'll finish off the bunch of you while I'm at it too, just to put you out of your misery, she mumbled to herself as she dished up the mashed potatoes.

* * *

Donna Jean stroked Kaitlin's long black hair with the hairbrush, counting, "Ninety-five, ninety-six, ninety-seven, ninety-eight, ninety-nine, and one hundred. You

98

have beautiful hair just as all the girls in this family have had. It is a gift from our great grandmothers down to us." Donna Jean smiled at her granddaughter and thought for a minute that she would just tell Kaitlin to pack up her things and go home again where it was safe.

"I know that your mother has told you how sick I am, " Donna Jean held up her hand to stop Kaitlin from saying anything. "It is not really the kind of time I had hoped to spend with you and I know it will be very hard on your mother and on you." Donna Jean shushed Kaitlin again, as she tried to interrupt.

"Shh, let me say this while I can, dear. I am your grandmother Doe, and you are my only granddaughter. I have a gift that was given to me by my grandmother that I must pass on to you. You are too young to carry so much right now, but my time is almost done and I have to ask you to be very strong to take this up."

Kaitlin looked closely at Doe, hair silver at the temples, making her sixty-year-old face seem older than it should. It wasn't fair that someone with so much left to do would not have the chance to live longer. But Kaitlin could see it in Doe's eyes; she understood that Doe had only a little while left.

"I expect that some of it will come to you now that you're at Bluehills. I can't make it come and I can't make it go away, but I hope to help you understand what's happening. I just want you to promise me that if anything strange happens or if you feel strange, that you let me know. I want to talk about it with you. Will you do that Kaitlin?"

Kaitlin nodded, still held by Doe's admonition not to talk, and Donna Jean laughed to herself, wondering what could be stranger than the conversation they were having right now.

* * *

Kaitlin rose from a bed of moss and dead leaves, still wet from spring rains. Leaves clung to her hair and legs and she swiped them away like cobwebs. She pulled aside a curtain of fog in front of her, revealing the gray of early morning just before sunrise. She shook off the sleep of the dead, as each sense took back its strength, smelling the rich loam beneath her feet, feeling cool dew left from the night before, tasting the bitter flavor of new growth in her mouth, and finally picking up the mournful, tired howl of an old hound. Her bare feet stepped carefully around broken twigs and old briars as she left the damp meadow for the steep hill in front of her. A sad keening called to her from the ridge as she carefully climbed to the top of the rise.

Kaitlin woke suddenly to find herself in the dark unfamiliar room. It was a strange dream, almost real like her other dreams, but it was not the terror that sometimes came to her. Relieved, but still confused, she focused her eyes on the dim shapes around her, trying to find her place in this unfamiliar room. She was standing at the window, trying to climb over the sill that set even with the window seat. She looked down at the long drop to the ground and wondered what might have happened if she had sleepwalked even a little longer.

CHAPTER 12

Kaitlin made her way slowly up the steep brick steps into the Congregational Church, holding one of Doe's arms while Laurel supported the other. Friendly faces under bright straw hats greeted them for the Easter service; eyes framed by crow's feet scrutinizing Kaitlin for her family resemblance and rough housewives' hands grasping Laurel's arm with warm welcome-backs. They were stopped in the cool entryway by Reverend Anderson's sincere inquiries and solicitations.

Kaitlin was pulled away by a sharp jerk on her elbow. A girl about Kaitlin's age, dressed in a sunny yellow dress and white patent leather shoes, stood behind her. Her hair, the color of hot cinnamon, was covered with an old and battered wide-brimmed felt hat, a man's hat, stained and pulled out of shape with time and use. "Hey, I'm Stormy. Come up to the balcony with me. Huh?"

Laurel turned toward the interruption and nodded as Stormy pulled Kaitlin toward the back stairs.

"Whatever you do, don't let them stick you down here or you'll be sitting between two sweaty widows smelling of baby powder and hair spray." Stormy laughed though Kaitlin was taken aback by her forwardness.

"What's up here, a better brand of baby powder?"

"You might say that. I've got nursery duty today. It's a

closed-off room with a big window onto the sanctuary and a speaker so you can hear the minister but he can't hear you. You get to rock the babies, and if there aren't any you can do whatever you please, you know, drink beer, smoke cigarettes, that sort of stuff." Stormy turned into a side room wallpapered with pastel lambs and big-eyed children.

"Are you the local crazy or what?" Kaitlin asked when she had determined no one's baby or mother was in the nursery.

"Well, that depends on what reputation you're bringing to this town. Aren't you the one living at the spooky Bluehills place?" Stormy arched her eyebrows so hysterically that Kaitlin couldn't help laughing out loud.

"How do you know that? I just got here yesterday."

"I live down the road from you. Word travels fast on party lines. Especially if you listen in when you're supposed to be watching soaps in your room."

"Were you up in the woods behind my house last night?" Kaitlin hoped she had solved one mystery.

"Are you kidding? No one goes back there. Haven't they told you anything? That whole farm is haunted." Stormy wrinkled her nose with such distaste that Kaitlin laughed at her reaction.

"Man, you don't know do you? They haven't told you anything? Every kid around here knows the stories about that place." Stormy shook her head as if she could not believe the total innocence of some people.

"Tell me. What should I know?"

"Well, the farm has a curse on it and it kills anyone who lives on it, that's all."

"What about my grandmother, she's done all right for sixty years anyway."

"Sure, she's still alive, barely, but she's been cursed all right." Stormy was so casual about the situation that Kaitlin could feel herself heating up with annoyance.

"My grandmother's just sick like anyone else that's all. You ought to be more thoughtful about other people's feelings." Kaitlin pulled open the door and went down the stairs to sit with her mother and grandmother, angry enough that she didn't follow the sermon at all, just rose for songs and prayers at the right time and replayed the conversation with Stormy in her head.

* * *

Whaley fingered the tablets that lay in his pink palm. He rolled them to the edge of his fingers and let them fall onto the quilt and mix with the colors of the patterned square where they lay. He poked at one, prodding it against the other two, then gently placed them in his hand once again. The pills felt cool and prickly against his skin. He stared out the window, trying to ignore the nagging voice that told him to throw them away.

Children played in the yard across the street, bouncing a red rubber volleyball on the concrete sidewalk, trying to get it up the porch roof in one toss. They laughed as the sphere rebounded off the low eaves, thumping their heads and knees in its course. A red-haired girl threw up her hands to volley it in the direction of the porch again and hooted with glee as it rolled along the shingles and followed the rain gutter to the corner of the house. The others stood frozen watching the red ball spin suspended at the corner of the house before it toppled back to the ground. They slapped high fives all around and went on with the game.

Donald rubbed the small disks between his fingers and wondered if his little girl had played like that. He wondered if her children, his grandchildren, he corrected himself, played these games. He placed the three pills carefully on his tongue and swallowed them dry. A bitter aftertaste hung on his mouth and his head began to ache with the whiny anger of the little voice left unsatisfied.

* * *

Kaitlin slept peacefully that night, no terrors disturbed her. She woke late the next morning and didn't realize she had company until Stormy let herself into her bedroom. She woke with a thump on her bed as Stormy, still dressed in the battered felt hat, but this time in jeans and a bright orange T-shirt, made herself at home.

"Hey kid! I brought my brother's bike along. Let's go for a ride." Stormy was already off the bed, browsing the picture collages on the walls. "Hey, I know some of these people. They must be your great this and thats, huh?"

"Don't you knock or telephone ahead or anything?" Kaitlin threw off the quilt and reached for her brush, trying to make herself presentable.

"Don't you ever get out of bed before noon? This is Spring Break. Time is wasting and we have a lot we need to do before you have to go to school next Monday. Let's get out of here." Stormy had opened Kaitlin's dresser drawers and was looking for appropriate clothes. "We'll need some sandwiches and some drinks to take along."

"Do I get to ask where we're going?" Kaitlin pulled a T-shirt over her head, dressing as quickly as she could.

"Into the haunted woods of course!"

* * *

Their bikes bumped roughly over the rutted track that led from the gravel road onto the State Land. Stormy's carrier held their sandwiches and a dented tin canteen of water. Kaitlin followed, trying to memorize landmarks, in case Stormy deserted her in this wilderness. They were still in open fields but the trees loomed ahead, a dark wall cut through by a narrow path.

Stormy stopped her bike and fixed Kaitlin with a one-eyed stare. "Are you sure you really want to do this? This is your last chance to turn back to the safe world of television sitcoms and instant cocoa. Once we enter the haunted forest, you will never be the same."

"You are so melodramatic! Let's get this over with." Kaitlin spoke with bravado she really did not possess but she didn't know any other way to handle this strange girl.

They slipped from the hot sun into the shady light of the thick trees. The trail remained well marked with yellow stakes and was plainly clear of the thick underbrush that grew to either side. The path wound smoothly past the giant trunks of maples, oaks, and elms whose limbs overhung the girls, dripping of morning dampness and new growth. They rode silently for a long time going deeper into the woods and winding downhill with each turn in the path.

Kaitlin's first impression was one of beauty. The new growth was a bright yellowish green adding a fresh prominence to each bush and tree limb. Birds were thick here and they chattered overhead in the trees. Soft moss cushioned old logs and tree stumps, and young ferns were already covering the old winter debris. As the girls headed down hill, however, the cool shade felt chillier and the old trees stood barren except for patches of gray and green lichen and fungi. The soil was black with humus; pale toadstools and puffballs grew in the thin light.

When they reached a spot midway down a long slope, Stormy had them stop at a group of weathered boulders. She opened the pack and served up peanut butter and jelly sandwiches and apples. "This is where we stop for sustenance. We will need our strength for the rest of the journey and you need to know more before you decide if we should continue. Now I will reveal the true tales of this land to you."

"Stormy, you are the most impossible person I have ever met." Kaitlin used her half-eaten apple to gesture to Stormy to continue.

"Two people died here in these woods before you and I were born, and it is said that they still wander here, restless because they were murdered before their time. It is said that they were chained together in a prison gang being marched through here as hard labor for their terrible crimes. They were swinging axes and pounding rock when a freak storm began at the top of these very trees.

"A terrible funnel reached down to the earth and snapped their chains, releasing them from their guards and the other prisoners. They were lifted into the air and rode the funnel trying to break it to their will. The first prisoner was bucked off into the trees onto these very rocks where we are sitting. He died a slow and horrible death waiting for his friend to rescue him. You see these red streaks in the rocks? Those are his bloodstains and even though the prison guards have tried every year to wash them clean, these bloodstains still come back each spring.

"The second prisoner was not as lucky as the first one. He was finally tossed off below this hill into the middle of a horrible quicksand pond where a pack of rabid dogs had also been marooned. When he landed in the middle of them, the dogs were so ferocious they literally ripped him to pieces and ate him in great whole chunks. But he didn't die before he watched them eat his arms and legs and tear all the skin off of him. He screamed so loudly that the farmers who lived around here had to lock up their dogs to keep them from going mad."

"Oh, you are so gross, Stormy! Do you think I'm going to believe all that? Where do you think I'm from, Disneyland?" Kaitlin stuffed the rest of her sandwich into the pack and reached for her bike. "Come on you liar, I dare you to go down to the haunted quicksand pit with me."

Kaitlin pushed off with her bike and rattled down the winding trail that became more narrow and muddy as they descended. Stormy came up the rear warning her to watch out for the swamp that would come up quickly. A sudden turn in the path brought Kaitlin around a weathered old willow and right up to the water's edge. She stopped quickly and pulled the bike back from the water just as a small black water snake dropped from one of the bushes into the water in front of her.

Kaitlin screamed, dropped the bike and reversed her steps, returning to the backside of the tree at the same time Stormy arrived. Stormy's bike hit her hard, throwing them both into the mud and ripping a nasty gash into Kaitlin's shin. Kaitlin looked down to see a gush of crimson blood running down her leg and into her shoe.

The blood held Kaitlin in a trance of shock and adrenaline. It seemed as if she were completely alone with only the coppery smell of fresh blood, the sucking sound of mud grasping at her feet, the taste of dirt and decay in her mouth. She felt as if the thick wet air were filling her lungs until they were too heavy to draw air, as if the air were blocking her throat, as if the air and the smells, and the gray light were strangling her, cutting off her breath.

Kaitlin was gasping now, sucking for air, wheezing as her lungs failed her, pulling at Stormy in a panic of suffocation. She felt herself being pulled up, Stormy pounding on her back and yelling something into her face. Then Kaitlin faded away, red replaced by black.

* * *

Mike's fist swung out at empty air as Petty Officer McDougle dodged its arc. "Hold it sir, it's me! Lunch is over, it's time to rise and shine."

Mike rubbed his red eyes and scratched at the four-o'clock shadow already darkening his jaw. He pulled himself to sitting on the worn couch, smoothing out his rumpled uniform as he ran the fingers of his other hand through his short hair. "Christ, McDougle! How long have you been around here that you don't know better than to touch a man in uniform when he's sleeping?"

"Long enough to know some men don't hear their wake-up calls, even when they got a briefing in ten minutes. And you better shave before you go in with those big guns. Shake a leg, boss."

Mike studied his reflection in the dark shine of the filing cabinet as he stretched. He couldn't make out much but it was probably just as bad as the distortion looked. He'd already completed two shifts in a row and hadn't been dismissed yet. He wished he'd brought some aspirin or deodorant with him. If Laurel had been home, she'd have brought down a sandwich too and given him a backrub. He shook his head.

"Guess it's just as well the family is out of town, huh sir?" McDougle grinned like he'd just been reading Mike's mind. "You sure wouldn't be seeing much of them anyway 'till this crisis gets resolved."

Mike hated that smirk but McDougle always knew what to do or say, ten minutes before he was told.

"Well you got that right, McDougle. Of course I might sleep better when I had the chance, if I knew they were home. I can't push away the idea that they're all alone in that big old farmhouse in the middle of nowhere."

"Sounds safe enough to me sir. You don't get a lot of trouble out in the country."

"McDougle, did you ever see *Deliverance*? The movie where those guys take a canoe trip in the Georgia wilderness? That's how Laurel's homestead feels. Like being completely isolated from the rest of the world but knowing that eyes are following you. Like you're on somebody's menu for supper." Mike shivered and reached for the bathroom door. "Hey, see if you can get some snacks or something while I'm gone. I got a feeling it's going to be a long stand-off and you and I are going to see a lot more of these walls than we want."

* * *

"Why didn't you tell me you were some kind of epileptic or something? Stormy had torn the bottom off her T-shirt and wrapped it around Kaitlin's leg. She had soaked another piece in pond water and was washing Kaitlin's face with it.

"I'm not. But sometimes I get a real bad feeling and I get scared and have a panic attack. I've never fainted before, though. It was just that the fear was so real, worse than usual." Kaitlin was dizzy and found herself trying to stop the spinning with her out-stretched arms.

"Yeah I have a real bad feeling about this too. You can't tell anyone what happened. My mother would kill me if she knew I was down in these woods." Stormy wrung out the rag again to wash splattered blood off herself.

"No, I mean a different bad feeling. I think your story is true. Something terrible took place in this spot and there is still a bad feeling around here. I think we should get out of here now!" Kaitlin rose to her feet, glad to know she could still do it and moved toward her bike.

"Jeez, you're giving me the willies! Are you some kind of a fortune teller or something?" Stormy didn't hesitate in getting her bike as well.

"Or something," Kaitlin agreed as they turned to walk up the path that had brought them to the bad place.

CHAPTER 13

A nother spring rain beat at Kaitlin's window as her mother cleaned and bandaged the gash in her leg. Laurel gazed at the photos that papered the bedroom's wall with old memories. They held a lot of stories, some happy and most not. She took a large collage down to point out each face and history for Kaitlin.

"Look at this Kaitlin. Your great-great-grandmother was still alive when this was taken. Our dark looks come down from her. She was Native American you know, from some southern tribe that had been broken apart during the Indian wars in the 1800's. She said she promised her ancestors she would always live on this land and that her children would always live here too. I guess she was right." Laurel sighed and wiped the glass covering the photo clean with her skirt.

"There's your great-grandmother too and here's grandma when she was still a young woman. Doe was very beautiful wasn't she?" Laurel held the picture up for Kaitlin to see and she moved closer to admire the family.

"Who are these other children, Mom?" Kaitlin pointed to two boys and a girl who stood beside her grandmother.

"That one is your grandma's brother George and here is her brother Ray, and that's your Great Aunt Carol Ann.

Aunt Carol Ann is still alive and we'll have to go visit her." Laurel dreaded the visit but knew this was one of the jobs she promised to take over for her mother.

"What happened to George and Ray?"

"It's a very sad story, Kaitlin. They were still young when they were killed in a farm accident. Uncle Ray was trying to plow under the marshland near the far woods one summer when it was dry. The back tire must have hit a soft spot where there was some underground spring. The tire sank, tipping the tractor over on top of him. His brother, George, ran down from the garden he was hoeing and slipped in beside Ray. He tried to use his legs to lift the machine up enough to pull Ray free but he only succeeded in messing up the balance and the whole thing slipped back down and killed them both.

"They must have laid there a while before they were found. I was told they died with their hands clutching each other and their eyes wide open with terror. It broke my grandmother's heart and they say she went to bed after the funeral and never got up again. She was buried two months after them.

"Doe was working in town then, and she had to come back to the farm to take care of her father and Carol Ann. Her father died the next spring with a sudden heart attack. He was out checking his trap lines and was gone most of the day before Doe found him. It looked like he had caught some kind of animal in his trap that had chewed off its foot to get out. The animal may have still been in the trap when your great-grandfather came to check and probably gave him a shock so bad it brought on the heart attack. Some people said it was a wolf, but of course there've been no wolves around here for a hundred years. It's the only thing to explain why he just didn't kill the animal. His gun was on the ground nearby him, still unfired."

She turned to Kaitlin and found her looking suddenly pale and faint. "Hey, are you all right darling? I shouldn't have told you that gruesome story. You're as white as a sheet." Laurel moved closer to Kaitlin to put her arm around her.

"It wasn't a wolf, was it? It was a great white dog."

Kaitlin stared straight ahead as she mumbled the statement.

"Kaitlin, are you okay?"

Kaitlin turned toward her mother's concerned face. "I just have a feeling about it, that's all."

* * *

Laurel parked the car in front of the rest home, a three-story, brick building with heavy institutional screens that could double as bars. The structure looked like a prison or a warehouse but certainly not like the kind of place you would choose for your retirement. She wondered if she should say anything more to prepare Kaitlin for seeing Aunt Carol Ann. She had warned her that the old woman might not understand what they were saying and probably wouldn't know who they were. She wondered if she could prepare herself for this as well. When her mother was gone, Aunt Carol Ann would be her responsibility, not one she looked forward to.

"Ready Pumpkin? Let's do it."

They entered on the ground level and passed through long cool corridors looking for the elevator. The walls were the usual light green but were fresher than most institutional settings. Rooms off the hall revealed hospital beds and IV stands, their occupants hidden away under crisp white sheets or behind blue folding curtains. The odor of antiseptics, disinfectants, and astringents floated lightly on the air. Somewhere a man was weeping loudly.

The elevator let them off at the visitors' lounge, a large sparse room with windows that overlooked the town below. Though the day outside was bright and hot, the room was stale with cold, recirculated air. Aunt Carol Ann was already sitting in her chair near an orange plastic, visitor's couch. Laurel knew her immediately; Aunt Carol Ann had not changed in the intervening years since Laurel's last visit. She was like someone suspended in a dreary, frozen world, eyes staring straight ahead, hair hanging loosely, mouth moving in a constant silent conversation with herself.

"Aunt Carol Ann, it's Laurel. I've come to visit."

Carol Ann clutched a small white stuffed animal,

squeezing and pinching at it as she sat.

"Aunt Carol Ann, I'm your niece Laurel, I've come to see you." Laurel touched Carol Ann's shoulder trying to rouse her from her otherworld state.

"Mom, I don't think she hears you."

"I know, Honey. You have to get her attention first, then sometimes she follows what you're saying."

"No, Mom, I don't think she wants to hear you. I think she doesn't want to know we're here." Kaitlin shifted on her feet uncomfortably. "It's a feeling I have."

Laurel looked at her daughter carefully. Kaitlin seemed a little peaked, maybe a little nervous. "I'm sure you're right Kaitlin, but I think we need for her to be with us for a little while and not just locked inside because she's afraid of us. We are here to help her, she should know you and I won't hurt her."

Laurel reached for Carol Ann's chin and slowly turned her head toward them. "Aunt Carol Ann!" she spoke louder hoping to catch her attention. "This is Kaitlin, this is my daughter Kaitlin, your great niece. Say hello to Kaitlin."

Slowly, Aunt Carol Ann's face turned, and after just a moment her eyes seemed to focus as she faced Kaitlin directly. Her eyes widened and she said "April."

"No, Aunt Carol Ann, this is Kaitlin, I'm Laurel."

"April is back. April is back. April is back and the white dog is loose." Aunt Carol Ann pulled harder at the toy in her lap. "April is back and the white dog is loose."

"No, I'm Kaitlin." Kaitlin was obviously nervous now and stood staring into Aunt Carol Ann's eyes and flinching under her direct gaze.

"April, the white dog is loose. You have to go away. Go away now! The white dog is loose, April. Go away now."

Laurel could see Aunt Carol Ann was becoming agitated. She knelt so that she could step into her view between Carol Ann and Kaitlin. They both seemed upset, so Laurel reached a hand to each one, stroking shoulders and saying softly, "This is Kaitlin, I'm your niece Laurel."

"Eenie, meenie, minie, moe. Catch a doggy by the toe. When he's dead, don't let him go. Eenie, meenie, minie, moe." Aunt Carol Ann beat out the rhythm against the chair using the toy to punctuate each line. "Eenie, meenie, minie, moe. Catch a doggy by the toe. When he's dead, don't let him go. Eenie, meenie, minie, moe."

"Aunt Carol Ann, shh! It's okay. This isn't April, this is Kaitlin. Shh, please calm down." Laurel looked around hoping desperately that a nurse or aide might be near enough to help her.

"Eenie, meenie, minie, moe. Catch a doggy by the toe. When he's dead, don't let him go. Eenie, meenie, minie, moe." Aunt Carol Ann was shouting now, almost wailing as she repeated the rhyme. "Eenie, meenie, minie, moe. Catch a doggy by the toe. When he's dead, don't let him go. Eenie, meenie, minie, moe."

Laurel stepped back, frightened by what she saw. Kaitlin, staring into Aunt Carol Ann's eyes with alarm and Carol Ann staring back into hers, chanting louder and more shrilly with each repetition. Laurel ran into the hall hoping to see a nurse's station nearby and caught the attention of a white-uniformed woman she found there.

Laurel and the nurse broke the two apart, Laurel leading her daughter away and the attendant rolling Carol Ann back to her room. Once their eye contact had broken, Carol Ann stopped raving and rode silently out of the room. Laurel had goose bumps up and down her arms thinking of the strange connection the two had made. She hugged Kaitlin, who remained speechless and led her out of the building and into the sun.

"Are you all right, Baby? What happened in there?" Laurel rubbed Kaitlin's arms trying to break the spell or trance or whatever had taken over her daughter.

"I don't know Mom. I feel sick." Kaitlin turned and threw up in the flowerbed that bordered the sidewalk. They walked slowly to the car and Laurel asked her no more questions.

* * *

The nice lady nurse pushed her chair through the long hallways, worn brown tiles filling her view. The nurse leaned into Carol Ann's chair and tipped Carol Ann's weight back against her body to ease the wheelchair over the doorsill. Carol Ann's head flopped back and for a minute she was staring at the nurse's starched white collar. She was close enough to make out the tight weave of the white linen threads and the tiny white stitching that edged the pointed ends.

"There was blood in the snow," Carol Ann told her. "There was blood in the snow and hunks of fur and flesh everywhere."

"Is that right, Honey?" The nurse parked the chair beside Carol Ann's bed and set the brakes so it couldn't roll away.

"I could barely follow the tracks through the snow and I didn't see it at all until I came up over the hill in the woods. It was white everywhere. The tree branches were all heavy with snow and it had piled up higher than the wild grass, but there was blood at the top of the hill."

The nurse stepped over to the bed where she pulled back the sheets and covers. "A real snowy day, huh? I like snowy days, don't you?"

"The top of the hill was all black and red and white. Just those three colors and at first I didn't understand. I thought someone had tossed old clothes around or something, so I went up close because that was where the tracks stopped. But the red was blood in the snow; blood and pieces of torn up body. Its throat was ripped open like a big bloody mouth and at first I couldn't find its face, half buried in the snow. I thought I'd found some awful monster, some Abominable Snowman who'd died there."

The nurse faced Carol Ann in her chair, bent her knees so she could wrap her arms around Carol Ann's chest, then pulled her to a stand. Carol Ann tottered on her useless legs but the nurse pivoted them both in a slow purposeful dance that ended with Carol Ann sitting on her bed.

The nurse let out her breath and smiled. "Good job, Carol Ann. You were a big help." Then she turned to the bedside table where Carol Ann's injection stood ready.

"I stood right over it, trying to look into the deep open mouth that was all red. I was trying to figure out where I was when I found the eyes. The eyes looking up into heaven and the real mouth was open with little white teeth showing. There was a layer of snow over it, but I could see the blue of dead lips. I fell down on my butt in the snow and I couldn't see the face any more, just that big red mouth, ready to eat me alive.

"I lost myself in that red mouth and then nothing was white at all. Everything was red blood and shredded muscles and skin that wrapped around me like ropes and that big red mouth swallowed me whole."

"I like winter too, honey," the nurse interrupted. "In fact, I think that's my favorite time of year. Sometimes on the weekend, my boyfriend and I go up to Iron Mountain and we ski all Saturday and Sunday and then go home."

The shot stung and Carol Ann began to feel warm and sleepy. She fell back onto her pillow and looked up at the ceiling. The old water spots began the flow together and for just a minute Grandma Alana was there, grinning toothlessly at her. Then she fell asleep to no dreams.

* * *

That night Doe came to tuck Kaitlin into bed. She sat lightly on the bed and said, "I think something strange happened today. Do you want to talk to me about it, Kaitlin?"

"Doe, who's April? What became of to her?" Kaitlin had been quiet all evening and had not touched the soup and toast Laurel had made for her.

"April is someone Carol Ann remembers all the time but the rest of the family has tried to forget after all these years. She looked very much like you and I heard Carol Ann thought that you were April today. April was our little sister. She was very special to us but she died a long time ago."

"How did she die Doe? It was something bad wasn't it?" Kaitlin watched her grandmother's face and saw her smile fade and her eyes water with her memories.

"April wandered into a terrible snow storm. She was lost under the snow for months before we found her body. Carol Ann followed her into the same blizzard and it was hours before she found her way home to us. She has never been the same since that day. The doctor thought the cold and the shock of losing April caused Carol Ann to have a massive stroke, even though she was just a young girl herself. She had been so fragile since the summer before, never entirely well. We took care of her at home for many years, but now I'm too frail to look after her. I needed you and your mother to come home so Carol Ann will have someone after I'm gone."

Kaitlin felt her own eyes water now and she reached out to hold her grandmother. She hardly knew this woman, but she knew she loved her dearly; there was something to the family blood that drew them close. Kaitlin spoke softly almost into her grandmother's ear as they hugged, "Is there really a curse on this farm and on our family?"

"There is something here that makes us have to be very careful, Kaitlin. My Grandma Alana made this for me and told me to wear it always." She fished under her blouse and pulled up a small leather bag hung from a leather cord around her neck.

"What is it?" Kaitlin asked staring at the sack.

"I don't really know. Alana was a full-blooded Indian but her people had been torn apart many years before. She never even told us the name of her tribe, but she held on to their old superstitions and some of their medicine ways. I think this has herbs and maybe small shells or stones in it. It is supposed to ward off evil and she made one for each of us to wear, always.

"Kaitlin, my Grandma Alana had some very unusual powers; she could tell you things before they happened and she could smell bad air from something dangerous or evil. She read signs in the way a tree bent or the way a wave lapped the shore. Some people thought she was strange like a witch because she could sense things about them.

"All the women in our family have been more sensitive than most people. Your mother can find things people have lost, can't she? And doesn't it seem as if she knows when you are sad and tries to cheer you up even if you haven't said anything? Doesn't she sometimes know who is calling when she first hears the phone ring? Don't you sometimes know she's thinking about you when you are away from her? Don't you sometimes have feelings about certain places or people?"

"Yes, I do, but I'm afraid to tell people because they laugh at me or get mad at me." Kaitlin's eyes were wide now thinking of incidents that had happened recently.

"Kaitlin, I would like to talk to you more about this. I want you to tell me any feelings you have or any dreams you may have while you are here. I also want you to wear this now and never take it off." Kaitlin's grandmother raised the cord over her head and placed it around Kaitlin's neck.

"No, Doe. You should keep this." Kaitlin felt warm where the bag touched the skin on her chest.

"Kaitlin, I'm almost done here. What could be taken away from an old woman like me? Besides, I have you and your mother to take care of me. I have everything a person could want. Now you should go to sleep. I've given you a lot of things to think about and I want you to talk to me about anything." Kaitlin's grandmother reached over and switched off the bedside lamp. Then she stepped slowly and quietly from the room while her words echoed in Kaitlin's head.

* * *

Kaitlin walked through a noble, old forest where Spanish moss hung from high branches of pines and cedar that crept into each sunlit space. She followed a game trail through the trees until she came to a clearing where water sang over smooth rocks. An old woman sat on her knees by the stream with her back toward Kaitlin. She wore deerskin around her waist and bright shell beads around her neck. As she bent over the water she chanted and bowed first to the East, then the South, then the West. Finally she turned and bowed toward Kaitlin who was standing toward the North. With her head bowed she held up a small leather sack and cord that Kaitlin took and placed around her neck. The old woman then raised her head and smiled at Kaitlin. Her face was Aunt Carol Ann's.

CHAPTER 14

Kaitlin found herself in the woods with Stormy again. Stormy had used the 'back-up-on-the-horse' argument and persuaded Kaitlin to come as long as they didn't visit any swamps. It really was a kind of adventure and her mother didn't seem to mind Kaitlin's exploration, or maybe it was just that Laurel's mind was taken up with caring for Doe. Anyway, it was good to have a friend right away, even a crazy one, and not to be left on her own in the big gray farmhouse with its empty rooms and sad memories.

"So what scary stories are you going to tell me about today? Or haven't you had enough time to think up anything new?" Kaitlin looked over at Stormy whose red hair was pulled back into a ponytail.

"Listen, I'm not making any of this up. I swear to God! I just know a lot of local history and when it comes to your grandmother's farm, there's a lot to tell." Stormy rolled her eyes like she couldn't believe she'd ever be accused of exaggerating.

"Well you can tell me all about ghosts as long as you keep me away from any real danger. My mother would thank you for that." Kaitlin pushed off with her peddles and Stormy sped after her as they bumped down the shaded dirt road.

Stormy signaled a stop at a place where the road covered an old viaduct that led the stream out of the woods. They climbed down the steep side, almost slipping into the water where the stream left a wide shaded pool.

"We can swim here next summer. It can be our secret place." Kaitlin smiled in agreement with Stormy, although she wondered how many snakes liked to hide out in that cool concrete pipe and wait for stupid girls to come wading there.

They returned to the road, and in a short while, pulled off onto a faint double track that led into the forest which bordered Doe's farm at the back. Entering the dim woods, Kaitlin was struck by the size and age of the trees. "This looks like a national park. I thought only the Redwoods and Sequoia grew so big."

"Yeah, it's neat isn't it? It's like an ancient burial ground, you know, something sacred and secret all these years. A couple of years ago, a guy who was a buddy to the governor tried to get permission to buy these woods and put up a fancy subdivision. Your grandma put up such a big stink, guys from Washington, D.C. came out to see what the deal was. She said this was a national treasure and it had to be protected."

"My grandmother did that? I didn't know she was an environmentalist."

"Well, I've got a theory about that too. I think she wanted to keep people out of these woods because there's something that's dangerous back here." Stormy stopped her bike and looked seriously at Kaitlin.

"Stormy, now you're giving me ghost stories again!"

"No, really! Your grandma said that this place had been home to Indian people long before any white folks came this far west and that it was a religious place for them. She said she'd have Indian activists down here faster than the D.C. bunch if they pushed the subdivision. The funny thing is that there's no record of these Indians and I think she was just bluffing, but those D.C. guys came hiking down here with daypacks, cameras, and surveyor equipment. When they left, they agreed it was a legitimate sacred site and told the state government not to touch it or they would declare it a Federal monument."

"You really aren't making this up are you Stormy?"

"Cross my heart and hope to die. Those guys left here like they'd seen a ghost. I was down there by the pipe and I saw them stumbling out of the trees. They weren't even talking to each other and their faces had gone all pale and sweaty. They nearly jumped out of their skins when I came up onto the road in front of them and they swatted me away like they were real mad about something. And I don't think they were in these woods meeting with the Godfather. I think they ran into something supernatural and they didn't want to tell anyone."

"Why are we going back here then? Honestly, Stormy I don't know why I should do this when all you try to do is scare me."

"Come on, you'll be all right. I want to see what they found. I've been out here lots of times but all I ever see is a hawk, or squirrels, or sometimes a turtle. I think you have to be a bad person to get scared out here. And everyone knows I'm practically an angel." Stormy shook her ponytail and started off again.

"Hey, wait up. I'm coming, but we leave here when I say!"

* * *

He crawled from the dark comfort of his den, awakened by some sound or smell in the woods. Groggy, he rubbed his nose against the ground and its new grass, raked his muzzle with his paws, and sniffed the air to see if he could locate the intruder. The constant pain at the back of his head flared up even in the shallow light of the forest and the voice that had been with him all these years was whispering again. He was not sure which he hated more, the pain or the inside voice which tormented him. He whined and stood to shake off the debris that had accumulated in his fur through his long sleep. Hunger gnawed at his insides making him restless; the voice whispered relentlessly, distressing him to anger.

As the whisper grew louder, he bit at himself, scratched at his head, and rolled on the dirt, trying to get the bad thing out of him. But there was never an escape.

Sleep did not stop it, eating did not stop it, and killing did not stop it, though all these sometimes slowed the words and bad thoughts. Now, the something inside was hungry for blood, for life. It would not be quiet until he found some prey.

Stepping gingerly into the woods, Yuki began his long hunt.

* * *

The double track soon petered out and became a single narrow footpath, apparently seldom used. It was hard to make the bikes follow the stony path and several times the girls stopped to pull fallen branches out of the way. Despite their exertion, Kaitlin shivered under her jacket, feeling herself go colder as they went deeper into the woods. Though there was great beauty here, the place set a somber mood over her, making her depressed and grouchy. She hoped they would turn back soon and thought of suggesting it, when Stormy, just ahead of her, stopped suddenly and announced that they had arrived.

"Look, doubter. Isn't this spectacular?" Stormy stood at the top of a great hill that overlooked acres of deep woods but was clear enough at this point to provide a vantage of it all.

Kaitlin dropped her bike to the ground and gazed at the wide horizon of green, broken only by the cleared fields of her grandmother Doe's farm. Her eyes stopped there, wondering what her mother and Doe were doing right now as she watched them. Some movement at the edge of the farthest field caught her eye. It looked like a small girl and a black dog; the girl waving in her direction. Kaitlin shuddered, suddenly cold and queasy in the warm sun. A chill shook her as if she had taken on a high fever. She used her deep breathing, determined not to collapse again.

Kaitlin's rapid pulse almost choked her words off as she spoke. "Stormy, look. At the edge of that bare field. Do you see them?"

Stormy raised her hand over her eyes to shade them. "Right by the creek? No, I don't see anyone. Are they still there?"

"Stormy I can see them plain as day, a girl and a black

dog. She's waving at us. Can't you see them?" Kaitlin desperately wanted Stormy to agree.

"Okay, I see the field, I see the creek, I'm looking down the whole length of it but I don't see any people or dogs. Are you sure that's what you see?"

Kaitlin watched the girl and dog turn away and disappear in the direction of the creek. The fear subsided as they left her field of vision. "Yeah, I saw them, for real. They're going now. Who could that be? Does some other girl live around here who might walk on my grandmother's farm?"

"Until you moved in, I was the only girl in six square miles. Mostly there aren't many kids at all. Just a lot of old people who've lived here all their lives. Their kids are all grown up and gone. Except for my family who didn't have better sense."

"I saw her before too, from my bedroom window. She looked like she was just staring right at me, like she knew where I was." Kaitlin shuddered again and turned toward Stormy. "Let's get out of here, I don't like this place."

* * *

Instinct led him due south following deer trails and waterways until he came up close to the dilapidated farm buildings. A small tar-papered house sat close to the road, a flock of scrawny red hens scratching in the back yard for bugs and worms. He was not happy to be so near to man smell, but the whispering urged him on, circling him around the old barn and sheds until he found what he was after.

Behind the shabby one-story house, a thin young woman stretched out on a dirty plastic beach chair, trying to catch an early tan. She fretted with the aluminum legs, trying to lock the chair in place so it wouldn't collapse on her. Beside her, a wicker laundry basket sat with a thin gray sheet stretched over it, shading the tiny baby inside. Despite Yuki's fretting, the voice told him to stay, and he felt a part of him ignore the dusty chickens and stare at the skinny woman and the plump baby with a hungry longing.

Yuki paced restlessly, tempted to escape into the

woods, but something inside commanded him back to the edge of the yard where he could watch the two. Yuki tried to shake off the command and whined with frustration, but as always, the inner voice controlled him anyway.

A phone rang, startling Yuki from his daze, and he watched as the woman patted the baby, then ran into the house. He could hear her light laughter and chatter through the open window but she stayed inside, as the baby gurgled and kicked in its makeshift bed. Something screamed at him inside his head, to go now, to get the baby.

Yuki's feet obeyed the inner urge, moving forward, drawing closer to the baby, as the infant's smell excited and enticed him. Yuki ran the last few yards, drooling with eagerness. He stood over the basket looking at a tiny bundle of blankets and pink skin inside. Desire pressed him closer until he nosed the sheet aside, opened eager jaws, and closed his sharp teeth on the baby's diaper, snatching it from its nest of blankets. Something sang in his head, cooing and laughing with anticipation, making him feel better as he fled with the heavy parcel that wriggled and cried as he bounced along.

Yuki retreated for the woods, glad to be away from the farm and intrigued by the bundle he carried in his jaws. He ran silently and swiftly without stopping, until he was deep in the old forest. The infant shrieked in his ears and Yuki caught the bad smell of its droppings as it protested the tearing branches along the way, but still Yuki's head rang with good words whispered with delighted expectation.

Yuki finally dropped to his stomach in the middle of a wide space in the trail. Without hesitation, his jaws tore away the white cloth that was wrapped around the baby. Yuki, exhilarated, danced away from the noisy infant, then crept closer and fed his hunger. Yuki edged toward the squirming baby, nipping at the skin lightly, the salty taste of flesh swelling his tongue with pleasure while the baby's howling deafened his thoughts.

Something inside encouraged Yuki, prodded at him,

and he dove in again, this time biting deeply into the soft belly of the wailing child. Blood filled his mouth and ran down his throat in deep satisfying drafts as he sucked in the infant's dying breath, then lifted the carcass and moved off the trail to finish his feast. Yuki was a mix of emotions, dread and satisfaction, loathing and enchantment, but when it was done he just felt full. The thing inside was quiet for now and even his perpetual pain had diminished. Yuki barked his momentary joy, running through the trees with new vigor.

* * *

The girls said little on the ride back to Kaitlin's. The trail had been longer than they expected and both of them were sweaty and tired in the afternoon heat. Kaitlin was feeling a growing nausea and uneasiness coming on, but she didn't want Stormy to know she was having such feelings about the woods. Kaitlin tried to concentrate on the puzzle of the girl and her dog while Stormy brooded out loud about school starting again on Monday. They almost missed the steaming entrails in the path and would have passed by, never knowing, if Stormy's pant-leg had not become caught in her chain.

"Gross! What is that stuff?" Stormy stepped away, staring with fascination at the mangled mess in the dirt beside her.

"It looks like something's insides," Kaitlin's mouth screwed into a grimace and she felt her face growing clammy. She quickly stepped off the path and vomited violently, feeling worse, rather than better, afterward. Every cell seemed to scream, "Danger! Run!" As if in confirmation, the forest air was wrenched by a long and gleeful howl.

"Criminy, it's wild dogs. We've got to get out of here now!" Stormy was already on her bike and Kaitlin leapt on hers trying to keep up with her friend. Pedaling furiously, they put some distance between themselves and the ghoulish howling. By the time they finally reached the road, Kaitlin's legs were shaking with exertion and both girls were panting heavily. They stood at the side, chests heaving, as they caught their breath and slowed their heart rates.

The roar of a large engine flung them into the roadside ditch in a wash of terror as a high-powered truck set on huge wheels sprung from the marsh opposite them. Its tires dripped black, tarry mud as it spun around on the dirt road and rolled off again, returning to the watery bottoms beyond the road. The girls could hear the driver whooping and smashing a bottle against the door of his truck as it slammed into the wet earth. A little farther off, another engine ignited and a horn blasted, challenging the first driver to a game of chicken.

Abandoning their bikes, Kaitlin and Stormy pulled themselves from the wet ditch, watching the two big-wheeled vehicles lunge and dodge in the muddy bog, tearing up the sod and quickly destroying the area with their deep ruts and smashed bushes.

"What are they doing?" Kaitlin felt her anger rise as the drunken men played their games in the fragile marsh.

"They're mud-bogging, the sport of jerks." Stormy spat in the direction of the trucks and raised her hand in a one-finger salute neither driver saw.

Kaitlin laughed, and leaned against Stormy, exhausted by fear and exertion.

"I'm sorry, Kaitlin. I'm some kind of jinx or something. Those dogs aren't usually a problem until summer. I shouldn't have taken you back there."

"You're right. You do first, and think later, and I don't like being caught up in this all the time. No more adventures. Can't we just be ordinary friends who sleep overnight and listen to tapes and talk about guys?"

"Hey, face it Kaitlin, you and I are not ordinary."

* * *

Kaitlin offered to take Doe's lunch tray upstairs and suggested her mother take a nap while Kaitlin kept her grandmother company. Laurel nodded with a tired smile, untied her apron, and followed Kaitlin up the stairs. She gave Kaitlin's shoulder a squeeze as she turned off to her own room.

When Kaitlin entered, she found Doe sitting at the window as if she were watching the forest. A smooth round stone was in her lap and her left hand rubbed it gently. Kaitlin noticed immediately how much deeper and darker her grandmother's eyes had become and how much thinner she looked in just the week Kaitlin had been here. She swallowed back the thoughts that crowded in, and smiled broadly for her grandmother.

"Grandma, I brought lunch for you; cream of potato soup, applesauce, wheat toast and hot tea." Kaitlin set the tray at the table and Doe pulled her chair closer, catching her breath and wincing with the effort.

Doe set the stone beside the tray, "Come sit with me, Kaitlin. Let me catch up with you and everything you've done this week."

Kaitlin caught herself staring at the stone, well rounded and pink with a few lines of gray circling its middle.

"Ah, this is my worry stone. When I am not feeling well or things are going badly, I rub the stone and it takes the worry and hurt away from me. Here feel it." Doe held out the stone to Kaitlin who took it in her hand.

The stone's coolness soothed her palm, hot from carrying the soup and tea. Kaitlin used her thumb to rub its smooth surface, surprised to find a few rough spots at the edges. Doe, sensing Kaitlin's discovery, nodded, "Life's troubles smooth us down but we are not past all the rough times yet. I want to give this to you and you will make it smooth all the way around in your time. This I know." She smiled at the girl and Kaitlin's heart felt lighter, holding the stone close to her breast.

"Doe, I went into the woods today and I had a very bad feeling there. It made me feel sick and afraid." Kaitlin kept rubbing the stone and it did feel as if the stone were absorbing her bad feelings as she spoke of them.

"Kaitlin, I need to tell you a story about what is in your blood for you to understand. It was not so many generations back that your ancestors lived as nomadic Indians. Our line comes down from powerful people, chiefs and prophets of their tribe. In the last generation before the tribe was scattered, twin brothers were born who were the most powerful yet.

"One brother was a great war chief and one brother was a great prophet. The prophet's visions came to him in dreams and told him that our people must keep our old ways and not mix with the whites who were settling around us. Because his prophecies were so strong, many Indians believed him, even those outside our tribe. His brother, the chief, became a great warrior leader for the other tribes and led raids on the whites to defend our lands.

"One day, when the war chief had to leave the village, he left his brother the prophet in charge, and told him not to antagonize the whites while he was gone, but the prophet was a poor leader and he disobeyed his brother. The whites returned his attack, destroying the women and children and old men left in the village. After that, the whites brought powerful forces and gathered all the people of the remaining tribes and took them away, to the barren deserts of the west.

"The prophet's daughter fled with her children and came to this place of power. My grandmother told me the women of this line must carry on her work, to pay for her father's foolishness. We are left with a legacy to guard this powerful place and never leave it. In return, our women have powers to see what others do not. But our power comes from the land and it must be balanced and protected carefully.

"When I was still young, the balance shifted and now we guard others from the power of this land. Kaitlin, you have a power to recognize danger and evil. These feelings are a part of it. You must pay attention to your feelings and use them to warn others."

"Doe, there was a wild dog in the woods. We heard it howling and we saw part of something it had killed. I don't know what it had killed, but I knew with all my heart that something evil had passed by, some deep and terrible thing. Are the wild dogs the danger in the woods that I'm supposed to warn about?"

"The wild dogs are dangerous but that is not the evil. There is something much deeper and I have never had the strength to know for certain what it is. Something was released there some forty years ago and I have felt the residue of it all this time. Still I am not able to rid this place of its disease. I think that when it could not kill me outright, it crept into my bones and into my organs to make me sick."

"Oh Doe, why would you stay here all this time with so much awful happening to you?"

"This land is my heritage. It is your heritage as well. Our people have been on this land as long as time can remember and we are the last there are to protect the land. April would have been strong but she died too soon.

"I have such hopes for you Kaitlin. I can feel the power in you. I called you here because it is your job now, and I think that you will make the land right again."

Kaitlin sat back on the bed, embarrassed and uncomfortable, wondering if her grandmother was really as crazy as Aunt Carol Ann. Her face flushed, thinking that part of it might be true, and wanting to tell her grandmother that she was just a child, too, and that she didn't want this job, didn't even understand half of what her grandmother was talking about. Kaitlin wanted to leave, to take her mother and grandmother away from here to a place where the land didn't make you sick or terrified.

CHAPTER 15

Whaley woke with the taste of stale beer and cigarette butts in his mouth. He hadn't smoked in years but he recognized that morning-after bar smell hanging from his clothes. He coughed and clots of phlegm came up, gagging him for a minute before he could swallow it. Still dressed, shoes and all, he must have barely staggered home last night. He pushed himself off the bed and headed for the upstairs bathroom. He could smell his infection, even through the barroom reek. Time to change his dressing and be on his way. He didn't want to run into Mrs. Jackson. Didn't want to explain last night to her.

The sun was just rising by the time he made for the sidewalk. There was little traffic and he gave in to his constant urge to walk. He was free, he could just keep walking if he wanted, wear out the soles of his shoes, walk until his feet were just stubs. He chose to go east this morning, to walk into the sun, to feel its fresh warmth on his face. Pulling his hat brim down to cover his eyes, he started off at a steady stride, down long broken sidewalks, along the gravel sides of blacktop roads, and across newly plowed fields where his feet sank into the moist furrows and left deep impressions behind. Sometimes his shoulder twinged but he shifted under his thin shirt and jacket and kept going, keeping his mind away from it.

He was long past the city limits when he stopped at a corner store to buy a beer to wet his whistle. The man inside sneered when he placed his order but he took Whaley's money all the same. What did that bastard know anyway? A man built up a fearful thirst walking. Gravel crunched beneath Whaley's thin soles as he walked along the highway, sipping at one beer, holding two others in the big pockets of his old jacket. Cars whisked past taking morning-shift workers in for the day.

He whistled between sips of Stroh's from the longneck bottle and as the morning warmed up, he slipped into old songs he'd sung as a young man. It struck him that he was headed somewhere but he couldn't put his finger on where. A warm buzz filled his head and the words of the old songs were harder to come by. He shrugged away his confusion and the shoulder complained but he concentrated on his feet and forgot the pain.

* * *

Kaitlin stood nervously at the end of the long driveway, waiting for the school bus that would take her into town. Her stomach rolled and fluttered and she was glad she hadn't eaten much for breakfast. She took deep breaths to calm herself, until she thought she was going to hyperventilate. Wouldn't that look dramatic, she thought, fainting on the bus steps on her first day of school?

She heard the growl of the big engine before it crested the hill. The yellow bus tossed up billows of dust as it rattled down the gravel road, looking for all the world like a rampaging caterpillar. Kaitlin waved, wondering if the driver would know to stop for her but she was rewarded with a screech of brakes and a noisy cranking as the door was opened to her.

Kaitlin lifted her knees high to climb in and the door clanged shut behind her even before she could make the top step. She grabbed the metal seat brackets to keep her balance, and moved down the empty aisle to a worn green seat. The metal walls echoed with the pings of rocky bumps as the empty bus bounced along the country roads.

She didn't even look at the bus driver until she was planted firmly in her seat and could study his reflection in the wide mirror that monitored the aisles. He nodded back at her and Kaitlin dodged her head in embarrassment, wringing her sack lunch in her hands.

The bus pulled up to a rambling white house, half hidden behind thick lilac bushes, and Stormy, in her old brown hat, climbed aboard, quickly followed by assorted younger brothers. Kaitlin smiled and slid over to the window so Stormy could sit with her, but Stormy quickly turned away and made her way to the back of the bus. Kaitlin got ready to change seats at the next stop but the girl who got on slipped into the seat beside her before Kaitlin could move. Kaitlin tried to catch Stormy's eye, but she was staring out the side window.

"New, huh?" The girl smiled and waited politely for an answer.

"Yeah, I'm Kaitlin. I'm in the sixth grade. How about you?"

"We'll be in the same room. See that guy over there?" Tricia pointed to a tall boy about three seats ahead. "That's Carson. He's in our grade too. The kid with him is my bratty brother. He's in third grade but he thinks Carson is a super-hero or something." She laughed, reminding Kaitlin of Allison and home. She settled into her seat, pleased to make a new friend but still worried about Stormy's sullen behavior.

By eight o'clock, the sun was streaming in the bus windows and Kaitlin was hot enough to take off her jacket. She pressed her nose to the glass, catching her first glimpses of the elementary school. It sat back on a broad street lined with maple trees. The classroom windows were painted with Easter bunnies and spring flowers. Kids were grouped in knots of two or three around the playground and for the first time, Kaitlin thought she might like it here.

* * *

Whaley was shocked when he found himself in front of the elementary school. Not a modern school, but built a long time after he'd last been here. He'd attended the high school that had stood on the same lot. A three-story red brick building put up some time in the 1890s; it had been a lot like the old prison hospital buildings he just left. He'd heard it had been torn down and replaced with this low brownstone, but the effect of seeing the place so changed was startling.

The old fight songs came to mind and he sang these softly to himself as he walked around the perimeter of the fenced-in playground. A couple of the huge maples he'd loved as a teenager were still there. He'd lost his heart under those trees, and he'd fought for her there too. He was just a skinny redheaded kid in those days but he'd won his true love and they'd married just two weeks after graduation that year.

The rumble of a school bus shook his reverie and he watched as boys and girls in jeans and backpacks unloaded. A few dragged band instruments in black cases and one child carried a wire cage with white mice inside. Bicycles pulled up to racks near the front doors and cars lined up behind the bus to drop off kids and pull out again. Another bus bounced into the circular turnaround and Whaley was about to leave when he saw her.

At first he thought it was Kitty again, her red hair in braids down her back, her lanky body shuffling along in worn jeans, but Kitty was grown with children of her own. Whaley stared, trying to be sure, and the girl turned to face him, almost as if she could read his mind. She looked at him curiously for a minute and then recognition filled her face and she ran toward the fence where he stood.

"Poppy! Is that you Poppy? What are you doing here, Poppy? When did you get out?" She beamed at him, and it made his eyes water to see her smile, just like her mother used to when she'd come to visit him up at the prison.

"They let me out last week, honey. I been meaning to come to see you kids and your mother. I'm just taking things gradual at first. You know, gotta take it a step at a time. How's my granddaughter doing?"

Stormy rolled her eyes. "This isn't my favorite place to be, you know. I can't stand being locked up like this." Her neck and cheeks turned red as she realized what she'd said. "You know what I mean Poppy?"

"Oh, that's something I know too well. Can't take a prancing filly like you and lock her up sweetheart. You just always stay free. Right?"

"Yeah, Poppy, I do, but it's harder here, that's all."

In the distance, the school bell rang and Stormy turned to watch the other children head for the doors. "I have to go Poppy. You'll come see us won't you? I'm so happy for you." She squeezed his hand through the fence and was gone before he could say anything more.

Whaley watched her on the long walk across the grass field. A boy with a safety patrol belt, sneered at her at the door, but she swung her braids and ignored him. The sun went behind a cloud and Whaley shivered, his sweat cooling in the draft that gathered at his back. Despite the chill, his wound throbbed with heat and pressed against his skin like it would soon break through. He opened the second bottle of beer and took a long swig before he wiped his mouth and moved on.

* * *

Kaitlin and Tricia were swarmed by other students as they left the bus; a confusion of new names and faces encircled Kaitlin. She could barely see over the heads of the girls who had crowded around her, just enough to watch Stormy cross the wide playground by herself. Distracted from the questions she was being asked, Kaitlin wondered about the old man who stood talking with Stormy at the far fence. A shiver of apprehension ran through her, then someone asked about Kaitlin's old school and she was too busy answering to think about Stormy.

Finally, Tricia pressed through the crowd and took Kaitlin inside to her new classroom. Mrs. Kozyra, a young woman in maternity clothes, showed Kaitlin where she could put her things and pointed out her new desk, already labeled with her name. Kaitlin stowed her school supplies and sat restlessly at her desk, fidgeting as the students filed in after the first bell.

Kaitlin was seated next to the tallest boy in the class; she recognized him from the bus and thought he lived not too far from Bluehills. Carson shyly pushed his math book to the space where their desks touched and Kaitlin looked on as they went through the day's lesson. Carson doodled on his scratch paper, drawing baskets and bouncing balls. Kaitlin added a tall skinny caricature of Carson to her own paper, pushed it over where he could see it, and watched him cover his mouth to keep from laughing.

Kaitlin tried to pay attention to Mrs. Kozyra, but found herself watching the other students around the room. She saw Stormy, sitting in a back corner by herself and wondered at how quiet she was in school. Kaitlin noticed that the other students left Stormy on her own, and that cheerful Mrs. Kozyra criticized Stormy's questions, left her out of the discussions, and dismissed her last for recess. Stormy seemed like a different person, subdued and awkward in the classroom. At recess she was wild; too loud, too rough, and too clumsy.

The ride home was quieter, Kaitlin found herself exhausted from the nervous tension of the first day. As the bus emptied, she moved to the back, sliding in beside Stormy.

"So, what kind of a friend are you, leaving me all on my own on my first day?" Kaitlin asked the question with a friendly nudge to Stormy's elbow but Stormy pulled away as if she were angry.

"A good friend that's what. You don't need a weirdo like me hanging around ruining your first impression on everyone. Besides, you didn't look like you were lonely." Stormy said this to the window, avoiding eye contact with Kaitlin.

"I thought you said we weren't ordinary? If that makes us both weird, that's all right with me, but you're my friend and I don't give up friends just because they're not popular. Am I making myself perfectly clear?" Kaitlin shoved Stormy's shoulder to make her look at her.

"Well that may be easy to say today but you might feel different later. I just wanted to save you trouble down the road."

"Stormy, you never worried about putting me in danger before, don't start changing your ways now. I'll decide who I want for my friends, you don't need to make those decisions for me. From now on, we stick together, okay?" Kaitlin draped one arm around Stormy who turned a wan smile on her.

* * *

Whaley's legs ached as dusk settled in. Long shadows grew from trees clumped in front yards and made odd angles and movements against the pavement. He could hear children's voices echoing in the distance but he couldn't be sure if they were happening now or were some memory from this morning looping through his brain. Inside the houses, lights flashed on and dinner conversations floated through open windows and thin walls. At first he thought the voice he heard was from one of those houses, but it spoke his name insistently until Whaley looked up to find its source.

The street was empty except for him, straddling the centerline as he stumbled along. No one's door stood open, the fence gates were shut tight; he saw no one at any of the lighted windows. Whaley stopped walking so he could focus his blurry vision better. There. Was there something darker inside that shadow? Someone standing against the trunk of that willow? Whaley stepped closer, trying to be sure. A pain lanced through the lesion at his shoulder and he felt something free itself and drip beneath his shirt.

"Who's there?" Whaley leaned forward peering into the darkness that massed under the immense willow. "Someone talking to me?"

His vision flickered and the darkness seemed to shimmer and waver. A man stood in front of him, muscular and lean, a glint of blonde hair falling over his forehead. He turned from his lean waist and flexed his biceps for Whaley. Two small glowing red eyes burned from the dragon's head.

Whaley gasped and patted his pockets, looking frantically for his medicine but he knew it was back on the doily-topped dresser, untouched today.

"It's your old friend, Donald, and I sure enjoyed

meeting your little granddaughter today. That flame red hair must be hot to touch."

Whaley was suddenly filled with nightmare visions of his granddaughter, pieces of bloody meat hacked from her body while her uncovered heart beat wetly in a long hand-etched gash. He watched as bloody fangs devoured her throbbing flesh. Whaley screamed and rubbed at his eyes, trying to push out the horrible sights.

"You son-of-a-bitch! You torture me all you want, but you keep your perverted shit away from her! You ain't real," he shouted. "You never been real. You're my hallucination, and I'm telling you to go away."

Whaley watched as the man seemed to fade back into the shadows, mixing with the dark until only the dragon's eyes still glowed. A faint laugh echoed around him, a sinister laugh that seemed to twine around Whaley like a clinging web.

* * *

The ringing startled Laurel who had fallen asleep in the recliner, an open paperback in her lap. Laurel grabbed the phone quickly, knowing it was Mike, calling to say goodnight at his usual time. "Hello Honey," she answered, still sleepy.

"Well, I guess you were expecting an admirer." Laurel smiled at the sound of Mike's warm and familiar voice.

"A lover, actually. Am I close?"

"If you were close, I'd be there right now, tucking you into bed."

"Well, you just hold that thought for another two months and I'll make it worth the wait." Laurel sighed, betraying her own longing.

"You know, I've waited before I brought this up, but how is Kaitlin doing?" Mike's concern traveled through the lines, blunting the casual flirtation of a minute before.

"I think she's better, really. She hasn't had a night terror once since we got here. Some bad dreams, but I've actually slept through the night every night. She's had a couple of panic attacks but she's using the deep breathing to shake them off. I think it's been good. Keep your fingers crossed."

"That's great, Honey. I was afraid to ask, but I'm relieved, really. I guess you were right about your mother being a healer."

"Actually, Mike, Doe hasn't given her anything I know of. They've talked a little, but I guess the change of place is responsible or maybe the medicine is starting to work. I just hope it keeps getting better. She's been quiet, but her eyes are not so dark-ringed, and she's made a friend already. She started school this week; I guess that's the real test. I want so much for her to be able to make it here."

"Hey, I want us all to make it there. I miss you both. I'm keeping a countdown and the guys are giving me a bad time about moping around the base. I'll be there at the absolutely earliest date I can.

"We got some stuff going on here, you probably read about it in the paper. I figure it'll be cleared up before it's time for my departure anyway. I just want you two to be real careful, don't make me worry about you, too. Navy's keeping me as busy as I can handle. I love you, Baby."

"I know Mike. I love you too. Just behave yourself at that retirement party when it finally comes. I want you here in one piece."

Laurel hung up the phone and wondered at how well they lied to each other. How could they banter and flirt when their lives were in so much upheaval? Mike had forced his cheerfulness; she knew it wasn't natural for him. She would have felt better if he'd been honest with her. She knew retirement was like death to him. Mike was back in Washington dying and she should be with him. But her mother was dying here and she had to come. She twisted the corner of the paperback's cover. Had she made the right choice? Had she had any choice?

And why had she lied to Mike? If everything was getting better, why was she so nervous, so jumpy? She felt an air of expectancy around her as if they were waiting for something to happen, as if they were being brought together for some important thing. It's Doe's death she thought, and sighed. How will Bluehills go on when Doe is gone? What will happen when the power shifts?

CHAPTER 16

Carson carried the two poles casually over his shoulder, swinging a cardboard container of bait from his other hand. Kaitlin led him down the old ruts that curved toward the creek. The tall grass caught at their pants and their shoes scuffed up dry clods of dirt as they walked. Kaitlin startled when a frog jumped into her path and blushed with embarrassment when Carson laughed at her. She pelted him with dandelion blossoms and ran the rest of the way down the hill.

"I told you I'm not exactly a nature person. If you start teasing me about fishing, too, I'll just go back to the house and leave you out here all alone." Kaitlin panted, catching her breath under the old elms that lined the rutted truck lane.

"That's a pretty scary threat."

Kaitlin folded her arms and turned back toward the house.

"No, wait! I won't tease you, honest." Carson smiled and batted his eyelashes in a 'pretty-please' look that made Kaitlin laugh.

They turned toward the last stretch of road that led to the creek and were surprised by the creatures that rose up from the tall grass at the foot of the hill. Like dinosaur skeletons rising from the mists of time, there stood piles of old metal bones, still connected and identifiable. The red of the old McCormick combines and balers had gone rusty brown, but the John Deere equipment still displayed forest-green paint in patches on the metal. There were corn pickers, cultivators, and old tractors almost entirely surrounded by waist- and shoulder-high weeds. As they came closer, they could see that each McCormick still exhibited a ragged white sticker saying "Be Careful."

Kaitlin and Carson studied the solemn graveyard in silence, cautiously stepping around five or six enormous rakes at the end of the line of machines, metal claws curled and ready to strike. One last piece of equipment stood between them and the creek, a machine so old it was built with a wood frame and metal wheels. Its brown, rusty metal and gray wood stood revealed like the bones of some fallen beast.

Kaitlin shuddered as a cloud separated her from the sun, and Carson merely whispered, "Weird."

They followed the creek to the west toward where Kaitlin remembered seeing the pond. The noon sun was hot on their faces so they took off their shoes and waded in the shallow creek, the spring water quickly numbing their toes.

"I've lived around here all my life, but I've never been here on Bluehills Farm or back in these woods." Carson rubbed his foot over a slick, wet stone in the creek bed.

"How come?"

"I don't know. I guess my mother's a little superstitious about this place. She doesn't like me to go off by myself, and she always figures there's a kidnapper waiting somewhere for me." Carson pried the stone out of the sandy creek bottom and launched it into the tall reeds of the marsh, beyond the creek. A large pheasant swooped up from the reeds, surprising both of them.

Kaitlin jerked back from the water, then stopped to watch the big bird glide over the marsh. "That was neat!"

"We should come back here sometime just to watch for birds. I bet there's quail, and heron, and red-wing blackbirds out there."

"Yeah, and skunks, yellow-jackets, water moccasins,

itch weed, and lots of other exotic things." Kaitlin pulled herself up to the damp sand beside the water so her feet could thaw while she walked.

The noise of tumbling water alerted them to the old wooden dam before they turned a sharp bend in the creek. The land rose in a small hill and the creek water poured over a four-foot structure of wooden logs and moss-covered rocks that held back the pond. They clambered up the hill to a still lake decorated with water lilies and bordered by cattails. On one side of the pond, a clear field of rich black earth stretched back toward the house. On the other side, tall marsh grass waved in the wind, and at one end, towering elm trees draped their limbs over the water.

Kaitlin knelt down to look closer at the white soil clinging to her tennis shoes. She held a clay-like lump in her fingers, finding tiny snail shells, some still whole in the marl.

"Have you ever seen anything like this?" Kaitlin held the wet clay up to Carson who looked closely but shook his head.

"No, that's cool, isn't it?"

They found some old fruit boxes, turned over like benches and set in the middle of a narrow peninsula that jutted out into the pond. A couple of the crates still looked sturdy, so they dragged these closer to the water and baited the hooks.

"It's easy, really." Carson showed Kaitlin how to cast the line, then reeled it in and waited for her to try.

Kaitlin whipped her pole back, a little too hard, almost catching Carson's shirt with the hook. She slowed down and tried again, getting the hook and sinker to sail out over the water. Kaitlin laughed, pleased with herself, and Carson took the pole to show her how to tug the line to attract the fish.

Kaitlin was happy in the afternoon sun, watching her bobber dip in the water as a dragonfly used it for a buoy. She looked across the pond to the marsh that stretched as far as the forested hill. A cold breeze caught her as something moved in her line of vision. There, a black tail flicked behind a bush and a minute later she was looking directly at the dark-haired girl and her dog. Kaitlin stood, shading her eyes to see them more clearly. Goosebumps rose on her arms as a chill ran through her and the world shut down around her, her attention fixed on the mysterious pair. Kaitlin's pulse raced and she couldn't swallow, a foreboding of disaster filling her.

Beside her, Carson was shouting excitedly and the pond water splashed loudly, but Kaitlin couldn't take her eyes off the girl. She seemed to look directly into Kaitlin's eyes and Kaitlin couldn't break away, even when she sensed that Carson was also standing, moving toward the water. The girl's mouth moved and Kaitlin held her breath, straining to figure out what she was saying, then the girl disappeared, completely vanished, though Kaitlin had not even blinked.

Kaitlin wilted, her heart slowing and her breath returning, though the chill in her bones persisted. The world around her reasserted itself and she turned to the sound of a "Whoop!" Carson stood at the edge of the grassy peninsula, spooling in his line, the pole bending and the water splashing high, as a large fish jumped at its end. Carson reached out to grab the line with one hand, putting his lead foot into the water.

Suddenly, Carson was down, his foot sinking below him and pulling his whole body into the pond, his head barely above the water line. Carson's arms flailed and he sank below the ripples entirely. Kaitlin watched in frozen shock, rooted to the shore, waiting for Carson to come up, but instead, bubbles lifted to the top of the water.

"Oh God, Carson," Kaitlin screamed, and found she could move again. She stepped to the edge of the water and tried to reach out, but felt her foot slip in the slick mud. She jerked her foot out of the sucking ooze and frantically looked for something she could use to reach out to Carson. There, under the elm was a pile of old limbs. She ran to the pile, tugged a branch from the dirt and dragged it to the water's edge.

For a minute, Kaitlin couldn't be sure where Carson had gone under. She searched the surface with her eyes, biting her hand, and trying to remember. There, small bubbles were still coming up. It had to be the place where Carson had gone under. Kaitlin pushed the long limb into the water. She couldn't see Carson in the muddy water so she pushed until she hit against something. Once, the limb bumped, then twice, and still Carson didn't respond.

"Oh, please God. Please let me save him." Kaitlin dipped the limb into the water again and almost lost her footing as something pulled at it. She sat on the ground, gripping the branch tightly and inching backward, praying and pulling, with all her strength.

Carson's head broke the surface of the water and he rose, coughing and spitting muddy water into the pond. Both his hands clung to the limb as Kaitlin pulled him to shore. When his arms could reach the grass, Carson dragged himself from the pond, one shoe gone, pants white with pasty wet marl, and his throat clogged with pond water and scum.

Kaitlin helped Carson stand and watched him spit up more water, heaving into the grass, until he was able to suck in a great gasp of air. She pulled off her sweatshirt to clean his face and helped him sit on one of the crates.

"I thought I was dead!" Carson coughed again and rubbed the shirt through his hair and over his muddy clothes. His face was pale and he shook with the after effects of his panic. He wrapped his arms around himself and rocked on the crate, trying to still his own agitation.

Kaitlin's hand clutched the leather amulet inside her shirt. "I thought you were too. God, I thought you were!"

* * *

Something pinged at Kaitlin's window, drawing her head up from her math assignment. She moved to the window, just as another rock struck, leaving a little chip in the glass. Quickly, Kaitlin unlatched the middle section, leaning out. "Cut it out, Stormy. You're going to break it."

"Well, get your butt down here and open this door. Have I got a treat for you!" Stormy was dancing below, her hat waving in one hand, a crushed box in the other. "Come on. This is important!"

Kaitlin pushed open the door, holding her finger to her mouth to shush Stormy. "Quiet, Doe's asleep and I think my Mom is too. What are you doing here at this time of the night?"

"I had to finish my homework before I came. This can't wait for the weekend." Stormy held the flattened cardboard box so that Kaitlin could read its cover. A shrouded, purple figure dominated its black cover and Stormy held the box at arm's length with great respect and wonder. The word Ouija was printed in flowing script across the front.

"I got it at a garage sale, this afternoon, with my mother. It was only fifty cents and my mother thought it was some board game. Do you believe it? I think it was meant for us. Do you know what it is?" Stormy could hardly contain herself.

"I saw one in *The Exorcist*. Why would we want to mess with something like this?" Kaitlin was conscious of a feeling that came when she touched the box, not frightening but a kind of tingling at least. She wondered if she should ask Doe about this before they tried anything.

"This is just what we need to find out who that girl is that you keep seeing. The Ouija calls spirits and they have to answer your questions and tell you the future. You can't keep any secrets from them, so we'll find out." Stormy headed for the stairs to Kaitlin's room.

"I don't feel good about this," Kaitlin protested weakly.

"Oh, come on. What could happen?"

They settled down on the window seat facing the vast old woods that stretched over the hills beyond the barn. Stormy carefully withdrew the Ouija Board and the triangular pointer that would spell out its messages. Kaitlin admired the illustrations, a smiling sun in the corner near 'YES' and a sober-looking quarter moon in the corner that said "NO." The letters of the alphabet stretched in two arcs across the board with numbers from one to nine and zero just below. At the bottom were the words 'GOOD BYE' which Kaitlin figured would be all right with her.

"We need to get things in the right mood," Stormy announced as she turned off the lights and the Oldies radio station that Kaitlin had playing. She reached into her pocket, fishing out an old candle and matches. "We have to be totally serious or the spirits will not respond." She placed the candle on the dresser and lit it.

Stormy placed the arrow-shaped message indicator on the board and demonstrated how Kaitlin should place her fingertips. "Don't try to move the arrow, the spirits will do that, just follow where it leads you and don't take your fingers off the plastic. We'll have to warm it up first, you know, some easy questions."

The girls sat with the board between them, hands poised and eyes closed as Stormy hummed a passable version of the funeral dirge. "Oh spirits wake up and hear us call. You can answer our questions all. Are you with us?"

They sat without moving for several minutes, the candle flickering and their breath gently moving the air, and then, the triangle began to totter and vibrate ever so slightly. Kaitlin felt her hand being pushed toward the 'YES' and snickered at Stormy who shook her head seriously and concentrated on the next question. "Does Kaitlin truly like Stormy for a friend?"

Kaitlin obliged by falling into the game with her own pressure toward 'YES'.

"Does Kaitlin have a boyfriend?"

The arrow pointed to 'YES'. "Ooh, Kaitlin! I guess some of us are just born lovers. You ask a question, Kaitlin."

"Who is my boyfriend?"

'C, A, R.' Kaitlin pulled her hand off the triangle. "Come on Stormy!"

"Hey, I am not doing that, okay?" Stormy thought for a minute and then asked, "Is there danger here?"

The arrow forcefully moved to 'YES'.

"What kind of danger is here?"

The arrow began to move in circles as if it were searching for something. It moved to the 'D' and stopped, then to the 'E' and stopped, on to the 'A' and stopped, next to 'T', and finally to 'H'. "Death!" Stormy's and Kaitlin's eyes met over the board.

Kaitlin jerked her hands away. "I've had enough of

this game, Stormy. How do you expect me to sleep tonight?"

"No, honest, Kaitlin. I am not making it answer this way. I didn't even know that's how you spelled death. This is important. We can't run away from this. We need to know!"

Kaitlin put her hands back on the triangle. "Yeah, this is real important. I hope you are enjoying yourself."

"Who will die?" Stormy asked.

Kaitlin jumped away from the board, wiping her hands as if they were filthy. "No, you can't ask that, I don't want to know. I won't help you ask that."

"All right, I'll ask if we can stop the death. Would that be okay?" Stormy looked expectantly at Kaitlin who agreed and sat down at the board again.

"Spirit, can we stop the death from happening?" Kaitlin held her breath as the arrow remained motionless, and then it moved to the letters. 'F, I, N, D, G, H, O, S, T'.

Stormy persisted, "What ghost? Find who?" The arrow gradually spelled out 'I, W, A, I, T'.

"What does that mean?" Stormy looked over at Kaitlin.

"I wait. This spirit is waiting for one of us or both of us to be dead!"

"Who are you?" Stormy looked around the room as if she expected the ghost to appear in front of them.

'A, P, R, I, L'.

Kaitlin sprang up from the window seat. "That does it, put it away. I won't touch that thing any more." Kaitlin's hands were trembling.

"Who is April, Kaitlin?"

"She's the ghost. She's been dead forty years and she's waiting for me!"

* * *

As Kaitlin closed the door behind Stormy, she heard her mother's voice from the stairs. "Kaitlin, who was that?"

"It was Stormy, Mom. She just left for home." Kaitlin turned toward her mother who was pulling a sweater on as she hurried down the stairs.

Betty Fry

"Kaitlin, will you go up and sit with Doe?" Laurel
flipped through the directory on the telephone desk.
"She's not doing well at all. I just gave her another dose
of her pain medication. I'm going to call the visiting
nurse and see if she can come out to give her an injection
or something. She's awful bad, right now."   Laurel
reached out to squeeze Kaitlin's shoulder, making Kaitlin
realize how serious this was.

"Sure, Mom." Kaitlin moved quickly up the stairs, her
mother already in conversation with someone on the
phone.

Kaitlin tapped lightly on her grandmother's door,
then let herself in, easing the door shut again behind her.
Doe's head rested lightly on the fluffed pillows, her eyes
closed, so Kaitlin sat in a chair pulled close to the bed.
More of Doe's hair had turned to silver in the last week;
it fanned out around her face like a halo. Kaitlin felt
compelled to stroke Doe's hair and as she touched it
lightly, Doe spoke, her eyes still closed.

"Kaitlin, are you wearing the amulet I gave you?"

Kaitlin's hand went automatically to the leather bag
beneath her shirt. "Yes, Doe. I never take it off."

"That's good, Dear. The amulet will protect you."
Doe's breath caught and she sighed slightly as she shifted
her weight in the bed. Doe's eyes were still closed and the
lines around her mouth pinched a little tighter with the
movement.

"Doe, I saw someone today. There's a girl and a dog
I've seen before. I think it's April. Is that possible?"
Kaitlin whispered, close to her grandmother's ear, not
wanting Laurel to hear the question.

"Promise me again, you'll always wear the amulet."

"Yes Doe, I'll always wear it." Kaitlin thought about
the Ouija Board and tightened her hand on the amulet.

"Doe, is it April that I'm seeing?"

"I loved April, Kaitlin. You look so much like her. She
was very special to us all, but sometimes a ghost is not
the same as the person, and April died such a hard
death. You must be careful." Doe's words came slowly, as
she stopped to take a breath between each one. Her
breathing was so forced and shallow, Kaitlin grabbed her

146

hand and held it, gently wishing her strength into Doe.

"Kaitlin, are you wearing the amulet?"

"Yes, Doe, I will always wear it. I promise you." Kaitlin's stomach tensed, and she leaned forward, still holding Doe's hand.

The door swung open and Laurel came in carrying two steaming cups of Ginseng tea. "Thank you, Kaitlin. You better get to bed now. I'll stay with Doe." Laurel put the tray down on a nearby table. She gave Kaitlin a long embrace when she stood to leave and rubbed her back like she had when Kaitlin had been a small girl, crying over some cut or bad dream. Kaitlin hugged her hard and gave Doe one long, last gaze.

* * *

Kaitlin's room felt cold and empty, the small lamp feebly lighting her desk, the overhead lights glaring off the black window. She pulled old books from the shelves that stood under the family pictures. The books smelled of must and their yellow pages offered up fanciful drawings of fairy tales and rhymes. Kaitlin stared for a long time at an illustration of an Indian girl watching her brothers dance into the sky where they sparkled as yellow stars in a deep blue horizon. The Indian girl wore tasseled buckskin and a beaded headband with one blue feather. The Indian girl sat beside a roaring bonfire whose sparks rushed up to the sky after her brothers. Her large dark eyes looked in wonder at the dancing boys.

Kaitlin set the book aside, remembering the box of old photographs under the bed. She pulled out the tattered brown box and shuffled through the dusty images of babies, wooden front porches, and teams of horses. There was a family in high, starched, white collars and tall, laced boots. Here was a woman in long black skirts sitting at a library table. Here was a very dark woman with an austere face and tall black boots; she stared solemnly into the camera; looking as if she could see right through the paper into Kaitlin's eyes. Here was a dark-haired girl, about Kaitlin's age and build, in a short-sleeved cotton dress and white anklets. A large black dog with a scarred face sat at her side in front of a blossoming apple tree. The girl's gaze was steady and her mouth was warm. Kaitlin felt as if she were looking into a mirror, a strange mirror that reflected another time. On the back of the photo were the words, April and Duke, 1951.

Kaitlin felt the tingling chill that she'd noticed earlier, but she was not really frightened. She set aside the photo and methodically went through the box pulling out each snapshot of April or her dog. Here was April at about three years old, crying loudly as her brother kept a large bucket of huckleberries from her (April and Ray, June, 1943). Here she was grinning through an oversized slice of watermelon (April, July, 1946). This one showed April at about seven, still a tiny girl perched on the huge back tire of her father's tractor (April and FarmAll, 1947). A final one showed April pulling a sled in the winter snow, a dark knit cap pulled over her head, hair in braids lying on her shoulders, rubber galoshes buckled on her feet (April, December, 1950).

Kaitlin stared at the smiling images, imagining a girl like herself, growing up in a big family on Bluehills farm. She imagined she could smell strawberries and fresh straw, that she could taste mashed potatoes and hot rolls, that she could hear the hens clucking and cows mooing in the pasture, that she could feel the first snow flakes melting on her cheek and a father's callused hands. Kaitlin could see the creek sparkling in the sun and watched the grass bend as the big dog waded through it.

'I wait' buzzed in Kaitlin's head but wouldn't quite settle anywhere. Kaitlin yawned and put the box of photos away, keeping April's pictures out and lining them up against her dresser mirror. Maybe tomorrow she would be able to figure out what this was about, but tonight she needed her sleep.

She turned out the light and went into a restless slumber, images of babies with old faces and crying children mixing in with the purple hooded figure on the Ouija Board. She tossed the blankets off and twisted her sheets but eventually she fell into a long continuous dream.

She lay beneath starched sheets tucked in so tightly that she couldn't turn over and she found it hard to breathe. She turned her head toward the window and she could see a glow in the woods beyond the barn that seemed to move steadily toward her. She watched the glow move down the hills and over the marshland at the edge of the last field. She saw it hover over the creek as it crossed the bridge and come up the rows of small corn that had just been planted this spring. The glow hesitated at the barn, then came slowly up the hill.

She heard the door latch down stairs turn and knew that the glow was moving up the steps, she could see its cool light under the door now and as the door swung open, it was in the room with her. The glow was white and cold, freezing cold like the winter's worst day. It rose from the floor and stood over her bed, sending its frigid breath across her chest, filling it with snow until she couldn't draw any breath.

She looked down, surprised to see how thin and withered she was. She raised her hands to push away the cold and found them bony and liver-spotted, her nails yellowed and broken. A draft engulfed her as the glow sat upon her chest and she saw white fur blow across her eyes. She struggled with the pressure on her chest, but she couldn't move the weight off, and as it shifted, the creature turned icy eyes upon her. Moonlight lit its frozen orbs and she could see her own reflection. She was Doe.

.

Part 4, 1950

"A time to cast away stones, and a time to gather stones together; a time to embrace, and a time to refrain from embracing; A time to get, and a time to lose; a time to keep, and a time to cast away;" --Ecclesiastes 3:5-6

CHAPTER 17

hristmas vacation was everything April had daydreamed for when she was supposed to be doing sums in school. The radio played all her favorites, *All I Want for Christmas Is My Two Front Teeth*, *Baby, It's Cold Outside*, *Rudolf the Rednosed Reindeer*, and the newest, *Silver Bells*. Donna Jean was home for a week, teaching April how to play Canasta and showing Carol Ann how to do the box step. The girls rolled their hair using bobby socks as curlers and the boys went ice fishing every day.

April's favorite time was early morning, when the sun lit up a brilliant blanket of fresh white snow, unmarred by anyone's footprints. April was the first one up; Papa slept late when there was no garden to tend. She loved it this way, with the whole world belonging only to her, each corner waiting to be discovered for the very first time. April waded through the unmarked snow, Duke breaking his own path in front of her.

April whistled Duke back to her. Duke needed no rope now, but still he took off after every wild animal he could scent out, so April tried to keep him within her horizon line. Papa would chew into her if she let Duke get lost or go off for days the way dogs wanted to do. April pulled her sled behind her, making for the hill of the far hay field. It was a long slow slope, unobstructed by trees and made smooth with the last hay mowing. She was sure the new snow would make her sled fly down that hill.

April stopped to brush snow from the tops of her boots. The snow was deep enough in this valley that it was creeping into her boots and with much more of this, April's socks would be soaked and her feet frozen. She scanned the hill for Duke and could see him off to the east along a windbreak of trees. April figured it was too cold for much else to be out so he probably wouldn't run too far.

Another ten minutes brought her to the top of the long-sought hill. An unbroken sweep of white lay before her. With a running start for a good push-off she would ride a long way without stopping. Marking off a good projection point in her head, she pulled the sled back, bent down to grasp the back of it with her arms and pushed it forward toward the brink of the hill. Rushing forward at full speed, she threw herself prone on the wooden sled, steering with her hands as the full-speed glide began.

It was a wonderful sensation; the blades cutting through the new snow, sending ice crystals stinging into her face; the wind tugging at her hat and pulling her coat collar open; the view flinging itself past her and leaping into her path. White surrounded her in flashing detail and in half-seen visions.

Without warning, the white in front of her shifted shape and rose from the flat panorama. Almost on top of her, she realized a white dog was racing up the hill toward her, the wild white dog that had leapt at her that night by the barn. She wrenched the left runner to the side swerving away from the dog and picking up speed on a steeper grade of the hill. The white dog spun and changed directions, barking and snapping at her as she prayed the sled would escape it.

A jarring bump at the bottom of the hill sent the sled airborne for a long silent second and then April landed hard, not on the frozen ground as she expected, but crashing through thin ice hidden under a shifting layer of snow. The sled seemed to hang in the water, but before

April could roll off, the back end dipped and both she and the sled slipped into the bruising cold.

April's boots filled with water, her snow pants soaked through, and icy hands pulled her down below the level of the white snow and the glassy surface. April's open eyes frosted over before she could blink but she kicked out in panic and rocketed back to the surface, flailing for the snowy edge which broke off at her touch.

The air around her was filled with gnashing teeth and thunderous growling, but louder to her ears, was the cracking of the ice, the splashing of black water, and the rasping of her breath as she sucked in air before sinking once again.

April tried to kick, finding her legs moved as if they were wading in cement. The kick brought her above water once more and again she reached for the icy edge. Suddenly warm breath on her neck spurred her with terror and she thrust herself to the side to avoid the teeth she could feel at her back. She scrambled in desperation but the struggle just caused the ice to break more quickly.

"No!" she shrieked just as her mouth filled with icy water and she went under again. She was sapped of energy and will. Her legs were numb and would not obey her own weak commands. April's face hung in the thick water, slippery with wet grass. Her lungs were bursting, demanding air. April thought she would have to breathe in, this time, before rising.

The teeth followed her, fastened onto her collar, jerked her upward and backward, the ice breaking away as she was dragged closer to the shore. Finally her kicking feet struck bottom and she pushed backward onto the solid sod at the edge of the swampy pond. Even as she felt the earth beneath her and air rushing into her lungs, she batted out, striking the dog away as she rolled out of its grasp.

Duke yelped, then moved in to lick her face.

"Oh my God!" April reached up to embrace the whimpering black dog and used him as a support to pull herself out of the water. Shaking uncontrollably, she held Duke close to her, trying to gather warmth from his thick fur. He licked her face and climbed onto her shoulders, barking and leaping over her. Duke pulled at April's sleeve, dragging her to her feet and pulling her into a walk. Stunned, April wiped her own face to clear her vision, then made straight away for the house, noting drops of red strewn on the snow leading into the woods.

Long after Mama had warmed her at the fire, April continued to shake, knowing that death could come like a white wolf in the snow.

* * *

Yuki cowered within his shelter, listening to the men's harsh voices echoing in the empty woods. They had thrashed through brush, slopped through the marsh, and frightened all the game into hiding as they invaded his territory. Yuki jumped when their rifles buckled his dreams and he tensed with each whiff of their wet wool coats and oily rubber boots.

Yuki stayed in his den for three days, nursing his wounds and his humiliation. Flashes of the girl and the black dog flickered in his thoughts, paired with rage and hurt. Yuki was half-grown, half-starved, and half-knowing; but he would be more and he would remember. He ignored his empty, aching stomach and thought one thought, growing greater with each breath he took. Yuki would hurt them, he would kill them, he would give them back the agony they had given him.

* * *

Alana fretted in the little kitchen, banging pans and thumping chairs, until Ezra rose from his bed and shuffled in to see what the racket was.

"Hell woman, what are you on the warpath about? You got nothing better to do than raise the dead this early in the morning?" Ezra pulled the grimy coffee pot to him but found it cold and empty.

"There's something wrong at Bluehills. You got to walk up the road and call them. I don't know why we can't have a phone like everyone else. You got to get me a ride to Bluehills. I don't like what's happening up there."

"Woman, you got no idea what's happening there. You just keep your trap shut. You near scare a body to death the way you go on. You think you got mind reading powers? You tell me what I'm thinking right now and then you go and do it. I'm not getting them all riled up because you're having one of your days. Damn dumb Indian woman, you got to let go of those old ways of yours because nobody cares anymore." Ezra raised his arm to backhand her but Alana quickly moved away from him.

"You want to read the future why don't you tell me where the fish are gonna bite? Why don't you tell me when they'll raise my social security? Why didn't you tell me when my boy was going to drown? Why didn't you keep him home that day? What good are you?" He raised his arm again but this time wiped his eyes quickly on his sleeve, then slammed down the empty pot and walked out to the screened-in porch that faced the lake. He reached into a case that stood near the door, pulled out a bottle of beer, and mumbled, "Damn woman, why didn't you save my son?"

CHAPTER 18

Papa carried April into the doctor's office, his rough stubble scraping her hot face as he bent his head to test her fever. "She's been awful bad all night, Doc. She can't hardly breathe and she's burnin' up with fever." Papa coughed a little to clear his throat that clenched up on him as he spoke. He laid her on the leather-covered examining table and stepped back for Dr. Faust to get a better look.

April turned her burning face to the doctor's shelves where all kinds of wondrous and frightening things were kept. Her eyes stopped on the small skull that grinned back at her, its jaw moving just enough to make its teeth chatter with each footstep on the old wooden floor of the office. Or maybe the skull chattered because it was always cold in this room. April wondered again, as she always did when she came here, what small child had left this skull behind to watch Dr. Faust as he worked on other patients?

Dr. Faust's hands, colder even than the room, moved over her body, positioning his unfriendly stethoscope to listen to her chest and back. She knew a shot of penicillin, the all purpose wonder-drug, would follow and she tightened in anticipation of its sudden sting, reminding herself that a prescription for an ice cream cone would be forthcoming as well.

Instead, Dr. Faust left the room and April could hear him using the phone out at the desk, asking for the hospital and ordering a room and an oxygen tent. She asked her father to hold her hand, now suddenly afraid that she really might die. She closed her eyes tightly and wished herself to sleep so that she wouldn't know what they were going to do to her. She kept them closed as Papa wrapped her in the blankets again and carried her out to the car.

* * *

The noise in the kitchen was almost deafening, inmates scraping food into fifty-gallon barrels, tin dishware clattering into the automatic washers, and men shouting over the roar. Cash held the sprayer over the tin trays, ripping food away and into the industrial drain below. Satisfied, he loaded each into the metal rack that sat beside the silvery sink waiting to be transferred to the conveyer that would run them through the dishwasher; state prison duties appropriate for an inmate known for good behavior.

Behind him, Cash could hear Whaley and Malott trying to talk over the noise of the kitchen equipment, though they fell silent when Cash turned to smile at them. Whaley gave him a hard stare and the two moved toward the end of the conveyer where they could unload and stack the clean dishes.

Cash could read them like a book. They thought they knew something about Emilio's sad departure. Cash remembered his fine performance for the prison board. Wasn't it a shame how Cash had slept soundly through the night as Emilio tied one shirtsleeve to the top of the cell bars and the other sleeve around his neck? No officer, he hadn't heard a thing as Emilio threw himself off his bunk. Damn shame the fall hadn't snapped his neck. Must be terrible to die slowly by strangulation. Yes sir, the boy had seemed depressed lately, seemed his mother was heartsick over his conviction.

Yeah, it was quite a shock to wake up and see a sight like that. Damn nice kid, that Emilio. He probably would have gone straight when he got out. Think he had a wife and baby waiting for him to come home. Don't know why a man wouldn't wait for all that instead of taking this easy way out. Yes, it's awful hard to lose a good cellmate like that. It may take a while before he found another one as nice as that kid.

No sir, didn't know how he got that cut on his ear. Maybe he had a run-in with someone earlier or maybe he just cut himself shaving. Yes sir, that was peculiar.

Cash looked over at Whaley and Malott, catching a furtive glance from Malott. "What's the matter boy? You got something to say to me?" Cash moved in on the pair, pressing himself close enough to jab his fingers against Malott's chest.

"You ought to speak up, mister. I can't hear you so well in here." Cash pressed hard against Malott, pushing him backward into Whaley who held his hands out trying to calm down the situation.

"Hey, Cash. We ain't talkin' about you anyway. Back off and give us some room here." Whaley smiled weakly while Malott continued to glare at Cash.

"Sure thing, fellas. Why didn't you say so?" Cash turned away, then lashed out with a bent elbow into Malott's jaw and a forward kick to Whaley's midriff. Malott growled and lurched forward but Whaley caught at his shirt and held him back.

"He ain't worth it. Let it go." Whaley had a firm hold on Malott now, pulling his arms back away from Cash.

Cash leaned forward and smiled into Malott's face. "True, you ain't worth it." He spat in Malott's face and turned away, while Whaley fought to control the man, but Malott was squirming and squealing like a pig being dragged to the butcher block.

Malott slipped from Whaley's grasp and fell to his knees, his hands blotting his face as if he were trying to smother a fire. Puzzled, Whaley struggled to pull Malott up to his feet and managed only to pry one hand away from Malott's face. Shocked, almost frozen in place, Whaley gasped as he watched smoke rise from Malott's ruined face. One eye was already misshapen, like melted plastic. A steaming hole in Malott's cheek revealed the white enamel of an exposed tooth. Whaley released Malott's hand and stood away, watching his pal roll and scream on the cold tile of the prison kitchen.

A guard, diverted from his rounds, started toward their end of the long room. Cash grinned broadly at the uniform, motioned toward Whaley and Malott, and directed him their way. "Guess that guy got ammonia or something in his eyes."

Cash went back to his dirty dishes. Bet they wondered how a man could stay so good-looking and young, locked up as long as me. They better be careful, or they might just learn my secret youth formula someday. Cash smiled at the wall, whistling *It's a Good Day*, as he sprayed down the dented trays that piled up beside him and daydreamed of fresh air and the warm weather work gangs.

* * *

Winter faded away into long gray days April spent inside. She tried to draw, but each cute animal or smiling face she started ended as snapping teeth and flashing white. She tried to sleep, but kept waking with muddy water choking her and ice closing over her. She tried to play with the new 'Susie-doll' Santa had brought her, but kept seeing its neck covered in blood. Each day Papa and the boys came in from the woods with nothing to say. Soon, they went back to their other chores and the white dog was forgotten. Mama looked at her with sad gray eyes but didn't make April talk about it.

Sometimes Grandma Alana came and they cut out paper dolls, all in a row with their arms connected together like chorus dancers. Sometimes Grandma Alana made her warm ginger milk and talked about how she had grown up here at Bluehills Farm. Grandma Alana told funny stories about chickens that chased cats, and how her brothers tied her braids together when she slept. Sometimes she made a bad smelling tea of dried herbs that she had collected last summer and April drank it for her while Grandma Alana pinched April's nose and made her laugh. She pulled out dried plants and named each one, making April recite their uses and where they were found.

An early spring brought muddy roads, runoffs carving gullies into the old rows of the cornfield, and a new calf, spindly-legged and cow licked. The cowslips bloomed rich yellows in the black mud along the creek, violets grew in Mama's orchard, and Carol Ann went mushroom hunting, bringing back a basket of deep brown morels for frying. April finished her class report on Michigan, illustrated with a drawing of red robins she'd seen scratching for Mama's flower seeds in the side yard. The spring sun made April feel good again and she started to venture out, first picking lilacs in the yard, then going with Carol Ann to gather wild strawberries. As June moved into summer, the girls ventured farther to bring in blackberries and later huckleberries to be canned for winter pies.

Papa woke April and Carol Ann early, on his way to the garden. They dressed quickly, covering themselves with long overalls and flannel shirts. Carol Ann pulled out work gloves and straw hats for each of them. April tied Duke up outside so he couldn't follow them, then, loaded with rubber galoshes and tin pails, they shuffled down the dirt road, looking more like scarecrows than girls. They cut into the State Land where a sandy two-lane path between two giant maple trees was blocked by a large iron bar to keep cars from trespassing.

Near the road, they could still make out a crumbling stonewall covered with grape vines. The old stones marked an old homestead abandoned during the Great Depression. Tiger lilies and snowballs planted by some long absent hand still thrived among the maples that crowded into what was once someone's front yard. April tried to picture a great brick house set in these woods and wondered what they could have farmed here among the trees which dominated these wilds.

The girls followed the lane until it became a path designated by wooden markers topped with bright yellow paint. Carol Ann shushed April with her finger to her mouth and they could both hear voices coming quickly up the path behind them. They snaked through the grass and stood behind the nearest bush as a group of well-muscled men shuffled down the path they had just vacated.

A guard in a khaki uniform and wide brimmed hat led

the procession and another followed at the end. Both wore holsters with black handled guns poking from them. The rest of the men were dressed in identical loose blue denim pants and shirts. Some had tied bandannas over their heads and others wore baseball caps with the bills pulled down low. Many of them were colored and one man looked Mexican.

April peered between the bushes, eyes large, watching the men's feet kicking up dust along the path. She had never seen the convict work gang so close. They sometimes stopped at the house for water from the well, but Mama always made the girls go in the house away from the windows while she stood on the back steps keeping her eye on them. Muscles bulged out of the short-sleeved shirts and several had tattoos on their arms. Some had greased hair slicked back into duck tales but most of the dozen or so men wore close-cropped hair. All were deeply tanned and some already showed sweat stains beneath their arms. The line passed quickly and April crept around the bush ready to move on.

The last prisoner turned his blonde head just as April was stepping out from behind the bush. He caught her eye and froze her in mid-step. His gaze held her pinned like a fluttering bird caged in a man's hands. His frozen blue orbs telegraphed a message to her; I know you, I could crush you. A sense of malicious evil swept through her and she knew she would flinch and her heart would pound whenever any man looked at her again.

He smiled and then licked his lips and put his tattooed hand on his crotch, the spider's legs bending around the bulge there. The guard, McLaughlin, nudged him hard in the back with his stick and the convict walked on, dismissing her like trash pitched out of a car window, leaving April feeling dirty, as if he had seen her in just her underpants.

April gagged, holding dry heaves down with a hand pressed against her mouth. She cleared her throat and spit into the grass trying to rid herself of the feeling. She turned to see if Carol Ann had noticed, but Carol Ann's back was to the path and she was gathering up the pails and boots. The rest of the walk was ruined for April who kept seeing the man's tongue sliding out like a snake's.

* * *

Cash chuckled as he shuffled along, hanging back just a little to irritate McLaughlin who followed him with his baton and sidearm. He slicked back his gleaming blonde hair with one hand and smoothed his pants with the other. He enjoyed the sudden warmth the girls had given him. The older one was a precious little piece, but the younger one, she was something more, something delicious and dangerous. He'd seen her and her sister before, when the work gang had been closer to their house. They looked like little bits of fluff just budding and right for the picking, but the little one was more than he'd reckoned. She was a serious treat who deserved special attention, and he knew the man for the job. He smiled and licked his lips again.

Cash closed his eyes as his feet moved along the fresh dirt path ahead of him. He could imagine the warm sun on his back as he took them one by one in a haystack behind the barn. Oh yes, he could make them squirm and scream against his hands when he took them. He'd bind and gag the little one to watch while he took her big sister first. Let her see how much it would hurt and let her watch while he took everything her sister had. Let her see him swell and grow big with life while her sister bled and struggled under his blade. Let her watch while he covered sister's mouth with his own and sucked the life out of her. Let the little girl watch her sister suffocate and convulse under him while he grew stronger.

Then while he was large and full of her sister's life, wet with her sister's blood, he would mount the little girl. Oh, he liked them so young and innocent. He liked the taste of their terror and the way they fought and scratched. She would fight so hard because she'd know he wasn't playing games. She'd know he was the real one, the one come to take her to her death. She'd fight for her life, but he would take it; take it with great pain so he could gain from her struggle. He would take her life slowly, chewing off pieces of her while she screamed into her gag, slapping her awake if she fainted; he wouldn't stop until his tongue found her beating heart. Then he would drink her life away while her dark eyes pleaded with him to stop. Oh, the pain she would suffer; she would make him live forever, if he could kill her like that.

"Slimy, bastard pervert."

The remark pulled Cash out of his daydream. "What's that you say, Whaley?" he spoke softly so the guard wouldn't interrupt their conversation.

"You heard me. You're a sick, dirty pervert. So help me, if I ever catch you with one of those girls I'll cut your balls off."

"Well, Whaley, maybe you don't know how real men like them, young and juicy." Cash reached forward to pat Whaley's shoulder. A gentle, friendly motion the guard wouldn't object to.

"Why is it, whenever you open your mouth, nothing but filth comes out? I hope to God you rot in some deep and special part of hell for perverts."

Cash's hand tightened on Whaley's shoulder and grew warmer. He felt his nails extend and dig through Whaley's shirt, into his skin. "I expect there is a very special place in hell for me, and for you too." The spider's legs on his fingers danced and his sharp claws sliced into Whaley's flesh like venomous stingers.

McLaughlin poked him hard with his stick and told him to keep his hands to himself. Cash smiled again. It had been a long time since he had fed, but when he had those girls, this puny guard-man would throw down his stick and beg for mercy. The begging would make him all the more tasty.

* * *

After a half-mile or so of clear-cut path the girls veered off, heading down a steep hill that rapidly dropped into a much gloomier and older section of the woods. Mosquitoes swarmed over them, stinging even through their flannel and jean coverings. The girls followed a deer path now, which barely separated the trees to let them pass. The ground grew damper and occasionally they slipped and grabbed onto limbs to keep from falling.

The breeze came in moist gusts, carrying a musty smell of mold and decay. The light faded as the girls moved lower into the dense swamp at the foot of the hill. Trees were replaced with ancient huckleberry bushes that stood above their heads shadowing dark, slimy water. The heavy air made the girls quiet and they whispered as they pulled on their boots and waded into the murk. Carefully, they stepped off tufts of sod, then scanned the limbs above them for snakes before moving forward.

April kept close to Carol Ann, placing each foot in the same spot Carol Ann's had just left. April kept glancing back to get her bearings, nervous they would become lost in here, hoping there would be no need to make a fast retreat from some threat. April was sure that a careless step would put her up to her hips in black stagnant water and mud that seemed to twist and roil around her like some slithering snake. She looked up, trying to catch a glimpse of sunlight though the dense leaves, but clouds must have gathered overhead, for the gray remained unbroken.

Carol Ann stopped moving, and motioned for April to come up to her right. "We'll start here, see how loaded this bush is. I'll go around this way and you go around the other direction and we'll meet on the other side. Come on, I'll hold your hand and you step over to that tuft there." Carol Ann held out her hand; April hesitated, then swallowed and took a giant step across the murkish water to the next tuft.

"Hold your bucket under the berries and just beat at the branches they're on. They fall right off, see?"

April watched her sister, then did as she had done. "Yuck, there's all kinds of leaves and bugs in there."

"Yeah, but don't worry about it now, we'll clean them up later in the blower. Just fill your bucket. I'll see you on the other side." Carol Ann made a step to the left, letting the branches snap back between them.

April worked silently, picking out a green worm now and then and sampling the rich purple berries as she went. She succeeded in getting around to Carol Ann's side and they moved on to another bush. They were getting into a rhythm and April's pail was starting to pull heavily on her elbow when they first heard the baying of dogs.

* * *

Yuki caught the scent of the female again, wandering, in heat, somewhere in this part of the forest. Yuki, at the head of the pack, howled in triumph alerting the stragglers to the trail he had picked up. A ragtag assortment ran with him: some summer vacationer's Irish Setter with burs caught up in its long fur, an old hunting dog with white hairs invading its Black Labrador face, and a heavily-built Rottweiler who stood as wide as he was tall. Big dogs caught up in freedom and hormone-produced adrenaline. Yuki led them, his dominance articulated in his unusual size, his rippling muscles, and his sense for survival.

Summer was good to them with game easy and plentiful, water abundant, and the occasional female stray available. They fell back to ancient instincts, stalking small prey, grouping to bring down deer, stealthily avoiding men. They grew healthier and stronger than they had been on leashes, in fences, and by firesides. Their jaws and teeth exercised on raw flesh and marrow. They bathed in fresh water lakes and rain showers. They ran, wrestled, and copulated with vigor in newfound freedom. Best of all, they were a pack, each knowing his own place in the order of dominance; and with the pack dominant over any other creatures.

Yuki's muscles flexed in his legs and shoulders as his long strides kept him ahead of the pack. In this moment, he knew only joy, no pain, no loss. His companions ran hard to keep up with him. Now, gripped in the chase for propagation, they knew only one purpose, followed only one trail, and bore down on only one clear and demanding obligation, propelling them forward.

* * *

A far-off baying alerted April to the dogs. She wiped her hands nervously on her jeans and tried to breathe deeply, the way Grandma Alana had shown her. She silently prayed the dogs would go the other way, and leave them alone to finish their job. The next howl was closer and April couldn't control her shallow breathing.

April was shaking as she called out, "Carol Ann it's

that dog. We can't stay here. Come on, we've got to leave," but the dogs were almost on them before Carol Ann could answer.

The girls could see the dogs clearly, splashing at the edge of the swamp, then climbing up the same game trail the girls had taken down to the huckleberries. The animals flew gracefully over the ground, weaving in and out of the trees with brief splashes of red, black, and white visible among the trunks. The leader's howl was taken up by the others, and for a time, the trees echoed with a mournful baying that rang in the girls' ears long after the dogs were out of sight.

April was halfway out of the marsh, ignoring the risk and leaping from one sod tuft to the next. Her urgency made Carol Ann grab her half-full bucket and scurry to keep up.

"We have to get home, now, before they can come back. We have to let Papa know where the pack is." April was almost hysterical with fear, but Carol Ann caught April's shirt before she started up the steep trail.

"Wait, let them go first. We don't want them to find us. Be quiet." Carol Ann shook her sister to get her attention, then held her finger to her mouth to warn her to speak softly. "Take off your boots so we can walk faster. Put your berries in my pail. I'll carry them for you. We'll go this way toward the road behind Quiggley's. We can get to their place first and they'll give us a ride to the house. OK? Can you do this?"

April nodded at each part and complied quickly, counting on Carol Ann to lead her to the back road without a trail to follow. The girls did no more berry picking that summer.

CHAPTER 19

The summer grew hotter and muggier as it went on, brewing up thunderstorms most afternoons. Donna Jean went to a drive-in movie with a boy from town, but it stormed so bad, her date had to bring her home early and she was grouchy for the whole next week. Mama worried about her cousin Bob who was stationed near Seoul and made each of the children write notes to him throughout the early summer. Papa complained about Donna Jean wearing lipstick and made her wash her face clean before going out of the house. The boys and Papa spent long days tending the corn, weeding the truck garden, and waiting for the hay to get dry enough to cut.

It was hard to breathe, even outside; it was like walking in the hot fog of a steam bath. Summer always meant a lot of work, but most of it was done in slow motion. The clothes hung out on the line refused to dry in the stagnant air. The kitchen walls wept with sweat after each batch of canning. April made extra trips to the pump, keeping the water pails full of fresh cold water. Mama made a gallon jug of sun tea every morning but it was empty by dinnertime. The ice in the icebox melted away quickly, the ice truck made extra rounds, and Mama nagged Papa to buy an electric refrigerator like the rest of the world had.

The afternoon was turning nasty; the air in a dead calm, the sky a sick greenish-yellow, a low rumbling off in the distance. Mama had the radio on, listening for storm warnings. Its static said more about the approaching storm than the announcer. With each loud burst of noise, Mama looked out the southwest window, watching for any change in the clouds boiling up in that direction. She checked the lantern and the kerosene stove and set them at ready by the back door. She prepared a cold supper and put the matches and candles where they would be handy if the lines went down. She fussed about Papa, Donna Jean, and the boys who were baling hay in the far field, and called for Carol Ann to come home from the Quiggley's house.

Mama's preparations made April nervous. Mama had a hundred superstitions and signs for ill omens and April could see a great number of them were adding up today. When Mama pulled her black hair back, like today, and her gray eyes glinted in their own portentous way, April was reminded that Mama carried Indian blood and in some dark and mysterious way could read the earth better than other people. April shuddered and decided to seek cover out of the kitchen. Grabbing a book, she trotted down to the barn and made a spot to read up in the hayloft.

* * *

Grandma Alana lay on her bed tossing with a high fever, sweat running in rivulets down her blanched face. From time to time she leaned over the side of the bed and vomited into the bucket Ezra had placed beside her. Her distended abdomen stabbed with pain that made her cry out and she messed the sheets twice before the old man stopped changing them. At times she seemed delirious and cried out that the snake was loose in the woods, that his fangs would poison them all, that the Windigo was walking.

When the wind buffeted the house and the old man could see the water funnels across the lake, he tried to move Alana but she could not be budged. Even the smallest turn made her scream, so Ezra sat beside the bed holding her hand as the battered windows exploded and the rain cut through the screens to soak them. Ezra was not a religious man, but he prayed loudly, if only to block out her screams about the venom that would drown them. Ezra shook with terror at the storm but her words held greater fear for him.

* * *

Whaley's shoulder throbbed in the muggy heat. It had been tender ever since Cash dug into it, but today it was the devil itself; it felt almost as if something were inside him, about to hatch. That thought hung with him all through the long morning until he could swear he felt things crawling about on his back. His mind kept seeing creepy, black spiders wriggling their way out of the wounds in his skin. He tried to keep working, swinging his ax high and hard, but each time his blade split the wood he thought of his skin splitting and releasing more many-legged creatures to crawl inside his shirt. The shoulder ached and itched but he worked all the harder trying to ignore it.

At noon the men broke for lunch and Whaley reluctantly removed his shirt, reaching over his own shoulder to brush away whatever vermin had been plaguing him. His skin was hot to the touch and his fingers came away wet and gluey with green and yellow pus.

"It's festered up pretty bad, Whaley." Cash grinned down at him. "I wouldn't be surprised if you took on a horrible fever and died. Course you'd suffer something awful before the end." He laughed loudly and wandered away, holding his belly and whooping into the noon sun.

The old guard, McLaughlin, washed the wound with whiskey he'd been carrying in a pocket somewhere and contrived a bandage from several handkerchiefs tied together. He put Whaley on light work piling up the brush scattered by the trees they felled, but Whaley's fever grew in the still hot air.

When the storm finally hit, Whaley wasn't sure what was real and what was a fever dream. A great bolt of lightning flashed around them and Whaley saw bony skulls where men's faces should have been. He watched black clouds boil and reach down long arms to twist and snap the great trees around him. But, the most terrifying sight was Cash, twirling and dancing like a demon in the funnel itself.

* * *

Duke napped in the cool shade below and April was almost asleep herself when the dinner bell started ringing and she could hear Mama calling them in. Mama's call was insistent, so April hurried down the ladder two rungs at a time. April couldn't see Duke, but didn't think she'd better waste time looking for him. Mama had thrown open the big storm doors to the cellar and was waving from the top of the stairs. The sky was mountainous with purplish-red clouds boiling over each other, and the wind was starting to whip the trees around. April ran for the cellar and Mama grappled with the big doors, fighting with the wind to pull them shut. She hesitated and then slipped the latch closed just as another gust tried to lift the doors up from the frame.

Carol Ann was already below, just getting the lantern lit, but Papa, Donna Jean, and the boys must still be out in the field. The wind was howling now and April could hear the screen doors slapping against the house at both the front and the back. She could also hear a pail or barrel being tossed about, above the cellar doors, and the cows had begun a terrible bawling. An ear-splitting crack resounded from the orchard side of the house and then the wind's velocity grew until it sounded like a freight train was roaring at them.

Mama huddled with the girls in the southwest corner, against the damp stonewalls. April never liked the cellar with its cobwebs and scurrying mice, but right now the musty dirt floor and cold walls felt strong and secure. Mama put newspapers down for them to sit on and she pulled a blanket around them. April didn't realize how cold she was until Mama did that.

Carol Ann nursed the lantern flame enough to light their faces and April could see how afraid they all were. The kerosene smelled bad but no one wanted to extinguish the light. April wondered if Papa, Donna Jean and the boys were flattened out on the ground in this or if they had taken to the truck to sit it out. April hoped they weren't pounding on the cellar doors to get in, because she didn't think they could be heard over the storm. She wondered where Duke was and if he was going to be all right out there.

The roar of the wind lessened a bit only to be replaced by the pounding of hail stones. The icy balls rattled the cellar doors and a few forced their way through the crack between the doors. Soon a small pile of white had accumulated on the third step up. A great peal of thunder shook even the cellar walls, then the deluge began.

A river of rain poured from the sky and rushed down the cellar steps in a steady stream Mama tried to dam up with newspapers. She managed to direct the water toward the wood box, keeping their corner dry until it began to seep in between the stones forming the walls. Then the girls and Mama stood on the dry places still remaining and listened to thunder shaking the house.

A last immense blow almost split their eardrums and reverberated through the stonewalls and solid floor. "That one hit in the orchard or maybe one of the maples," Mama said. "We're gonna have quite a mess to clean up after this."

The bolt seemed to be the storm's last punch and the wind died down, leaving a slow drizzle pattering against the storm doors. Mama figured it would be okay to climb out now and guessed that almost an hour had passed. Just as they were unlatching the doors, they heard Papa's horn honking and ran out to the driveway to exchange stories.

* * *

The work gang was deep in the woods hacking out a new hiking trail when the tornado passed over. The trees flung themselves about like Russian dancers; hail the size and velocity of golf balls pounded at the convicts, and then blazing bolts of lightning attacked from every direction. With no clearings or ravines in sight, the men separated, each diving for some hiding place or shelter.

Cash stood alone in the deluge, arms stretched wide, head thrown back in raucous laughter. Lightning bolts crashed around him as he twirled among the trees like some Pan intent on dancing with the storm. Flashes of searing light outlined him among the dark trees and he seemed to crackle and pitch with surges of electrical energy. As the storm moved away, Cash slumped wearily, breathless and suddenly drained.

Ancient trees that had stood for a hundred years had toppled among younger, suppler ones. Twisted limbs and splintered trunks marked the area through which they had just worked. Cash could hear a man screaming from somewhere nearby and wished he would shut his hole. Damn fool had probably broken a leg, if not worse, and his screaming was making it hard for Cash to concentrate. Aside from the screaming, Cash heard no other members of the work gang, and assumed he was alone.

Truly alone for the first time in two years, Cash dropped to the wet ground, covered his eyes with his large dirty hands, and during the lengthening intervals between screams, simply listened to the quiet. He could hear droplets falling from limbs hanging overhead, he could hear water running in a stream not far away, and finally he heard the call of a meadowlark. He concentrated until he could hear his own heart beating, mosquito wings gliding, and even the moss growing. The storm had come for him, to set him free.

Following the sounds of the screaming man, Cash determined to shut the fool up before he attracted attention. In a few minutes he came on Sweeney, trapped beneath a fallen tree, clutching his knee and rocking in agony. When Sweeney saw Cash standing over him, he dropped back to the ground, mouth clamped shut, sweat running down his pale face.

"Hey, it's okay Old Man. I'm here to help you." But as Cash approached, Sweeney tried to push himself backward, wincing when he moved his knee and going whiter with the effort.

Cash reached down to stroke the man's face but Sweeney batted his hand away, saying, "Leave me the hell alone." Cash smiled, and snapped the back of his hand across Sweeney's wide face.

"I am the friend you've been praying for. That's right,

I'm going to help you right out of here." Cash smiled slickly as he lifted his heavily booted foot and slammed it down against Sweeney's head. The blow knocked Sweeney onto his back, both hands clutching his battered head. Cash squatted down beside him, leaning close enough for his hot breath to disturb wisps of hair on Sweeney's head.

"You ought to be so much more grateful than you are. Few men ever meet someone like me and live as long as you have. But I've thought about you right along, wondering how you'd taste deep in my craw. I figured you for the type who'd beg right at the end, thinking I'd be merciful, but I like it when the pain lingers and grows. I like to see a man's eyes go all bloody. I like to hear him choke on his own puke. I especially like it when he stops wanting to live and starts wanting me to kill him." Cash stood, drew back his booted foot and slammed its steel toe into Sweeney's torn knee. Sweeney roared in agony and almost blacked out.

"I think you and I could have a wonderful time if we had the whole afternoon, don't you?" Cash gripped Sweeney's chin with one hand and his jaw with the other, twisting them in opposite directions while Sweeney's garbled moaning echoed through the trees. "What's the matter, can't make up your mind? Let me help you along."

Cash deftly drove his heel into Sweeney's hand, crushing the bones against the rocks beneath them. He ground his heel back and forth, making Sweeney howl and jerk. "Well, this is awful entertaining, but I do have a full schedule today and you're not really the show I'd been hoping for."

Cash wiped his boot in the grass, checking the sole to make sure it was clean, then raised his foot directly over Sweeney's face. "Say good-bye, Old Man. It's been nice knowing you." Cash slammed the boot into Sweeney's skull, watching it give way under his heel. Not satisfied with one crushing blow, he kicked Sweeney repeatedly until his skull was peculiarly flattened on one side, blood running from the ears, nose and mouth. Cash stepped back and wiped his shoe on the wet grass, then dropped to the ground close to Sweeney's battered face.

Cash brought his lips against Sweeney's ear, inhaling the fresh odors of blood and gray matter, flicking his tongue out to lick a yellowish gob from Sweeney's cheek.

"I suppose that will go onto my good behavior report," he laughed into Sweeney's ear. Good behavior meant only one year in jail and eighteen months on this damn work crew. Good behavior because they caught him in the rape but never connected him with the rape-murders in Ohio and Indiana. Damn stupid hick sheriffs thought they had protected their women and children so well. Cash laughed again, remembering how the last girl's father and brother had come up on him in the barn before he could reach the knife in his boot and stop the bitch's screaming.

"But now, little girl, I'll be back. Just going to have a little fun on the way." Cash thought of how his knife would disembowel her and how he would press his lips over hers and breathe in her last life's breath as she thrashed under him. Remembering how he'd done it to the others made him hard in his wet pants. He thought of the little girl he'd seen the other day. Thought of how he would collect her life too, how it would make him strong, make him live forever. He laughed again, a long oily laugh with no humor in it.

Cash embraced Sweeney's cooling body, aching for the life that quickly dispersed in the humid summer air. Unsatisfied by the quick death, Cash stood again, prodding at Sweeney's pockets for anything useful. Kicking Sweeney's limp body, he moved away and into darker parts of the forest where the funnel had not touched down.

The undergrowth caught at his pants and several times he swerved to circle around thorny thickets or standing water. Cash was energized, eager to be gone from here and heady with his new freedom. He couldn't be sure which direction he was going because there was no open sky to reveal where the sun stood, but Cash felt he was headed steadily downhill.

Cash started to lay out a plan of escape. He thought about hunkering down here in the woods for a few days, especially if he found berries to eat, but figured this was the first place they'd start looking after the storm. He'd noticed a farm or two around here. Could be if he followed the road and waited for dark, he'd be able to grab a car or a truck and put some distance between himself and this place. He sure hoped this was a washday, he'd need a change of clothes if he didn't want to look too conspicuous. Cash interrupted his planning to catch his breath and get his bearings if he could.

The woods were dense enough there were few clues for him in any direction. Cash figured the storm had hit about two o'clock and about two hours had passed since then. Daylight was lasting a long time right now so he had maybe four hours of sun left before it would be too dark to move around. Still, he'd want to be out of these woods before dark or he wouldn't make any progress at all. There was still no clue as to direction, but Cash reasoned a straight line would bring him to a road sometime soon. He picked a direction and set off but his beeline was interrupted by undergrowth before he'd gone 20 yards. This was going to be slow.

* * *

The pack laid low most of the afternoon. Short tempered and nervous, they stayed close to the den, little scraps erupting between dogs, until Yuki flattened back his ears and intimidated them into silence with his deep menacing growl. Restless and occasionally whining, they cooled off in dirt beds and waited for the first cracks of thunder to announce the start of the storm.

The breeze ceased, as if the earth was holding its breath, and the animals in the woods did the same. The sky changed to a sickly green yellow and the forest sounds abated. Nothing stirred, squirrels sat frozen in their nests, eyes wide and staring, mice huddled in tunnels as if they had settled for the night. Birds hung on the branches, alert, but staying close to the nest. Nothing flew in the yellowing sky.

Suddenly, the sky exploded in boiling clouds and whirling winds. The trees were battered by abrupt gales and healthy green leaves were torn from their branches. The wind scooped up loose dirt and sticks and scattered them with ferocious blows against the hillsides. Then the rain fell in rivers of water, crashing around boulders, lifting fallen limbs, stripping bushes of their berries, and joining together to overrun streambeds.

Squeezing together in the hole the dogs had tunneled under fallen tree trunks, wincing at nearby lightning, and shaking with the peals of thunder, the pack weathered the storm. Yuki lay close to the opening, his head shrieking with pain as his old wound emulated the storm. Each crash of thunder reminded him of the gun and his mother's death. As the storm grew, so did his anger and impatience.

When the rain ceased, and the wind and lightning moved on, the animals nervously stretched and nosed out of their shelter. The dogs were muddy from the runoff but not one was injured. In the open, they snapped at each other, leaping up on their back feet in exhilaration. The pack tore away from their den; they were wired from the electricity in the air and pumped with adrenaline from fear-gorged glands; hungry for excitement. Howling in the still air, the dogs ran full speed, noses to the ground, seeking a good chase.

* * *

Cash's catnap was broken with the sudden baying of hounds from some distance behind him. It was an eerie sound in the otherwise ominously silent woods. The howls echoed off the trees and hills, overlapping each other, making the noise seem endless. Cash first thought of wolves and laughed at himself, thinking it was just someone's farm dogs startled by the work gang coming in. Still, the howling made his arms goose-pimply and caused the hair on the back of his neck to prickle. Cash wondered if he had been missing long enough for the sheriff to have brought out bloodhounds to track him. He decided he'd rested long enough and took off in what he hoped was the same direction he'd been headed before.

He was surprised to be moving down hill all this time. It hadn't seemed as if the land ever was so high around here that he could still be moving downward. Now the air was noticeably damper and heavier and the smell of dead leaves and stagnant water drifted up to him. Cash lost his balance on the wet clay beneath his feet and slid a good distance down the hill on his seat before a downed limb stopped his slide with a blunt jar to his ankle. The late afternoon light was diffused by a green canopy of leaves and thick branches. Cash found himself at the edge of a large marsh.

Cash pulled himself to his feet and found one foot had been badly sprained. It wasn't holding his weight well, so he dropped back to the ground and groped in the dim light until he located a supple limb that would support him as a walking stick. The marsh presented a major setback. Cash would have to change directions to skirt it and still hope to hit a road before it was totally dark. The damaged ankle complained with each step, but another chorus of barking spurred him on.

He remembered that water would foul a dog's ability to track him and wondered if he should move into the swampy pond to cover his trail. He couldn't tell how deep the black oily water was, and the thought of snakebite gave him reason to be careful. Cash decided to hug the edge of the marsh so he could make for it if the dogs got too close.

Cash stumbled into the wet mud, tripping over hassocks of grass, but kept moving. The dogs were close and they didn't sound friendly. The dogs sounded frenzied, wild, and dangerous. Cash was getting short of breath, his pulse thundered in his temple, and his ankle bitched with each wrong step but Cash couldn't slow down. He couldn't stop. These were wild dogs, angry dogs, and there was no question, they were on his trail.

* * *

Noses snuffled at the wet ground. The scent was fresh but it wasn't their usual game. It was man smell with a sour taste of brutality. A bad man, one who would throw rocks, who would sneak around the gas tank in the orchard at night, one who would beat a horse to death, one who would eat babies. One man, reeking of pungent evil and slow deaths. Yuki hesitated, but the others weren't afraid of the man smell; they were angered by the bad man smell and they all were euphoric with survival relief. It felt right to track the bad man, to hunt him down. The pack moved on quickly, the trail fresher with each stride.

Branches rushed out to slap at the dogs, twigs crackled underfoot, and the wind blew back their sweaty ears and cooled their panting tongues. Noses to the ground, they flew over downed trees and through tall grasses. The bad man was near, the evil one was close, and they snarled involuntarily with each new whiff of his scent. The pack moved as one in an ultimate pursuit. The dogs built up speed as the land sloped downward and broke through the brush in time to see the bad man at the edge of the water.

The pack ran in unison, no longer howling, legs pumping and teeth bared, aimed at the bad man near the water. The dogs foamed in anticipation. This was the most important chase of their lives. They had spent hours at doorsteps and in front yards guarding their homes against evil like this. The air reeked with the stink of wickedness and the smell roused coarse fury in each animal. Almost as one, they leapt over the water and came down hard on the wretched man's back as he tried to pull his feet up from the muck.

* * *

Cash flew forward as the dogs' heavy bodies pounded into him, his head striking hard against a submerged stone there at the edge of the water. The blow sent stars and flashes before his eyes and then he was blinded by murky water and the deep blackness of the bog. He struggled up from the muck, tossing off one dog, then another, but they kept coming at him, mad with fear and loathing. Fangs tore into his flesh, ripping muscle away from bone. Cash fell back into the water.

The water closed over him like the crushing fist of an angry giant, suddenly roused from a long sleep. Cash's limbs thrashed and struggled to push him out of the muck, but deep inside, the part of him that savored others' pain fell suddenly still, aware of the presence of another power. Cash fought the terrible weight that pressed him into the frigid mud, but he was helpless in its power. The great dark hand of dank and slimy water tightened around his body, snapping his ribs and compressing his lungs into a useless mass. Mud forced itself between Cash's clenched lips, strangling his screams; silt rushed into his nose, filling his lungs with heavy earth.

Cash summoned his deepest reservoir of power, an ancient core of evil that boiled from his gut and flooded through his limbs as he struggled to push up from the bottom. His arms sank deeper into the mire, then hit a rock or tree root. His will surged and he exploded from the water, almost standing as the pack flew at him more urgently, two large dogs leaping on his back, tearing at his neck, and knocking him forward.

Pushing up again, Cash used one powerful arm to grasp Yuki by the throat and pull his snapping jaws away from his chest but closer to his face. Cash's own jaws snapped open, exposing lengthening fangs as his primal growl grew into a beastly howl.

The water rose in sinewy cords to lash around Cash's legs, tearing him from his feet again and submerging him in the filthy murk, still clenched in his deadly embrace with Yuki. Twisting around Cash, the water tightened, grinding his bones into pulp and squeezing the last of his life out of him. Bubbles flew up from the gloomy deep, heavy with Cash's last curse. Foul, death-tainted breath broke into the frightened dog's mouth, then Cash stopped thrashing and loosened his grip on Yuki's fur. Yuki yelped in terror as the pain in his head splintered into a thousand burning fragments through his body.

The dogs splashed away, still growling at the smell of corruption and depravity. Puzzled by the cessation of struggles, disappointed in the hunt's anti-climax, they shook themselves and milled around waiting for Yuki to find another trail to follow. Yuki sat stunned, transformed by what had happened. Man was soft, man was easy to kill, man held no more fear for him, and now stirring deep inside of Yuki, was a great new compulsion to destroy.

CHAPTER 20

George and Ray pushed through the front door, shirtless and sunburned. "Hell, we been working all morning but I don't think we're going to get the electricity back on until tomorrow."

Mama frowned at George for his cussing but set ice tea and glasses out for the boys. "Where's your father?"

"He's going up to see Bruno and Ross, and Mr. Johnson to see what needs fixing at their places." Ray spooned sugar into his tea until it made a thick pile at the bottom of the glass then stirred it slowly and drank it down without stopping.

"Papa said to have you fix lunches to take out for everybody. He said you'd know if he'd be home for supper by whether or not there's electricity to cook with." George wiped his mouth with his arm and poured another glass of tea.

Mama cut thick slices of homemade bread and cold ham for sandwiches, filled a jug with fresh well water and added a bag of tomatoes to the basket. She washed the boys' red backs with vinegar to reduce the sting of their sunburns, made them promise to wear their undershirts, then sent them out the door.

* * *

April and Donna Jean bounced along in the old Chevy, April's head almost hitting the car roof with one big washout. Donna Jean slowed down, then came to a complete stop, a large limb blocking the driveway to Grandma and Grandpa's house.

"April you're going to have to help me with this one." Donna Jean hung her head out the window to estimate the size of the problem.

The girls dragged the huge limb aside and April, nagged by a feeling that something was terribly wrong, ran on up to the house while Donna Jean pulled the car into a space close to the back door.

"Grandma!" April yelled through the screen, then, not getting any answer, pulled it open. The smell of vomit hung over the small cabin like a cloud, almost sending April back out the door. She moved into the main room, stepping over broken glass and making out a lump under the bed covers.

"Grandma Alana, are you all right?" April could see the vomit now, pooled on the top cover and in a pan on the floor beside the bed. She ran back to the door to fetch Donna Jean but she had gone around the other way.

Donna Jean was already on the back porch, standing over Grandpa Ezra, who lay passed out with a beer bottle between his legs. The porch roof was sagging at one corner and the windows had burst here as well.

"Grandma's awful sick, I think. You better come see." April turned away from the old man and Donna Jean stepped over him to come inside.

"April, go fetch some water from the kitchen. We're going to have to clean her up, maybe take her to Dr. Faust's if she's able." Donna Jean pulled back the filthy blankets and felt Alana's forehead. There didn't seem to be a fever but Alana's color was bad, a lot like the old people Donna Jean worked with after school at the rest home, the ones who didn't talk or move any more. Donna Jean held her warm hand to her grandmother's cheek and Alana's hand reached up to squeeze it weakly.

* * *

April hung close to the radio listening to the reports of storm damage that had replaced the *Amos and Andy* show, and waited for Papa to come back. Her mind wasn't much on the news as the announcer listed the number of houses destroyed and people killed in the most violent tornado to hit the region in fifty years.

She heard Papa's truck before she saw it and ran out to the end of the driveway, hoping Duke would be in the truck bed, happy to be home.

"Did you find him?" she called as the truck pulled in, but Papa drove up to the house without stopping and April could see the back end was empty. She started to cry as she slowly made her way back to the house.

"Goddamn it April, I done everything I can think of. I've been up every damn dirt track in these woods, I've tried honking the horn on the truck to get his attention, and I've traipsed over half of creation. I got nothin' to show but sore feet and a nearly broken axle. I'd appreciate it if you'd thank me instead of standing there cryin'." Papa slammed the truck door hard and stomped up the front steps, angry and discouraged.

Mama had the table set and a beer open at Papa's place. Mama raised her eyebrows but didn't say anything. Papa settled in at the head while the children took their places. Carol Ann and April sat quietly; even George and Ray seemed to know enough to keep their mouths shut. Donna Jean's place was empty; she was helping Ezra with Grandma Alana.

"That Goddamn dog is probably after some bitch in heat right now and he can just starve out there 'till he brings himself home. I ain't losin' no more time over him. Damn woods is full of dogs. I saw dog tracks everywhere I went. He's probably part of the damn pack by now." Papa sipped his beer while the rest of the family ate dinner. He wasn't yet in the mood to enjoy his food.

"Papa you got to find him. Maybe he got hurt in the storm and can't get home. I've been callin' all day and I know he'd come if he could." April had also left her food untouched, though she'd been tramping the fields and the edge of the woods for hours looking for Duke.

"April, you need to drop this. Your father has done everything he can. That dog will come home when he's ready and there's nothing you can do to hurry it up." Mama spoke more harshly than usual and April just put her head down on the table and cried again.

"Something terrible has happened to him. I can feel it," April stammered through her sobs.

"Get up to your room, April. You can't take on like that at the table." Mama and Papa exchanged glances but didn't say anything else as April left the room. The boys snickered and Carol Ann kicked them under the table, giving them her most powerful glare.

Laughing, George and Ray went down to the barn to milk cows and do their other chores while Carol Ann helped Mama clear the table. "Mama, what if Duke doesn't come home? Can I go look for him tomorrow? I'll be all right in the woods and Papa can do what he needs to do."

"That would be awful nice, Honey. I hope you find him because I think it hurts your Papa more than it hurts April." She gave Carol Ann a long sorrowful look and they went on with their work in silence.

* * *

Duke loped through the woods, his joints loose from exertion, panting heavily in the hot summer air. He was filled with excitement, drunk from independence as he ran through the trees. His nose picked up the spoor of the other dogs and he hurried along, expecting to catch up with them soon, to be a part of the pack. Ancient instincts held him sway and he delighted in the way the wind lifted his ears and the bushes brushed his coat. He stopped in the soft, sandy shade of a large maple tree and threw himself into the dirt, rolling onto his back and wiggling until every itch had been reached. Duke leapt to his feet again, and catching a whiff of bacon and coffee in the air, he ran toward the welcoming smell of man.

As Duke burst through the bushes into a little clearing, he saw the boy, about George's age, dressed in a flannel shirt in the cool air. The boy held an old shotgun, worn from two generations of use, but polished and gleaming in the early morning sun. Duke caught the smell of the oiled iron and spent gunpowder. Thrilled by the prospect of hunting, Duke leapt in the air, barking joyously, and running full-speed at the startled boy.

The buckshot hit at the same time the long gun exploded. Full force, at close range, the pellets struck

Duke in the face, riddling his skull and muzzle with lead shot, and downed him like an anvil. Duke twitched as blood spurted from his neck and head, then fell back, unconscious.

The boy approached him cautiously, nudging Duke's chest with his booted foot. The dog lay stunned and unmoving. The boy cocked the gun again, placed it against the dog's forehead and pulled the trigger again. He hadn't braced for the kickback and brought up the gun's muzzle as he fired, grazing the top of the dog's head as he stumbled backward.

Taking off his hat, the boy wiped sweat from his face, then hurried home.

* * *

Carol Ann trudged along the path to the huckleberry marsh, making better time without boots and pails and without April to slow her down. She pulled a sturdy whistle from her shirt, a shiny steel one with a little wooden ball inside that spun each time she blew it. Every few yards Carol Ann blew the whistle and called for Duke. She had wrapped a length of twine through her belt to use as a leash, and one hand kept pulling nervously at it as she made her way deeper into the woods.

Between whistles, Carol Ann stopped walking, listening intently, swatting away the yellow jackets that circled her face. She scratched at new chigger bites on her legs and chewed on a stem of sassafras that had grown beside the path. The forest sent back the sound of wind in the trees and insects humming in the grass, but there was no sound nor sign of dogs, Duke or otherwise.

Carol Ann reached the place where a smaller path broke off toward the marsh and decided to take it. It was sweltering today and the shade of the deeper woods appealed to her. She made her way down the narrow game path, slowing when the slope steepened. The stillness of these woods laid heavily on her and she stopped blowing the irritating whistle. Carol Ann called for Duke, her voice softened in the thick growth, and she felt like a trespasser in some ancient cathedral. This place had some power of its own, like something holy, or primal, or even primitive evil. Carol Ann shivered and wrapped her hands about her arms, trying to shake off the chill that had just played over her.

Carol Ann kept moving forward, paying close attention to where she stepped, and telling herself she would turn back soon. It was late afternoon and Mama would be mad if she were late for dinner. It would get dark in here early and she wouldn't be able to find a black dog in all these shadows anyway. The pack might be somewhere back here. Carol Ann shouldn't go so far by herself.

At last, Carol Ann reached the edge of the marsh where the silence was overwhelming. Each time she took a step, she could hear the damp mud sucking at her foot, her shoe slipping down from her heel. Carol Ann's breath seemed so loud it blocked out her thoughts and, when a tree shifted in the wind, it sounded like a ghost groaning. She cautiously edged along the water trying to see across the narrow clearings in the bushes, listening intently for splashing or panting. Carol Ann stepped into a clearing where the bushes parted for a long view and almost stepped on him.

Her eyes set on the bushes, Carol Ann stumbled when her foot struck the dead man's shoe. She had righted herself before she realized that she was standing in water, straddling his bloated and discolored body. A scream was trapped in her throat as she recognized the man shape floating in the water. Her eyes wide in terror, Carol Ann backed away, tripping again, this time on tree roots that crept down to the water. A growl to her side froze her, fear washing through Carol Ann like liquid fire, and when she could finally breathe again, she slowly turned her head to see the great white dog.

Carol Ann's throat spasmed with the gruff sound of terror and in that instant, time stretched into infinity around her, she saw the bared teeth, the raised fur, the strangely scarred head and the eyes that flamed with blue-white fury and black desire. Carol Ann pushed out her right hand in defense and edged backward until her left hand struck the base of the rough-barked elm that had tripped her. As she moved, the dog crept forward, head lowered, ears flattened, a menacing growling swelling out of its chest. The distance between them grew even smaller until Carol Ann could feel the dog's hot breath on her outstretched hand.

With a shrill cry, Carol Ann turned and reached for the lowest branch, pulling her leg up just as the white dog's teeth caught her pants leg. She kicked out hard, jerking with all her strength, and managed to fling the dog off her ankle and pull herself to a higher branch. Carol Ann's screams pierced the quiet as she pulled herself farther up the tree until she was well above the ground and just short of branches too small to hold her weight. Then the strength she had borrowed from her fear disappeared, and she clung weakly to the tree's rough trunk.

For a horrible moment, Carol Ann thought the dog would reach her, after all, either by jumping high enough or climbing after her, but after a few fruitless tries, the dog simply circled the tree, growling and looking up at Carol Ann with mad eyes of fiery ice. Time ticked by so slowly Carol Ann was afraid her arms would not hold her up any longer. Reluctantly, the dog moved away from the tree and took up his station where the dead man lay, swollen in the summer heat, face down in the water.

The dog tugged at the dead man's pant leg, pulling his body closer to dry ground. Carol Ann could see that the man's lower leg had been gnawed through and the water had whitened the exposed tissue and bone. She prayed the body would not turn over. Carol Ann was sure that seeing his face would cause her to faint and fall from the tree. She shifted so she couldn't see the water, and in doing so, bumped the whistle that rattled inside her shirt and reminded her that she could call for help.

Twining one arm around a solid branch, Carol Ann used the other to fish the whistle out of her blouse and pull it up to her mouth. Taking a deep breath, she blew the whistle as long and hard as could, rested, and started again. Soon, someone would miss her and begin the search. They would hear the whistle and take her from here, before she, too, lay with the body in the swamp.

   * * *

Mama checked the clock again. It was half past five and Carol Ann knew to be back by five to help get supper ready. Mama laid green onions out on the cutting board and diced them with a wide-bladed knife. She looked at the clock, it was 5:35 p.m. Mama put the sliced potatoes into the frying pan and added the onions as spattering grease and steam rose to fog the kitchen windows. She looked at the clock and filled the glasses for the table. Mama opened the oven to check on the bread and let the door fall back too hard, almost burning her. She looked at the clock, then moved into the hall and sat beside the phone, hoping it wouldn't ring.

Mama wiped her hands on her apron and lifted the telephone receiver, covering it with one hand, the line was still busy. Mama went back to the kitchen and pulled down plates for the table. She laid out the silverware and plates, brought out butter and salt and pepper and checked the clock. Mama went back to the phone, lifted the receiver and politely waited for a break in the conversation, when she would ask to use the line.

The mention of a black dog caught her ears and she covered the hand set with her apron to listen more carefully.

"Hell, one of them wild dogs almost got me yesterday when I was out early hunting rabbits. A big black bastard come crashing through the brush at me. Jumped right at me but I had my gun ready and blasted him square between the eyes. Thing fell right in the middle of his jump like a brick off a truck. Scared the shit out of me! I run all the way back up to the house and didn't stop until I had the door hooked behind me. Thing's still layin' out there but I'll let the birds have him before I go back and bury it."

Mama recognized the Memmer boy's voice, just out of high school last year. She pressed the receiver to her ear to catch any more he might say.

"Damn thing come right out of the woods in back of the house. I guess the shot must've spooked the rest of them. I didn't wait around to find out."

Carefully, Mama replaced the receiver on its hook. She sat by the phone table and mopped her face with her apron. She'd tell Papa when they were alone and send him down to fetch Duke's body. They'd do it early, before April was up, and bury him in the hay field. Better if April thought Duke was still wandering.

It was almost six now and she had to get dinner on the table. Where was Carol Ann? By now Mama was boiling mad that Carol Ann would pull a stunt like this. When Papa pulled into the driveway with George and Ray, she put supper on the table and waited until eight o'clock when the chores were done before she asked them to look for Carol Ann.

* * *

Mama sat by the phone with a hanky in her hand while April watched from the end of the driveway. It was almost ten o'clock before April first caught sight of the lanterns George, Ray, and Papa carried. She saw their lights coming out from the entrance to the State Land and she caught the glint of Papa's gun barrel as the lanterns swung. She ran back to the house to let Mama know they had returned, then she took off down the road at a fast clip to meet them. All the way, she strained to count if there were three or four figures heading toward her.

As April drew nearer, she could see that George was carrying two lanterns and Papa was carrying Carol Ann like she was five years old again, hoisted piggy back, her arms wrapped around his neck. Papa moved slowly with his burden and when April was close enough, she could hear Carol Ann singing some slow flat rhyme over and over again, a tuneless mumbling that sent cold shivers through April. She ran up to them.

"Carol Ann, are you all right?" But Carol Ann pressed her head into Papa's shoulder, eyes staring blankly ahead, lips weakly mumbling something April couldn't understand. Papa shifted Carol Ann's weight so he could carry her in front of him, head buried in his chest.

"Go tell your mother to call Dr. Faust out and tell her to call the Sheriff too. Hurry up! We're going to need them both." April raised her hand to Carol Ann's long curls, patting her head before turning toward the house. Carol Ann seemed smaller and very fragile to April, like a broken doll, sagging in Papa's arms.

* * *

The Sheriff and his two men slogged through the marsh in heavy, well-made waders. Their over-sized flashlights gave a lurid glare to the dark surface of the scummy water. They hung yellow tape to rope off footprints or marks they'd inspect closer in the morning and leaned over their boundaries to flash pictures in brilliant strobes that left Papa half-blind.

Papa could hardly stand, he was so worn through with exhaustion, but the men repeated their questions and asked Papa to show them just where Carol Ann had sat, and where she'd seen the dog pacing, and where the body had lain when she'd first seen it. Papa answered patiently, knowing he'd never let them bring Carol Ann back here in the daylight, remembering her deep, terrified eyes.

When the Sheriff seemed satisfied they would not find the other missing convict before morning, he and his men hoisted the body onto a makeshift stretcher, with Papa at one corner. Slowly, they threaded their way along the narrow game trail that wound up the steep slope. At one point, one of the Sheriff's men slipped, his corner dropping downhill and the corpse fell with a sick, wet thud to the ground. Papa coughed and looked away, sickened by the exposed bones and torn remains.

It was after three in the morning before all the depositions had been recorded, and the corpse examined. Papa crept into the bedroom where Mama lay awake beneath the covers, Carol Ann sleeping uneasily beside her. They held each other for a long, quiet time and they talked about what should happen next. By four o'clock, the sun was just waking the sky to a weak gray and Papa rose, still dressed, to fetch Duke's body. By his reckoning, a burial would be the best way to put some closure to the last couple of days.

A light mist still lay over the grasses, leaving a heavy morning dew. Papa's shoes and pants were damp before he had gone twenty yards across Memmer's field to the large stand of trees at the back. Papa scanned the windbreak of trees looking for an opening that might be a natural path into the woods. He was rewarded with a bright space in the dawn silhouette that he followed into a small clearing. Surrounded by bushes, this looked like the right place unless the boy had been deeper into the wood lot. Kneeling, Papa checked the ground for footprints and saw where heavy boots had torn into the dirt in a rush to get out of there. He also saw bloody and matted grass forming a pitiful path made by a dog dragging itself into the undergrowth.

Following the smudged trail on his hands and knees, he soon came to Duke's cold wet body. "Oh my poor old fella," he sighed, though it was difficult to tell if the words were for the dog, or for himself. He'd held together all through the long night, but now he cried quiet tears of anguish. His chest heaved in deep, sad sighs but he swallowed back his pain. His hands felt along the dog's side and up to its shattered head. Papa's hand shook with heartache as he touched the ruined eyes and nose.

As he gave Duke's muzzle one last stroke, the dog whimpered and licked his hand.

Part 5, 1995

"A time to rend, and a time to sew; a time to keep silence, and a time to speak; A time to love, and a time to hate; a time of war, and a time of peace." --Ecclesiastes 3:7-8

CHAPTER 21

A thumping on the stairs woke Kaitlin from her troubled sleep. She heard a man's voice outside her door and sat up quickly, checking her alarm clock, to find it was only 5:00 A.M. The voice moved down the hall, and with it the noise of something sliding against her wall and into her grandmother's room. Kaitlin rose quickly and pulled her quilted robe around her.

Kaitlin opened her door but found the hallway empty. "Mom. What's happening?"

Laurel came from Doe's room and grabbed Kaitlin's hands. Her eyes were red with dark circles as if she had been up all night. "Honey, Doe's not doing well, so I called for an ambulance. These men are going to help me get her to the hospital."

"Mom, I dreamed," Kaitlin hesitated, watching the lines in her mother's face deepen. "It doesn't matter right now. Do you want me to do anything?"

"Just stay here, Baby. I'm going to take Doe to the hospital and I'll stay there until I'm sure everything is all right. I'll call you as soon as I know anything. Dad said he'd call today and I know he's going to want to talk to you." Laurel kissed her daughter's head, then turned back to her mother's room.

Kaitlin followed her into her grandmother's room that was now brightly lit with the overhead lights. She flinched at the glare then slipped behind one of the emergency medical technicians so she could see what was happening. A tall slim nurse in a burgundy jumpsuit was talking quietly with Doe as she adjusted an oxygen mask over Doe's face. Kaitlin could hear Doe's ragged wheezing until the facemask covered her mouth.

As the EMTs moved Doe over to their stretcher, something fell from her hand. Kaitlin reached down to pick up the worn worry stone and tried to place it back in Doe's palm. Doe shook her head and pushed the stone back in Kaitlin's hand. She winked one eye, then winced as her tender abdomen was jostled onto the stretcher.

The EMTs carried Doe swiftly out of the room and down the stairs to their waiting vehicle. Laurel climbed into the back and sat holding her mother's hand, the door was slammed shut, and with lights flashing, but no siren, the ambulance moved away, swallowed by the dark morning.

Kaitlin was completely alone in the old house for the first time. She moved from room to room, touching the polished surfaces of tables and mirrors, pulling the curtains closed, and switching on the lights in each room. Finally she found herself in the large white kitchen, sitting on a red vinyl stool at the counter. She put her head on the counter and wailed, for she knew deep in her heart that her grandmother was sick because she had dreamed it true.

* * *

Carol Ann heaved in her sleep, tossing the blankets off the side of the bed as she struggled. Her garbled mumbles grew louder as she twisted in the sheets, crying out. Charley, the night duty attendant hesitated at her door, and seeing the piled covers on the floor, walked softly into the room. He could see well enough by the moon, so he left the lights off and bent to retrieve the blankets. His head was down when Carol Ann's gnarled fingers snatched at his collar and jerked him to her.

He tried to push away, startled and breathless, then caught himself, knowing he'd have to unhook himself gently from her bony fingers. The old lady spooked him in the dim light, her pasty face as wide and round as the moon at the window. Her toothless mouth contorted and she tugged him closer, trying to tell him something. He was close enough to see goose bumps rise along her arms and her cold fist seemed to suck the warmth away from his hands as he tried to release himself. She shivered with a sudden chill and he bent again to pull the blankets up to cover her.

Carol Ann let Charley hold her hand and bring the blankets up to cover her but she wouldn't let him go when he tried to leave. She clung to the man, warning him.

"It's so cold, so white and cold." Her witch's voice made his stomach drop and he tried again to pull away. The old woman was remarkably strong and her fingers would not budge.

"It's so cold, so white and cold inside its heart. It killed April and left her in the snow. It killed Papa and watched him slowly freeze to death. It reached inside and twisted his heart into a knot and watched the blood turn to ice inside of him."

Charley swallowed hard and tried to shake off the willies she was giving him. He reached over to push the assistance button and called into the corridor. "Clarice, I need some help down here."

Still the old woman held him tight, her lips trembling and turning blue in front of him. Her eyes were round, the whites reflected a shine from the window, and he noticed for the first time she had no eyelashes and no eyebrows. He pressed at her hands again but she held fast.

"It's so cold and so white, it's not earthly. It's an ice demon and it collects the dead. It took George and Ray. Stood on their chests and pressed the air out of them until they were stiff and cold. It laughed at their pain and their fear."

"Clarice!" Charley yelled louder, frightened by her ramblings that reminded him of the gypsy crone in the old werewolf movie. He felt like she was laying a curse on him. "Clarice, I need you now!"

"It took Doe's boy into the woods. Made him suffer a long time before it let him die. It's so cold inside where something alive should be. It told me all of it. Talked to me at night when the others were asleep. Told me things

I shouldn't know. It's so cold. Talks to me. So white and so cold. It's walking again, it's strong again."

"Charley, what's the matter with you?" Clarice stood at the door holding a hand over her mouth but shaking with laughter. "My God! You can't handle a poor old bed-ridden invalid?"

Carol Ann dropped her hands and Charley stepped away. "Christ she had hold of me like a bear trap."

Clarice doubled over with laughter, now, unable to contain herself. "She is one dangerous woman, Charley. You better carry your shotgun next time you come in here or she'll eat you alive."

Charley wanted to be angry but his queasy stomach and watery bowels wouldn't let him. He hurried from the room and down the hall to the employee rest room where he scrubbed his face and hands trying to make himself clean again.

* * *

Yuki crept to the edge of the pasture where the mare and its foal lay sleeping in the new grass. He kept his head low and inched forward one paw at a time, his snout filled with the salty smell of horseflesh. He felt powerful tonight, huge and fearless, invincible. An owl hooted from the direction of the barn and he watched it glide overhead off on a hunting trip of its own. Carefully he crept, licking his chops, pushing back the urgent whine that tried to crawl out of his throat, holding down the excited barking that threatened to give him away.

He startled when a pheasant flew up to the right of him. He had been so intent on the foal, he hadn't noticed the bird smell that filled the air around him in a whoosh of feathers. The mare twitched her ears and whinnied, then tucked her head to the ground once more. The foal kicked and rose awkwardly from the grass, nuzzling his mother for milk but she pushed him away.

Yuki froze in the dark, watching the clumsy foal hop away from his mother, awake and curious in the dark. Yuki's ears flattened and he barely breathed as the youngster sniffed at the ground and moved closer to the edge of the barbed wire where Yuki lay hidden in the tall grass. The mare snickered but the foal explored further, tripping over rocks in the pasture and nosing at clumps of grass that made him sneeze.

Yuki's heart beat hard as he snaked under the fence, his white fur catching at one of the pointed barbs and leaving a thatch behind. Yuki saw nothing but the foal, stepping closer to the edge of the field, unconscious of his stalker. Yuki smelled nothing but the sweet milk and grass-edged breath the foal expelled with quick uneven snorts. Yuki tensed like one great muscle waiting to spring, waiting for the distance to close, waiting to strike.

The foal danced away from the fence, then back, following the smell of wild oats that grew thick just beyond the wire. Yuki waited, and the yards between them became feet. Tightening his back legs, tensing his forelegs, holding his abdomen absolutely still, Yuki didn't breathe, didn't even let his heart beat. Feet became inches. He sprang.

The foal screamed when Yuki's feet sank in but he fell with the dog's weight and lay trapped on his side. Terrified, the foal kicked out but found only empty air as Yuki climbed on his back, wrenching at the foal's neck, tearing open the soft white hide at the throat. Blood splashed out of the torn artery and the smell incensed the foal who struggled harder, sending fountains of red onto Yuki. The foal was weakening before the mare was on them.

Yuki dragged the foal toward the fence as the mare galloped at him, rearing on her hind legs and whinnying a harsh cry against the night. Yuki held his grasp but twisted his body and narrowly dodged her flying hoofs. Again she rose, wild eyed, teeth bared, and chest heaving with her shriek. Yuki growled and jerked the struggling foal backwards, just enough that the heavy hoofs pounded into the young one's groin. The foal shuddered in Yuki's grasp and gave up its fight.

The mare stumbled backwards then ran forward, building momentum and rearing once more. By now Yuki was almost under the fence. He tugged once more and this time as the mare came down, her legs caught up in the barbed wire, ripping her shins and chest. An electric spark crackled in the air and she backed off with a loud grieving neigh.

Yuki pulled the heavy carcass away from the fence and waited. The mare galloped full speed into the fence, almost jumping, but balking at the last as another shock of electricity jumped out at her. She paced beside the fence braying helplessly as Yuki tore into the warm flesh and swallowed the tender meat in great choking chunks.

***

Whaley scratched at his eyes, blinked blood from them, and scratched at them again, trying to clear the terrible vision that was etched into his eyeballs. The girl had turned toward him, auburn braids swinging as she turned to face him. Her features had flowered into red and merged into a great beating heart that hemorrhaged blood onto the sidewalk.

Whaley ran, eyes clenched tightly closed, blood running like tears down his face. He ran on blistered feet, feeling his way down the center of the street, running from the waves of blood that poured after him.

Whaley wheezed and gasped for air as he climbed the porch steps of the boarding house. He'd run as long as he could, in a fever to get out of the dark, to get off the street. Sweat dripped from his face, running salty into his mouth, chaffing the corners of his lips. He wiped his mouth with the back of his hand and grabbed for the doorknob, but his hand slipped off. Cursing and looking over his throbbing shoulder, he wiped his hands on his pants and tried again. He had a good grasp but the knob wouldn't turn, the door was locked.

Whaley swiveled to watch the street, unable to leave his back to the shadows. He patted his pants, shirt and jacket, reached deep into each pocket and came up empty. He'd forgotten his key or lost it somewhere. Panicked, he caught himself hyperventilating, forced himself to slow his breathing, recited his relaxation training, and willed his pulse to slow down. The shadows danced in the street, seemed to twist and slither on the sidewalk, but there were no red dragon's eyes, no oily voice, no demon's silhouette.

He muttered to himself, under his breath; no eyes, no voice, no demon. Still, he watched the street as he leaned on the doorbell, knowing he would wake Mrs. Jackson, but too frightened not to. He could hear the bell clamoring inside as he watched the shadows ebb and flow around the trees. He mumbled louder; no eyes, no voice, no demon. No steps on the stairs either, no metallic click of the dead bolt. His breathing became more rapid and the tree limbs seemed to be reaching down for him from the trees overhead.

He turned to the door and pounded, begging and crying to be let in. "For the love of God, open this door now!"

"Mr. Whaley, Lord God-a-mighty! Do you know what time it is?" The landlady's voice came through a gap in the half-opened door, a security chain still firmly in place.

"Thank God, open the door! Let me out of the dark. Open the door, I beg of you."

"Mr. Whaley, you reek to high heaven again, and you're not making sense. You just calm down and wait right here. I'm going to have to call the hospital and I'll get someone out here to help you."

"No!" he screamed. "Just open the goddamned, fucking door, you bitch! Open it now!"

She slammed the wooden door in his face and he could hear the dead bolt click shut again. He pounded his shoulder against the door but it held solidly against him. Too desperate to look behind him, he raised his heavy shoes and began to kick at the door. The wood creaked under his blows and he could feel it start to give, at the same time he heard the siren.

He looked up to see blue and red flashers turning the corner. They were coming to take him, to lock him away. If they locked him up, he would never be free again.

Terrified, he stood twisting his head from the lights at the end of the block to the shadows and dark trees that shifted and reached in the dark. They would lock him up forever this time. He turned and ran into the dark, afraid to stop, afraid to hide, able only to keep running.

CHAPTER 22

Stormy's pounding on the front door woke Kaitlin, still seated at the kitchen counter, head buried in her arms, neck aching, and eyes burning. She took a deep breath to clear her head before opening the door and stepped back as Stormy released a pile of old newspapers and journals onto the floor. The musky, yellowed pages scattered across the floor, raising a cloud of dust and the stink of mildew.

"Stormy, what is all this? Are you trying to catch up on your back reading?"

"This is a gold mine. I dug all this up from my Grandmother Elinore's trunks. She saved everything down in our basement. You should see the stuff I had to go through before I found these. Do you know she still had every Plaster of Paris ashtray my mother made in elementary school?"

"Well thank you for sharing that, Stormy, but I'm not doing too well so if you'd like to get to the point I'd appreciate it."

"Listen, my grandmother cut out every newspaper article about anybody she ever heard of around this place. She kept a lot of information in her diary too, and it turns out that she was good friends with your Grandma Doe's family before everything fell apart. She even had a crush on your great Uncle George and he and my grandfather had a big fight over her. I might have been some cousin twice removed or something if things had worked out a little differently.

"So, I just figured the more you know about this April ghost, the better your chances of fighting her off." Stormy sneezed loudly as she scooped up the papers and headed up the stairs to Kaitlin's room.

The girls settled themselves on the braided rug and systematically placed the papers and then the journals in order from oldest to most recent. Some of the clippings occupied broad headlines from the local town paper while others were just snips of announcements torn from back pages.

"See, you didn't believe me about the convicts being murdered back in that swamp but it's all right here. I must have heard that story a hundred times." Stormy, hesitated and for a second she seemed to blush under her freckles.

"Seems that your Grandma Doe's sister, Carol Ann, found one of the bodies and was almost attacked by the dogs herself. Look, it says she sat up in a tree half the night waiting for someone to find her. I wonder what that was like with a dead body below her."

Kaitlin's mind flashed with a scene of trembling muscles clinging to weak green limbs as a snarling dog leapt and snapped at a frightened girl in the dark. She shuddered and wondered how bad this was going to be.

"And look, there are all kinds of accounts about a pack of wild dogs terrorizing the woods around here. This old man was attacked when he was out ice fishing, but your Grandma Doe's brothers fought them off. This one says that dead sheep were found on several nearby farms and a letter to the editor complains that the game wardens weren't doing enough to get rid of the problem." Stormy flipped through the articles she had read earlier, pointing out the main reports in each, until she pulled up one with a yellow, faded picture of April and a large black dog.

"This is the main one. Seems that April's pet dog was blind, and he wandered off into a God-awful blizzard one morning before anyone was up. April must've gone off after him and they both froze to death in the woods. They didn't find April's body until spring. Look at this." Stormy pointed to a particularly descriptive passage she wanted Kaitlin to read, but Kaitlin sat stunned, caught up in a vision of her own.

The teeth were sharp but it was the eyes that killed; they laughed with each lunge as pieces of flesh were torn away and tossed into the snow. She saw intestines unravel, stretched across the white ground and watched blood soak into the snow with a quiet steaming. She saw the white dog choking down hunks of pink flesh and dancing with excitement.

* * *

It had been a bad night, the worst of his life until he'd found an all night truck stop that sold bottled wine and liquor. Whaley clutched the bottle of Old Rocking Chair to his chest. Necessary medication; oblivion for a few hours as he curled himself into a ball in a grassy ditch near the railroad line. The morning train had dredged him up from a dark cave where he had safely hidden from the demon. He giggled out loud and took another sip, saluting the train as it passed. The hot liquid burned the skin at the back of his throat but a few more swallows would take away the spikes that stabbed through his head just above his eyes. A few more swallows would help him forget the yellow crust that stuck to his shirt and cracked open as the pus swelled and grew inside.

He was dusty from his feet to his waist. The ditch was formed in soft loam heavy with clay and it left red blotches against his pants whenever he shifted his weight. His skin itched like ants were crawling under his clothes and his acid stomach roiled and burned with each new sip of whiskey. He made himself stand, knowing only to walk.

He muttered as he rose, "Damn ants chewing on my ass. Damn booze burning up my gut." He laughed a high-pitched giggle that echoed on the early morning air. "Fucking night is gone and I'm alive. I'm a crazy, drunk, old coot but I'm alive."

He held the bottle high, extending his arm to the rising sun. "I'm alive and I'm free, you bastard." He took another quick sip, eyed the half empty bottle, capped it and stored it away in his pocket. It was time for a walk. A long walk. Time to look in on Kitty and the children. Time to go home before fate got hold of him.

* * *

Kaitlin gagged and ran for the bathroom, leaving dry heaves to echo through the hall back to Stormy. This had never before happened to Kaitlin when she was awake. She had never had a dream about something that had already happened. She dropped her head to the rim of the toilet and wept copious tears, trying to clear her head of the suffering she felt.

Stormy stood behind her, speechless for once, then grabbed a washcloth and wet it for Kaitlin. Stormy used her finger to raise Kaitlin's chin and gently washed her face. "I'm sorry, Kaitlin. I didn't know, I'm so sorry to do this to you."

Kaitlin pulled Stormy closer and begged, "You have to help me do this. I think I am going to go insane. I think I'm psycho or something and I don't know how to make it stop. I am feeling all these things like they are happening to me and I can't make it stop."

Stormy squeezed Kaitlin's shoulders and looked into her eyes. "I don't think it's you. I think something evil is doing this and we have to fight it or it will just get worse. Don't give up on me, Kaitlin! No one else would ever believe me."

Stormy helped her stand and the two girls went back to the papers. This time, Kaitlin lay on the bed, not touching or looking at the articles, while Stormy recited each event as unemotionally as possible.

"It seems that your Grandma Doe's sister, Carol Ann, followed after April but somehow managed to find her way home again, all frost bit and mumbling nonsense. My grandmother's journal says that Carol Ann was never right in the head after that. They had to take care of her like a baby, and after a while she couldn't walk anymore, and she didn't recognize her friends or anything."

Kaitlin interrupted, "I know, I saw her at the rest home and she was all freaked out because she thought I was April. I didn't think of that before, but I guess mental illness runs in my family. What if I end up in a home, a basket case like her?"

"That's why we have to figure out how to stop all this. If this is some kind of curse, we have to stop it now. This has been going on way too long. Those dogs were just the start of a long string of bad luck. Your Grandma Doe's grandmother and grandfather died in a house fire when their old pot-bellied stove blew sparks out into the curtains. Your Grandma Doe's brothers got themselves killed when they were out plowing a field, and that was followed pretty quickly by their mother's death. Your Grandma Doe had to come back to run the farm and she wasn't here long when her father died of a heart attack while out checking his traps.

"Years later after your Grandma Doe's husband died, there were two young boys lost in these woods and their bodies were never found. My grandmother's journal says that some people also thought maybe your grandmother did them in and hid the bodies, but no one who knew her ever thought that was possible.

"Your Grandma Doe wouldn't let anyone move in to help out. She just kept temporary help that would come and go, and no one was allowed to get too familiar with the place. She put up 'no trespassing' signs all over her property and when people asked to run their fox hounds through or use it to get back to the State Land, she wouldn't let them.

"My grandmother's journal says that your mother, Laurel, was sent away to boarding school when she was a teenager and went back East for college so she wouldn't be around this accursed place, but your Grandma Doe would never leave and she wouldn't put this place up for sale either. She's clung to it all these years all on her own like it was her own private hell to take care of." Stormy looked as scared as Kaitlin felt when she had got to the end of her recitation.

* * *

Dust rose up from the dirt road and hung in the air behind him like a lingering cloud trail. Whaley shuffled through the thick sand of the shoulder, the cool soft dirt sifting between his toes like talcum, soothing the oozing blisters which had broken and run in his thin socks. He carried his shoes in one hand and the pint of whiskey in the other. He felt safe in the daylight; the sun seemed to keep the demon away. He whispered as he walked, a hoarse croak that carried him onward.

He told himself the story of his life, repeating the early parts over and over again. Picturing Elinore when she was just a teenager. Remembering how they played in the creek, pretending they were getting married and the sandy creek bed was really the church aisle and the overhanging branches were the arched ceiling. When the time came, they had run away to get married and spent a weekend honeymoon in Detroit before they went home to face her father.

He was going back now. Back to the creek where they'd played. Back to the old farm where Elinore had grown up and where Kitty lived now with her children. A shiver flashed through him but he shook it off with a long swallow of Old Rocking Chair.

It was daylight and he was going home to family. He couldn't keep the demon away while he was with strangers but home was a good place. If he'd never left Elinore's farm he'd have never gone to prison, never become a warped and twisted old man. Maybe the farm could cure him. Maybe the farm could kill him.

* * *

"Her own private hell?" Kaitlin tasted the words in her mouth and they seemed to fit after the flashbacks of trauma this speech had produced in her.

"Well, those are my grandmother's words. I guess she thought an awful lot of your Grandma Doe, and she hated seeing all this happen to her." Stormy looked out the window for a minute and then turned back. "It wasn't just your family either, Kaitlin. All the farms and houses that border on these woods have had troubles over the last 40 years. There have been other children lost, and barn fires, and heavy winters, and droughts, and you name it. Seems like we live in a pretty depressing place." There was a catch in Stormy's voice as she spoke that made Kaitlin look at her more closely.

"Stormy, did something real bad happen to you or

your family?"

"You swear not to tell this to anybody else?" Stormy waited until Kaitlin nodded and urged her on.

"Well, I know that story about the convicts so well because my grandfather was on that chain gang. He wasn't really a bad man. He just had a temper and he got in too many fights. But after that storm, he wasn't the same anymore. He got to seeing things and hearing voices and when he should have been out of jail and back home, they locked him away in the state hospital instead.

"It's bad enough that the town kids all think I'm some kind of bad seed; I don't need them to think I'm looney tunes too."

"Stormy, I'm sorry. No wonder you're so patient with me."

"Yeah, well, that was pretty bad, but it got a lot worse. My Mama said growing up around here wasn't that great but, she did all right with it I guess. When she got married, she moved my Grandma out to the farm. Things were pretty good for a while, until I was six years old.

"My Daddy was coming home from work late one night and when he came over the last big hill before the house, he missed the curve and smashed head-on into the tree that stood in a fork in the road. He wasn't drinking or asleep or anything so they thought he must have tried to avoid something in the road. Somebody's dog or something. But I always wondered, because they said his left arm, you know, the one you would hang out the window on a summer night like that, was all bit up and scratched, like maybe something attacked him as he drove by, and that's what really killed him."

It was Kaitlin's turn to hug Stormy. "Stupid me, I never even thought to ask if you had a father or anything. I'm awful sorry it had to happen to you. God, Stormy, this is way too much, all this laid on me at one time. I didn't sleep much last night and my grandmother's in the hospital. We've got to talk to her about this. She's been trying to warn me about something but it's like she doesn't know how to make me really understand."

* * *

It was late afternoon as Whaley cut through the hay

field to the rise that looked over the house itself. He put his shoes on before he stepped into the stubble. There had been an early cutting of hay but it had been so dry, it hadn't grown much. The sharp stalks poked at his thin soles and caught at his socks as he took long strides across the Timothy.

Open blue sky hung low over him but the woods in the distance seemed dark and ominous. Whaley shivered in the hot sun, watching the shadows that gathered under the thick trees. He wondered whether he would dare to hole up tonight in the old barn that stood at the end of the cow pasture, and worried about rats the size of cats that used to frighten him as a boy.

He knew he couldn't approach Kitty today. Not yet, not while he was stewed to the gills. He wondered when he would dare to dry out. Not yet, not while he still had his visions. Not until the land had washed him clean again.

The steep hill ended in a sharp bluff that stood above the farmhouse and there they were. Kitty was hanging clothes on the old line behind the house, and Stormy, a slimmer version of her mother, was dragging a basket of wet laundry through the grass behind her. There were the little ones, Billy and David hammering on a wobbly saw horse near the old pump house.

Whaley smiled and his eyes watered as he settled into the grass. Kitty was red-haired like him but had her mother's lanky body. Stormy was the picture of her mother but the boys looked like their dad, long dead now. How he wanted to go down. Go down and beg their forgiveness, sit at their table, and sleep under their roof. How he wanted to settle into the old place, to be someone's grandfather, though he'd never really gotten to be someone's dad.

He watched Stormy bend from the waist and thought of her willowy grandmother, until the light seemed to falter and the shadow of a cloud came between them and the sun.

The shadow chilled him and when he looked again, Stormy had changed. Her face ran with long streaks of blood and she held up bloody hands, dripping onto the clean clothes. Kitty turned toward her screaming daughter and she was drenched in blood as well. The boys came running to their mother, arguing, then they swung their hammers at each other, shattering skull bones and sending hunks of gray matter to splatter against their mother's apron.

Kitty fell on them, biting and scratching the boys, trying to part them and Stormy fell into the fight as well. They rolled and fought in the grass as the carnage grew bloodier.

The oily voice laughed in Whaley's ear where he sat, shocked rigid. The scene changed and they were normal again, still working at the clothesline and playing at the sawhorse.

"You think I only come at night? You think I can't touch you here on this little farm? How far I've come and how little you know." The voice cackled and gasped in his ear, like someone who is laughing too hard to breathe.

Whaley's head fell into his lap and he wailed. The long desperate cry of a man who suddenly realizes he has opened the door to his family's death.

CHAPTER 23

The hospital corridors were lit by cool white fluorescents softened by mauve carpeting and gray walls. Laurel frowned at the decor, pointing out to Kaitlin that it was clearly designed to reduce one's anxiety in one of the few places where anxiety would be an appropriate emotional response. The hum of the circulating system accompanied them on the long trek to Doe's room and Kaitlin thought about air filters and ventilation vents, anything but her grandmother's illness. Signs at each corner directed them, first to the right, then a left, then another right. So many sick people, so much misery. Laurel gave Kaitlin's hand a squeeze and led her up to a reception counter where a radio played some soft-rock tune as the nurse, with a tag naming her as Kandi, gave them both a wide, artificial smile.

Kandi pulled up Doe's file on the computer to give Laurel an update on her condition. "She's been moved out of intensive care and she's stable now. She's been resting all afternoon but was awake and alert for dinner. I'll take you down to her new room and make sure she's doing all right before I leave you." The nurse smiled broadly, picked up a covered clipboard to bring along, then led them down still another hall.

Kandi knocked before she took them into Doe's room,

revealing a small and fragile woman lying beneath white sheets and yards of tubes and wires. An oxygen tube was plugged into her nose and an intravenous was taped to her inner arm. Wires led from her chest to a machine that hummed and beeped in regular soft tones.

Doe coughed a little to clear her throat and then smiled at them. "It's pneumonia, that's all. A little ampicillin and they'll be sending me home. How are you two doing?"

Laurel shook her head. "As well as can be expected with a mother in the hospital. Mike called last night and said he's hoping to get here as early as late July. He's already got an offer on the house." Laurel told her mother about the garden she had started which was now going to weeds. She figured Mike had piled laundry up to the top of the washer by now and wondered out loud what kind of impression the Realtor had of the place.

Donna Jean nodded, agreeing with her daughter's worries. "Laurel, I've had some money set aside to spruce up the house, but I just wasn't feeling up to it. It would sure cheer me up to come home to some fresh paint and anything you'd like to do to fix up the old place. It's yours now and you should make it the way you'd like it to be."

"Oh no, you're just trying to get us out there to scrape off the old stuff. You always were clever at getting me to do the chores. The house is great, but a little new paint wouldn't hurt." Laurel joked, trying to make her mother laugh. Kaitlin knew Laurel didn't want to talk about inheritances and settlements. She knew Laurel didn't want to think of her mother gone from Bluehills Farm.

"Well, as long as I'm asking for favors, do you think you could find some sinful, chocolate ice cream down in the cafeteria and bring it up to me? I don't have much appetite for the food they've brought me, but I sure have been craving ice cream."

"Of course I will, mother." Laurel hesitated, a puzzled look on her face, then she smiled at Kaitlin and turned to leave for the cafeteria. Kaitlin started to go with her mother, but Doe called her back.

"Kaitlin, keep me company while your mother's

gone." Donna Jean pulled herself back up on the pillows trying to sit a little higher. Kaitlin stepped over to help her and almost flinched, feeling how light her grandmother had become, as if she had been shrinking away over the last two weeks.

"I feel like you want to talk to me alone, Kaitlin. Is that so?"

Kaitlin stuttered, not sure how to say it. "Some things are going on I don't understand, Doe. I have had some real bad feelings around the farm. The kind of feelings that make me sick to my stomach, I'm so afraid."

"Yes, Kaitlin. I thought that might happen to you. It used to happen to me too. If I stood where something terrible had occurred once, it was like some of the poison of that time was still there and I'd be sick. You'll learn to carry it a little better, not get so sick, though you never get over the feeling of wanting to be sick."

"Doe, I've been reading about Bluehills Farm and people who lived around here. Why has there been so much trouble since April died?" Kaitlin didn't look at Doe's face. She felt as if she had accused April of something bad, yet knowing that was wrong.

"Something happened when April died, or maybe just before. Bluehills had been a beautiful place with a powerful good that served our family for generations. My grandmother said it was like the power of the place shifted to something wrong; as if a layer of wet, rotting leaves had been laid over a bright fire, making a heavy smoke that choked and sickened us. I was never strong enough to break its curse. I never held the power April would have had. I've just tried to protect people from it. That's why I sent your mother off when she was young. Please remember I wouldn't have brought you back, but I think if one of us is not at the farm, the curse will go a lot further and more people will be hurt."

"Doe, what am I supposed to do? I don't know how to protect anyone. I don't even know how to protect myself."

"Kaitlin, you have what you need inside of you. It is the gift of your blood, but part of that gift is also the land. You can draw power from the land. The bag I gave you to wear has bits of things taken from Bluehills Farm. You and the land have to work together. It is something you have to grow inside of you."

"Doe, I've seen a ghost. I've seen April and her dog. I'm afraid." Kaitlin almost cried when she said it. She bit her lip and reached for a tissue.

"Kaitlin, you mustn't be afraid. You have more power than I ever had, and more power than April would've had. It is so important that you stay at Bluehills Farm. Don't ever take off the amulet. Listen to all your feelings and learn from your dreams. Warn people when you can, and protect them." Doe's small, bony hand gripped Kaitlin's with a strength Kaitlin didn't expect. The hand warmed hers and soothed her like a balm.

* * *

Whaley followed the train tracks through the whole hot day and by late afternoon, he had finished the bottle of whiskey. He mumbled as he fingered through the money left in his pockets. Not so bad really, but it wouldn't last him too long unless he cut back to cheaper alcohol. What was it the alkies drank? Thunderbird or Mogen David. Strong and cheap and came in big bottles. He'd better get this right if he was going to be a practicing convert.

The country store had what he was after under the counter. The clerk, a pleasantly chubby-faced young woman pressed him to buy some food too. She smiled so pretty, he didn't mind her intrusiveness. She reminded him of Alice who used to work the day shift on his ward, years ago before she got married and started having kids. Alice in her white uniform and her tray of meds. This girl was another Alice for him. Meds still in the bottle but as long as they kept the demon away, he could be happy.

It was starting to get dark as he left the store and made his way through back lots that led away from town. He smiled happily when he saw the scrap yard. Acres of cars parked in long rows, waiting for vital parts to be transplanted in somebody's '72 Chevy Nova or '78 Toyota station wagon. A big sign warned, "Guard Dog on Duty" but Whaley moved quietly through the grass without attracting attention.

The back door of an old Ford sedan opened easily and he slipped into its musty interior. Stale, but there was no odor of mice or mildew and the seat sure beat the grassy ditch where he'd spent the night before. He patted the pocket that held the Thunderbird and settled into the soft upholstery, chewing on the bologna and mustard sandwich the Alice-girl had sold him. Tired, he reached across to push down all the door locks before he slept, safe and dreamless for the moment.

* * *

The moon was full tonight, lighting the woods as if it were day. Yuki's coat bristled with electricity and his senses were as bright as the night. Enhanced to a fine tune, he listened to moths fluttering in the bushes, smelled fresh eggshell in bird nests high above the ground, and watched the black barn cat slip among the shadows in the orchard. He stood large in the silver light and moved with a whisper from the apple trees to the smooth-packed dirt driveway. His feet were keenly aware of the pebbles beneath them and the tiny shadow each grain threw off in the glare of the phosphorescent lighting.

Yuki held his muzzle high and sang to the moon, a tune of pure malevolence, an invocation of evil. The very air had changed, the earth's vibrations were different, the balance had shifted and drawn him to a place he had long avoided. He sensed every tension within the house acutely, the gap that left the house vulnerable, the weak growth that failed to fill its space, the victim that promised his fulfillment. Yuki danced at the doorstep, sniffed around windows, and nudged at their closed latches. He leapt from the brick porch to the grass, circled the yard, and then raced to the hill from which he would watch and wait.

For a brief, rare, moment he felt no pain.

* * *

Kaitlin lay alone in the house. Her mother had gone back to the hospital after dinner and had not returned. Kaitlin had carefully checked all the windows and doors twice, left on enough lights to make a clear path to the kitchen, then retreated to her room. She lay beneath the heavy quilt even though the day had been warm. Her stomach ached with a dull, throbbing pain that kept her from getting comfortable enough to sleep, her lower back complained as well, and her whole body seemed tense and sore.

Kaitlin finally gave in to the disagreeable notion that she should take some Tylenol and threw back the quilt to step down to the braided carpet beside her bed. In bare feet, she shrugged a robe around herself and made for the medicine cabinet. Moonlight illuminated her room but the harsh glare of the hall light caught her unexpectedly and floating discs of color swirled in her eyes as she squeezed them shut and searched for the light switch.

As soon as the hall went dark, she heard it, a doleful cry that worked its way from the cold soles of her feet through the top of her head, searing her with its cutting tone of retribution. She thought she would wet her pants with fear as she stumbled down the hall to the bathroom, slamming and locking the door behind her. She sat on the toilet seat, hugging herself and rocking back and forth, until she realized that the sound was gone. A clicking sound from the porch made the hair on her arms stand straight and she pressed herself against the small bathroom window quickly enough to watch a white wraith disappear down the driveway and into the fields.

Kaitlin shuddered again and flipped on the overhead. This time, she welcomed the glare and the flat two-dimensionality it gave to objects in the room. She opened the cabinet and took out two Tylenol, hesitated, then took two Tums as well, to fight the acid that had climbed up from her stomach. She drew a hot bath and sat in the steamy water until the adrenaline-jitters had subsided, leaving her tired and aching in its wake. She made her way back to her cold bed, and tugging the blankets over her head, finally slipped into a cocoon of sleep.

* * *

Laurel paced in the waiting room wishing she were a smoker or a drinker so that she'd have something to relax her nerves. Her mother was asleep now, but her signs were poor. How does it happen so fast? she wondered. They'd had a great afternoon and Laurel had started to think of what she would do to surprise her mother when she returned home, something to brighten up that old gloomy house. The doctors said the pneumonia was responding to the medication, but . . . Laurel sniffled, trying to breath deeply, to keep her composure.

Donna Jean was bleeding internally, her abdomen was swelling and pressing against her diaphragm, making it more and more difficult to breathe. There was nothing they could do but give her intravenous morphine and make her comfortable. The pneumonia had weakened her but it was the cancer that held Donna Jean's body under siege. Her pancreas was so badly damaged, Donna Jean's blood pressure had steadily dropped and she was drowning inside. The doctors and machines were fighting against the failure of her heart, kidneys, and respiratory system. They were fighting, but they were going to lose, Laurel thought. If not tonight, then next week or the week after. This was one condition for which there was no turning back the tide.

Maybe today was a good day to die. Donna Jean had spent time with her and with Kaitlin. She had been alert and relatively painless. She almost seemed relieved of some burden, as if she were ready to retire to a respite she had earned a long time ago. Laurel's chin wobbled as she thought this, and a tear ran down her face. She sniffed into the soggy tissue she had clutched for the last hour, and took another deep breath. The doctors would be done now, it was time to go back into the room.

Donna Jean's room was mint green, intended to be a soothing color, but too cool for Laurel's tastes. The curtain had been pulled around her bed even though the other bed lay empty beside her. Laurel pulled it away and found her mother watching the stars and city lights that made a peaceful view from her window. Donna Jean patted the bed and caught up Laurel's hand in hers.

"I want you to always know that whatever I did for you as a child, I did because I loved you." Laurel could hardly hear Donna Jean, her voice was so weak and Laurel's heart was pounding so hard. She leaned her head closer to catch every treasured word. A small moan escaped as Donna Jean tried to turn her body toward Laurel. Laurel bit her own lip trying to keep back grief.

"I love you all. I want you to know that I love Kaitlin as if she were my own and I would not pass this on to her if there were another way." Donna Jean lay back on the pillow with her eyes closed. "Oh God help me," she cried out, and a long moment of silence passed between them.

Laurel held her mother's hand and gently rubbed her arm and shoulder, feeling Donna Jean tense again with the next wave of pain. She could hardly speak as she whispered, "I love you Mama."

She clutched Donna Jean's hand as a deep rattle grew up from her mother's throat and tore something from Laurel's heart before its sound faded away. She watched as Donna Jean's face relaxed and she felt her hand go limp. Laurel sat a long time still holding her mother's hand as the warmth slipped away from it. Then she rose from the bed, pulled the blankets up a little higher around her mother, kissed her cheek one last time and stood at the window looking into the dark night.

Her mother was gone; she was surely an orphan now. All grown up and a mother too, but just as surely an orphan as if she'd been abandoned at birth. So much at stake and she didn't know where to turn or what to do to protect her own. She stared into the silvery moon outside the window, looking into its wise old eyes and tight mouth. There were no answers there.

* * *

Kaitlin was muffled, swaddled, wrapped tight in cotton or something else soft and smooth. A yellow light diffused through the veil that surrounded her and she felt as if she were floating on a cloud high above any fear or pain or anything that could hurt her. Kaitlin smiled as the feeling of well-being flowed through her.

Grandma Doe's voice spoke clearly and directly to her, with no tremor or weakness about it. It was like listening to a song, it sounded so clean and fresh. "Kaitlin, I came to say good-bye and to wish you well. I leave you with your gift and with all the love that surrounds you. You are strong and all you need is inside of you."

Doe's voice moved away, humming a quiet and dreadfully beautiful tune. And as the voice became more distant, the yellow light dimmed and Kaitlin was trapped and smothered by the heavy folds around her. Gravity tore at her and she felt herself falling a long and terrifying fall.

Her feet were tangled in the heavy quilt and the sheets were wet and sticky beneath her. Kaitlin tugged back the blankets and found spots of blood soaking her nightgown and sheet. She lurched off the bed, then realized that what she had expected so long had finally come. She was having her first period. She had become a woman.

She pulled herself from the bed and thought about the dream, such peace and then such terror. She felt so alone in the empty house, as she realized she had dreamed her grandmother dead. She fell back to her pillow, sobs wracking her body.

CHAPTER 24

L aurel pulled into the driveway, still in a daze of fatigue and sorrow. She let herself slump over the steering wheel, thinking of how she would frame her words for Kaitlin, then remembered the engine and turned off the car. She reached across the seat for the blue plastic bag holding the few things Donna Jean had taken to the hospital with her. Laurel sorted through the clothes, reaching down to the bottom of the sack, to pull up a locket that held her picture and Kaitlin's. She slipped the chain around her neck and held the locket in her hand, picturing it next to Doe's heart these last few years. For a moment, she felt her mother, warm and alive again.

Slowly, Laurel opened the car door and swung out, dragging herself up the steps and onto the porch. A flicker of the curtain at the window let her know Kaitlin had seen her come up. The front door flew open and Kaitlin's arms were around her, squeezing her tightly.

"Mom, I'm so sorry. I didn't mean to do it. I would never have done it. I loved her so much." Kaitlin wailed in her mother's arms, frightening Laurel like nothing had before. She pushed Kaitlin back, studying her face and shaking her a little to stop the hysteria.

"Kaitlin, what's happened to your face? Are you hurt?" Laurel could make out rough scratches down

Kaitlin's cheeks and purple bruises forming around her eyes.

"I dreamed Doe dead, and I never meant to. I never wanted it to happen." Kaitlin was hitting at herself, ripping out hair, and pounding her head with her fists.

"Stop it Kaitlin! You did not kill Doe! Stop it!" Laurel was shouting now and shaking Kaitlin harder. "Stop it! Cancer killed Doe, you had nothing to do with it."

"No, Mom. I dreamed it real. I did it. She would still be alive if I hadn't had that dream." Kaitlin tore out of Laurel's arms and ran up the stairs toward her room.

Laurel ran after her, grabbing Kaitlin in the hallway and forcing her into the bathroom. She held Kaitlin with one hand and ran cold water from the tap with the other. She forced Kaitlin's head under the tap until the girl was gasping for air. Laurel wrapped a towel around her wet hair and another around her shoulders. She forced Kaitlin to sit on the toilet and knelt in front of her, holding both of Kaitlin's hands.

"You did not make Doe die. She was riddled with cancer and she would have died next week or next month. You had nothing to do with it. I was there, Kaitlin. She was ready to die, she wanted to die. You can not make anyone die by dreaming it." Laurel pulled Kaitlin into her arms and lifted her onto her lap. She rocked Kaitlin as she had when her daughter was a preschooler, rubbing her back and stroking her wet hair.

"Hush, Kaitlin. Doe is dead, but you had nothing to do with it. It was her time and if you dreamed it, that was just because you loved each other so much. But Doe is resting now. She doesn't hurt anymore, she's not afraid, and she's not sick anymore." Laurel's voice quavered and her own hot tears mixed with Kaitlin's.

"Oh, Kaitlin, you didn't kill her. You poor baby. You mustn't think you did." Laurel rocked her daughter as their crying subsided. "You mustn't think you could ever kill anyone."

* * *

The scratching nudged at his ear like a pesky mosquito, an annoying irritant that wouldn't go away until he chased it off. Whaley shook himself awake, instantly regretting it. His tongue was swollen and thick inside his cottony mouth. His eyes hurt even in the dim early morning light and each scritch-scratch against the roof of the car bore into his head like a dentist's drill. He lurched to an upright position and pounded a fist against the car's roof, rapping sharply against the bare metal where the inner upholstery had fallen away.

A heavy weight shifted and the springs of the car bounced as a large white dog leapt from the roof to the hood and peered through the windshield at him. His eyes were icy like the cold light before dawn and his lips drew back in a snarl that made Whaley flinch and raise his arm to cover his face. The dog stared and then it spoke in the demon's voice.

"I have a job for you old man. There's a little girl I want to collect. Red haired like you was once. Pretty girl but head strong like you were once."

Whaley clapped his hands over his ears, squeezed his eyes shut, and started to pray. The Lord's prayer was all he knew but he repeated it over and over again to close out the evil sound of that slimy voice. "Deliver me from evil" he chanted over and over again until he chanced lowering his hands. The voice was silent.

He opened his eyes and the dog was gone, the windshield filled only with the weak rays of the newly rising sun. In his head, he continued to repeat his prayer, but all he could see was her bright hair, head lolling loosely at the end of a bruised and strangled neck.

He broke from the car, falling in the wet grass as his stiff legs failed him. He rolled onto his back and searched his pockets for the last of the Mogen David. He had to keep the demon away, could not listen to the horrible voice, had to get away from here. He had to leave, remove himself to where he couldn't hurt his family. He had to walk and never stop walking. He had to travel, far enough to outrun the demon.

* * *

Kaitlin was soaking in the hot bathtub when she heard the phone ring. She eased lower into the water and lifted a steaming washcloth over her face, letting it clean the deep scratches she had made. She could hear Laurel talking in her bedroom; it was Dad, Kaitlin knew by the soft tones her mother used with him. She pulled herself from the tub, wrapped a towel around herself, and joined Laurel in the bedroom, sitting on the quilted bed, waiting for a chance to talk. Laurel handed the phone over, gave Kaitlin a quick sad smile, and left the room.

"Hi Dad." She knew at that moment how much she missed him. How she wished he was there to give her a bear hug, to check all the door locks at night, to load a gun if necessary.

"Are you okay, Pumpkin? I'm awful sorry to hear about Doe. It's hard on your Mom; I have to count on you to take care of her."

"Dad, are you coming? Can you come for the funeral?"

"No, Honey, I can't get off right now. We're on an alert status. There's some crisis in Europe and all leave has been canceled, even for emergencies. You know I want to be there. I hate not being there for you and Mom. I really need you to take care of your Mom for me. Will you do that?"

"Dad, we want you here, we really do."

"Kaitlin, you've got to hold things down for a while. I'll come as soon as I can. Then I won't ever leave you two anymore. You've got to hang in there until then. Can you do that?"

"I don't know, Dad. It's a lot harder than I thought."

"Kaitlin, I think you are a lot stronger than you imagine. Mom really can't do this without your help. You have to be strong. Okay?"

"I'll try, Dad. You know I'll try." Kaitlin hung up, wondering how she was going to be strong enough for two when she wasn't strong enough for herself.

* * *

He hung up the phone softly but turned and pounded his fist against the office wall where he stood. Mike reached for the pencil jar, lifting a half dozen wooden shafts in his hands. He flexed, snapping them with a loud satisfying crack, then pitched them into the wastebasket with a clatter of frustration. He was such a total failure, a complete jerk, a major loser. His whole life was collapsing around him and what was he doing about it? Nothing! He was trapped. He was bound up by the chains of duty and they were pulling him apart and there was nothing he could do.

His life in the service was almost over. He was supposed to ease out career men like himself, give them new starts, new opportunities. He spit into the wastebasket. Who the hell were they all trying to fool? He'd watched his men go one at a time, shaking hands and patting his back and they all felt the same way he did. They'd trained for one job, they'd given up most of their lives doing it, and now they were good for nothing. Men who ought to be looking at promotions and higher commands; instead they were out looking for jobs as security guards and bus drivers.

His wife and child were so far away and they needed him but he was obligated to serve a military that wasn't obligated to serve him. Always the good soldier. Just one more sacrifice for the nation; like moving every year had been, like being out to sea half his life had been, like service in the Gulf War had been. Where were the long-sought commissions, where were the military honors, where were the men in his service? Erased as easily as a line in the budget. How could he have put all his life into this without knowing he was just penciled in?

He refilled his coffee and shook out two aspirin from the plastic bottle in his desk. The hot liquid burned as it went down so he tossed a couple of antacids after it and shuffled the files at this desk again. At least the alert put some of these dismissals on hold for another day. No one to fire today. No men and women to look in the eye and to lie to about how much their service meant to their country. Just his own wife and daughter.

* * *

Kaitlin sat in the front row, lost in the padded armchair that faced the blue coffin. She clutched her mother's hand on her right and a bundle of tissues on the left, but she had stopped crying; worn out with grief, too tired to cry anymore. Behind them, dulcimer music played softly, friends of Doe's had asked to do this for her, as a last gift. They sat in a back parlor, in a circle around their instruments, softly hammering out light tunes Doe would have liked.

The other guests shuffled quietly into the chapel, stopping to give their respects to Doe. She looked like an angel, lying on a blue satin pillow, birds in flight embroidered above her with the words, Going Home. She was surrounded by gladiolas, daisies, lilies, and chrysanthemums in bright yellows, pinks, and whites. The flowers filled the chapel with the heavy perfume of flower shops and candle stores.

Kaitlin stared straight ahead at Doe's cold, powdered face. Her dark hair was pulled back, her high cheekbones prominent, and her full lips a little too bright. She looked like an Indian medicine woman, Kaitlin thought. All solemn and wise, but silent. She looked like Doe, but Kaitlin knew there was nothing of Doe here at all. Doe was gone; she had not even lingered for this last ceremony of passing.

Kaitlin missed her father badly and she wished he would come through the undertaker's front door, grab her up and carry her out of here, like some fairy-tale rescue. Her Dad would swing her in his arms and she could be his little girl again. Mike would protect them and it wouldn't be up to Laurel and Kaitlin to fill the big old house with noise and to lock it up tight at night against the curse that sat outside under a white moon, watching them. Mike would tell Kaitlin that the dreams were nonsense and meant nothing. Laurel couldn't do that.

But Kaitlin's father was not here. Her father was not here and her mother was not much here either. Laurel walked through the last three days in some kind of stupor or valium haze or whatever it was that allowed her to nod pleasantly at relatives she hardly knew, and to speak on the phone as if she actually enjoyed the condolences and sympathy.

Laurel was encumbered in the ceremonies of death; sitting at the funeral home during the visiting hours, accepting casseroles and cakes, and letting Sadie Johnson organize the supper that would follow. They'd had no peace from the comforting of Donna Jean's longtime neighbors and friends. It seemed so many people felt indebted to Donna Jean or at least felt close to her over the years.

There was business too, and it seemed it couldn't wait. An attorney had already called with papers to settle the estate into Laurel's possession, the insurance company wanted specific forms completed in triplicate, and the bank accounts had to be transferred to Laurel as well. Then came the calls from Realtors who wanted to interest Laurel in subdividing the property, from the speculators who were willing to invest Laurel's inheritance, and from charities who claimed long relationships with Donna Jean.

Laurel shuttled Kaitlin from one place to another. She'd dressed and primped Kaitlin for meeting old ladies with blue hair and businessmen in black suits and red power ties. Laurel responded calmly and respectfully to all, but throughout the three days, she squeezed Kaitlin's hand, kept Kaitlin's chair close to hers, and even asked Kaitlin to sleep in her room.

The low buzz of conversation stopped as the preacher cleared his throat to begin a long prayer. Kaitlin's ears pricked up as the minister said her name, something about Laurel and Kaitlin being the last of the generations on Bluehills Farm and how all our prayers were with them. Kaitlin sighed, and wondered if prayers would ever be enough to make her a normal person again. She wondered how long it would be before she dreamed her own mother dead. Kaitlin wondered how many more days she could go without sleeping.

The ride in the funeral home's limousine was blissfully free of interruptions. Kaitlin leaned against her mother and even drowsed a little, a dreamless nap for which she was grateful. The two women, neither a child anymore, Kaitlin thought, must look extremely well controlled behind their blank faces and the tinted limousine windows. No one would recognize the turmoil that lay just below the thin skin that protected them.

The graveside ceremony was brief and simple, ashes to ashes and dust to dust. Laurel and Kaitlin stayed to say good-bye to the last visitors. Both were reluctant to trade the bright grassy garden for the noisy buffet set up in the church basement. Laurel sat on a concrete bench among the family graves while Kaitlin examined each headstone in sad succession. Her grandfather's marker rose beside the fresh mound for Doe and to their right were stones for Doe's mother, father, brothers and finally, a white marble lamb which marked April's grave.

"Our beloved child, taken from us too soon, we wait to walk with thee."

Kaitlin knelt on the grassy mound, its lilacs burned away by the hot summer sun. She wondered what April must have been like. Why would April come back to hurt her? she asked, almost out loud. Kaitlin sensed only innocence in this stone, in this grave. There was no feeling of malice or danger. There was sadness and loss but no feeling of revenge. Kaitlin patted the ground, as if this would reassure them both, then turned to her mother who was calling her to the car.

* * *

The visit was much harder than Laurel had already dreaded it might be. She doubted that Aunt Carol Ann would understand the difficult news she had to share but she had not expected her own great reluctance to enter the prison-like care center where Carol Ann was kept. Kaitlin stayed at Laurel's side as she had this whole week, making her feel less alone and powerless, but she could feel Kaitlin's uneasiness reflecting her own. This place made them nervous though they knew duty would keep them visiting regularly.

Aunt Carol Ann was waiting for them in her chair in the tiled day room. It was easy to spot her across the large room. Her lips moved in some personal cadence and her hands twisted at the stuffed animal in her lap. Her brown eyes fell sightlessly on the window, failing to recognize the hot summer landscape in front of her. Abruptly, Carol Ann jerked upright in her chair and turned her eyes toward the doorway, pinning them with her sudden attention. Laurel felt paralyzed in that brief second, as if an electric charge held her in her spot, then Carol Ann turned back to the window and the world came on again.

Laurel started resolutely toward her aunt, knowing there was no escaping responsibility. Kaitlin carried the box of cream chocolates they'd brought to help get Aunt Carol Ann's attention and to establish some friendship there. The two women pulled their chairs close to Carol Ann's and waited as her head rose to make eye contact.

"Aunt Carol Ann, this is Laurel. I've come to see you again. Do you remember Kaitlin?" Carol Ann watched without expression as if she were waiting for Laurel to tell her something that was actually true.

"We've brought you some chocolates. Kaitlin, show Aunt Carol Ann the chocolates. We've come to visit you." Laurel patted Carol Ann's knees and Kaitlin offered her the box of candy.

Carol Ann held the box in one hand and the tattered white stuffed dog in the other. She stared into Laurel's face and asked, "Is Donna Jean dead?"

Laurel swallowed hard; she hadn't expected anything so direct or so astute. "Yes, Aunt Carol Ann, Donna Jean died four days ago. We buried her yesterday next to your mother and father up at City Cemetery. Donna Jean asked us to take care of you and to be your family now. Do you understand?" Laurel expected Aunt Carol Ann to become distraught, to start chanting like she had when they had last visited her, but strangely, she did not. She remained coherent as she turned to Kaitlin.

Kaitlin pulled back as Carol Ann's eyes stared at her, frightened of what the woman might do or say, but Carol Ann spoke quietly. "You find April. Donna Jean wants you to find April."

CHAPTER 25

Kaitlin moved toward the dusty road and settled on the big rock under the old maple tree where she'd said she'd wait for Stormy. The rock was warm to the touch even in the skimpy shade of the old tree. There were piles of rocks like these at the corners of each field. She imagined some long ago grandfather using a horse and harness to wrestle the giant boulders out of the way of his plow and to drag the rocks to the side where they built up like small fortresses.

Shriveled corn plants spread out in front of her, their dead leaves moving listlessly in the afternoon heat. Spring had died away in a haze of summer heat that dried up the new shoots as they opened and carried topsoil away on hot winds. There had been no rain for six weeks and the lush green countryside was disappearing under a light coat of brown dust.

Near the end of one row, a gray robin scratched at the dirt like a farmyard hen. One wing hung low, apparently injured. Kaitlin guessed that even the insects were getting scarce now that water was so sparse and an injured bird would have a hard time of it. She watched wondering where the bird's bright-colored mate might be. The bird reminded her of Laurel, mateless, wounded, going through the motions of everyday life without much animation. Kaitlin felt a pang of guilt for leaving Laurel alone in a house full of memories, but Laurel was not really good company yet.

The drab robin continued to peck in the sand until Kaitlin noticed a shadow flickering around it. She shaded her eyes and looked up to see a strange hawk, white, pure white, like some kind of dove or sea gull but rendered dangerous by clawed talons that reached lower with each circle. The robin remained unaware of the oncoming threat, still searching the dry dirt for some loose kernel of corn or some scurrying beetle.

Kaitlin rose to her feet, reached down for a stone to hurl at the bigger bird and ran forward, shouting at the hawk, "Get out of here." Both birds panicked with the interruption, the robin bobbing off down the row of corn and the hawk rising to the air again with screams of frustration. Kaitlin tossed the stone after the hawk, feeling her own frustration and an unreasonable enmity toward the hawk.

Kaitlin returned to the rock, angry with herself for being so easily upset. Her head ached with the tension created by her feelings of responsibility and confusion. She replayed Aunt Carol Ann's words in her head, not understanding what they meant. 'Find April. Donna Jean wants you to find April.'

Did she mean April's grave? Kaitlin thought not, she'd been there and nothing special happened. Did she mean where April had died? Perhaps, but Kaitlin was not going to go there alone. Maybe Stormy would help her. Did she mean catch up with the ghost vision of April? That possibility gave her the shivers. She didn't think she could really bring herself to chase a ghost who wanted her dead, unless she started to believe the ghost was just her own hallucination.

Kaitlin watched Stormy turning the corner on her bike, moving slowly, putting up small clouds of dust as she rattled down the road. Stormy still wore the battered brown hat, despite the heat of the summer, but she had given up her long jeans for ragged cut-offs that were almost worn through in the seat. Under her hat, light headphones sat on her ears, their cord snaking down to a compact Walkman tucked into Stormy's pocket. Kaitlin smiled seeing her friend, and thought, that it felt good to smile again.

"Hey, girl friend! Whatcha been up to?" Stormy put up five fingers waiting for a high five then reduced them to one as Kaitlin tried to slap her hand. Kaitlin laughed so hard she had to hold her stomach in to keep it from hurting.

"So I haven't seen you in a week and you've become Aretha Franklin or something?" Kaitlin was laughing tears now picturing Stormy in her cutoffs and felt hat in a Motown act.

"Jeeze, it's good to see you again! You couldn't have a clue how bad it's been." Kaitlin covered her mouth to quiet her giggles and let Stormy have a chance to say something.

"Well, while you have been partying and living the high life, I have been making a plan for us." Stormy pulled off her backpack and started unzipping pockets. She pulled out a county map with the corner that detailed their area boxed in red. She also pulled out a hand-drawn close-up of the farm and the State Lands that bordered it. Finally, Stormy produced a rough drawing of the house plans for the old farmhouse.

"You said we have to find April. I figure we better start looking. I think maybe you could be some kind of human Geiger-counter, you know, maybe your 'feelings' would heat up as we get close to something important." Stormy pulled a ruler and a pencil from the bag now, spreading her sketch of the map across the boulder Kaitlin had been sitting on.

"We just have to lay a grid over these, then search each one systematically and keep notes on what you're picking up. Are you game for it?" Stormy stuck the pencil behind her ear and gave Kaitlin a questioning look.

Kaitlin nodded, "Yeah, I'm ready as long as you're with me. Where do we start?"

"Right here." Stormy used her ruler to slap the diagram of the house. "It's too hot to work outside."

* * *

Yuki paced on the ridge. Usually asleep during the day, he found the tension in the air made him nervous and agitated. His eyes felt grainy and his nose dry in the dusty heat. Some secret appetite stirred deep inside him that he didn't understand except to recognize that a skinny rabbit or field mouse was not going to satisfy it, not that there had been many of those this summer. Even the local dogs, who usually joined him in the summer when some bitch in heat had led them away from their doorsteps, hadn't shown up this year. Too hot to chase, too dry, he didn't know.

Yuki kept watch on the house where the woman and the girls hid away from him. Their odors carried far on the dry air and each one tantalized that hungry desire inside of him. It had been a long time since the foal had obliged him and opportunities had been few.

A door slammed down below and Yuki watched as the woman wandered from the house down the long driveway to the little car. He could see she was distracted, not paying attention to what was around her, vulnerable. Her weakness stirred his appetite and he licked his chops as he watched the car exit from the driveway onto the dirt road. Maybe later, maybe she would be gone until it was dark, and he could creep close, be waiting for her in the bushes beside the stone porch. He would like that, leaping from the shadows and catching the flash of fear in her wide eyes. Yes, he and his inner companion would like that very much.

* * *

Kaitlin shifted her weight carefully from one beam to the next. She couldn't stand straight in the narrow space so she doubled over, using her hands to help balance her feet on the beams. Plasterboard had been hammered into the beams from below, with an occasional nail left sticking up into the air, threatening to catch a misplaced hand or knee. The room was just a crawl space with a cobwebbed window at each end that allowed just enough light to see the dust motes dancing into her lungs and nose.

Old fruit crates and cardboard boxes housed mouse droppings and tiny worm casings. The boxes were filled with treasures like an old tailor's dummy, ancient school texts, and World War II ration booklets. Most of the boxes had probably not been disturbed since they were first placed there, though two frayed boxes by the door to her closet held Christmas decorations.

"Stormy, the trail is cold. I bet she never even came in here." Kaitlin was feeling claustrophobic in the stifling heat of the closed-up attic.

"Come on, we may find some of her old toys or books or something she used. It might give you some clues about her."

"Stormy, you said I'd be the human Geiger-counter and I'm telling you there is nothing here. Let's get out." Kaitlin backed toward the trapdoor and Stormy reluctantly followed.

The fresh air at the door to her room was a great relief and Kaitlin crawled quickly out so Stormy could get her share.

"We've done the whole house and I don't pick up anything. Maybe I'm not so clairvoyant as you believe. Or maybe April doesn't want to be found." Kaitlin's head throbbed and she wondered if she'd have noticed anything anyway with that pain.

"We haven't done the cellar and it's a lot cooler down there. What do you say? Let's give it a shot."

The girls latched the trapdoor from Kaitlin's closet, washed their hands in the bathroom, then made for the kitchen where the door to the cellar stood, locked tight. Kaitlin searched through the odds and ends drawer until she came up with an old skeleton key that fit the lock. Cool air wafted up from the cellar, reminding Kaitlin of the damp richness of the woods.

Kaitlin followed Stormy down the stone stairs, her knees going weak and her stomach loosening as she felt a strange familiarity in the earthen room. Kaitlin probed with the flashlight, exposing deep shelves, still holding a few filled bottles of vegetables and fruits, and housing boxes of empty canning gear waiting for summer's harvest. She continued to the east wall where a break in the shelves made a small alcove, set back from the center of the floor.

Kaitlin dropped to her knees on the hard-packed floor and closed her eyes. She held herself like she did when she prayed, listening and trying to feel what was happening in this spot. Her throat closed in a little, feeling raw as if from crying. She recognized that tightness, having held back a lot of sobs lately. She tried to make her mind blank and open to the feelings. Her eyes began to water and her nose began to run. Kaitlin felt incredibly sad here, overwhelmed with grief and then she knew, as if she were watching a video on the back of her eyelids.

Here was the black dog, a good dog, in pain, badly hurt; his eyes ran with white, and blood streamed from his head and ears. She reached out and stroked his side gently and she spoke soft reassuring words. Her hands grew warm with the stroking and she could feel his chest heave with a deep breath. She patted the good black dog.

Kaitlin opened her eyes, breaking the spell. She rubbed her hands together, making sure they were hers again, then pulled herself to her feet, grabbing at Stormy. "She was here, I was her, for a minute. I saw the dog, all torn up and hurting."

"What do you mean Kaitlin?"

"Stormy, you were right. It was like it was real. I could feel her dog. I moved my hands like she did. I don't know how, but I was April." A chill ran through her, leaving a trail of small Goosebumps on her arms.

* * *

The girls hesitated at the mouth of the barn. The doorway stood in a half-light cast by storm clouds moving in from the west. The long thin clouds promised dry sheet lightning and thunder. Inside, the dry air stirred with their footsteps, sending up clouds of old corn dust and hay particles.

A cursory inspection of the downstairs revealed nothing more than the dismal home of spiders and other crawly things. The grain bin greeted them with the smell of fermentation and the cow stanchions stood empty, showing worn indentations from the necks of long dead cows. The chicken coop was a dry, foul place; perches were piled with hard coats of old bird droppings and gray cobwebs draped every corner and rough extension, though it looked as if even the flies had deserted the dreary room.

Outside the pens around the barn stood just as empty in the yellow light of the impending storm. The pigpen was overgrown with yellow weeds which now rooted in dry, cracked clay. The pastures stood empty of animals but filled with an abundance of thirsty thistles, quickly going to brown, in the unrelenting summer heat.

The barn was as lifeless as the house had been. Kaitlin picked up nothing, no feelings, no visions.

The girls surveyed the loft from below, wondering if it was worth it to climb the rickety ladder to its heights. Kaitlin shrugged, "Why not?" and they ventured into the old bales of moldering hay that rested under the sagging roof.

Gray sunbeams, entering through numerous small holes in the leaky roof, speckled the pyramids of old bales with dancing spots of dim light. A brilliant flash of heat lightning accentuated the darkness between spots as the girls climbed higher and the cloud cover grew.

"Don't you think we ought to get down from here before we're struck by lightning?" Kaitlin looked nervously through a crack in the boards of the wall nearest her. The sky was a queer yellow at the horizon and an ominous purple where the clouds covered the sun.

"Criminy! That stuff's just sheet lightning. It's not going to strike anywhere. Besides, this barn probably has lightning rods or it wouldn't have stood so long." Stormy was already above Kaitlin, almost to the small window that was perched at the peak of the roof.

Kaitlin frowned, figuring Stormy probably didn't know what she was talking about. Oh well, she guessed she might as well get one good look from that high window that faced the back of the farm before she packed it in and came down.

Kaitlin placed her foot in a small hole between the bales to give herself a boost up to the next level. It was then she felt it, a cold smooth slithering over her ankle where her sock and pant leg separated. She froze, praying to God that it was not a snake, then looked down to see a long gray rat's tail whip deeper into the hole where her foot was lodged.

Kaitlin screamed and jerked herself upward, screaming again as small pink feet trotted across her exposed hand. She flailed the hand into space, carrying its small passenger in an arc several bales over to her right. Involuntarily following the creature's flight, her eyes fell on several more of the gray rats, the largest of which sat up on its back feet staring at her with beady black eyes.

Kaitlin screamed a third time and scrambled still higher to get away from what seemed to be a living tide of gray hide and quivering whiskers around her. "Stormy, oh God, help me, they're all over."

Stormy turned ever so slowly from the window, seeing for the first time, the invasion that was on them. She struggled to her feet, covered her own scream, then reached a hand down to pull Kaitlin up as she climbed. Giving her a rough jerk, she dragged Kaitlin up to the top bale beside her then searched frantically for something they might use to fight off the fearless beasts.

Kaitlin backed away from the flood that followed her, slamming herself into the wall and rattling the old cracked window that illuminated this end of the barn. She turned quickly to see what she had struck and in that glance, all hope fled from her, for there across the far field, at the edge of the woods stood a girl and a black dog staring at her.

* * *

Yuki crept through the old pasture, using the husks of dried out thistles and itch weed to cover his approach. He could smell them nearby, little girls with soft clean thighs and high weak screams. His mouth watered with a desire to taste their salty skin and to feel their strong young pulses. They were in the barn, the hot wind carried the smell of disturbed hay dust and the sound of creaky ladder rungs. He crawled forward on his belly, his desire inching him onward even when reason bade him to wait until it was darker.

The pit of his stomach rumbled as his appetite awakened deeper urges. He could smell the sweat that trickled under their arms and gathered at the back of their knees. He could pick up the sound of denim rubbing against tanned calves and the quiet bending of dried alfalfa stalks as light feet stepped onto the bales. Yuki raised himself into a half crouch now and rushed forward, careless of being seen, thinking only of what awaited him in the barn.

The sweep of the car's headlights and the roar of its motor startled him, causing him to retreat inside the barn, back into the deep shadows brought by the early storm-clouded night that gathered around him. He waited, knowing he would deal with this one first, then take the two who hovered above him.

* * *

Laurel pulled the car around to the back of the house, thinking it would be a shorter run to the back door if these ominous clouds decided to break open on her. The darkness was bizarre, this early on a summer evening. She shuddered to think what kind of storm such clouds might unleash. She switched on the radio before abandoning the car to see if there were any storm warnings or tornado watches she should know about, but all she could tune in was static and a fitful reception of some soft-rock tune she didn't recognize.

She switched off the headlights, turned off the ignition, opened the door, pushed down the lock and swung the door shut behind her. She turned toward the barn, thinking she heard some noise from that direction, then swung back toward the house, and there he stood. Between Laurel and the back porch stood a monstrous, longhaired, white beast, growling and slathering.

Teeth bared and red lips curled back, white foam dripping from his jaws, fur standing on end, a demon with sharpened fangs and curved claws stood poised for a final lunge. Laurel's heart crashed into overdrive and time froze into single frames around her. As slowly as melting snow, she stepped back fumbling for her car keys and the car door handle. The dog's back legs began their ejection, lifting the creature like a powerful spring released. Laurel instinctively raised her left arm to cover her face and dropped directly to the ground. The creature flew with all the grace and precision of a silver bullet launched from a gun barrel, his jaws snapping where Laurel's face had been a split second before.

Laurel hit the ground, bruising her shoulder and hip, and without thinking, scuttled for the cover offered by the low chassis of the car beside her. She slid through soft dirt, her torso protected just as the dog's front claws landed hard on her still exposed arm. His teeth sank into the bare flesh above her wrist and his head twisted cruelly, dragging her arm out from under the car. Laurel reached up with her free arm, grabbing at the metal rods and connectors that hung there, burning her palm on something and grabbing again. She clenched her teeth and clutched the car's frame while the dog ripped and tore at her exposed arm.

* * *

Stormy missed it on her first panicked search, but something unconscious drew her eyes back to the handle of the pitch fork leaning against the old gray barn boards. She dove for it, then turned to swing the fork wildly at the rats who were now pouring out of every cranny among the bales and moving like an army toward Kaitlin, who stood frozen, staring out the small broken window.

"Kaitlin!" Stormy screamed at total capacity and the spell was broken. Kaitlin turned and, kicking with all her might, stomped at the swarming vermin gathering around her. Stormy's fork raised and lowered, skewering two and three at a time until she had to fling them off to start again. With the fork lunging up and down in front of them, feet beating at the twisting and churning stream of gray fur, the girls fought their way downward until they stood on the floor of the loft. An old rope was neatly circled and hung on a beam there and Kaitlin unwound it as Stormy continued to pierce advancing rats.

With hands nipped and bleeding in several places, Kaitlin threw herself off the loft, feet squeezed together around the rope and hands loose. Kaitlin dropped rapidly down the rope as a fireman might slide down his pole. Rubbing her red and burned hands at the bottom, she swung the rope back to Stormy. Stormy yelled a warning, then tossed the pitchfork down and swung out on the rope. Moving more slowly, Stormy dropped hand over hand to the bottom where Kaitlin stood with the pitchfork at ready.

They stood without moving, back-to-back, watching for the attack, but no rat moved. Laurel's scream broke their concentration, and turning toward the house they saw a white fury snarling and lunging at something under the car. Another scream let them know, too well, what the something was.

* * *

Soft flesh ripping away in pleasing strips of pain. Screams soaring inside his brain in echoes of ecstasy. Blood splashing on his tongue, adding fire to his frenzy. Yuki's claws and teeth tearing at the meat and bone which would bring him closer to the steaming entrails in her soft belly and the pounding heart within her frail chest wall. All his senses were engaged in an orgy of bloodlust and adrenaline.

Then the cold iron spikes drove into his hind muscles, startling him out of his pleasure and diverting his attack from the woman under the car. Yuki turned, snarling and dodging from the attack. There stood two young girls, ripe and ready to be picked, some excited and delighted part of him pointed out. He stood for a moment mesmerized with desire for the young flesh in front of him and heightened by the fresh blood that pooled at his feet. The fascination was shattered as he saw the taller girl raise the pitchfork again and hurl it at him with terrific force. Yuki jumped to the side, averting the second blow and reassessing the situation.

Now the girl he called April smashed a rock almost at his feet. He reversed and his hind leg faltered, feeling the pain of the wounds the fork had inflicted. He backed away again, feeling blood run down his leg, growling his frustration at losing his kill. The pitchfork was raised again, and Yuki hobbled out of range, the voice inside howling in rage as he was defeated.

CHAPTER 26

L aurel woke groggily, fighting off wooziness and the biggest headache of her life. She licked at her dry lips and tried to remember when she had come down with such an awful flu. She turned to her side, thinking she would get up for some water, but felt her arm tethered to something. Turning, she found an intravenous needle inserted and taped to her right arm, a tube drooping from a plastic bottle of clear fluids suspended on a metal pole beside her. Confused, she rolled her head to the other side to find her left arm wrapped in heavy bandages and set in a splint against her chest. At that moment she remembered.

Laurel felt for the gravel that should be beneath her, and it registered that she was in a high bed, between clean white sheets. A black TV screen grinned down at her from its ceiling swing and a Formica table spanned her thighs. A small, plastic pitcher of water sat beside a paper cup tempting her to drink.

Laurel laid back on her pillow, needing to know how long she had been here and where her daughter was. She reached for the call button, remembering its placement from her recent visits with her mother. She pressed once, then again and again, unable to stop herself. A nurse came rushing into the room, a worried look on her face.

"Mrs. Taylor, you're awake! You must have a lot of

questions." The nurse was an older woman who looked like she knew her way around patients and doctors. Her metal nametag reflected the fluorescent lights and read, Bernice.

"Is my daughter all right? Is she here?" Laurel wanted to ask calmly but her voice quivered.

"Your daughter is fine, Mrs. Taylor. She had some small bites and scratches that have been treated and she's in the waiting room right now. We'll let her in to see you after the doctor has a chance to check you over to make sure you're doing well." Bernice fussed with the IV line, took Laurel's pulse, and made a notation in her chart.

"I'm going to fetch the doctor right now. As soon as she gives the okay, then your daughter can visit with you." Bernice pulled the curtain away from the bed and stepped out into the hallway. She let the door swing shut behind her.

Laurel held her breath as she waited for the doctor. The seconds seemed to move as slowly as minutes and her mind began to flash back to the snarling dog and its terrible, ripping teeth. For a moment, her stomach lurched, and she closed her eyes and breathed slowly trying to relax. White teeth snapped at her, and she jumped when she felt a hand on her shoulder.

"I'm sorry to startle you, Mrs. Taylor. I'm Dr. Burcalow. I'd like to see how you're doing." The doctor was probably only ten years older than Laurel, her red hair showing gray at the temples. Her open face revealed laugh lines and kind green eyes.

The doctor reached out to take her wrist but Laurel held up her hand, stopping her. "Please, first, the nurse said my daughter was hurt." Laurel caught her breath again, waiting.

Dr. Burcalow nodded, and patted Laurel's hand. "She had some very minor injuries, not due to the dog. She was very upset about you, so the emergency room people gave her a sedative and right now she's probably feeling a little dopey. I'm going to let her in to see you in just a few minutes." Dr. Burcalow's voice was calm and reassuring.

"You went through quite a trauma and your arm was badly torn up. Do you remember a large dog attacking you?"

Laurel nodded and shuddered, more frightened now that the scene returned to her.

"Your daughter and her friend fought the dog off you and called the paramedics. You were unconscious when they brought you in and you've already had some surgery on your arm. You lost quite a lot of blood but I'd like to see how you're recovering before we decide if we need to do a transfusion." Laurel nodded again, though she missed most of the doctor's words while the dog's attack kept replaying in her mind.

"You are a very lucky person and we think that you won't lose any functioning in that arm. You are going to have some scars that are likely to cause some interesting conversations. We'll probably have to do more surgery once the tissue is healthy again, but you shouldn't be limited at all once that arm has healed.

"Mrs. Taylor, this has been an unusually traumatic episode for you and for your daughter. Your daughter and her friend demonstrated exceptional maturity and courage in rescuing you, but I am worried that both you and your daughter will have some emotional after-effects from this. I'd like to have you talk to our resident psychologist before you are released. If you grant permission, I'd also like Kaitlin to talk to her today or tomorrow, before she returns home. Would you sign a release for her to do that?"

Laurel's mind, caught in a circle of replay, was distressed by the words 'psychologist' and 'after-effects.' "Doctor, are you telling me that my daughter is not well?"

"Mrs. Taylor, your daughter has been wrenched by several powerfully emotional events lately, just as you have. I understand that you just lost your mother. Remember that Kaitlin lost her grandmother and now she almost lost her own mother; indeed, she was sure that you were dead when she dragged you out from under that car. I can tell that she's a very strong girl, but I think that she, and you too, for that matter, need to talk this through with someone. This kind of experience can haunt you for years, and I don't think you want that for Kaitlin. I also don't think it would be healthy for Kaitlin if you carry this trauma on with you either. So, all I'm asking is to give permission for Kaitlin to receive some counseling before she goes home, and maybe later, if the psychologist thinks she needs it."

Laurel nodded, pressing her good hand against the bandaged arm to stop her trembling. "Of course, I see what you mean."

"We have Kaitlin on a sedative right now, and I'd like to check her in for the night just so we can keep an eye on her as she comes off the medication. The psychologist can see her tomorrow and the nurses can treat her cuts again before she goes home. I can arrange to have her share this room with you if you like."

"Of course, Doctor. Thank you very much." Laurel's eyes watered and she knew she couldn't contain the tears. "Thank you for taking care of me; I thought I was dead too." Laurel brought her hand to her mouth, unable to continue talking. The doctor simply reached out and patted her arm.

Dr. Burcalow smiled gently, "I'm going to bring Kaitlin in now."

* * *

Kaitlin eased into the hospital bed as silently as she could, hoping not to disturb her mother's rest. The hospital pajamas they'd given her to sleep in were thin and the room was cold, but Kaitlin was exhausted, and knew she would fall asleep quickly. She turned over to get a better view of her mother, still tied to tubes and wrapped in gauze. Kaitlin's heart went cold, thinking once again, that she could have prevented what had happened. Doe had warned her to pay attention to the signs and she knew now that the attack on the robin was just a premonition of the attack on Laurel. She was also learning that seeing April and her dog always meant danger.

Kaitlin rubbed her temples, the tension headache building there. How could she be so stupid, to miss the obvious? How could she let her mother be hurt so badly?

Here she had a gift from God, or someone, and she was too stupid to use it right. Then again, why did she have to have the gift if she was too stupid to use it? Laurel would be papering the living room right now, if her daughter hadn't been so dense. Kaitlin cried quietly, knowing the damage was her responsibility, whether she wanted it or not.

Kaitlin slept, red tear tracks drying on her face, blankets pulled high to her chin, body folded tight, knees to her chest. Her sleep, like Laurel's, was broken by jerky motions of her hands and head, low mumbling cries, and rapid eye movement. A nurse, checking on them both, turned off the overhead lights and closed the door to the hallway noises.

* * *

Mike chewed his lip as he waited for the hospital operator to connect him to Laurel's room. Beads of sweat formed on his forehead and he wiped the perspiration away with an oily handkerchief he pulled from the pocket of his work clothes. Morbid possibilities danced in his head, chasing away all of Sadie's reassuring words.

"Laurel!" His voice cracked with his anticipation and he took a deep breath, reminding himself not to upset her.

"God, Laurel. Are you and Kaitlin all right? I just heard. It took Sadie Johnson a while to track me down at the base." He pressed his ear against the receiver and held his hand over the other ear to hear better her gentle voice over the grumbling lines.

"Mike, I'm so glad it's you. I'm cut up a little, but they'll let me go home in a sling in just a couple of days. Kaitlin is a little scratched and shook up but you know she's a trooper."

"Listen, I'll come right away. I can catch a ride on a Navy plane and be there before tomorrow. I'll come take care of things." Mike could hear the pain behind her lies. He wondered how bad it really was.

"Mike, aren't you on special alert? They're not going to let you go right now, just for this are they?"

"Christ, I'll go AWOL if they won't release me. You need me, I'll get to Michigan somehow."

"No, Mike, don't do anything crazy. That would make me really happy if you ended up in the brig for the next year or lost our pension or something like that. Really, no stunts, please. I want you here so much, but it's only a few more days before you'll be retired. Besides, I hear there's a fly-by planned for your retirement party. You can't give up something like that. I want you to stick to the original plan, really."

"Christ, Laurel. I ought to be there with you. I'm sure they'll grant a hardship release in this case." It was always so frustrating when she resisted, and he knew from experience that she seldom changed her mind.

"No, Mike. Once I get you here, I'm going to hang on and never let you go. I don't want you having to go back and put in more time. We're so close. Please, don't come until you've sold the house and packed our truck. I've got Sadie Johnson here to take care of us. You know that tough old lady is more man than you are!"

"Laurel, it's not right. I love you and Kaitlin." It's hopeless, he thought. She is not going to budge.

"Then grant me this wish. Don't come until it's final, then we'll never part again. Promise me."

"I'll be there in two weeks then. Just make sure you keep your end of the deal." Mike lowered the phone gently in its cradle, figuring the steps he could take to speed things up. He had to get there; he felt it like a second heart pulsing through his being.

***

Kaitlin sat straight upright pressed to the back of the Naugahyde chair, feet swinging, just short of the floor. A nurse had found a toothbrush and comb for her but she was dressed in yesterday's clothes, streaked with rust-colored stains from her mother's arm and smudged with car grease and gravel from the driveway. The small bites and scratches on her hands and ankles burned and itched today, even though they'd been redressed this morning.

A secretary looked up from her keyboard and smiled at Kaitlin. "It won't be much longer now I'm sure. Would you like a magazine to read or maybe something to doodle on?"

"No thank you, Ma'am. I'm fine." Right, she thought. I look like I was dragged behind a car to get here and I feel the same, but I'm just fine.

The inner office door opened and a woman dressed in worn jeans and a cotton plaid shirt stepped out. She was slight, with sandy blonde hair and rimless glasses that covered smiling eyes. She held out her hand to Kaitlin, "I'm Dr. Howard, you must be Kaitlin. Please come in and make yourself comfortable."

Kaitlin stepped through the inner door, and instead of seeing the couch she expected, she found two cushioned chairs and a low coffee table. In one corner a bright red toy box held stuffed animals and dolls, small dishes, books, and drawing supplies. Behind the psychologist's desk, a bulletin board of children's drawings, cartoons, and greeting cards made a colorful collage. Kaitlin relaxed and sat in one of the soft chairs while Dr. Howard took the other.

"Dr. Burcalow asked me to see you today. She told me that you went through a very terrifying experience and that it might help you to talk to someone about your feelings and fears about this."

Kaitlin sat speechless for a minute, wondering how much she really should say. Could she tell this stranger about the leather pouch she wore around her neck for protection? Should she ask Dr. Howard how one was supposed to find a ghost who only seemed to appear at inconvenient times? Should she tell her about warning signs? Would Dr. Howard think she was crazy? Was she crazy?

"Maybe you should just tell me a little about yourself. Where you go to school. How long you've lived here. That sort of thing." Dr. Howard leaned forward, attentive for Kaitlin's reply. There was no notebook or tape recorder in sight. Just the teddy bears in the toy box and the Snoopy dog on the bulletin board.

Kaitlin went through the 'Hi, I'm new here' speech she'd made several times at school this spring, Dr. Howard interrupting occasionally to ask questions.

"Kaitlin, how do you feel about being away from your dad?"

"I don't like it but I understand it. He's in the Navy. My mom and I have been on our own before. We do okay."

"Tell me about your grandmother. Were you close to her?"

Kaitlin's lip trembled now and she honestly answered, "Yes. I hadn't seen her very much before this year but I got to know her pretty well before she died. I miss her a lot. I wish she were here right now."

"Do you ever have dreams about your grandmother?"

Kaitlin felt the bright red blush moving up her neck to her cheeks. What could she say about her dreams without making herself sound crazy? She might be crazy.

"Yes, I dreamed about her before she died," and that made her die, Kaitlin thought, but didn't say out loud.

"How did you feel after that dream?"

Kaitlin stared at her shoes. She wants to know about feelings too. Am I wearing a sign that says 'Crazy Girl' on my chest? She tried to think of the right words before she answered.

"I felt sad, and she died the next day."

"A lot has happened to you lately. What do you do when you are feeling sad or afraid?"

Kaitlin felt the psychologist's eyes searching her face as if she could read what Kaitlin was thinking. Should I tell I wake up in terror? That I have panic attacks in the middle of the day? That I hunt for ghosts in my spare time?

"I don't know. I guess I don't do anything special. I just go on with what has to be done, like the funeral or the dinner afterward." Kaitlin knew her whole face was red now and she couldn't meet the doctor's eyes. She played with a button on her shirt and shifted in her chair.

"Dr. Burcalow told me that you were playing in the barn when your mother got hurt and that you and your friend were bitten pretty badly by a nest of rats up there. What were you thinking when all that happened?" Dr. Howard patted Kaitlin's shoulder so that she couldn't avoid looking at her.

"I was really, really scared. They were coming out

from every crack around us and my friend and I were fighting them off so we could get down from there." And then I saw April and froze, she thought, and started to sob.

"I couldn't move at first. Stormy got me out of there and when we were down on the ground I heard my mom screaming. It was all like a horrible nightmare." Kaitlin's shoulders shook and her chest heaved with great gasps as she tried to catch her breath around the sobs that broke through.

Dr. Howard patted Kaitlin's hand and held a tissue out to her. "It was a very bad thing that happened to you. It's okay to cry. You can cry any time you need to. It was a terrible thing that happened and anyone would cry about this. It's okay."

Kaitlin curled her body tightly, her face to the back of the chair and her feet under her and wailed with all the strength she had left inside of her. She cried for her grandmother, she cried for her mother, but mostly she cried for herself. She was caught in some awful dream and she couldn't do anything but finish it. It wasn't the rats that scared her, it wasn't the dog, it wasn't even April that scared her. The thing that frightened her most was knowing this was not the end. This was just working toward something more terrible than she could ever say, and the scariest thing was knowing that if she could feel it, then it would be so.

Part 6, 1951

"Thou shalt not be afraid for the terror by night; nor for the arrow that flieth by day; Nor for the pestilence that walketh in darkness; nor for the destruction that wasteth at noonday." --Psalm 91:5-6

CHAPTER 27

Papa drove the old truck slowly to reduce its jolting over the gravel road that led back to Bluehills Farm. He kept one hand on the steering wheel and used the other to stroke the dog that lay beside him on the truck's seat, careful to touch only his uninjured flank. Each time Papa shifted, the roar of the engine brought a small whimper from Duke and Papa shushed him with gentle petting and "Good old dog, we're going home."

At the house, Papa pulled musty old blankets out of an attic trunk and piled them into a soft bed in the cellar for Duke. Tiptoeing around the kitchen, he heated water and tore old rags that he used to clean the dog's worst mud and blood, wanting to make the sight of him less of a shock for April. Then, not wanting to put off the inevitable, he went upstairs to April's room and woke her quietly.

"April, I found Duke for you." Papa shook his sleepy daughter, preparing himself to break her heart.

"Oh, Papa, I knew you would find him." April rubbed her tired eyes and threw her arms around her father.

"Honey, I found Duke, but he's been hurt. He's in awful bad shape, but I brought him home so we could make him comfortable. I want you to come see him right now, but you need to know that I'm wakin' you up so you can say your good-byes." Papa held April by the shoulders, looking her right in the eyes, making her understand that he was serious. "Do you understand?"

April nodded, her eyes wide and filling rapidly. "Duke's gonna die?"

"We're all goin' to die someday, but I think this may be Duke's day. He's hurt awful bad and I don't think you'd want him to keep hurtin' this way. Do you understand?"

April nodded and pulled on her robe and slippers. Papa could see she was close to crying now, but she swallowed hard and hugged him again, saying, "Thank you, Papa, for bringin' him home." They went down the stairs together.

* * *

April crept quietly across the packed dirt floor toward Duke, afraid to startle him with any sudden movements. Her eyes brimmed with tears and she quickly covered her mouth when she saw his terrible wounds. Duke's eyes were gone completely, and in the place of tears, two streams of pus ran down his jaws. His muzzle was swollen immensely and caked with dried blood. His mouth lay open and he sucked air weakly into his throat. His ears were ragged and bloody, and his whole head looked bloated with bruising and infection.

"Duke," April whispered his name softly, "I love you, puppy." His tail wagged weakly and she reached to stroke his side. He continued to wag and tried to raise his head. "No, puppy." She pushed him back on his side and sat for the next half-hour petting him slowly and steadily, then made up her mind and headed upstairs to the kitchen.

April rummaged through the lower cupboard until she found Mama's box of cleaning rags and pulled out the whitest of them. She pulled a chair over to reach the top shelf and took down the hydrogen peroxide and an eyedropper. She filled a wash pan with hot soapy water then pulled an old work shirt over her clothes. These supplies were all ferried down to the basement and for the last trip she warmed a cup of chicken broth, left over from Mama's stew, and took it down as well.

Speaking softly to Duke, April gently cleaned away the rusty, dried blood and yellowed pus that stiffened the fur on his face. She placed drops of hydrogen peroxide in each open wound, holding Duke's head still with a damp towel. He lay quietly through the whole operation, never growling and never jerking away from her. When each abrasion had been cleaned and disinfected, she took the now cool broth and soaked a bit into a clean cloth that she squeezed onto his tongue. He swallowed, gagged, but swallowed again until all the broth had either been taken in or spilled.

When April turned away from her task, she saw Papa standing in the doorway watching her. He nodded, then brought over clean blankets and lifted Duke as April pulled away the dirty bedding and placed clean bedclothes down for him. They said good-bye, and turned off the light as they went up to breakfast. Duke lay clean and dry and home again.

* * *

Yuki hunkered down beside the brush pile that served as his shelter, deep in the middle of Bluehills. Pain sliced his head like an apple, digging at the core until he whimpered and closed his eyes, trying to sit without moving. Somewhere at the center of the pain an oily voice spoke to him, edging Yuki away from himself and into the bottomless pit of some putrid force he recognized but didn't understand. Yuki whimpered again, this time in fear. Since he had killed the man, he had carried this sickness with him. He couldn't out-run it, and he couldn't out-wait it.

The voice slipped along Yuki's desires and needs, twisting each drive, perverting each motivation to something foreign and unclean. Yuki dropped his head to his paws, rubbed the side of his muzzle and clawed at his skull. His keening cry set birds to flight and sent field mice into their tunnels. Yuki tried to stand but fell to his side, jaws snapping, mouth foaming, legs beating at the air. His body writhed with seizures until he fell still, deep in coma, while he battled for his very soul.

* * *

Alana rose from her bed for the first time in a week. A

blue moon reflected off the lake, breaking into a shimmer as the night's steady waves spilled on the sand. Alana lifted the hook on the screen door and stepped out onto the grass. She muffled the door's closing so she could be left alone for this important task. Slowly, still feeble from her illness, Alana made her way to the edge of the water and followed the sandy beach until she was beyond sight of her little cottage. She lowered herself wearily onto a smooth rock that jutted out over the small ripples on the shore.

Alana raised her face to the moon and studied the lines in its visage. Sorrowful eyes looked back at her and the moon's mouth was circled by marks of hard-set grief. Misfortune hung in the air she breathed, suffering weighed down her shoulders, and adversity lapped at her very feet. Alana's despair was so complete it had almost killed her, portents worse than any Alana had ever known had come to them, and Alana cursed the ignorance that left her helpless to protect her people and her land.

Still, Alana lived, and so did her hope. She reached into the water, scooping up the wet sand from its bottom, sifting through until she held several water-worn stones in her palm. She pressed these together in both hands and turned her face into the full moonlight. Alana hummed softly, searching for the sounds that she recalled her grandmother using so many years ago. Slowly, the chant grew, rising from her old woman's lips into the silvery night. The night wind lifted the prayer above her and scattered it over the surrounding hills and forest.

* * *

Don Whaley fought his way up from a long dark tunnel, the incline so steep he was exhausted by the climb, but far below lay snapping jaws that would eat him alive if he slipped back down. As he neared the top, he could almost see light beyond and he could hear voices murmuring around him. At last he seemed to reach the opening and he threw his arm over the rim and pulled himself out of the darkness. His eyes opened to a bright white room. Sunlight dazzled him as it fell in his eyes and reflected off the white enamel paint of the walls, the fresh white linens, and the white metal footboard of his bed. A white uniformed nurse leaned over him, removing a thermometer from under his tongue.

"You're back among the living! You gave us quite a scare. Never saw a man with a temperature so high live to survive. That was quite a nasty injury you got."

Whaley's eyes adjusted to the light and he pushed himself up on his elbows. The infirmary was full of other men from his work gang; some with casts on arms or legs, or bandages wrapped around their heads. One man was hidden behind a white curtain and he could see men's shoes and white trousers under the edge of the drape. The ward was strangely quiet, just a moan now and again, but no one was talking. The men looked dazed, haggard, and bruised. One turned to look at him, then another, until two long rows of patients stared only at him.

He could feel the poison inside him. The fever had subsided, but he could draw a line that followed the path of the poison from his festering sore to deep inside his chest, crawling toward his heart. He looked down to see his heart beating through the white sheet and when he looked up again at the nurse. Her face had changed.

She wore Cash's face, leering and gloating over him. His wide smile open to reveal sharp fangs and a long red tongue. Whaley began to scream and could not stop.

* * *

Carol Ann tossed in her sleep, unable to turn away as the dead man rolled over in his watery bier. Horrified, she watched his face slip away from the mud until the blue lips and livid forehead rose from the brackish water. Trembling, but frozen, Carol Ann watched as eyelids lined with green algae moved upward and opened, revealing red coals of seething desire beneath. From beneath those glowing eyes, a black tongue eased out of dead lips which pulled back to reveal gleaming white fangs. The face shifted as white fur ringed the eyes and mouth and Carol Ann stared helplessly into Yuki's lunging jaws.

Carol Ann kicked at the quilt and her scream rattled

the windows of the room, waking April from her hard-won sleep. April leapt from her bed, grabbed Carol Ann by the shoulders, shaking her and shouting at her to wake up. The commotion brought Mama and Papa from the next room and Papa lifted Carol Ann in his arms holding her tightly until she woke, sobbing and gasping for air.

* * *

Ray stooped to read the marks of the dog's trail in the fallen leaves on the muddy ground. The trail was cold but clearly marked in the damp soil. Ray didn't understand the dog's thinking though, he seemed to have gone in circles, sometimes staying in one spot long enough to push the leaves around and tear up the ground, then moving on. Ray pressed his gun closer to him, figuring that this dog must have rabies, and chilling at the thought of running into him face to face.

Ray heard a branch snap to his left and looked over to see George breaking through the brush. "This looks like the only clear path he left. I can see that other dogs have been here but their trails lead straight out of here and none of them look fresher than a couple of days ago. I think this dog's on his own now."

"Yup, but I don't think we really want to find him. This dog's gotta be loco or rabid or both. Look at how this trail wanders around like he's not in charge anymore!" Ray used a stick to poke at something sticky which held brown, wet leaves together. "He's foaming at the mouth, for sure."

George adjusted his orange hat, pulling the bill down more snugly on his head. "What do you reckon we should do?"

"Let's leave it to the Sheriff. He's got men out here lookin' for that other convict and they got more fire-power anyway." Ray stuffed his hands into the pockets of his pants and rocked back and forth on his heels, waiting for his big brother to tell him what they'd do.

"Okay, let's get outta here before those guys start shootin' at us." George broke open his gun and took out the shells. "Mama don't need nothin' else happenin'." The boys turned back toward the marsh and the path that would lead them home.

From beneath a nearby bush, blue eyes watched their progress as Yuki waited for the smell of oiled iron and gun powder to drift away in the distance, then crawled out of cover and made for his shelter deeper in the Bluehills woods.

CHAPTER 28

April rose early and rubbed frost from the window so she could see the big rusted thermometer on the pump house. The mercury stood at 10 degrees; summer's green lawn and garden were buried under a layer of white snow. Such cold in early November would surely mean a hard Michigan winter with a lot of wood to cut and stack for the furnace.

A soft noise pulled April from her winter thoughts and she turned to look at Carol Ann who tossed in her sleep and made sad little mewing sounds that chilled April more than the frost outside. Carol Ann had started back to school, though she made Papa drive her each day, still afraid to walk past the woods that were on the way. Yesterday, Carol Ann made a joke for April and sometimes she came down to help with Duke.

April pulled on old jeans and a sweater. She carried her shoes as she walked through the sleeping house and stopped in the kitchen to put them on before going out to the cellar stairs. She could hear Duke whining in the cellar; he always knew her footsteps on the old boards in the kitchen, just above his bed. April shushed him through the floor and hurried so she wouldn't wake anyone.

April threw back the storm doors and made her way down to the cellar. She could see Duke wandering across the floor to meet her. April winced when Duke collided with the wall beside the stairs. He was learning, but when he was excited, he still ran into the rough stonewalls. For weeks, Papa had carried Duke up the stairs several times a day to do his business outside, but April was teaching Duke to climb the stairs by himself. Soon, they would surprise Papa.

As Duke reached the foot of the steps, April cued him, "Climb." The dog raised his paw and lowered it carefully on the step in front of him and pulled up the other leg.

"Climb." They made their way one step at a time up the rough stone stairs until Duke was on level ground again. Immediately, he lifted his head to sniff the air and trotted off in the direction of some enticing scent. Occasionally he stumbled into a small hole or over some dish or tool left in the barnyard, but the freedom made him prance.

Duke stopped at the shady side of the barn to nose in the dirt. Digging more energetically, he quickly uncovered a bone and dropped to the cold ground to chew on it. April could see Duke was tired already. Gently she dislodged the dirty bone from his teeth and used it to lead him back to the cellar stairs. Going down was much harder. Holding one end of the dirty bone with one hand, while Duke held the other end in his mouth, April used her free hand to place each paw securely on the next lower step as they went down.

April led Duke back to his blankets where he settled with his bone, chewing contentedly. Duke had survived the shooting but had become a very old dog in the process.

* * *

Grandma Alana added wood to the fire and stirred up the coals until the smallest limbs began to snap and take the flame. She rose from the old stove, her face red from the heat, and looked over the cold children who stood at the door, pulling off their boots and mittens. The boys were getting big and April's red cheeks shone like apples. Alana shook her head, pushing back the black thoughts that perched above her heart, talons digging painfully into her. She smiled and called them into the kitchen where the cookie jar stood, filled just for them.

Grandpa Ezra pushed open the back door, coming in from chopping wood for the winter woodpile. He cuffed George and Ray playfully, made them measure up against him for height, and then reached over to tug at April's long black braids.

"You sure look like your Grandma, little one. You better watch out or you'll end up married to some old ornery cuss like me. Right woman?" Ezra shifted his eyes to Alana, and she made sure she nodded in agreement, before he went into the other room to turn on the radio.

Ezra sat before the tall wooden cabinet, turning knobs and dials looking for the news. Snatches of *Kisses Sweeter than Wine* brought a growl from the old man as he quickly changed the dial. He was satisfied when he heard a commentator extolling General McArthur and criticizing American policy in the Far East. He leaned his chair back against the wall, pulled off his boots and propped up his feet in front of the stove.

"You ain't gonna get no fish out there today." Grandpa Ezra pinched a bit of chewing tobacco in one hand and tucked it into the back of his mouth. "It's gettin' too damn cold to sit out on that ice anyway. Wind'll cut right through you. This is gonna be one hell of a winter."

Alana frowned as she wondered if the old man had any idea how true his words would be. She pulled the steaming kettle from the top of the pot bellied stove and poured the water into cups of cocoa, sugar, and salt. Stirring each one thoroughly, she looked at her grandchildren and prayed for each one, wishing their cups held some potent herb that could protect them all.

* * *

The November ice lay clear and gleaming in the cold air. April stood on the shore, hesitant to follow George and Ray onto the lake. Flashes of last winter's near drowning flew up before her eyes like startled birds.

"Come-on, it's at least three inches deep. You ain't gonna fall through this." George pulled the tackle box, its wooden runners skating across the smooth ice. Ray followed with the ice auger, chopping at the ice with its sharp blade to punctuate George's point.

April tugged on Duke's rope. "Okay, easy boy. It's going to be slippery." Slowly the two tagged behind the boys as they made their way out toward the center of the lake. April carried the wool blanket Grandma Alana insisted she take along for her and Duke to sit on while they watched the boys fish. April held the blanket in front of her figuring it would cushion her if she fell.

They moved out onto the ice, the light covering of frost making a crunching sound beneath their feet and the ice making loud cracking sounds as they moved away from shore. "It's just because it's so cold," George insisted when April threatened to turn back. "It's not going to break on us when it's as cold as this."

Still, the thought of going through the ice set April on edge and she moved slowly, stepping only where she could see the boys had safely tread. Duke synchronized his steps to hers and they soon found themselves some distance behind the boys who were headed for a prime fishing spot near the other side of the lake. April broke from their trail and cautiously made her way to the south shore where Uncle Ross lived.

April was startled out of her concentration by a grumbling 'Watch your step, young lady!' from Uncle Ross. His thin frame was covered in thick winter clothing from head to toe. He wore snow pants, a heavy army jacket, a scarf wrapped around his neck and face, and a red woolen cap with flaps pulled down over his ears.

"Damn poor fishing this time of the year. It's hardly worth it to sit out on this ice. Freezes up a man's joints something fierce and you don't even have a decent supper to show for it. You out here by yourself?" Uncle Ross frowned, waiting to scold her for foolishness.

"No, look -- George and Ray are over there. I'm just trying to catch up with them."

"Is this that damn blind dog? What good is he except to eat your food? I told your father he should've put him out of his misery when he first found him. Now look at you dragging him out on the ice. You be careful he don't eat the fish they bring up."

"Yes sir. He's a very well behaved dog, he won't make

any trouble."

"Well, you just see to it. I'm going over to Mr. Johnson's for some coffee and some of his berry pie. You pass my regards on to your mother and tell your father I need him to come down here and take me to the store in the next couple of days." Uncle Ross eyed her closely as she promised to pass on the message.

"Don't forget now, girl, and be careful of the damn fishing holes out here. I don't want to come back and fish you out of here." April continued to nod and then watched him move out across the icy plain to the camp side of the lake. She noticed even his steps were economical, short steady strides that came down compactly on the ice. She watched for a long time, reluctant to continue her careful trip across the ice.

The boys were already past the center of the lake and Duke's feet were probably freezing up from staying in one spot so long. April kept her eyes down as she moved, following her brothers' footprints and looking out for spots that might have been opened earlier by other fishermen. She glanced to the side and saw that Uncle Ross was already halfway to his destination. April patted Duke's side and kept moving until she was in the middle of the lake.

Suddenly, April was overtaken with panic, a phobic reaction to being over the deepest part of the lake with only clear ice holding her above the deadly, cold water. She wished she had not stayed so far behind, because now, there was no one near her to help. April wished she had not been so determined to come along, despite her fears of the ice and water. She was breathing too rapidly, the harsh winter air burning her lungs; her chin trembled and though she wanted to call out to her brothers, she couldn't make any sound at all. She was sure she would freeze to death before anyone noticed. Just, please God, don't let her fall through the ice again.

* * *

Yuki hunkered down at the edge of the woods watching the cottage door. A man lived there, different from the others he'd seen, a different color, a different smell about him. Yuki still didn't like the man smell but this one left food in a tin dish away from the house. At this time of the day, the food was still warm and Yuki could not resist its tantalizing odor. The winter was already hard, the summer pack had left him, gone back to their farms or found new ones. They wouldn't survive this kind of year anyway, but Yuki would, even if it meant coming so close to the disgusting man smell of houses and machines.

Yuki waited under cover of branches that lay low to the ground. The door opened, the screen door slammed to and the old man carried his dish across the open yard. "Come on fella, I got your lunch here. Oooee, it's good today! We got some biscuit leavings and bacon grease. You're going to like this. Here you go boy." The man set the dish near the trees and backed into the house, still coaxing the dog with warm rich tones.

Yuki waited until the door closed again and the man was inside. He saw the man come to the window and waited longer until he had stepped away. When Yuki could sense he was no longer watched, he inched out of the branches and made for the dish. It was good, the bacon grease making his mouth drool even before he reached the tin plate. Yuki ate heartily and licked the dish clean of every drop, then, skitterish, he ran back to the woods and on to the lakeshore.

Feeling satisfied, feeling happy, Yuki pranced along, running onto the ice, chasing his tail in circles and letting himself skid on the slick surface. He usually didn't like a clearing like this but today he felt good, a rare feeling that called for play and action. The lake had become deserted during the last few weeks; no one to hide from, his guard was down when the chunk of ice hit him and he turned to see the not nice man shouting at him, "Get away, bastard. Get out of here."

* * *

A noise caught April's attention and she turned toward Uncle Ross' side of the lake, maybe he was still closer than the boys. Maybe he would look back and she could make her frozen arms wave to him. But when April turned in his direction, she was shocked out of her own panic by a more frightening sight.

Uncle Ross was down on the ice, his arms lifted upward pushing away a great white dog that lunged repeatedly at his throat and stomach. April felt as if she had been punched hard, but a sound escaped her, a gasp of surprise, and her feet started to move again, as she rushed to help him. She was horrified, but moving, and started screaming for George and Ray as loudly as she could.

Duke's hair went up, he started to growl and bark fiercely as he ran beside April, matching his strides to hers. April could see that Uncle Ross' heavy clothing was nullifying the dog's attack but she could also see the scarf was coming undone, slipping away from Uncle Ross' face and neck. There wasn't much time.

April looked toward George and Ray; they had changed direction and were running toward Ross, faster than she and Duke could go. They had left the sled but George carried the ice auger. They shouted as they ran but April was too far from them to hear what they were saying. The boys reached Uncle Ross first, and swinging the heavy iron auger, George was able to push the dog off the bundled figure in the snow. George kept swinging as he fought off the dog even as Duke and April neared them.

Duke was growling ferociously now and jerked the rope from April's hands as he picked up speed and headed for the struggle. He ran as if he were sighted, following some scent or sixth sense of his own. Duke came between George and the white dog, teeth bared and mouth frothing. The white dog lunged but was stopped by Duke's teeth and the wickedly sharp end of the auger. Badly injured, the white dog yelped and retreated with Duke still coming at him.

April reached the group and jumped to grab the end of Duke's rope. She knew his bravado would not save him if the white dog returned the attack. April yanked hard on the rope to pull Duke back as Ray grabbed his tail and back legs to keep him from chasing the white dog. It was over, for now, but April's heart beat with a dread premonition that it was not over for always.

CHAPTER 29

*A*pril ran, terrified, through a black night and *numbing cold with the gray wolves howling behind her. The trees seemed to conspire with the pack, reaching bare black limbs down to catch at her clothes and to scratch at her face. She sucked in air until her lungs burned with cold fire and her legs shook with fatigue. She couldn't run any more; she slipped to the ground beside a downed log, lying in a tired heap with her head tucked down and her arms wrapped around her belly as the howling was almost upon her. The lead wolf, icy white in the light of the full moon bound over the log that protected her and before he tore into her, he put back his head to howl.*

April sat upright on her bed, throwing back her quilt, and still hearing the wolf howl in her dream. No, it wasn't the dream. It was Duke howling from the cellar. She took a deep breath to calm herself and made for the door. She would have to let him out before Papa got mad. She was wide-awake anyway and this wouldn't take long.

She bundled up in her boots and coat and made for the cellar storm doors. She drew back the latch to lift the doors and Duke was there at the top step, waiting to be let out. He was anxious to go; it seemed he hadn't totally recovered yet, but he was insistent on keeping his bed clean. Duke sauntered toward the barn, following his well-learned route, and April went back in the house for a few minutes.

April lay on the davenport, still dressed in her coat and boots, and closed her eyes while she tried to warm up. In minutes, she was asleep.

* * *

It was so bitterly cold the wind cut through Yuki's fur like a long-edged blade. The cold split his bones from the inside, making an agony of any movement. His ears were deafened by the silence, the nothingness. He wanted to howl, to break the dark night into pieces. It was lonely, so very lonely and cold, it burned in his heart like frost bite. The gash in his side pierced him with pain with each breath he took, the old injury in his head thundered with each heartbeat, and his wounded thoughts left him with no peace. The inner fire was stoked with hate and longing to pay back all the hurt he had been given. The night was deeply black but his eyes saw every shape and possibility ringed in shades of crimson and scarlet. Yuki waited for the one who had caused all this damage.

For ten days Yuki had waited at the edge of the woods where he could watch the farm and its people. He had waited without shelter and without food. He waited for a little girl with long black hair. He waited for her to come out alone, to walk the snowy paths that would bring her into his world. When she came, Yuki would end it all. He would rip her apart, he would drink her blood, he would eat her heart, steaming in its empty cavity. He would make her die and he would take her strength as she left.

* * *

April startled awake knowing immediately that she had fallen asleep and should not have. She wiped drool from her cheek and rubbed her eyes. It was still dark outside but when she checked the clock, it was already six in the morning. April winced, she had left Duke out for hours, she had to hurry. She stumbled to the back door, still groggy from sleep and stepped down from the back porch. The storm had built up incredibly. April could hardly see the barn in the thick snow that came at her. Already, the wind had pushed several new inches into drifts around the pump house. The cellar door, still open, had let snow pile up on the steps leading down. Papa would be mad but maybe Duke had come back on his own.

April scuttled down to the cellar, hurriedly whistling and calling out Duke's name, but there was no response. It was too dark in the lightless hole to see, but April knew Duke would have come to her without pausing. She returned to the top, threw the storm doors shut and started for the barn. Maybe Duke had settled in among the bales of hay and stayed warm all this time.

The wind battled her as April tried to reach the barn, making her weave against it to maintain a straight line. Snow was piled against the chicken coop door drifting it closed but the big doors stood open to the hayloft and granary. The remaining moonlight outlined the doorway, making the barn look like a great open mouth.

April stepped inside the doorway, hearing a tiny scuttling somewhere in the loft and seeing deep shadows within the dark barn shift against the roof. She didn't see Duke anywhere and when she whistled and called to him, there was no response. Swallowing her regret, she mounted the ladder to the loft and climbed up to the high window that would give her the best view of the south end of the farm.

The sky had lightened perceptibly, but perhaps, only because the moon had lost its clouds. April strained her eyes, scanning the backfields toward the creek, the marsh, and finally the forest. She thought she might have seen a black spot moving slowly across the frozen marsh toward the woods. Then she heard it, a low strong baying much like her dream and recognized it as Duke's hunting sound.

April scrambled awkwardly from the loft, her heavy rubber boots holding her back as she tried to slide down the bales quickly. She grabbed a short length of loose twine and tucked it into her pocket, buttoned the top and bottom buttons of her coat, and headed out into the wind once again.

The snow seemed to be coming thicker now than it had earlier. April was surprised how hard it was to see even the outhouse in the blizzard. She moved closer to the pasture fence and kept it within her vision as she slogged through the knee-deep drifts leading down to the creek. She heard Duke's excited howl once again, and knew he must be tracking something of great interest to him. April had to catch up to him, Duke would never be able to find his way back to the house again.

April wished she had put snow pants on before leaving the house. Now she was afraid to go back, knowing that she might lose track of Duke's position if she wasted any time, but the drifts were over her boots and her nightgown kept hiking up around her knees, leaving them open to the wet new snow. April brushed off her knees and hurriedly put her bare hands back into her coat pockets. Her knuckles had gone red almost as soon as she had left the barn and her ears and eyes were stinging from the cold as well. Mama was sure to give her a licking if she caught her out like this. 'It'll be your death!' Mama would say.

"Duke!" April shouted but the wind blew his name back into her face. A whistle would be worse she knew. There was nothing to do but to keep moving fast and hope to catch up to the dog, who couldn't be making very good time himself.

* * *

The trail was fresh and if Duke moved quickly, he would not lose it in the snow. It was the bad smell Duke had sensed for several days but they had never let him loose to hunt it until now. A strange odor, some of it dog, some of it man, all of it bad, hurting, death, decay, and evil. His world was black, completely and ultimately black but in his mind he saw a bad man laughing. A bad man laughing with his head thrown back and his large mouth open, showing the sharp white teeth of a big dog. Duke must protect the family. He must not lose the track. Nose pressed to the frozen ground, Duke moved forward, falling into holes, walking into bushes, slipping on icy puddles, he kept moving.

* * *

The plank bridge over the creek was icy and April had to slide slowly across, first one foot and then the other.

She almost cried for the delay but knew the ice on the swift running creek could not hold her either. It was this, or turn back and she was not going to lose Duke now that she was so close. The air carried another baying sound from his direction and April tried to shuffle a little faster, almost losing her balance on the board. She shuddered, her fear of the ice and water almost freezing her to the spot. She had to get Duke before he was hurt again.

April made it to the other side, grabbed a handful of tall brown weeds to help pull her up the steep bank and then only the frozen marsh lay before her. It stretched like a vast maze between her and the forest where she could now see Duke toiling his way up a wooded hillside. April knew she would have to jump from one grass tuft to another, or at least stay away from any large icy patches which might now be deep with collected rain water and snow melt. Closing her eyes, she made a brief prayer, then concentrating all her attention, she began the long strides from tuft to tuft, which would take her to the other side of the marsh.

Eyes on her feet, April looked no farther than the next three steps. She avoided bushes as she needed to and deliberately turned away from large open spaces. Occasionally she looked up to see if Duke might still be in her line of vision and brushed the snow off her now wet hair. April's cheeks felt like stone slabs laid over her bare skeleton and her teeth chattered loudly as she moved. She pushed her nightgown down with each blast of wind and rubbed her knees while her hands were down. April's toes had lost all feeling and she shook with uncontrollable shivers despite her constant movement. She chanted quietly to herself, "Find Duke, keep going."

April was surprised when she suddenly became aware of the solid ground in front of her. She had made it to the woods. The trees sheltered the ground so less snow had built up here. April could easily see Duke's shuffling path among the trees and knew she could really catch up now. She lifted her head to gauge the slope of the hill in front of her, and saw that the most direct route would also be the most trying. Still, she dared not to veer off, for fear the wind would soon obliterate the trail she had found.

Hitching her nightdress above her knees, she grabbed hold of a nearby sapling and pulled herself upward.

April had almost reached the top of the hill when the sound of snarling and growling rent the air. She was too late, Duke had met his quarry, whatever it was, just over the hill. The noise was so loud and violent April was sure he must have come upon a wolverine, though she had never really seen one. She tried to pull up a rock sticking up from the frozen ground but found it immovable. April snapped a fair-sized branch from a nearby oak, to use if she needed it, then she pushed on, over the hill.

* * *

The feeble farm dog had caught his scent and obligingly followed Yuki out into the woods, out of sight of the house. It would be easy now for Yuki to dispose of him once and for all. The black dog would soon taste blood and feel his insides freeze in the winter air. Yuki moved slowly, looking back to make sure the blind dog was still on the trail, once doubling back to give the path a fresher scent. Yuki salivated with excitement as he bound over the hill, waiting in ambush. Though Yuki was hungry and cold, the aspect of fresh blood invigorated him and he playfully pounced on twigs under the snow as he waited for his prey.

Yuki saw the black tail first, standing straight up, then saw the ears, close to the ground, nose still following the trail. He held back, biding his time, as the black dog came over the rise, then leaped from his position above the trail and directly onto the black dog's back. Yuki's teeth sank into the loose folds below the black dog's chin and Yuki threw back his head ripping into the dog's jugular. The black dog fell onto his back, breaking Yuki's hold on his skin, and lashed out with snapping jaws into Yuki's vulnerable underside. The dogs scratched out madly with their feet, which sent them spinning on the slippery snow like a discarded tire. The black dog snagged Yuki's ear, ripping it to streamers with a jerk of his head.

Yuki pulled himself to his feet and smashed into the black dog's stomach, biting and ripping, until finally, blood ruptured from a mortal wound. The black dog howled in agony but continued to snap at Yuki's head even as his lifeblood flowed. Yuki dove in to rip again, when he was knocked aside by a sudden blow from behind. Turning quickly, fangs ready, he saw the girl and dove directly at her.

* * *

Frozen at the brink of the hill, April gasped and clutched her club. It was the white wolf from her dream, tearing Duke apart in front of her. Just like her dream, she felt she could no longer move, could not protect him, until she heard Duke's agonizing cry and suddenly woke from her paralysis. April flew full speed down the hill to where the dogs were entangled in their bloody embrace. They took no notice of her, but continued to struggle in the snow. April raised the heavy stick above her head, waited for the white dog to be on top, then she swung with all her might, smashing the white dog and tossing him off of Duke.

The white dog turned, and frozen blue eyes, lit by the fire of fury, trapped April where she stood. She was in the nightmare again, only this time it was real and she knew she could not shake herself awake. The white dog pushed off from the ground, flying at her chest. April shoved outward with the oak club; the dog's weight crashed into it hard enough to jolt her arms into her shoulder sockets with the impact. He fell back, for only a second and threw himself at April again. She dropped the club, arms too numb to hold its weight. Her hands pulled across her face instinctively as the white cannon ball crushed into her.

His heavy feet knocked her to the snow and pressed the breath from her lungs. April fell back, crashing heavily onto the frozen ground. She punched out, fists digging into the dog's snarling jaws, pounding into his raging eyes. April crunched her chin to her chest, protecting her throat as the dog ripped at her winter coat, pulling buttons off as he tossed his head back. April stretched her arms back, reaching for a rock or stick or anything on the snowy ground that she could use as a weapon. Her hands came back empty; she arched her back to reach just a little farther exposing her neck. The dog's bloody white teeth tore her throat; great gouts of blood splattered them both, falling hotly in April's eyes and turning the dog's face to scarlet in front of her. She reached forward with both hands, circling his clenched teeth and pushing the jaws away as he continued to ravage her.

April's hands began to weaken, her arms fell back, and she felt her stomach release and chest muscles sag. She faded, ever so slowly, ever so warmly, she slipped away from the scene. April felt herself rise above the ground and look down to see a little girl, ravaged and mutilated, lying in a pool of blood, a white dog sporting a brilliant red mantle on his coat as he tore at her body, a wounded black dog convulsing in a broken heap nearby. April stood apart, suspended, feeling no cold, no fear, and no pain, but aware that another spirit was reaching for her.

Something foul, putrid, and perverse lanced out from the white dog, like a diseased white snake with jagged fangs seeking to devour April. She could smell its corruption, feel its gruesome intentions, and see its vicious expression, but she did not move. She hung above the earth, hypnotized by icy blue eyes that captured her with their venom.

A shadow fell over April and as the spirit snake's eyes released her, she looked up to see Crow Woman soaring above her. Her black wings were spread to full extension and her long black hair streamed behind her head as she dived at the white snake/dog, knife-like talons curled for her attack. Fangs and talons clashed, hisses and shrieks erupted in the swirling snow.

April faded out, her pale spirit blending into a blazing white light unlike any sun she had ever seen.

Part 7, 1995

"There shall no evil befall thee, neither shall any plague come nigh thy dwelling. For he shall give his angels charge over thee, to keep thee in all thy ways." -- Psalm 91:10-11

CHAPTER 30

Mike lashed the last of the furniture together inside the crowded truck. He pushed the doors tightly closed and secured the bolt and padlock that he hoped would hold the cargo securely as he crossed the country. He made one more check on the tow bar and the wiring that led from the truck to the brake lights of the car he pulled. He looked at the house one last time, tossed a stuffed duffel bag into the front seat, and swung up behind the wheel.

This was it. He just wished to God he'd been out of here a week sooner. He'd rushed through the paperwork and packing in order to leave this morning, but what had he been doing last week when his wife and daughter needed him? It had been like that for a lot of his Navy life, stationed somewhere out at sea when he should have been home with his family. Laurel was strong and Kaitlin was even tougher, but sometimes they depended on him. He couldn't think of a time when it had been worse than this. And where was he?

This was good-bye to an old life and hello to another. This was leaving the ocean behind and heading for the farm. This was being with his wife and daughter again, holding them tightly and planning a new future, no more ship duty for six months at a stretch, no more last-minute orders, no more shoe polishing or saluting. This was dry dock and retirement, freedom from routine, and no external discipline. His life was his own for the first time since he was twenty.

Slowly he nudged the truck around his cul-de-sac, waving good-bye to the neighbor who was out washing his car. He shuffled his way through the gears as he drove out of the subdivision, braking for dogs in the street and kids on bikes. He rolled down the window to catch the morning breeze, unfolded the map on the seat beside him and decided he'd stop in Spokane for lunch.

* * *

Sadie Johnson drove slowly; making the trip home much longer than it had ever been for Kaitlin. "Now listen to me child. I told your mama this and I'm going to tell you. I can stay and help you at the farm as long as you like. I was practically living there anyway before your grandma died and I'm getting a little homesick." She turned to give Kaitlin a smile and a quick wink. Kaitlin couldn't help but smile back.

"You don't have to worry about any wild animals either. The sheriff and the game warden have men out tracking that dog and when they find him they'll shoot on sight. They'll bring him in to be examined and make sure he didn't have rabies, or if he did, they'll start your mama on treatment right away so she doesn't have anything to worry about there. You'll never see that monster again." Sadie emphasized her words to be more convincing, but Kaitlin wondered if that were really so.

"Yesterday, I called an exterminator in and he has that whole barn laced with poison. There's not a rat out there who feels well enough to stir out of his corner today and they aren't going to be bothering you anymore either. I had him do the house too, just to be sure.

"Kaitlin, I just want you to know that I'm looking out for both of you just the way your grandma asked me to. I should have been there the other day too, and I'm going to stay with you two until your daddy gets here and settles things down."

Kaitlin wished her father could come sooner. She had talked to him yesterday and he needed only to get the house papers signed and the moving truck packed before he came. At least when he got here, they'd be together for good. Or would it be for bad? she wondered. What kind of life could they make on the farm if it was cursed?

"Sadie, you knew my grandmother a long time didn't you?"

"Honey, we were in diapers together and when my mother died your great-grandmother nearly raised us up together. My father and your great grandfather were good friends for all their years. You are talking to someone who could practically be your great aunt." Sadie Johnson patted Kaitlin's hand and Kaitlin wondered why she'd never married and had her own family.

"There is a curse on Bluehills Farm, isn't there?" Kaitlin said it softly, afraid to say it at all.

Sadie Johnson answered softly too. "Yes, child. I think there is something about that farm that has brought grief to your family all these years. But you ought to know, honey, that there is something about your family that just won't let them leave Bluehills either.

"Your Grandma Doe wanted to leave so bad, but after her mama died she came back to take care of the place. When she found her papa dead, I thought she'd sell out and find a home for Carol Ann but she told me she could never leave.

"For a while, things went real well too. We were all so happy when Doe got married and it seemed like there'd be a family on the place again and things would be good like they'd been in the old days. Doe had your mother and her twin brother the next year and she was so happy. Then, just a couple of months later, her husband Johnny was drowned over in the pond. Some people thought water moccasins had infested the place and that he probably choked because of the poison before he drowned."

"Wait Sadie, I didn't know about the pond, and I sure didn't know my mother had a twin, or a brother at all."

"Oh honey, I suppose Laurel doesn't want to talk about it much. Her brother was such a sweet soul, and he died so bad. He went off in the woods hiking with a friend of his and they were never seen again. Folks around here set out in search parties every weekend for months, just in hopes of bringing back the bodies, but we never found any trace of either boy. Some people believed they must have been kidnapped and taken away to live somewhere else, but Doe said she knew they were dead and had a memorial service for her boy even when the parents of the other boy wouldn't give up."

"I think Doe was trying to tell me something about my inheritance but she died before she told me everything. It wasn't money or anything like that. She said the women in our family had a special gift." Kaitlin felt shivers just saying this out loud and she waited for Sadie Johnson to give her that 'crazy woman' look.

Sadie Johnson kept her eyes on the road, going only forty-five on the freeway while the traffic rushed past her at seventy miles per hour. Her black hair had gone mostly white, emphasizing her weathered brown face and wizened expression. Her black eyes turned to Kaitlin, but she was nodding.

"I know your grandmother was something special and I know she guarded Bluehills Farm and she also protected us from it. She could tell the future sometimes, and when she told me to do a thing, I would do it. Some people wouldn't listen to her and they came to bad ends. That used to tear her up something fierce, when she'd try to warn someone and the thing would happen anyway. Sometimes she just had a general sense of disaster and that would upset her mightily because she didn't know exactly what would happen or who needed protection.

"Once, I was supposed to go to Detroit with a young man I liked very much. Donna Jean wouldn't let me. Almost tied me to my bed to keep me from going and my young man went anyway. He was killed in a terrible car accident. For a long time I wished I'd been killed too, but I learned to listen to what your grandmother said.

"Donna Jean's grandmother was different too. Folks around here would ask her for advice on when to plant and who to marry and things like that. She was a full-blooded Indian almost as dark as I am and she kept a lot of Indian ways. She walked in the forest all the time and I think she collected herbs and special stones and things. Sometimes she'd make all the kids drink some awful tonic or carry a special shell or some other thing she'd found. When I was a child I thought she was just a strange old lady, but I knew the grownups were a little afraid of her.

"Donna Jean wouldn't ever leave the farm, even though she couldn't keep it up right by herself. It was a beautiful place when we were children, the barn was new and bright red. Your great-grandfather kept cattle and pigs and chickens. His fields always brought in the biggest yields, and in winter he always got the best game. Donna Jean wouldn't remarry, said she wouldn't bring any more people to Bluehills than she had to. Then, when she took sick, she got it in her head that you and your mama needed to come home. There had to be a Bluehills' woman here, is what she was thinking."

Sadie Johnson was quiet and Kaitlin didn't know what else to ask. She knew it wasn't just any Bluehills' woman the farm demanded, it was her.

* * *

Stormy sat across from her, chowing down on Sadie's tuna salad sandwiches and a tall glass of milk. A few flesh-colored Band-Aids remained but she looked largely untouched by the ordeal that had put Kaitlin into the blue funk to end all depressions. Stormy had shoved her hat back on her head so that her high forehead was prominent above her green eyes. She even had freckles there, Kaitlin noticed.

"So what are we going to do? Any more ghost hunting on the agenda?" Stormy reached for a third sandwich, trying to fill out her lanky frame, Kaitlin guessed.

"Shh! Don't let Sadie hear you. She doesn't have to be told I'm kind of loony-tunes." Kaitlin shrugged, "I don't know what to do. We didn't find much in the house or the barn that would give us any clues. I've been to the cemetery and there isn't anything there. My great aunt is certifiably crazy you know. Maybe we should have thought this through before we took the advice of an institutionalized, senile, old woman."

"Sure Kaitlin, and this curse, or whatever, is probably what drove her crazy. I sure don't want to have to go uptown to that place just to visit you on the weekends. I think some part of her is perfectly sane and that's the part that sent us after April. How could you think anything else after what happened?" Stormy talked around her sandwich, spitting a little onto the table as she spoke, but her exaggerated clumsiness didn't make Kaitlin smile.

"You know, Kaitlin, there's still the woods. Something weird always happens when we go out there. April's got to be in the woods."

"Right, Stormy, and some rabid dog is out there too. I'm sure Sadie is going to pack us a picnic lunch and say, 'Have a good time girls, be back in time for supper'."

"Kaitlin, I wouldn't exactly announce it. Wait 'till Sadie takes her nap, then we go for a little bike ride; maybe try for some off-road racing."

"God, Stormy! And what's going to come after us this time? Maybe snakes or rabid squirrels or maybe the birds will think we're doing another Hitchcock film. I'm not going out there. I'm going to wait until my mother is doing better and my father is here to go with me."

"Okay, okay. We'll go later. Just don't wimp out on me, Kaitlin. "

* * *

Carol Ann's chair was parked too close to the wide screen television, the lurid colors of the game show wheel washing over her as the hostess spun its kaleidoscope of numbers. The volume was high, so her mumbling rhymes were not noticeable to the elderly man who sat on the couch or the frail young woman propped with her portable oxygen in the recliner near him. Carol Ann recited the number over and over so she wouldn't forget.

A nurse popped her head through the recreation room door, smiled at the patients and was gone again. She just wanted to make sure they were all right, but she had papers to file and reports to type. Most of the staff were busy straightening up for the late afternoon visitors they received each day.

Carol Ann released her grasp on the worn stuffed dog in her lap. Her hands dropped down to the brakes that held the wheels of her chair in place. With an unusual degree of function, she swiftly released the levers and gripped the tread. A quick jerk with both hands took her backward away from the screen. She turned her head, surveying the room; suddenly clever and clear-headed, she directed the chair toward the wide doorway.

The hallway was empty; most of the residents were napping and attendants were washing down basins and counters, emptying bedpans and spraying air fresheners. Carol Ann heard two women laughing at the front desk as they loaded a cart with fresh flowers sent over from the funeral home. Some of the plants would go to the foyer and the dining room, and one would head for one of the women's car trunk and be taken to her mother-in-law as a birthday gift. Carol Ann gave her wheels an extra push to speed past their doorway before they could turn and find her there.

"Don't forget the number. Don't forget the number." Carol Ann repeated the digits in her singsong voice.

Her arms began to ache and she slowed before she reached the end of the hall. An attendant came out of one of the rooms and she froze, staring at the wall. He patted her shoulder and went on, assuming someone else was moving her through the corridors. When he disappeared into another room, Carol Ann went back to her work, her wrists trembling from their exceptional effort and her lips moving as she repeated the number over and over again.

The nurse's office was empty, but she would have to be fast, before the woman returned. Carol Ann gathered the strength in her arms for one more turn and entered the office. She reached behind her and swung the door closed.

The phone sat squat and black at the edge of the desk. Its earpiece was strangely shaped and curved to rest against your shoulder. When Carol Ann had last used a phone, the receiver had been shaped like an ice cream cone and you talked into another piece, loudly, so your party could hear you. She reached for the phone and raised it to her ear.

A loud hum buzzed at her from the end she held against her ear. She'd seen other people do this before, though she couldn't remember when that might have been. It was all jumbled in a doughy mix of images over many years. She fit her thick hand over the keypad and hesitated while she said the list of numbers to herself again. Slowly, she pressed each key, saying the number out loud, and releasing her breath only when she'd reached the end.

She heard the rumbling ring through the phone and smiled at the image of calling her first boy friend. She'd been beet red at her end of the line but he seemed to smile right through the wires and she'd been glad she'd done it, even though Mama and Papa had kept her in her room for a week afterwards. The answering voice fractured the old memory and she suddenly panicked as she forgot what she was supposed to say.

"Hello. Hello. Is someone there?" It was April, she thought; no, the other girl.

"Hello. What number are you calling?"

Carol Ann liked the sweet voice, but something nagged her to speak. "April's waiting. You're afraid of the wrong one. April's waiting for you. Wear the amulet."

Carol Ann's voice cracked as the words came out and as soon as she'd said them she was confused again. Where was she? She dropped the phone and pushed away from the desk with her weak legs.

A tinny voice came from the black receiver where it dangled from its curly cord against the side of the desk. "Who is this? What did you say?"

Carol Ann was frightened by the voice and backed into the door jamming it tightly behind her. Still the little voice spoke to her from the desk. "Are you there?"

She pressed against the door and now she heard the doorknob rattle as someone tried to push it open. She was caught, she was afraid, she'd been bad. Carol Ann clutched the stuffed dog and picked at its eyes, "Eenie, meenie, minie, moe."

A beeping came from the phone and the noise at the door grew louder. "Arthur, give me some help down here, this door's stuck."

Carol Ann rolled forward, now frightened by the ruckus at the door. She squeezed her eyes tightly closed and pulled at the dog's ears and nose, "Eenie, meenie, minie, moe."

Betty Fry

* * *

Kaitlin dropped the phone back into its cradle and tried to rub the goose bumps out of her arms. She wished she had gone into town with Sadie Johnson; the house was so spooky when she was alone, and now this. She shivered and moved to the rocking chair by the front window where the late afternoon sun was warming a pool of carpet. She wished someone else were home. It felt like a waking dream, but she knew it was real. She rocked back and forth in the chair, hugging herself and holding back impossible thoughts.

Suddenly, the doorknocker banged, echoing through the empty house and jerking her to her feet. She inched her way to the window, lifting the lace curtains at their edge, feeling for all the world like the stupid girl in the cheap horror movie who always walks into trouble. She felt she should hide, but it was getting clearer all the time that there was no place to hide.

She saw the back of someone's jeans and white T-shirt, but was too slow to turn away when his head swung toward her. She let out her breath in a great whoosh of relief when she saw it was Carson. He smiled and waved. Her heart beat faster and lighter and she almost forgot the awful message on the phone.

She hurried to open the door and smiled for the first time in days. His face was red and sweaty from pumping his bike up the long driveway. He wiped his forehead on his shirtsleeve, then looked up to see Kaitlin smiling at him from the front door.

"Hey, I'm sorry, I didn't mean to scare you. I just thought I'd see how things were going. You missed the last week of school, so I cleaned out your desk for you." Carson reached around to a gym bag he'd dropped at his feet. "I just sort of piled all your stuff in here. I didn't read your notes or anything."

Carson's face was redder now, as he held the bag out to her.

"God, I'm really glad you're here. It's been a really weird afternoon." Carson gave her a puzzled look and Kaitlin tried to explain. "I just got a crank phone call or something.

"There's been a lot on my mind lately; you know. I haven't even thought about school. There's been such strange stuff happening around here, it's like the rest of the world isn't real anymore." Kaitlin bit her tongue, knowing she really sounded stupid.

Carson shuffled into the house, letting the screen door slam too hard. "I'm real sorry about your grandmother, and I heard what happened to your mother too. I guess you must have been pretty scared, huh?" He followed Kaitlin toward the kitchen where he unloaded the gym bag onto the kitchen table.

"I didn't think you'd ever want to come back here after, . . . you know." Kaitlin remembered how frightened they'd been at the pond when he'd almost drowned. She was embarrassed for dredging up that day again, and pulled two Vernor's from the refrigerator to hide her blush. When she thought she was composed, she turned to set them on the table next to the pile of notebooks and pencils.

"Well, I didn't let my Ma know. She believes this place is jinxed or something." Carson stuttered, and quickly twisted off the bottle top.

"I think she's right. Sometimes I feel like I'm in the middle of a really bad nightmare where all my family and friends are in danger but I'm frozen and can't do anything about it. Have you ever had one of those dreams?"

Carson nodded. "Sure seems like a lot of bad stuff happens around here. I used to think the woods were haunted. I don't know if that's because my Ma told me scary stories about it or because it really does give me the chills when I get close enough. I don't ever go back there, but sometimes even when I'm on my bike, it feels like things are watching. "

"You probably shouldn't have biked out here. They haven't found that dog yet. I wouldn't want to see you get hurt." Kaitlin's face warmed, but she looked straight at Carson and he smiled at her.

"Yeah, it's getting late too. Ma's probably got supper on the table and the dogs out looking for me. I better get going." Carson made his way down the porch steps to his bike, Kaitlin just a step behind him. "You think maybe we could go roller skating or something next weekend. If my Ma says she'll take us?"

Kaitlin nodded, watched Carson ride down the long driveway, and waved to him when he turned to look back. He was silhouetted by the sun as he headed down the dirt road toward his house. Kaitlin rubbed the worry stone in her pocket, hoping he would be okay.

* * *

Mike pulled off I-90 at the Billings exit. He'd traveled over 700 miles that day and would have kept going, but he knew he'd have a hard time finding a room between Billings and Bismark, once it got dark. He also knew he was running on adrenaline. He'd been up almost all the night before packing the truck so he could leave as soon as possible. He'd seen enough white crosses along Montana highways to be leery of driving tired.

Mike checked his watch and guessed it was already after eight o'clock Eastern Time. He wanted to see how Laurel was doing before he turned in for the night. Up ahead, a Super 8 Motel sign brightened a large parking lot that looked like it would let a truck the size of his turn around, even with an amateur at the wheel. He caught the word vacancy in the lobby window just as he pulled up.

The room smelled of stale tobacco but the air conditioner came on strong and the television had a passable picture on four stations. He sat on the hard mattress, holding the brown hotel phone to his ear, waiting for someone to pick up on the other end.

"Honey, it's Dad. I'm on my way, Pumpkin. I've already made it half way through Montana."

"Oh, Dad, I'm so glad you're coming. You don't know how much we've missed you. Mom's going to be so happy to see you."

"How's your Mom doing, Baby?"

"The doctor says she's going to be fine, but he wants her to stay in the hospital a little longer. They haven't found the dog that attacked her, so they'll probably start shots before they let her go home. Just in case, you know."

"Yeah, I know. How are you, Kaitlin?"

"Sadie Johnson's staying with me so I'll be all right. She likes to fuss over me. I think she's been pretty lonely with Doe gone. A couple of my friends came over today. I'll be fine. Just get yourself home to us Dad. It's awful hard without you."

"You tell Mom I love her very much. It'll take me another two full days of driving. You just take care of yourself 'till I can get there to take care of you. I love you Pumpkin."

"I love you, Dad. Drive carefully, Dad. We need you so much!"

"Good-night, Baby."

Mike hung up the phone, shaking his head. Damn it, he should be there now with Laurel in the hospital and Kaitlin in that spooky old house. Just a kid. Well, the best he could do was to push it and get there the day after tomorrow if everything went all right. Mike gathered up his wallet and keys and left to find something to eat, and maybe a beer. He needed to keep up his strength.

* * *

Yuki hunkered in the trees that closed in on the road, making the twilight darker here. The boy who had sped past him on the bike earlier, sat in the dirt at the side of road. Yuki smelled oily metal from the broken bike chain and the salty smell of the sweaty boy. It had been too long since he had eaten. The drought had done in most of the small game earlier in the spring and he'd had to lay low the past few days while the woods were full of men smelling of gun powder and polished steel. Yuki's stomach growled with hunger, and his hindquarter throbbed where the pitchfork had skewered him. He was feverish with infection, feverish with desire. Yuki crept closer to the boy, the inner voice hot with urgency, but his own instincts warning him to be careful.

The boy was big and healthy and Yuki could sense the nervousness coming off him. The boy looked up from his work frequently, checking the trees in front and behind him, then back to the chain, trying to hook the broken links together again.

Yuki kept himself as flat as possible, ears back, and head down. He inched forward, pushing the pain back silently, stalking the boy, careful not to give himself away. He'd have to surprise the boy if he were to make this one. Yuki held back, wanting to whine in anticipation, wanting to snatch at his prey. First one foot, then another, slipping under the low hanging branches, disturbing the dusty sand without a sound. Flies landed on his swollen hindquarter, but he didn't snap at them; dust crept into his flared nostrils but he kept from sneezing; saliva pooled on his tongue but he didn't even swallow.

The boy stood, picking up the bike and pushing it along the gravel. Yuki moved sleekly, the slightest limp from one back leg, keeping up, but not alerting his prey. Yuki circled back, deeper into the shadows and calculated the boy's speed, guessing where he might jump from the roadside bank and onto the boy's back. Yuki slipped through the trees, running lightly now, to a spot ahead of the boy where the woods were especially dense and dark. He froze there, hind legs tensed and hurting, like springs wound for the leap. In just a second, he would attack.

The car's horn blasted, startling Yuki from his position. He flailed back on the sore leg and dropped to his side. The car's engine roared toward them, dust ballooning out behind. The car pulled over between Yuki and his prey, a woman yelling from the window.

"Good Lord, where have you been? We've already eaten and finished the chores. Your father is fit to be tied. You'll be lucky if he doesn't ground you for this."

"Look, Ma! My chain broke, I couldn't get home any faster."

Yuki watched the boy load his bike into the car's trunk and climb into the back seat. Yuki backed away, a low growl rising from his chest. He retreated, frustrated and hungry.

CHAPTER 31

Donald Whaley sailed the winds of oblivion, totally immersed in the anesthetic of alcohol. He stumbled and drooled, soiled himself, and staggered on, knowing only one goal, to walk away from the ones he loved. He circled the county on two-lane blacktops and shaded gravel roads and every time his consciousness emerged enough to find himself too close to home, he turned about-face and directed himself elsewhere.

The rot of the earth was working on him, wearing him to ruined bone and stretched skin. His feet stank with fungal infection, his unshaved beard was sticky with wine and vomit, and the pulsing, protruding nest of gangrene in his shoulder soaked through his flimsy jacket and wasted the little substance he had left inside.

All the booze he drank did little to still the voice that brayed and wheedled inside him. The voice that lusted for the lives of his small family could be quieted only by his own hoarse whispers and protests. As long as he could stand, he walked; as long as he could navigate, he led himself away from them, but his money was almost gone, his voice was nearly vanished, and the reserve that kept him moving was almost exhausted.

* * *

Kaitlin talked to her Mom on the phone before she

got ready for bed. Laurel sounded groggy from her medication and Kaitlin just let her know Dad was on his way, then told her to get to sleep. Sadie Johnson snored in one of the empty bedrooms and Jay Leno was over before Kaitlin decided to turn off the light and give sleep a try. She lay awake a long time in the dark room, listening for scuttling in the walls or howling in the woods but nothing came to her except the lulling sound of crickets in the grass. At some point, she passed from waking to sleeping, without her knowledge.

The grass was high as she trampled through the dry field nearing the blackened edge of the railroad bed. The old ties smelled of creosote and cinders and the gravel bed reflected the hot noonday sun. The rails hummed softly with some far-off travel as Kaitlin followed the roadbed toward an intersection with a two-lane blacktop road. She could see there was no warning signal at the intersection and she could hear the vibrations of the iron rails increase ever so slightly in volume. Up ahead, a couple in a bright blue convertible pulled onto the tracks just as the car's engine stalled out. A young man pumped the accelerator without success. He stepped out of the car, wiping his forehead in the summer heat, kicking at the tires in frustration.

Kaitlin couldn't deny the hum in the rails any longer. She knew that soon she'd hear the train's wheels through the air as well. She stepped off the ties, moving down a mound of gravel to be far enough off the tracks that she wouldn't be hit by any flying sparks or rocks that might get kicked up when the train went by.

At the intersection, the car still sat on the tracks. The girl, long-bodied and thin moved over to the driver's side, turning the key while the young man pushed from behind.

Kaitlin could distinctly hear the train now, its whistle blowing at some intersection a half-mile back or so. She waved and yelled at the couple trying to get their attention but they were shouting at each other, angry with the car's lack of cooperation.

Kaitlin could hear the train's wheels pounding clearly now, less than a minute away. She screamed with all her might as she ran toward the couple. The girl behind the wheel pulled off her beat-up, felt hat and turned her freckled face toward Kaitlin.

Kaitlin drove her feet into the ground, gasping with effort, trying to get to the couple in time, but now she could feel the steamy heat of the train engine as it bore down on her.

Screaming, Kaitlin waved at the lanky, boyish girl who still held the wheel as the young man behind her pushed at the convertible's back end, trying to get the tires to budge off the tracks. For the briefest second, both the girl and the boy turned, then they froze, as the train bore down on them, its whistle blowing urgently.

Iron shredded the flimsy steel panels of the car, tossed the girl and the boy off to both sides in front of it. Brakes wailed and metal screamed as the car was dragged along the rails.

A spray of blood watered the cinders and gravel, and over it all, Kaitlin could hear herself raging, "No!"

Her own scream woke her, in a cold sweat, blankets tossed to the end of the bed, knees shaking, and stomach retching. Kaitlin dropped to the floor, pulled the wastebasket to her chest and heaved until she couldn't bring up anything more.

From the door Kaitlin heard Sadie Johnson, "Good Lord, child. You're sicker than a dog. Let me help you."

Kaitlin clung to Sadie Johnson, squeezing her arms hard enough to bruise them. "It's Stormy, I've got to help Stormy."

Sadie Johnson grasped the cross she wore on a chain around her neck and silently prayed a desperate plea.

* * *

The iron rails sang to him like a hymn he'd heard in church when he was a boy. Whaley sang along until the words slipped away from his hazy grasp. "Rock of Ages, cleft for me, let me hide myself in thee. Let the water and the blood from thy wound a healing flood." He gagged as bile rose in his throat and bit off the tune, spitting into the steep grading that led up to the tracks. He fell to his knees against the sandy slope but pushed himself up and used his hands to dig into the loose dirt to give himself enough purchase to climb the hillside.

He smiled in the early morning light as red glints flickered from the polished rails. He'd always loved the railroad. He would've lived and died on the railroad if things had worked out differently. Well maybe he could have half his original bargain after all. He crawled forward until his body draped over both sides of the track. Quite a speed bump he'd make. He laughed for the first time in days. He laughed with a heart unfettered, his misery finally abandoned.

* * *

Sadie Johnson wouldn't let her call Stormy until after five the next morning, even though they both sat awake in their rooms until the sun came up. Stormy's mother said Stormy had spent the night with her cousins in Napoleon and the oldest boy would be driving her back this morning. Kaitlin got the phone number but she'd already missed Stormy who had gone out with her cousin to help him deliver newspapers. Kaitlin was almost crying, and said it was an awful emergency; couldn't they find her and fetch her home? But Stormy's relatives had just the one car running and couldn't be convinced the matter wouldn't wait another hour.

Sadie Johnson, who had sat calmly at Kaitlin's side through the whole conversation, quietly took the phone and asked directions to their house. She drew out a map as she listened and Kaitlin bit her lip as Sadie drew a line with cross hatches where the country highway crossed the train tracks.

Sadie looked up at Kaitlin with frightened eyes then hurried to find her car keys. "Come on child, we don't have all day."

Kaitlin had never seen Sadie Johnson drive so fast. In fact, she'd never seen her father drive so fast. Thankfully, it was early and the roads were clear of traffic. Sadie jerked the wheel to swing them off the dirt road and onto the asphalt, leaving a long-hanging cloud of white dust behind them marking their trail from the house. The roads to Napoleon were mostly back roads, winding around ponds and marshes, drop-offs marked with thick wooden posts, and little clear distance for passing, but

Sadie Johnson drove like a 'bat out of Hell' as she kept repeating. Her hands gripped the wheel tightly, her head was tucked down, and her feet pressed the 'pedal to the metal'. Kaitlin wished for a helmet but mostly pleaded with God to get them there in time.

They were within two miles of the cousin's house when the road swung into a parallel with the railroad tracks. At almost the same instant, the train's whistle drew up on them. Sadie Johnson didn't pause for a second, forcing every ounce of power out of the old car, but slowly the iron engine overtook them and pulled ahead. Still Sadie kept the car flying, even with tears running down her face.

* * *

The whistle woke him from his first happy dream, and he smiled knowing it would not be long. He relaxed and rested against the cold rails, happy until the car horn wrenched him from his joy.

He raised his head and there they were, at a crossing no more than fifty yards away. A car on the tracks and two people shouting at him, one with long red braids and an old battered hat. Behind them the blue steel of a hammer-headed locomotive hurtled down the track, its whistle screaming and an anguished man swearing and waving from the engine.

Whaley broke from the paralysis that had frozen him in his stance. He ran toward the children, shouting and warning them off the tracks. Barely able to propel himself, he raced the train, gesturing and begging them to get out of the car. He saw the boy jump out behind the car and lean into the bumper, trying to push it off the tracks. He was close enough to watch Stormy's panicked struggle with the car's starter and the boy's confused expression as his eyes jumped from Whaley, to the girl, to the train. The boy shouted angry words at her and then the train was on them.

Stormy looked into the engine hurtling at them, then turned to Whaley. He saw the way her braids swung in the morning light and the way her eyes glinted with fear as she mouthed, "Poppy!"

* * *

Kaitlin could see the railroad crossing now, and the bright blue car on its tracks. She rolled down her window and screamed into the wind, matching the roaring blast of the train's warning signal. Kaitlin could see the alarm in the crewman's face as he jerked the whistle's rope in long deep pulls. She could hear the train brakes screeching and tearing at the rails and could feel sparks from the train's wheels flying up to sting her arms. Still, the train passed their car. Within the space of time it takes to drag breath through a burned and wasted throat, Kaitlin could hear the shearing of metal against metal, just as she had in her dream.

Kaitlin was out of the car before the train crew could rush forward to the mangled rubble of bright blue metal. Desperately, she looked for anything resembling a human hand, a scrap of clothing, or a lock of hair; but the twisted metal was drenched in gasoline fumes that seared her eyes and lungs and left wavery images of torn rubber and shattered glass.

Someone strong-armed Kaitlin away from the shredded pile of metal, just before an explosion rocked the torn remains, scattering bits and pieces of deadly shrapnel into the dry grass and rough gravel of the roadbed. Flames engulfed the bulk of the wretched vehicle, filling the air with the stench of burning fuel, synthetics, and flesh. Kaitlin collapsed at the siding, clutching the charred remnants of the old felt hat she had grasped just as she had been torn away from the wreckage. For the first time in her life, she felt empty; absolutely, stone-cold devoid of any feeling.

* * *

Whaley picked rocks out of his face and fingered the torn fabric of his pants, trying to make the shredded material stay in its proper place, covering the gash in his leg. He pushed himself up to his knees and dragged himself away from the tracks into the high grass. His back sagged like an empty paper bag pushed along by the wind. He scuttled into the wild oats that grew thickly in the neglected field and curled into a tight curve, his knees drawn up to his chest, his head bent over them and his hands crossed tightly against his shins. He lay with his festering shoulder open to the wind, and his ragged coat stretched wetly over the swollen flesh.

Somewhere inside, Whaley's soul crawled into its own nest, hunched like a toad hibernating in a thick insulating mud of dissociation. When he was safely hidden there, his body rose and shuffled toward the road, searching his pockets for a bottle of cheap wine. He belched and farted and talked to himself in a long and rhythmic litany of complaints. His mumbling husk walked on like some kind of golem fashioned of rags and sticks; a moving scarecrow draped over an empty cage of wire and straw.

CHAPTER 32

Mike eased the truck off the road, fighting the steering wheel. The truck had become several tons of dead weight in his hands as soon as the engine had given its last gasp and stalled out on him. His stomach churned as hot acid filled it. Why the hell had he decided on this damn shortcut? He'd thought he'd save a hour on this God-forsaken two-laner and now here he was, eating dust, with a dead truck, somewhere outside of Tamarack, Minnesota.

He made his way around to the hood, searched for the latch, then pounded his fist on the steaming metal when he couldn't find the catch. "Shit!" He pushed his baseball cap back on his head and told himself to calm down. He slipped his fingers under the hood again, fumbling in the tight space to find the release. Clumsily, his thick fingers nudged dirty metal and he felt the catch give way. Using both hands, he raised the hood, stepped up on the bumper and surveyed the damage.

Hot steam rose from the oily machine, but not near the radiator where he expected it. He prodded at belts and wheels but no obviously broken parts or gaps stood out. Damn stupid thing for a paper-pusher to be doing anyway. He didn't know enough about trucks to figure out what was wrong except the certainty he'd be beside the road a long time before he'd find a tow truck that could get the damn thing into a town. He knew it would be longer than that to get parts out from Duluth to fix the damn thing. Probably next to impossible to just trade into another truck out in these boondocks.

Mike jumped down from the bumper, leaving the hood up to attract help. He moved around to the passenger side, heaving the front tire a good swift kick, and felt better for it. He reached in for a can from the six-pack of coke he'd picked up, wondered how his acid stomach would appreciate the chaser, and looked around for a piece of shade where he could wait, stupid and helpless.

* * *

Clouds obscured the moon, making his nocturnal hunt all the easier. When traffic was virtually nil on the dirt roads and even the nearby freeway had slowed to only an occasional set of head lamps, he felt most free, using the clear smooth car paths to take him quickly from one destination to another. Though he never lost his repulsion for all things smelling of man, some inner fascination and urging dragged him from one settlement to another looking for another opportunity to snatch a precious bit of life away. The longing grew loud when hungry and quieted only when Yuki complied with its strange demands.

He had roamed a long way tonight but had found pleasant sights to entertain him, a man beating the dog who had barked a warning only minutes before, a sleepless child staring out her window at the empty road, and a woman weeping inside her house in the dark. He did not understand any of these things but inside of him the voice enjoyed them and whispered happy thoughts into Yuki's pounding head as he padded from one residence to another.

His tail wagged as he trotted along the road, a warm squirrel filling his belly. He smelled the man coming before he heard the noise of the tramp's clumsy steps in the soft dirt. The unwashed sweat of days on the road, the acrid belch of cheap wine and no food, and the sick decay of rotting flesh rolled toward him on the early morning breeze. An inner whisper rose from its slumber, sending anticipation through Yuki.

A slurring monologue kept pace with the stumbling feet, "Damn birds peckin' my eyes out of my head, damn red ants eatin' the skin between my toes, damn mosquitoes sucking me dry, damn fleas chewin' my hide. Whoa, damn rocks tearin' up my feet, damn wine burnin' my gut, damn cancer eatin' my bones, damn slime climbin' up my legs, damn dust cloggin' my lungs, damn it to hell!" The shambling bum fell on his rear at the side of the road, looked both ways, and swung back a second time when his eyes made out the great white wolf-like creature in front of him.

"Jesus Christ! What the damn hell are you?"

Yuki lowered his head at the man's shouting and growled his warning, baring yellowed fangs and glowering, icy, blue eyes. Though Yuki skittered when the man swung his arms out in his direction, the voice inside him was laughing with delight at the prospect of playing with the old drunk. Yuki found himself circling closer until he could nip at the old man's rancid pant leg. A jerk on the cuff brought a swift kick from the man, but Yuki was faster, leaping away from the tardy foot.

"Get the hell out of here dog!" The raggedy man felt clumsily around for a rock to throw and came up with only a brittle dead tree limb that fell apart as he pulled it toward him. "Go on! Get away!"

Yuki was intoxicated with the game, something cheering him on as he moved in close behind the man where he snatched at the thin elbow of the man's torn jacket. Using his front feet for pulling power, Yuki tugged at the jacket until both the man's arms were pinned behind him as he tried to shrug out of the worn material. Yuki let up on the jacket sleeve and leapt over the man's outstretched legs to lunge in at his naked belly. A tooth caught at the soft skin of the man's unprotected waistline and loosened a taste of blood and flesh that inflamed his longing even more.

Now Yuki was in a fever, dancing around the downed man, lunging into the belly, biting at the exposed neck, cutting into his buttocks. The man struggled to pull his arms from the jacket, to cover his soft underside and to protect his jugular, all the time shouting in unholy terror, "Damn devil dog, get off me! Go back to Hell, demon!"

Yuki pulled back when the laughing inside stopped. Now there was just desire, pure and lustful, an uncontrollable need to take the man's life. Yuki stopped seeing the ragged drunk and saw only flesh, heard only blood pulsing, and felt only the fresh wind of life coming from the heaving pile in front of him. With a great howl, Yuki threw himself on the man, knocking him flat and engaging his scrawny neck in a lethal vise of jaws and teeth.

An incoherent scream ripped the early morning light, and the dog, splashed with jets of crimson, inhaled the scream as if he were devouring a banquet. The old man shuddered, his legs kicking up puffs of dust on the road, then lay still. Yuki stepped back, appalled by the stench, but something inside directed him in dragging the body into the weedy ditch at the side of the road. The sun was rising as Yuki left the road and made for his den.

* * *

The church was filled to capacity with both families, young friends, and curiosity-seekers who had come to see the two closed coffins with their blue and pink flower shawls. A smiling school portrait of Stormy and another of her cousin stood on easels before the altar. An unbroken line of solemn mourners moved by to pay their respects as the stony-eyed parents sat on either side of the wide aisle and simply endured.

Kaitlin sat beside her mother whose arm was protected by a thick sling. Laurel had been brought directly from the hospital to the church and she slumped in the pew, dopey with painkillers and weak from blood loss. She had argued with the doctors to be released in order to be with Kaitlin during the funeral. Kaitlin held Laurel's good hand, squeezing it from time to time, just to be sure her mother was really alive and beside her.

Sadie Johnson sat on the other side of Laurel, hands twisting a white lace handkerchief embroidered in violet. Kaitlin could hear Sadie's deep sighs and her mother's tiny moans when she shifted in her seat and the pain surprised her with its sharp pinch, despite the medication. Kaitlin felt blank, dried out, drained of her tears and sedated with valium. She watched the formal blessings and the children's choir as if from far away, behind a thick glass that padded her against the reality and pain of it all. When the service was ended, Kaitlin could not bear to look at Stormy's mother, black mascara smearing the woman's face as she led her weeping family out of the church.

Kaitlin rose with the last song and felt a gentle tapping on her shoulder. She turned to look at the person beside her, but it was an old lady she didn't recognize, intent on the hymnbook. Something nagged Kaitlin's eyes up to the balcony where she and Stormy had shared Sunday communions of their own. Someone was sitting there. A girl, she thought, tucked into the shadows of the unlighted balcony. The girl wasn't crying, in fact, she smiled and nodded knowingly at her. Kaitlin swung around to see if Sadie Johnson or her mother were looking, and when she turned back no one was there.

CHAPTER 33

"**M**om, I don't want to live here anymore. I think we should sell this place and go back to our house in Washington." Kaitlin pushed the eggs on her plate around and met Laurel's eyes with a look of immovable determination.

"Kaitlin, I can't do that. This farm has been in my family since before records were kept, and I'm not going to be the one to let it go." Laurel was confused, the drugs making her perceptions hazy. She wasn't sure she had really followed Kaitlin's remark. She swallowed dryly and probed at her dull mind, wondering where this notion had come from and why now.

"I can't stay here anymore. I can't watch all the people I love be hurt or killed by this place." Kaitlin folded her arms across her chest and stared at her mother.

Laurel licked her lips and worked to focus her eyes on Kaitlin. She searched for the right words and put her hand out to cover Kaitlin's as she answered. "Kaitlin, you have been through two terrible losses but those weren't caused by the farm."

Kaitlin cut her off, "Almost three, mother. I almost lost you too. I don't want to wait here for you to get killed and then Dad. I want us to get out of here now, while we still can." Kaitlin balled up her fist and struck the table with her last words.

The movement jarred Laurel's arm, making the pain rise up in a swift wave that crashed through her shoulder, chest, and head. The pain and the noise made Laurel sharper, more alert. She felt annoyed by the intrusion, irritated by the tone of Kaitlin's voice.

"Kaitlin, don't you raise your voice to me! You know good and well that our house in Washington is sold. Your Dad is already on his way here. He doesn't have a job. We have to make this farm work just to support us. You don't think a Navy pension is going to send you to college, do you?" Laurel felt her own voice rising in volume and she tried to restrain herself but the words were coming out on their own now, each one biting where it struck. Her anger pushed away the dullness the drugs had laid over her.

"I promised my mother on her death-bed that I would stay on this farm. When she could hardly draw one more breath to keep her own heart beating, all she wanted was for me to promise that you would stay here too. I don't think it was selfishness that made her ask that of me either. I think it was heritage. This family has been on this land as long as time can remember and it is our heritage." Laurel rose from her chair, her fists clenched and her face turning red with emotion.

"You need to rein in your imagination, young lady, and think of the realities involved here. Bad things happen to good people and that's all that is going on here, not some demonic evil trying to destroy us all. I don't need that kind of talk from you right now. I need you to help me to get better and I need you to help us as a family, to make it right here and not run away." Laurel was shouting at the end of it, her throat still raw from the attack and the surgery. Her words fell harshly, then she was shaking with her own anger. Surprised at her reaction, she sat down, a hand covering her eyes. She had never spoken to Kaitlin like this in all the time she'd raised her. Laurel could not conceive of leaving here again, she realized for the first time.

Kaitlin shouted, half crying and half screaming at her mother. "This is not some fantasy I invented. How can you be too blind to see? You've brought me back to some kind of hell, and I'm going to be sitting in that rest home with Aunt Carol Ann soon. This is not a farm, it's a trap and we're caught in it, just waiting to be collected." Kaitlin pushed away from the table, hard enough to knock her chair to the floor. It fell with a crash to the tile floor. Kaitlin kicked it out of the way and ran from the house, the back door slamming shut behind her, snapping like a gunshot in her mother's ears.

* * *

Yuki stirred warily from his den, the throbbing wound in his hindquarters flaring with hot pain and stiffness. His head pulsed with stabbing jolts of pain with each heartbeat. His nose was hot and dry and he found it hard to raise his head. He inched toward the opening in the brush that let in diffused morning light. His tongue hung thickly from his mouth, coated with the dust stirred up by his movements. Finally, he nosed his muzzle through the opening and sniffed at the cool air.

The woods were quiet this morning. He tensed, concentrating to listen, but no voices or heavy footfalls came to him; no death troops searching him out. The thought of the police officers with their smell of gunmetal and sulfur enraged him. They jangled as they walked, metal keys bouncing against scratchy khaki; they coughed loudly and belched onions and sausage into the wind; they snapped branches underfoot and trampled tender shoots, announcing themselves in discords where they entered the forest. If Yuki found a policeman alone, he'd creep up on the man, go for the throat, and catch the blood that gushed from it in his own dry mouth. But for now, the woods stood silent and empty.

Yuki pulled himself forward, out of the brush that camouflaged his hiding place. Branches caught at his yellowed fur, rocks scratched at his underbelly, and burs tangled into his once proud coat. He was thirsty and hungry, his empty belly pressed against his backbone. He needed to hunt today, despite the risk, or he would soon be too weak from the infection to fight it off. He hesitated in the opening, intent on listening for noises; he suddenly became aware of how very quiet the trees were.

The woods seemed to stand still this morning as if the whole thing were suspended in some thick glassy liquid that made it hard to pass through. Yuki recognized the silence first, no bird song and no chattering from the squirrels, then he picked up the scent. The one warning that every wild creature recognized and dreaded. A thin veil of smoke sifted between the trees. Somewhere, fire was creeping in a slow, quiet advance through dry grass and dead leaves, heaving up a thick and distinct odor of destruction.

* * *

Kaitlin ran from the house, her tears almost blinding her as she stumbled across the barnyard and into the cornfield. She was desperate to escape this place. She wanted to go back to a life where worrying about being the new girl in town was the worst thing that happened to you. She wanted to fret about choosing what to wear to school today or getting her bike brakes fixed. She didn't want to agonize about which of the people she loved was going to die next.

She kicked at the ash dry ground, her sandaled feet catching dirt under her toes. She pulled off the sandals and continued barefoot among the baking rows of stunted corn plants. She tugged at the threads of her cut-offs, talking to herself in a quiet drone of misery. Finally her restless fingers found the amulet on its leather thong around her neck. She prodded at its contents, through the leather, wondering what power it was supposed to hold. She almost ripped it off, but remembered her promise to Donna Jean, and left the bag hanging.

The ragged row of corn ended at the creek bed and Kaitlin turned to take a worn cow path along the stream until it reached the old plank bridge that spanned the water. By now Kaitlin was drained of emotion. She walked like a zombie with no destination in mind, just a feeling that she should keep moving forward. The creek was almost dry here, with cracked mud along its side and dying water grasses browning in the sun. A small spill of water tracked slowly across the middle of the bed, too weak to move with any force.

The marsh on the other side had dried into a pasture of grassy tufts of sod that sat like islands above the black marsh silt, now exposed to the hot summer wind. Kaitlin's long legs took her from tuft to tuft across the wide field of rough marsh grass. Occasionally, a small pool of stagnant water still held a green frog or water bug whose home would soon be gone.

Kaitlin paused at the edge of the marsh where thick trees covered the hillsides. She looked back at the house wondering if her mother was watching. Kaitlin scolded herself for making more worry for her mother, but somehow she couldn't stop what she was doing. She realized for the first time since leaving the house that she was going to go into the woods. She was going to go into the woods where a vicious dog probably waited to attack her, and where a ghost-child wanted to lead her to some fate she couldn't fathom. She was going into the woods because her mother was right. It was her responsibility. It was something she couldn't keep running away from.

Kaitlin slipped her sandals back on, reached up to grab a tree branch, which would steady her as she scrambled up the steep hill, and hiked on, accepting her destiny.

* * *

Yuki kept running and found that the stiffness of his bad leg loosened up with the exercise. He had a long trek to water since most of the reliable springs and streams had dried up in the summer drought. All around him, he sensed other animals on the move as well. Mice scampered in the undergrowth off to his side and tree squirrels skittered along the thin branches overhead. Others seemed to be digging deeper into their tunnels below him. Everywhere there was the odor of watchful anxiety mingled with the increasing smell of charred wood, grass, and fur.

The breeze was picking up and it carried noises from almost beyond Yuki's perception. He could barely pick up the thin wail of sirens and the drone of low-flying planes at some far off edge of the vast forest. The air was becoming thicker and the smoke nagged his throat and made his eyes run. The horizon was turning a yellow gray and it was hard to see into the distance. The ache in Yuki's leg lessened with the adrenaline buildup that was triggered by the tension in the air. Yuki kept pace with the movement in the trees, silently, steadily, flowing with the others, headed away from the sounds and the smells of disaster.

* * *

Kaitlin moved with a purpose now, she was determined to find April. Perhaps if she had done this when Stormy first suggested it, she'd still have Stormy alive today. Perhaps April would teach her how to use this gift or perhaps April would take Kaitlin in payment for her own tragedy and put an end to the curse that hung over this land. Kaitlin didn't know, and she no longer cared; she was numb with loss and sorrow and she didn't care what happened to herself.

The woods quickly grew thicker and more difficult to cross, but Kaitlin was determined to keep advancing in a straight line. She had no inclination to veer around the clumps of itch-weed or sumac that grew up in the way. She methodically pressed down thorny wild rose bushes and climbed over rocky slopes. She was sweating, and pesky mosquitoes and deer flies buzzed her head as she pushed on. She broke off an old branch from a dead pine tree and used it like a machete to beat down the brush that stood in her way.

With some inner compass guiding her, Kaitlin navigated through the hills, following the remains of a dry creek bed when she could, though the weeds grew taller here and the obstructions were many. Kaitlin had a destination, and though she was not sure what it was, even the grumbling of her stomach, the mosquito bites on her arms, and the sharp rocks under her sandals could not disturb her concentration as she progressed slowly.

Suddenly, the bushes beside her shook with the lunge of a large animal. With only that instant of warning, the brush broke apart and an agitated deer thundered across her path, almost knocking her over as she fell to the dirt in alarm. She rocked on her heels, aware for the first time, of the forest, alive with an unusual amount of movement and noise. She glanced about, still not able to see the animals clearly, but keenly conscious of their chittering and scuttering in the leaves and grass around her. She sneezed suddenly with the smell of smoke, rich with the organic odors of grass and trees, bearing down on her.

Kaitlin looked up from the ground where she had been concentrating as she took each step, and found the air tinged with yellow wisps of smoke, obscuring her view. The smoke tickled at her throat and irritated her eyes. She looked up to see the tallest trees rocking in a stiff wind that crossed the beeline she had been following. She noticed the movement in the brush around her was directed at a perpendicular to her path. Still, she knew she couldn't vary; she held to her straight line and pressed against the crosswind of smoke and ash that beat at her.

* * *

Yuki's senses were hyper alert, as was his hunger. His own sense of self-preservation kept him traveling, losing no time running down the game that seemed to surround him, all on the same path, due east away from the west wind that carried fire. He felt the wind pick up, pushing his fur against the grain and growing hotter by the second. The fire was spreading fast on the gathering winds, the sound of cinders snapping and pinecones exploding had risen enough to be discernible above a constant low roar that announced flames eating at a vast and open spread of combustibles.

Yuki kept his nose to the ground searching instinctively for water and fleeing the danger at his back. For a brief time, he felt himself again, as if he were in charge of where he was going and what he would do, not the black rider inside that usually pulled him into danger where he felt sick and bad. The relief was destroyed, however, when Yuki picked up a new scent, an unusual scent this deep into the woods. He smelled the girl and with that instant recognition, the malevolent hitchhiker claimed him in his spell again.

The girl, deep in his own territory where there would be no man with a gun to shoot at him and no club to beat at him. The girl was here, coming to him as surely as the flames were leaping forward. He thought of tender thighs and flesh that would run red with young blood, and life, strong delicious life that would struggle and be captured inside of him. He thought of the girl and his deep hunger to have her. The fire forgotten, Yuki veered southward, his inner companion propelling him, catching the scent on the snatches of breeze that stirred up when the west wind rested.

CHAPTER 34

There was smoke all around her, and Kaitlin assumed this would be how it would end. April had drawn her out here for one more dramatic accident and then would take Kaitlin's mother and father until there was no one left to interfere with the farm again. Kaitlin shook her head for being so stupid but forced her way forward. Let April come in fire and smoke; Kaitlin was not so easy to frighten or kill. She would know the truth before she died.

A steady roar filled the acrid air and Kaitlin hurried. The temperature had risen on her right hand side, and her skin started to feel as if it were sunburned. She could hear distinct crackling to her right and when she looked westward, she could catch glimpses of fire through the trees. At one point a thunderous explosion shook the air and she looked to her right to see the top of a tall pine engulfed in flames that towered hundreds of feet into the air, like a giant torch bearing down on her. Kaitlin knew it was much too close, she started to run, lifting her feet from the ground to search out a path in front of her.

The fire came faster than Kaitlin could run. The dry, spindly pines around her began to hiss and pop as the heat forced them to combust. Kaitlin brushed ash from her hair as she ran and doubled over to catch air that was less smoky in her lungs. She veered from her straight path, trying to outrun the flames, and she started to pull ahead, when a tree fell directly into her path, its branches knocking her flat and pinning her to the needle-covered ground.

The pine had toppled when a larger, burning tree had fallen across it, pulling it down. Now fire was leaping from the larger tree to the newly fallen one as Kaitlin pressed back thick branches and tried to crawl out of rough bark and spiking needles that held her trapped to the ground. She screamed as old cones burst with flame and scattered burning pieces across her bare legs. She scrabbled at the ground trying to back out of the tangle of branches. The fire swept closer to her, and she pulled her hair back from the flames just before it could ignite. With one powerful shove, that ripped a long, deep furrow across her back, Kaitlin pushed herself free.

She struggled to her feet, just as fire was scorching her shoes. Thick, choking smoke immediately filled her lungs, wracking her body with violent coughs. She fell to her knees and considered lying down and ending it. Her eyes burned so she could hardly open them. Squinting through the smoke to find some way out, she saw April. April, standing just past the flames, beckoning her forward. April, her long black hair falling freely about her shoulders, untouched by the whirling smoke and exploding flames around her. April, solemn, silent, and calling Kaitlin to her with her dark, sad eyes.

Kaitlin dropped her eyes, as the coughing forced her to double over, but she stumbled a few steps in April's direction, determined to find her before she was done. Kaitlin leaned against a hot tree trunk to steady herself, then stepped away, conscious that she had to move fast to get to breathable air. She covered her mouth, still coughing violently, and ran from the inferno that was quickly surrounding her. For the briefest of moments, the wind died and she was able to get clear from the rapidly expanding circle of flame. A gap in the smoky air, where April had stood just a moment before, showed green ahead of her and Kaitlin stumbled toward the break.

The clearest path led downward and Kaitlin was

compelled to follow it. The trees here were greener despite the drought and the ground was damper, as if there was always water in this part of the forest, some central core protected from the elements by the vast acres of land that surrounded it. The walking was easier now, as Kaitlin moved downward, catching herself on tree branches to keep from sliding the entire way down the slope.

As she neared the bottom, the smoke grew more wispy and the air cooler. Kaitlin could smell water below, not just half-dried mud, but fresh, running water that made a splashing sound over rocks and logs below. A tree root tripped her, and despite her care, Kaitlin fell, tumbling head long down the steep hill until she rolled to a bruised and battered stop at the bottom. Kaitlin could hardly believe what she saw.

Here at the center of it all lay a large stream, more like a shallow river, rushing cool and clear even in the smoky mist. As the stream separated, it flowed around a small island crowned by vast trees, rising like a canopy overhead, their huge trunks seeming to support the very sky above.

Kaitlin sat catching her breath and rubbing her new bruises. Her eyes followed the trees down from lush branches to thick trunks, and there on the pebbled shore of the island stood April and her black dog, substantial as flesh and blood; no mere image. The hair on Kaitlin's arms stood straight as she stared directly at what she knew to be no apparition, no mask of smoke or distance between them now. April waited, without moving, her face open and patient, her hand stroking the solid black dog whose eyes glowed with reflected fire from the blaze sweeping down the hill behind Kaitlin. April lifted one arm, silently beckoning Kaitlin to come across the water.

April looked as real as Stormy ever had. The thought of Stormy rekindled Kaitlin's grief and determination to see this through. Kaitlin rose and took the first trembling steps toward April when she was knocked flat from behind.

The weight on her back was suffocating and Kaitlin felt her hair being yanked with a vicious twist. Kaitlin threw her arm back as hard as she could to knock away the mad dog whose claws dug into her skin and whose teeth snapped above her. Ferocious growls filled the air around her and Kaitlin found herself feeble in the dog's tenacious grasp. Kaitlin heard her shirt rip and felt it pulled tight around her neck. She struggled to reach her collar to pull the strangling material away from her throat. Succeeding, she screamed and kicked out, connecting with the dog's hard belly but failing to knock him away. She screamed again, her throat raw from the smoke and terror, as sharp teeth tore into her shoulder. With sudden clarity, she knew this was how she would die.

Kaitlin's harsh scream was answered by a flash of black fur flying over her head and connecting with the white dog who was pinning her to the ground and tearing at her flesh. For a minute, the weight of the two dogs crushed her face into the black, damp earth and suffocated her in its dank grasp. Then twisting, the two fell off to Kaitlin's side until she was free of the maelstrom of fangs, claws, and fur. She rolled aside, angling her body downhill, scrambling for the edge of the water. Behind her, deep growls and the gnashing of powerful teeth overpowered the roar of the fire. Kaitlin slithered across the forest floor, rocks and twigs tearing at her hands and knees, but the smoke thickened around her so that she dared not to stand.

The noise of the fire grew louder as she distanced herself from the ferocious fighting of the dogs. Kaitlin looked back to see the flames racing toward the dogs. The white dog with the icy cold eyes, the one who had attacked her mother, stood on his back feet, sharp fangs lunging for the other dog's exposed throat. The black dog, with eyes that reflected the very flames around them, gripped the white dog in powerful forelimbs and tore off its ear, gaining a scream of pain from the white dog. Their death dance broken, the dogs snarled and snapped, each trying to reach the other's vital organs, the throat or the abdomen.

Behind them, the smoke thickened into a choking gray fog that threatened to hide them from view. A tree on the hillside exploded in flame, sending a column of fire two hundred feet high and catching the tree next to it into its net. A conflagration was whipping down the hill toward them, but still the dogs fought in mortal combat.

Kaitlin, choking on the smoke, her throat searing from the heat, turned away from the pair and crawled toward the water. April still stood on the far shore beckoning to her. Kaitlin felt her death surrounding her and inched ahead, almost upright now. Kaitlin waded into the fast flow, ankles in the numbing water, then knees, almost pushed out from under her with the strong current. She continued, walking in up to her waist, the water freezing her legs as her arms blistered from the fire on the hillside shore.

Kaitlin looked back and as a breeze separated the thick black smoke for just a moment she could see the black dog heaving blood as it fought, the white dog locked to its throat with jaws that shredded the black hide while its back claws ripped open the Doberman's soft belly. A desperate keening erupted from the black dog, sounding enough like a man's death cry to chill Kaitlin, deep inside where the cold water did not reach, then the smoke closed over the beasts again and they were gone.

Kaitlin was blind, the smoke hid all the light of day away from her, her eyes ran with pain from the acrid fires. She fell to her knees in the stream, keeping just her nose and mouth above the water and slowly creeping onward, lifting one knee and then the other. She felt the water level lowering and dropped down to her hands and knees, keeping herself under the water now except for quick gasps of the black air. The water continued to lower and Kaitlin crawled now, using her hands to push against the wet gravel as she inched forward. When her lungs were at the end of their capacity, Kaitlin dropped her head onto the pebbled shore, using her elbows to push forward another five inches.

She was aware of the splashing behind her just as Yuki's fangs tore into the back of her neck. Yuki wrenched Kaitlin back into the deeper water, pushing her under the current that caught them both and tugged them along the rocky bottom. She choked as water filled her nose and she struggled to pull the animal off her back, clutching wet white fur with both hands. He thrashed against the current, bringing them both up to the surface again where she gasped for breath as the dog released its grip to do the same. Kaitlin's feet struck bottom and she pushed upward, standing shoulder deep in the pressing stream.

The white demon was in front of her now, blue eyes glowing with hatred and desire. She thrust her hands forward to block his teeth as he sprung to tear into her, slipping under her small hands and into her soft belly. Her arms clenched his head to her body as the beast struggled to rip at her abdomen. Locked by pain, Kaitlin's arms crushed the dog to her as they both went under again, fighting for air and for life.

Kaitlin's chin pressed against the leather bag that floated up from her neck and she thought of her grandmother. Trying desperately to be what Doe had promised her she was, Kaitlin pulled all her being into one bright spot centered on the amulet. Instantly, it seemed as if she stopped time itself with her intense concentration and in that space of time she thought only one thought, chanting silently for life. Her strength grew as she squeezed against the beast, finding the power deep inside of her to grind his body against hers as he thrashed and struggled to return to the surface and the life-giving air. The water churned around them, building in force until it erupted in a spray of white and crimson.

In the center of this vast, unnatural fountain, Kaitlin stood, whole and impenetrable. Power rushed through her, rising from the depths of the water in which she stood, channeling through her soul and crushing out the demented spirit of the Yuki/man/demon thing as it fought to enter her. Yuki's last agonized cry gurgled upward through the water and broke the silence of her spell. It was not the cry of a dog, or of a man, but that of a banshee's scream coming from the depths of hell. Kaitlin flung the dog's body off and into the burning woods, but knew she had thrown off more than a mere animal.

Kaitlin raised her arms, in awe of the power around and in her. She felt as if her strength was not just her own, but magnified by April's, and Doe's, and Lana's and the gathered power of generations of women before her.

In the midst of the smoke, and blood, and spray, she stood like a great eagle, pure and strong. Her arms moved like wings reaching into the sky. Around her the water exploded in droplets and streams until the very clouds above broke open and rain poured down in torrents on the blackened forest.

CHAPTER 35

Mike led the party of searchers as they moved slowly toward the single stand of trees still rising green above the vast acres of blackened trunks and still-burning root systems. It had been three days since Kaitlin ran from the house into this inferno and Mike knew only the last threads of hope sustained him. His orange overalls were blackened with soot, his gloved hands blistered around the shovel he carried. The thick fire boots he'd borrowed had melted and reshaped in a dozen places. He had not slept in 48 hours as he continued the search. He had to find his little girl and take her back to Laurel.

His exhausted legs stumbled on the last hill, propelling him down a long muddy slide to the edge of a fast-running stream. Beside him, he could make out the carcass of some large animal, and fearing to leave any body unidentified, he used the shovel to prod and turn the bones until he could be sure they were not human. The putrid mass fell away and he could make out the skull of a large dog or bear or something not human. He sighed with relief and, not for the first time today, he had to wipe at his eyes to hide his fear. The grove of trees was his last hope. There could have been no other escape in all the acres around this island, for the fire had torched every living organism it could reach.

Mike could not believe the rush of the stream before

him, running clean, sparkling in the sunlight and looking untouched by the destruction. Beyond this phenomenal stream stood the most beautiful old growth trees he had ever seen, true patriarchs of the immense forest that had once surrounded them. Standing in sunlight with full green leaves, sheltering a small, untouched piece of forest in the middle of total ruin. He waded through the stream, stopping to wash his face clean in the running water and praying that the island would hold what he sought.

He lurched as his boots filled with water and his soaked pants threatened to pull him down, but dragged himself through the strong current to the far side. As he stepped to the shore, he felt a peace and rightness that must always have been here, and for just a moment his dread turned to hope. He thought of this precious stand reseeding the woods around it and wondered if that had been its function the thousands of years it had probably stood here.

A rustling caused Mike to turn, and just there, among the ferns, he made out the sole of a girl's sandal and a small, blistered ankle, the rest hidden by the overhanging leaves. His eyes filled and ran over, his heartbeat swelling into his throat. He swallowed painfully and took a deep breath, preparing himself for the worst and praying for the best.

Mike threw down the shovel, tore off his hat and gloves and scrambled to the small foot. He felt at its pulse and laughed out loud, a laugh that echoed back to the rest of the party, still making their way down the hill. Mike's hand moved up the leg and he pushed the sheltering ferns aside, pulling at the girl's arms and raising her to his chest, pressing her head to his shoulder. It was Kaitlin; she was alive!

She opened ancient eyes to him. Staring at him for just a moment with a look that conveyed wisdom, understanding, and peace.

"Dad!" Kaitlin threw her arms around him. A hug much stronger than he would have thought possible held him tightly to her. "Oh Dad! It's okay. I had the most wonderful dream."

The End

Revised 3-1-18

ABOUT THE AUTHOR

Betty Fry grew up on a farm, ran barefoot in the newly turned earth behind her father's plow; waded in the icy, rushing creek; and fished at sunset in a boat on the lake, sandwiches in a box on the middle seat. She roamed freely in the deep Northern woods behind the barn with her dog beside her. The land whispered messages to her that she held close to her heart and kept in her mind as she matured. As a young adult, Betty traded this rural paradise for the neatly trimmed lawns and shaded brick buildings of college campuses where she studied the internal realities and behavioral expressions of usually broken and often haunted minds. She toiled on locked wards of state hospitals and detention centers, and in special segregated classrooms, private schools, and disrupted homes. As a working woman, she made long daily commutes, analyzed data, completed research, wrote textbooks, supervised interns, prepared lectures, and tried to lighten the loads of frustrated adults and confused children. Now Betty's life has come almost full circle and she breathes the cool air of Northern woods, sits on the dock of a deep mountain lake, and walks a winding path that hugs a rushing river, with her dogs beside her. She sits at her keyboard and once again delves into the internal realities and behavioral expressions of broken and haunted minds. If you enjoy your time reading *Season's End*, please leave a review to share your thoughts.

Made in the USA
Monee, IL
15 October 2020